He crossed the threshold.

Like any true gentleman, he removed his cowboy hat upon entrance. That simple gesture only revealed the handsome face beneath the shield of the brim. With his free hand he held on to an adorable little girl wearing a cute purple dress and matching cowgirl boots.

But the girl's hair had a serious wad of gum on one side.

"Good morning," she greeted. "I'm not open yet, but give me a few days."

"I'm Luke," the man said. "Your landlord. Sorry I'm late, but we have a hair emergency."

She hadn't expected her landlord to be so... handsome.

Jenn had no clue how her morning had gone from wondering how to finally approach her family, meet her landlord and unload her boxes to dealing with a wad of matted hair...not to mention the unexpected attraction to this stranger.

His bright blue eyes gripped at Jenn's heart and she couldn't let them walk away. Maybe she couldn't solve her family problems with a simple haircut, but she could brighten this little girl's day.

Julia Ruth is a *USA TODAY* bestselling author, married to her high school sweetheart and values her faith and family above all else. Julia and her husband have two teen girls and they enjoy their beach trips, where they can unwind and get back to basics. Since she grew up in a small rural community, Julia loves keeping her settings in fictitious towns that make her readers feel like they're home. You can find Julia on Instagram: juliaruthbooks.

Books by Julia Ruth

Love Inspired

Four Sisters Ranch

A Cowgirl's Homecoming

Visit the Author Profile page at LoveInspired.com.

A Cowgirl's Homecoming

JULIA RUTH

LOVE INSPIRED
INSPIRATIONAL ROMANCE

LOVE INSPIRED®
INSPIRATIONAL ROMANCE

Recycling programs
for this product may
not exist in your area.

ISBN-13: 978-1-335-59881-3

A Cowgirl's Homecoming

Copyright © 2024 by Julia Bennett

All rights reserved. No part of this book may be used or reproduced in any manner whatsoever without written permission except in the case of brief quotations embodied in critical articles and reviews.

This is a work of fiction. Names, characters, places and incidents are either the product of the author's imagination or are used fictitiously. Any resemblance to actual persons, living or dead, businesses, companies, events or locales is entirely coincidental.

For questions and comments about the quality of this book, please contact us at CustomerService@Harlequin.com.

® is a trademark of Harlequin Enterprises ULC.

Love Inspired
22 Adelaide St. West, 41st Floor
Toronto, Ontario M5H 4E3, Canada
www.LoveInspired.com

Printed in U.S.A.

Guide our feet into the way of peace.
—*Luke* 1:79

I can't let this opportunity pass
without praising God for opening this door.

Chapter One

The ranch is in trouble.

Jenn Spencer couldn't get the text from her sister out of her head. For the past few months she'd been on the verge of coming home, but that terrifying statement gave her all the boost she needed. She hadn't spoken to her family in years, but now it was time to put the past behind them.

Jenn glanced around the old building she'd be renting during her time back home—both the salon on the ground level and the apartment above. Her new landlord was late, but that gave her a chance to check out her new space thanks to the back door code she'd been given in the rental agreement.

The place certainly needed a fresh start... maybe that was why she'd felt so drawn to this old building when she'd seen the listing online. There were cobwebs and dirty corners that needed cleaning up in her own life as well.

And that revelation was yet another reason she found herself back in Rosewood Valley. Northern California had always held a special place in her heart, but three years ago tragedy forced her out of town. Thoughts that couldn't plague her now…not if she wanted to move forward. While her late husband was always in her heart and on her mind, Cole would want her to mend those tattered relationships and live her life to the fullest.

She needed to meet with her landlord before she could venture to the farm and take that monumental first step. She honestly had no clue how she'd be received, but she needed to know how she could help save the place and restore broken bonds.

One baby step at a time.

Pushing aside the past and vowing to look toward a positive future, Jenn propped the back door open and made a few trips bringing in storage totes. She figured she had to begin somewhere if she was going to get her new life started…no matter how temporary. If things didn't work out, she'd have to face the consequences of her actions and possibly move from her hometown for good.

The nice spring breeze and the warm sunshine drifted in from the back alley, already boosting her mood. After about five trips, Jenn checked the time on her cell and wondered what was keeping her landlord.

Just as she lifted a stack of shampoo capes from the tote, a soft clicking sound echoed from the back door. Jenn turned her attention to the little brown pup that cautiously pranced through, with his little toe nails clacking on the chipped tile flooring and his nose to the ground as if following a scent.

"Oh, buddy. You can't be in here."

She took one step toward the light brown pup with his unkempt curly hair hanging down in his eyes. The poor thing cowered at her voice and scurried beneath the shampoo bowl against the back wall. Before she could figure out what to do with this unexpected visitor, the front door opened with the most annoying jingle. That bell would have to go.

Jenn straightened and shifted her attention toward the entrance as a tall, broad man stepped over the threshold. Like any true gentleman, he removed his cowboy hat upon entering. That simple gesture only revealed the handsome face beneath the shield of the brim. With his free hand he held on to an adorable little girl wearing a cute purple dress and matching cowgirl boots.

But the girl's hair had a serious wad of gum on one side. Jenn cringed as a memory of her childhood with her three sisters flashed through her mind. Another time, another mess of gum, more reminiscing she couldn't have prepared for.

"Good morning," she greeted, realizing this was her first interaction since she'd been back in town. "I'm not open yet, but give me a few days."

More like a month, but she had to get started so she could build back her savings. She'd just have to work with the dated decor for now and prioritize her needs and wants. Needs would be utilities and groceries. Wants…well, there were too many to list. Paint and flooring would be a good place to start. Maybe some air fresheners and a vase with some cheery spring flowers.

"I'm Luke. Your landlord," the man said. "Sorry I'm late, but we have a hair emergency."

She hadn't expected her landlord to be so… attractive. Someone older, retired maybe, with thinning gray hair and a thick midsection had come to mind. Certainly not a thirty-something man that seemed to fit the mold of a proverbial Western cowboy.

"She said she wasn't open, Toot," the little girl whispered, staring up at her father.

Jenn chewed the inside of her cheek to keep from laughing. What did this little cutie just call her dad?

The man glanced at the girl, sighed, then turned his attention back to Jenn. "We have an emergency," he repeated. "She's getting birthday pictures taken later today and *somehow* there's gum stuck in her hair."

He gave her a side-eye, silently expressing his frustration at their current predicament. The muscle beneath his bearded jaw ticked.

"Oh, is that your puppy?"

The little girl broke free and started toward the back of the salon. A furry animal clearly trumped a gum fiasco.

"Honey, you can't just go after every animal you see," he stated. "You need to ask if you can pet her dog."

"That's not my dog," Jenn explained, shaking her head. "He wandered in right before you did."

Jenn had no clue how her morning had gone from wondering how to finally approach her family, meet her landlord and unload her boxes, to dealing with a stray dog and a wad of matted hair…not to mention the unexpected attraction to this stranger.

The girl poked her purple glasses up with her index finger then turned to Jenn.

"Can you get the gum out?" She picked up a thick chunk of hair beside her face and held it out for Jenn to see. "Toot bought me the cutest ribbon with purple flowers that matches my new cowgirl boots and I really want to be able to wear it for my pictures."

Clearly this sweet girl had a favorite color.

Jenn's heart clenched as another memory flooded her mind. Her own matching bows and boots, the excitement of breaking in a new pair as she helped her father on the ranch. But the love for boots had faded these past three years and Jenn hadn't touched hers since she left Rosewood Valley.

They were forgotten…just like her dreams.

"Paisley, she's not open yet. We can find someone else." The guy came to stand next to his daughter as he offered Jenn a warm smile. "I will come back to make sure you're all settled once I get her hair taken care of. She has an appointment with a photographer in an hour. I'm not normally this scattered but…kids."

He took Paisley's hand once again and started to turn, but those bright blue eyes gripped at Jenn's heart and she couldn't let them walk away. Maybe she couldn't solve her own problems with a simple haircut, but she could brighten this little girl's day.

"I'll meet you at that chair up there." Jenn pointed toward the front of the salon. "Let me find where my sheers and booster seat are and we'll get you picture-perfect in no time."

Luke Bennett always counted his blessings when he could, and right now, the great gum debacle was getting fixed and he nearly wept with gratitude.

He knew nothing about raising a little girl, let alone a hair crisis. But his late brother had entrusted Luke enough to put him on the will. When Luke had agreed to be Paisley's guardian, he'd done so never imagining he'd actually have to step into that position.

As Jenn bustled around looking in one tote then another, Luke crossed to her and lowered his voice.

"If you don't have the time, I completely understand."

Her delicate hand stilled on one of the lids as her vibrant green eyes met his. The tips of her silky blond hair brushed against one shoulder and the pang of attraction startled him. She had a subtle, yet striking beauty. No makeup, her hair pulled up in a high ponytail…she looked just like her sisters. Yet there was something about this woman that intrigued him. Perhaps the underlying hint of pain he saw staring back at him or maybe the mystery involving her return, he wasn't sure. And no matter if he found her attractive or not, he didn't have the mental capacity to take on anything else in his life… not to mention he refused to risk his heart again.

Luke hadn't realized when he rented the building online that his new tenant would be Jenn Spencer—one of the girls the Four Sisters Ranch was named after. The very ranch he had his sights set on. He'd proposed something risky to Jenn's parents about acquiring their land, but he'd yet to get a reply. He wasn't backing down…not when he had too much on the line. Time was certainly of the essence for so many reasons.

"I remember being a little girl and getting excited for bows and boots," Jenn said.

A wide but sad smile flirted around her mouth, pulling him from his thoughts. Something haunted her. He could see the raw emotion in her eyes but couldn't get caught up in her troubles…not when he had a whole host of his own to combat.

"It's no problem as long as you all don't mind I'm not set up at all and this isn't normally how I work." She laughed. "I've only been here a half hour."

"Mind?" Luke shook his head. "You're saving the day if you can fix this. I have no clue what to do with a seven-year-old's hair, let alone one with a tangled mess."

"Well, we'll see what we're dealing with. Don't give me those accolades just yet." She dug farther into the tote and pulled out a black pouch. "Here we go. Now we're all set."

Jenn's focus shifted to the dog still hunkered under the sink. "Any idea who he belongs to?

There's no collar and he just walked in from the back as I was bringing some things in."

Luke tapped his thigh with his hat and looked to the pup who stared back with cautious eyes. He inched closer, not wanting to scare the poor thing. And a quick glance had him smiling.

"Your he is a she," Luke confirmed, then shrugged. "If you care."

Jenn laughed. "I hadn't even thought to look. I've always had male dogs growing up, so I just assumed."

"I've never seen her before. She looks like some type of a Spaniel mix. I can call a few people while you're fixing Paisley's hair."

She nodded. "I can't thank you enough," he added, relieved this nightmare might be fixed and they wouldn't have to cancel birthday pics.

Who knew being a single parent could be so difficult? Each day brought on a new adventure. Of course those "adventures" could be called disasters, but he preferred to try to stay somewhat positive. He still had a garbage disposal to work on because a doll head had gotten stuck in there. He didn't even want to know how that happened.

"No worries," she said. "And forgive me for asking, but what did Paisley call you?"

Luke laughed and shook his head. "Toot. It's a long story. I'm so used to it, I don't think about what other people wonder when they hear it."

"Sounds like a special relationship."

Jenn smiled once again before crossing the salon toward Paisley. *Special friendship* was a very mild way of putting things, considering he'd gone from long-distance uncle to permanent guardian in the proverbial blink of an eye.

Moving from Oregon to California and trying to start a new life, a new business, and put all of Paisley's needs first while dealing with the grief of losing his brother and sister-in-law had been the hardest time of his life. Not to mention the rental agreement on his brother's home was up in two months. They'd been preparing to build so they'd just been renting a small cottage, which was where he and Paisley lived.

He honestly didn't know how people got through such tragic events without their faith. He'd gotten on his knees in prayer so many times, begging God to give him the guidance to take on the role of father and make the best decisions for this new life he and Paisley shared.

Luke pulled out his cell and sent out several messages, trying to shift his focus from his own problems and worries to the misplaced pup. Hopefully he'd hear something soon. He highly doubted Jenn had the time or the space to keep a dog considering she was new to town.

"You know, I got gum in my sister's hair when I was little?" Jenn said.

Luke turned his attention toward the pair. Paisley sat perfectly still in the salon chair with a black cape around her shoulders as Jenn seemed to be examining the damage.

"You did?" Paisley asked, her eyes wide with curiosity. "Was she mad?"

"She was at first until our mom took her to get a new haircut and she loved the new style so much, she thanked me for the accident. Now, my mom—that's a different story. I had to do dishes every night for a month."

Paisley smiled and a warmth spread over Luke's heart. Smiles had been few and far between as of late, and no matter how short the happiness, he'd take it. That's all he wanted for his niece. Yet a sliver of guilt hit him as he listened to Jenn speak of her family. The way her father had insisted on keeping the potential sale of the family ranch a secret had Luke convinced that there had to be underlying friction with the homestead. He wasn't trying to rip the family apart, he just wanted a piece of their farm. He couldn't feel guilty for trying to provide the best life for Paisley.

A piece of land with a barn would be so ideal. He could renovate the large building for the livestock he tended to and he could build a nice, modest home for him and Paisley to start their lives. There was no secret in town that the Four

Sisters Ranch had hit hardship. Wasn't this the best solution for everyone involved?

"I think if we cut just a little and make some layers around your face, we'll be good to go."

"Can I still wear my bow?" his niece asked, her eyes wide with worry.

"Absolutely." Jenn turned the chair away from the mirror. "I don't want you to see until I'm all done."

"Like a surprise?"

Jenn nodded. "This is definitely a surprise."

Luke kept his eye on the dog, who seemed to be perfectly content tucked in the corner. He'd been a veterinarian for five years now. While he specialized in larger farm animals, he'd learned early on that all God's creatures were essentially the same. They had true feelings, fears and instinct. This dog probably knew she was safe in here, but the pup still kept a watchful eye on them, just in case.

The girls chatted about hair and boots, and Luke realized how much Paisley needed female conversation. He made a mental note to add pampering into a monthly routine for Sweet P. Coming to a salon and having someone do her hair, plus girl talk, was exactly what Paisley needed in her life right now. Would this make up for all she'd lost? Absolutely not, but Luke planned on integrating positive moments every chance he could get.

Moving any female into his life on any level would be difficult. The scar left behind by his runaway fiancée still seemed too fresh, but he had to put that hurt in the very back of his mind because that chapter in his life paled in comparison to this current chapter.

He glanced back to the dog, who had finally fallen asleep. Likely someone in town was missing their family pet and hopefully they'd put a collar on her once she returned home.

"What do we think?"

Luke looked back just as Jenn spun the chair around for Paisley to see her reflection in the mirror. Jenn fluffed the blond hair around Paisley's shoulders and his niece's smile widened. His heart swelled with a happiness he'd been missing over the past few months.

"Do you like it?" Jenn asked.

"I look older." Paisley beamed. "I love it."

Jenn caught his eyes in the mirror. "Sorry about that," she said, cringing. "I wasn't going for older. I was going for gum-free."

Luke shook his head. "Gum-free was the goal," he agreed. "I think she looks beautiful."

"You have to say that," Paisley argued.

"Who says?" he countered.

Paisley pursed her little lips, thinking of a

reply, when his cell vibrated in his pocket. He pulled it out and glanced at Jenn. Her striking eyes still held his and his heart beat a bit quicker. Good thing he had a call to pull his attention away from the beauty threatening to steal his focus.

"Hopefully this is someone about the dog," he explained before he turned to take the call from a number he didn't recognize.

"This is Luke."

"Mr. Bennett, this is Helen Myers from Beacon Law Firm. Is this a good time?"

He glanced to the girls, who had eyes on him, wondering if he had news about the pup. He shook his head and covered the cell.

"I need to take this," he whispered as he moved to the back of the salon.

He had no idea why a law firm would be calling him, and this wasn't even the firm that had handled his brother's will.

"I'm sorry, what did you say this was about?" Luke asked as he got to the open back door.

"I didn't, but my client Carol Stephens is seeking guardianship for Paisley Bennett and I need to set up a time to meet with you and your attorney. She would like to make this as seamless as possible for the child."

A pleasant breeze blew in from the open back door, random noises from the alley out back seemed to echo off the buildings, and Paisley and Jenn had started chatting once again. But all he heard was that someone wanted guardianship of his niece. *His* niece.

"I don't even know who this Carol is," he stated, then rattled off his lawyer's name. "You can call her if you need any further information, but the will was clear on who Paisley would be with. The name Carol wasn't even in the documents so I doubt she has a strong connection to my brother."

"She didn't think her name would be in the will, but that's a long story and one of the many reasons we need a meeting. Carol was Talia's best friend and cousin. She's the only family member Talia has left, but she's been overseas in the military. She's home now and is seeking custody."

Luke's hat dropped from his hand. He leaned against the doorjamb and attempted to calm his breathing. Getting worried or worked up wouldn't help things and he had no idea if this call was even legit.

But he did know that he was the only family member left on this side and Talia apparently was the only family member left on the other. Was that what this would all come down to? A ball of dread settled hard in his stomach.

"I'm not saying another word," he informed

the woman. "If you need anything, you can call my lawyer, but Paisley is going nowhere."

With that sickening weight in his gut, he disconnected the call. Nobody could take his niece from him...could they?

Chapter Two

"I need help."

Jenn clutched the dog in her arms and raced through the doors of the vet's office. The tiny waiting area with only three chairs was empty, but she'd seen a truck out front so she hoped someone was available. Fear consumed her as she glanced around for anyone to fix this problem.

"Hello?" she called.

"Jenn." Paisley jumped up from behind the reception desk and came around, her eyes wide. "What happened?"

Shaking, Jenn looked toward the doors that led to the back, hoping someone would come out. Any adult or provider who could take over this dire situation.

"I think she ate some of my hair color," she explained, swallowing the tears clogging her throat. "Is the vet here?"

"In the back. Come on."

Paisley led the way as she started calling out for Toot. Any other time she'd still find that name amusing, but right now her nerves were on edge and her heart beat much too fast.

Luke stepped into the narrow hallway from a side room, his eyes wide as he took in the sight. She'd had no idea he'd taken over Charles Major's clinic, but now wasn't the time for questions or trying to get to know her new landlord any better. She knew the old vet, as Charles had helped on her family's farm for years. But she wasn't going to get picky now.

"Jenn," Luke called.

He moved quickly, taking the dog from her. He led them into another room down the hallway. Luke lay the dog on the sterile metal table and turned his concerned eyes to her. Even in the midst of this chaos, an unexpected jolt of awareness hit her hard. She couldn't allow her thoughts to stray or become too distracted by a handsome stranger.

"What happened?" he asked in a voice much too calm in comparison to her own nerves.

She explained how she was in the front display windows using her vacuum for the dust and cobwebs when she heard commotion in the back and found the pup in the dispensary. Hair color covered the fur around her mouth and paws, tubes of color were all over the floor.

"Please tell me I didn't kill this poor dog!" she cried.

What a day for her first transition back into town. She hadn't even gotten the courage to go see the farm or her parents yet because she'd been procrastinating by cleaning and running over her speech in her head for when she finally landed on their doorstep.

What could she say to make up for all those years she'd stayed away? When she'd left Rosewood Valley after Cole suddenly passed, she'd been so angry and heartbroken. She'd said terrible things to her father, blamed him for Cole's death. She'd wanted her family out of her life... and now she needed to make amends.

"I'm not sure what's going on yet." Luke went into full work mode, his focus only on the dog now. "Let me do an assessment and run some tests. Why don't you go wait with Paisley in the lobby and I'll let you know something soon."

"I'll wait here."

He shot those piercing blue eyes over his shoulder, but she held her ground and tipped her chin, silently daring him to make her leave.

In a flash, she recalled another time and place...another man. Cole used to get perturbed with her when she'd wanted to hang in the barns when animals were giving birth. He wanted space to work and didn't want her around if something bad happened. Always trying to shield and protect her from the messy bits of life.

Very likely that's why Luke wanted her gone now. But she wasn't going anywhere. Life was messy—there was no getting around that fact. She'd tried running from her past mess and now she had an even bigger one to clean up, so here she was back in her hometown and ready to tackle whatever she needed to set her life back on the right path.

Because she respected Luke and his position, she did step back to the corner to stay out of his way. Jenn marveled at the way he was so gentle yet efficient with the pup. Luke asked her a few questions as he worked and informed her he'd know more after the tests were run.

Just having his calm voice in her moment of panic really settled her nerves. As if his looks weren't enough of an attraction, now he had charm and comforting mannerisms...all qualities in her late husband that she both loved and missed.

She couldn't be attracted to her landlord. She didn't want that reminder of all she'd lost when her husband passed. A man with a child was everything she'd been hoping for, but that was another lifetime ago.

This phase in her life was all about a fresh start, repairing relationships with her family and saving her farm. Nothing more.

"Good news." Luke came back into the small exam room to find Jenn stroking the pup's tan fur. "Doesn't look like anything toxic in her bloodstream. I don't believe she ingested anything, but we will keep a close eye on her to make sure she's acting okay."

Jenn straightened and blew out a sigh. "That's a relief. I thought she was sleeping the whole time I was cleaning and I had no idea she'd gotten into anything. I'm not an irresponsible person—"

Luke gave her shoulder a reassuring squeeze. "It's okay. Accidents happen and I never thought you did anything on purpose."

A tender smile spread across her face. And as beautiful as she was, it was the red-rimmed eyes that tugged at his heart. She obviously had a soft spot for animals. She'd grown up on a farm and hadn't ejected the stray pup from her shop, and he was sure there was likely some code or rule against animals in that type of business.

Why did he have to find her so adorable in a way that completely surprised him? He'd seen her sisters around the farm and in town and not one of them, while each pretty in their own way, had even remotely ruffled his interest. He didn't have time to start a relationship and there were too many reasons he shouldn't.

The main one being he'd just found himself in a custody dispute and he still wanted a piece of the Four Sisters' farmland. Was that why she'd come home? Did she know they were thinking of selling? What had Jenn heard?

He had no idea what brought her home, but he knew he still needed to keep quiet. None of this was his place to address. Whatever happened between him and Will and Sarah Spencer was between them. If they wanted to bring their girls in on the proposal, that was their business, but until he knew for sure what Jenn was aware of, Luke would remain true to his word.

Luke couldn't help but wonder why Jenn hadn't taken the dog to her sister, Violet. Vi was the small-animal vet in town. Were the sisters not on speaking terms? Granted his office was closer to Jenn's salon, but still. Odd that she didn't go to family first.

There had to be a rift, but he shouldn't concern himself with anyone else's business. Not only did he have enough on his own plate, he'd been so burned before, the last thing he needed was to get swept away in someone else's woes.

"Can I take her home?" Jenn asked, breaking into his thoughts.

Luke stepped back. "Does that mean you're keeping her?"

Jenn reached up and tightened her ponytail as her eyes traveled back to the dog, who didn't seem to have a worry in the world.

"I can't just toss her out," she admitted. "I hope pets are allowed in the building you rented me."

Luke laughed. "Of all people, you think I'm going to say no to your pet?"

"She's not *my* pet," Jenn corrected, focusing back on him. "But I'll keep her until we can find a home."

Luke nodded. "Fair enough."

He went over instructions and what to watch for once they left. He also let her know he'd be stopping by just to check in. Maybe he could have her come to the clinic, but he didn't mind stopping at the shop to see her—

No. To see the dog. He had to get his head on straight and focus on what was important. Paisley and buying a portion of the farm, in that order. Nothing else mattered.

"Toot."

Luke turned toward the door where Paisley stood in the opening holding up a dog treat in the shape of a sugar cookie. One bite had been taken and Paisley's nose wrinkled in disgust. They'd had her birthday pictures just a few hours ago and he'd come into the clinic to work on inventory. Thankfully they were here when Jenn came with her emergency.

"These cookies are terrible," she told him. "Where did you get them?"

Luke raked a hand over his jaw. "Those are dog treats, Sweet P. They are just made to look like human cookies."

The little girl's nose wrinkled. "Oops. Sorry. They were at the counter so I thought they were for people."

Jenn snickered and he glanced over his shoulder, pleased to see a smile as opposed to the sheer terror he'd seen on her face when she'd arrived.

"It's always something," he muttered, shaking his head. "So don't feel too bad about the pup. Paisley's eating dog treats."

He truly didn't know how he could keep an eye on her, run a clinic, try to fight for custody and get land secured for their future. He wasn't giving up, but he wouldn't mind catching a break.

"Is Jenn's dog okay?" Paisley asked. "Can she have the rest of my cookie?"

"I think the dog will be just fine," Luke told her. "And, yes, she'd probably like the rest of the cookie."

"That's a good name for her, don't you think?" Paisley asked, looking to Jenn for an answer.

Jenn tipped her head and grinned. "Cookie. I think that's a perfect name."

As Luke watched the two ladies fawn over the dog and the treat, he couldn't help but see a life he once thought he would have. A wife, a child, definitely pets. But four years ago his fiancée decided that wasn't her vision at all and left him standing at the altar like some fool. He'd learned his lesson and hunkered down into his work from then on out…until now when his focus shifted from himself to his niece.

"What else do you own in this town?"

Jenn's question pulled him from his thoughts. "Excuse me?"

"My building, you're a vet… Anything else you own I should be aware of? I feel like I'm going to go get a gallon of milk and you'll be my checkout clerk."

Her quick wit had him chuckling. "No. This is all I do. You're safe to get your milk."

The building she was in had belonged to his late brother who had just purchased with intentions of renting. His family saga and tragedies weren't necessary to get into right now. She'd no doubt find out enough if she listened around town.

The cell in his pocket vibrated and he excused himself.

Will Spencer, Jenn's father.

"I need to take this," he told her, feeling a bit awkward as he did.

Luke stepped into the hall, hoping the man was calling with an agreement to sell or at least a counteroffer. He needed that stability now more than ever. A solid plan for the future would go a long, long way in proving that he was the only option for guardianship of his niece.

Chapter Three

"You always did love animals."

Startled, Jenn jerked around. Her heart leaped as she stared back at the most beautiful sight. Words caught in her throat and her eyes filled. She'd been so worried about coming home, but a piece of home had come to her.

"Erin."

The youngest Spencer sister stood in the doorway of the salon and all the years of absence seemed to settle right between them. Jenn had always been closest with Erin, though all the sisters had been the very best of friends growing up and working together as a solid unit on the farm.

What hit Jenn hard was seeing the same pitcher necklace around Erin's neck that Jenn wore. The piece every single Spencer woman owned and treasured held such a powerful spot in Jenn's heart. Even with the time and distance that separated her from her family, Jenn had never removed the precious necklace.

"I can't believe you're here," she said, unsure what else to say or even if she should close that gap between them—and not just the physical one.

Erin tucked a strand of her long blond hair behind her ear as she took a step inside and let the door close behind her. Jenn remained frozen, still insecure about how to respond here. She'd rehearsed in her mind a thousand times how she would react when she saw her family again, but right now, none of those variations mattered.

Maybe being caught off guard was the best-case scenario. Jenn didn't have time to think; she had to rely on her faith. She'd just assumed she'd see her family at the farm when she went later today.

"I wouldn't be anywhere else," Erin assured her. "I heard just yesterday that you were renting this building and I can't believe it."

"Why not?" Jenn asked with a slight shrug. "It's perfect to work and live, and the lease is only for six months."

Erin moved farther into the open space toward Jenn. "I guess I assumed you'd live at the farm."

"I'm not sure how welcome I'd be," she admitted.

Erin nodded in understanding, then chewed on her bottom lip. She'd always done that as a kid when she worried about something.

"How bad is it?" Jenn asked.

"As bad as it's ever been," Erin said. "But we're hopeful. Mom and Dad had to sell some cattle, but so far nothing else. I'm just concerned. They're getting older, the farm is still quite demanding, and with the drought last year, we lost so many crops and cattle." She sighed. "I'm just afraid… I can't even believe I'm saying this, but what if they sell the farm?"

"Did they say they were?" Jenn asked, refusing to even let that thought roll through her mind.

Another dose of guilt settled deep into her core. She should have been here all along and maybe she could have prevented this impending tragedy from taking place. The very thought of her parents having to make such a difficult decision to sell some of their livestock wasn't something Jenn had ever experienced before. She couldn't even imagine how tough things must be for her father to have made such a drastic call.

Guilt and anger consumed her for so many reasons. Jenn had let fear and emotions drive her away from the people she loved most. At a time she was hurting over the tragic loss of her husband, when she should have turned to her family, she'd pushed them away—going even further and placing blame right at their feet.

Over the past few years her mother had

reached out, but Jenn had been so ashamed of how she'd left things. The thought of coming home to where her husband had died on the family farm, and also facing her family, didn't seem possible. The mere idea of stepping back had held her captive in her own mind with her own dark thoughts.

"I'm going to see Mom and Dad today." Jenn realized her reasoning seemed inadequate and late. "I'm scared, but I'm going."

"Scared is good because it shows you care." Erin hesitated, then tilted her head. "You do care or you wouldn't be back. Right? I hesitated on texting you but thought you should know how dire the situation is…and you're still part of the family."

"I never stopped caring about you guys," Jenn whispered. "I stopped caring about myself and I'm glad you told me. It was past time for me to come home."

Erin took another step, and Jenn found herself moving as well. The second Erin opened her arms, Jenn fell into the loving embrace. She welcomed the familiar feeling and didn't bother holding back her tears. How long had she held all of this inside? The repairs Jenn needed to make with so many people might just start right here, right now, with something as simple as a hug.

Easing back, Erin smoothed Jenn's hair from

her face. "No tears. You're home now. Don't leave me like that again. I need my big sister and I can't help you if you won't let me."

Jenn swiped her damp cheeks. "I thought coming back would be harder than this. I can't believe you're not angry."

"Oh, I'm angry," Erin admitted. "But I still love you and I need a haircut."

Jenn couldn't stop her watery laugh. "You don't even know if I'm a good beautician."

Erin gave her shoulders a reassuring squeeze. "You're my sister and that's all that matters."

The warmth that spread through her shouldn't be surprising. God didn't guide her this far, on this journey, to fail. Jenn had to hold tight to her faith because there would be hard days ahead— there was no getting around that.

"Do you think the rest of the family will be this receiving?" she asked.

Erin's lips pursed and the silence gave Jenn all the answer she needed. Erin had always been quickest to forgive. As the baby of the family, Erin thrived on being the peacemaker, which was what made her such a wonderful kindergarten teacher. Or did she teach a different grade now? There were so many basic details about her family Jenn didn't know. She didn't know because she hadn't asked or checked in…not even with Erin.

While each Spencer girl certainly had their own unique personalities, their sisterly bond had never wavered.

Until that fateful day.

Thank you, God, for letting Erin be my first family encounter.

Jenn took this meeting as another sign that coming home was the right decision for now. She had to take this first step or she would never know if there was a chance at redemption.

"Did you tell anyone I was coming to town?" Jenn asked.

Erin shook her head. "I was hoping you'd go to the ranch before Mom and Dad found out. You know word travels faster than wildfire in Rosewood Valley."

"Going back to the ranch..." Jenn curled her lips to stop the quivering that accompanied her emotions. "I haven't been back there since that day," she whispered. "I don't know if I'm more afraid of seeing the place where Cole passed or seeing Mom and Dad."

"You can't move forward without facing your past," Erin explained. "One day at a time. One step at a time. Right?"

Jenn pulled in a shaky breath, but before she could say a word, the clicking of paws drew her attention toward the back.

"Your dog is adorable," Erin stated. "What's his name?"

"Her, and it's Cookie." Jenn didn't dare move toward the poor thing. She still seemed skittish, but she was taking an interest in the water bowl Jenn had put out. "She wandered in the back door yesterday and made herself at home beneath the shampoo chair."

"Well, she seems to be yours now."

The last thing Jenn needed was another unchecked box on her priority list. And while Erin had been spot on about Jenn's love for animals, she wasn't exactly in a position to take on more responsibility.

"Want me to stay here while you go to the farm?" Erin offered. "I can clean up and watch your dog."

"She's not mine."

Erin smiled. "So is that a yes?"

"I won't turn down the offer."

"Just go with an open mind and don't think that years of absence and heartache will be repaired in one visit," Erin warned. "You know dad. He won't admit defeat with the farm on the brink of foreclosure so he likely won't be ready to welcome you with open arms so easily, either."

No, he wouldn't, and honestly, she couldn't blame him. He was a proud man and she'd hurt him. Now he was hurting with the only land he'd ever known, too. Somehow, she had to repair everything and lift their family back from despair.

"I shouldn't have been gone so long," Jenn murmured.

"You're here now and that's what matters."

Heavy silence settled between them while Jenn tried to gather her thoughts. There were simply too many and she could be overwhelmed, but she had to remain strong now more than ever.

"You could always take her with you to the farm," Erin suggested, nodding toward the pup. "Dad always needs good dogs."

Jenn crossed her arms and shifted her stance as she narrowed her stare toward her sister. "Is that your way of pushing me to go now?"

Erin shrugged. "It's been long enough."

No truer statement. Unfortunately, that panic still lived within her, and three years was an incredibly long time for her faith to be tested and for doubts to creep in. But she'd held strong. She might have turned her back on her family, but she'd never turned her back on God. She was human; she had a roller coaster of emotions like anyone else. Life was full of highs and lows and what mattered most was how you dealt with those valleys. Jenn hadn't handled her valleys very well, so she had to find a way to crawl back up and not let those lows keep her down.

"I don't even know what to say to fix this," Jenn admitted.

"Sometimes you don't need words. You know actions are always louder, but the damage won't be undone quickly. Give yourself, and Dad, some grace."

Her little sister still had that voice of reason. Maybe paying attention to everyone older had made her wise beyond her twenty-six years. Her hair had gotten longer, nearly touching her waistline now. Her eyes were still a striking shade of green and she had more of a shape than that tomboy figure Jenn recalled.

"My haircut can wait. Now go. I'll get to sweeping or something." Erin glanced around the salon and wrinkled her nose. "Or get some air fresheners."

Jenn couldn't help but laugh again as she reached for her sister and pulled her into another embrace.

"I needed this," she stated. "I needed you."

Finally, after all this time, she was about to see what she was truly made of.

"Easy, girl."

Luke eased his hand along the mare's neck and gave a soft stroke. He'd come out to Four

Sisters Ranch after getting a call that one of the mares had taken ill. Thankfully Mary, the receptionist at his office, was able to watch Paisley for a bit while he ran out to check on the sick animal.

Mary was a godsend for sure. Her late husband, Charles Major, had been the vet prior to Luke so she knew not only the ins and outs of the office, but every person in the town and their history. There was no way Luke could have transitioned into a new town and new position without her. She didn't have grandchildren, so she graciously offered to watch Paisley.

His hands still shook from that phone call earlier from his attorney, though. Yesterday, Luke had called the lawyer that had handled his brother's will but had to leave a message. Finally she'd returned his call today and assured Luke that she would take care of anything that came up. But how could he not worry? A completely unknown source had threatened to take away the one family member he had left. The last tie to his late brother. The thought of Paisley not living with him had a heavy pit settling in his stomach.

"Sorry, I got held up."

Luke glanced over his shoulder as Will Spencer strode through the barn. The robust man always had on worn jeans, a plaid shirt and suspenders. His gruff voice and overbearing size could lead people to believe the man was mean or angry, but Luke had seen how Will was around his animals. The guy was simply a gentle giant, but a sadness always lurked in his green eyes.

Those same green eyes each of his girls shared, and that same sadness he'd seen in Jenn's. He might not know all the history there, but he'd heard it had been years since she'd stepped foot in Rosewood Valley.

"I haven't been here long," Luke stated, turning his attention back to the horse.

Just then the mare let out a deep, dry cough and Luke had a pretty good idea of the problem. He continued to run his hands over her neck, checking all of the swollen lymph nodes. The poor girl eased down and ultimately laid on her side. Poor thing must be exhausted.

Will came to stand just outside the stall. "Influenza?" he asked.

Luke nodded. "Seems like a textbook case." He glanced around to the different stalls, then to Will. "We'll need to separate this one from all the others. You know how contagious the flu can be, not to mention expensive if it takes hold of your other livestock."

Will's lips thinned as he propped his hands on his hips. Worry lines etched in the fine lines around his mouth and eyes. The man looked worn down and exhausted. The cost of the farm was getting to him, and Luke wished the stubborn man would just agree to the partial sale of the place and do what was best for all parties involved.

"Fresh hay and fresh water on a regular rotation will also go a long way to recovery," Luke offered. "But anything you can do to keep them separated is going to be best. Maybe keep the others in the pasture as much as possible."

"The other barn is too small for all of them, so the pasture will have to do."

When Luke first arrived in town six months ago, it hadn't taken him long to realize everyone here worked hard. The tight-knit community wasn't one of wealth, but of love and support. He completely understood why his brother loved Rosewood Valley so much and why he wanted to raise his family here.

"I'll do everything I can to help stop the spread." Luke came to his feet and dusted his hands off on his jeans. "I have some vitamins I can supply and I'll be sure to check in every couple days to make sure the others are healthy. Don't hesitate to call if she takes a turn for the worse. My line is always open."

"'Preciate that."

Luke pulled in a deep breath. "If you're ready to discuss selling, I can—"

"Not yet. We're just not ready." The farmer let out a sigh that spoke volumes for the thoughts no doubt swirling in his head. "Sarah and I are talking. I'd appreciate you keeping our conversations to yourself. My girls…they don't know what we're thinking. I don't want them to hear anything until Sarah and I know for sure. If we decide to go through with the sale, they will be devastated."

Tires crunching over the gravel drive pulled their attention to the open end of the barn. A small silver SUV rolled to a stop in the wide space between the barn and the two-story white farmhouse.

"Who in the world is that?" Will muttered.

The old guy looped his thumbs through his suspenders and started moving toward the visitor. But the moment Jenn stepped from the car, Will froze.

"That can't be," Will gasped.

Luke figured he'd be happy to see his daughter, but from the look on his face, this was anything but a celebratory homecoming. No, if anything this visit leaned more toward shocking and unexpected.

Jenn's eyes surveyed the area and came to land directly on him. That spear of attraction hit him hard once again. His headspace and his overloaded life right now didn't have room for dating, so he needed to push aside the fact Jenn was both adorable and maybe a bit vulnerable right now. He couldn't slay anyone else's dragons...not while he was fighting his own.

Luke figured he was all done with his work with the sick mare so he made his way from the barn and toward his truck. Whatever overdue reunion needed to take place did not involve him, especially since Will had requested his silence on the potential sale.

The fresh breeze kicked up around them, sending Jenn's blond hair dancing around her shoulders. He shouldn't find her this attractive or be so drawn to her, but facts were facts.

"I thought you didn't do anything else," she joked as he got closer.

"I'm the livestock vet," he explained. "I said you'd be safe getting milk."

A smile flirted around her mouth. But as she pushed her sunglasses on top of her head, he noted something other than amusement in her eyes. Fear? Worry?

"Good to know," she murmured. "I'm just here to see my parents."

"I was headed out. How's Cookie?" he asked.

"She seems perfectly fine, thankfully. I'm sure I'll be seeing you soon."

Luke simply nodded and headed toward his truck. They were bound together through the rental agreement for the next six months, so she'd be seeing quite a bit of him. He honestly didn't know at this point if that was a good or bad thing. He had a secret and he had baggage… but he also had a fascination that would be difficult to ignore.

Chapter Four

Nostalgia curled around Jenn's heart and squeezed. She hadn't counted on the rush of emotions that would hit her the moment she drove beneath that iron arch. Once a homey, welcoming entrance, now a depressing reminder of all she'd left behind.

The white iron had chipped away in many places and the welcome to Four Sisters Ranch didn't seem as warm and cozy as it once had. Paint had also peeled off various parts of the white two-story farmhouse. The wraparound porch didn't have the vibrant flowerpots at the top of the steps. The balcony off her parents' bedroom on the second floor seemed sad with no rockers. The small barn in the back no longer stood, though the one out front did. The large oak trees in the front yard remained tall and strong. The old wooden bench rested beneath, and that familiar tire swing her father had hung on her fourth birthday swayed in the spring breeze.

Some things remained exactly the same while

some seemed like time and tragedy had taken their toll.

The scuff of boots on the dirt pulled her attention back toward the barn. Jenn squinted against the sun as Will Spencer stood in the wide-open doorway leading to the stalls. Even from this distance, she could see he'd put on a little weight, but he still wore those red suspenders and plaid shirt. He said nothing, simply stared back, very likely wondering why she was here or showed up with no warning.

Now that she'd arrived, she wanted to run away. But that's what had gotten her into this mess to begin with. The back screen door of the farmhouse clanged and Jenn turned to see her mother on the back stoop. Hair piled on top of her head in a silver bun, a yellow apron covered her simple white T-shirt and jeans. On a gasp, her mother's hand flew up to her mouth.

Sarah Spencer raced down the back steps and made a mad dash to close the distance.

"Jenn."

Just hearing her mother's voice sliced through the awkward tension and warmed Jenn's heart. Her mother's arms came around her and Jenn closed her eyes, wanting just to live in this single moment right here. A viselike squeeze held her in place. She couldn't move, couldn't speak, as the tears slid down her cheeks.

Finally, after all this time, the fear that had held her captive for three years seemed to ease. For this one moment, Jenn had a surge of hope she so desperately needed. She wanted to believe that everything would be alright. She wanted to believe that she hadn't destroyed everything by her insensitive actions and yawning absence.

When her mom eased back, she gripped Jenn's face between her delicate hands. Just like Jenn thought, her mother had just come from the kitchen. Flour covered the front of her old yellow apron, which Rachel had sewn one Christmas.

"I can't believe you're here," her mother cried. "I've prayed for this for so long. I've dreamed of you walking in that back door."

She pulled her into another tight hug. Jenn glanced toward the barn where her father remained still, his weathered eyes locked on the scene before him. The fact he hadn't come over to see her absolutely crushed her. But what did she expect? Jenn had been the angriest toward him after Cole's death. She'd needed to place blame somewhere and her father had been a convenient target.

Would he ever forgive her? Had her words and harsh actions done irreparable damage?

"My baby is home," her mother cried, patting

Jenn's back. "Please tell me you're staying. Tell me you're not just passing through."

Clearly her mom hadn't heard the news about Jenn renting the old salon. She pulled away and offered a soft smile, hoping this could be the start of building the bridge to come back home.

"I'm staying for now," she agreed. "I just… I'm not sure if this is the place for me yet."

"There's nowhere else you belong," her mother insisted. "This is your home."

Jenn's eyes darted toward her father, then down to the gravel beneath her sneakers.

"Will, don't just stand there," Sarah called to her husband.

Jenn didn't want to stand here and beg for anyone's attention or affection, especially her father's. Maybe he couldn't forgive her. Maybe she'd been gone too long, had pushed too hard to keep people away.

But she remembered Erin's warning that their issues couldn't be fixed in one visit. Years of heartache all settled right here between them, and only additional time would help them unpack all of the emotional baggage.

When her father turned and went back into the barn, her mother gasped again.

"Just give him some time," Sarah explained

in that soft tone she'd always had. "Come inside and let's have some tea."

Jenn shook her head and swiped at her damp cheeks. "I don't think that's a good idea today, Mom."

But maybe tomorrow. She'd showed up. Her parents knew she was back, and that was enough for one day.

The worry in her mom's dark brown eyes couldn't be shielded. Her mother had always been so expressive with her feelings without saying a word. Sarah Spencer definitely wore her heart on her sleeve and made no apologies about being her true self.

"Don't leave town yet. Please."

Jenn took hold of her mother's hands and squeezed. "I'm staying for now."

She tossed a glance back toward the barn and realized this homecoming would go one of two ways: her father would never forgive her and she'd have to move on, or she could trust in God's timing and believe she was brought home for a reason.

And God had never let her down yet, so she was ready to put in the work to repair her broken family.

"Toot. These spelling words are hard."

Luke wiped his hands on the checkered towel

hanging from the oven door and turned to Paisley. She'd only been home from school for a few minutes, but she always came straight into the kitchen and had a seat at the round table and started into her homework.

That must have been how her parents had raised her. Thankfully Paisley kept up with her studies. Even being in the first grade, especially being in the first grade, it was important to have a routine...or so he'd been told by his therapist.

Navigating his way through parenting had been and still was a fast lesson. Trying to learn all the rules and tricks in a short time was impossible. But he wasn't giving in or giving up. Paisley deserved everything he had to give. He just wished there was some magical handbook with all the answers. After his failed attempt at a wife and family, he never thought he'd see the day he was put into the role of a father.

"Let's see what we've got here," Luke stated as he crossed the kitchen to the eating area by the windows overlooking the small backyard. "I bet we can get this in no time."

"Why are words so hard?" she complained, handing over her paper. "I like math much better."

Luke chuckled as he took a seat next to her and glanced at the words. Homework was where their evening routine began. She came home and he started a snack for them to share. He always made sure to have his afternoons free unless there was an emergency that took him to the clinic or a farm.

"Can't we just ignore the words and eat the mac and cheese?" Her bright blue eyes rose to his. "I don't want to work today."

"Do you have other homework?" he asked.

"No. Just those dumb words."

"Then how about we do half the words, have our snack, then do the other half?"

She wrinkled her nose and shook her head. "I'd rather go to the salon and see Cookie and Jenn. She's nice and really pretty."

Yes. There was no denying her natural beauty. In fact, that woman had rolled through his mind more often than he was comfortable with.

Luke pulled in a deep breath and sighed. He hadn't seen Jenn in a few days, not since he left her at the farm. He couldn't help but wonder how her visit went with her parents. Had Will told her about the land sale proposition? She likely would've confronted Luke if he had. He knew enough to know she had been gone for years, that her husband had died, and now she was back. Other than that, her life was none of his business so long as she was a good renter and paid on time. He couldn't let himself care about any other dealings with the adorable Spencer sister.

He'd fallen hard and fast for a charming, sweet

woman once before. He'd thought when he fell in love that they'd marry and start a family, but he'd been much too naive. Having someone wipe out his savings and leave him at the altar was quite the eye-opener.

Which was why vulnerable women were a thing of his past. He'd definitely learned his lesson and he had much more pressing matters at this stage in his life.

"We can't just stop in anytime we want," he explained, focusing on the here and now. "I'm sure we'll see the pup soon enough."

"Did you find the owner?"

"Not yet."

The timer on the stove went off and Luke set the spelling words down and went to drain the pasta. Thankfully he knew how to do basics, and simple meals seemed to make his niece happy. He hadn't ventured too far into experimenting with food. He got fancy the other evening and cut up hot dogs in the mac. With a heavy dose of ketchup, Paisley had deemed the dish a hit.

Once the pasta was drained, he added the powder pack of cheese. He was pretty sure that wasn't real cheese, but whatever. He wasn't trying to spruce up his culinary skills. He knew his strengths and being in the kitchen wasn't one of them.

"So how do you spell *house*?" he asked, stirring in the mixture.

"H-o-u-s-e."

"Perfect. See? You're already acing this test." Luke reached into the cabinet for a bowl. "How about *family*?"

Silence filled the room. He scooped her noodles while she thought, but when he turned back to face her, he noted her staring out the window with unshed tears in her eyes.

"Sweet P?"

She glanced his way as a lone tear slid down her cheek. "I don't like that word. Do I have to spell it?"

He placed the bowl down in front of her, then squatted next to her chair. He turned her to face him and took her delicate hands in his. His own heart broke for this situation life had thrust at them, but he had to embrace the fact they had each other and they could get through these tough days.

"Family looks a little different for us right now," he started, weighing his words carefully. "Family can come in a variety of ways and what makes a family are those people in your world that love you unconditionally. We have each other, right? It's okay to be sad and even be angry."

Her chin quivered and he wanted to turn her thoughts from that dark place that lived in her mind.

"Can you help me with something?" he asked, giving her hands a gentle squeeze. "Can you help focus on the good we still have? I struggle with that sometimes so I have an idea, but I can't do it without you."

Luke reached up and swiped the moisture from her cheeks with the pad of his thumb. He wished he could snap his fingers and obliterate all of her pain or take it all on his own. He never wanted to see tears in her eyes again, but he also knew this was unfortunately part of their growth forward.

"I can help you," she whispered with a sniff. "I'm sorry. I just didn't have a good day at school."

"What can I help with?"

She shrugged and glanced away. "Nothing you can do unless you have a mom for me. There's a Mother's Day project due next week."

Mother's Day. That holiday hadn't even crossed his mind. But they were in spring and that day would be coming up soon enough—the first one since the passing of Talia and Scott.

"Then we will make the absolute best project and honor your mother," Luke replied. "Tell me what all you need and we'll make it happen. Now is the perfect time to show what an amazing woman your mom was."

A soft, albeit sad, smile spread across Paisley's face. "She was the best. That's what I want everyone to know."

Luke nodded and came to his feet. He eased down into the seat he'd vacated moments ago. He didn't have a clue how to do a school project, so this would be another first. But he also knew there wasn't a thing he wouldn't do for Paisley. Maybe this project would be a way of healing even further and remembering all the good that Talia had brought into their lives.

"Then that's what we'll do," he confirmed. "Your mom will shine and you'll be able to feel her more than ever."

He hoped.

Luke had to make this sound like the greatest project, and it would be if he had any say.

"Now, what do you say you dive into your snack, we do some spelling, and then we dig through some pictures to get started?"

She inched forward and grabbed her fork. "Aren't you having some?"

He'd had enough mac 'n' cheese over these past few months to last his lifetime. He could go for a big juicy steak, mashed potatoes with gravy, some fresh-from-the-garden green beans.

His mouth watered and his stomach grumbled at the thought of the best meal, but he wasn't confident in mastering all of that quite yet. Besides, there wasn't even room for a garden here at his late brother's rental house. But if Luke got that piece of Spencer land...

"I had a late lunch," he replied.

She took a few bites as he glanced over the word list once again. Before he could give her another, she set her fork down and turned her attention to him.

"Sorry I cried."

Luke smiled. "Don't be sorry for having feelings. I cry, too."

"Not as much as me." She sniffed a little and adjusted her glasses. "I have to keep it all in at school so I don't look like a baby."

"Cry here all you want, but you don't look like a baby. Do I look like a baby when I cry?"

She rolled her eyes and snorted. "You're a big man. You can't look like a baby."

"Well, you are a strong young lady," he retorted, tapping the end of her button nose. "You could never look like a baby, either."

Paisley slid out of her seat and came up beside him. Her little arms wrapped around his neck and Luke's heart tumbled in his chest. He might not know a thing about how to raise a child, let alone about a little girl, but he understood loyalty and love for family and that had to count for something. He'd do anything for Paisley and he had a feeling she'd do anything for him. They were a team now.

"I'm glad I have you," she murmured against his shoulder. "Even if you do make mac every day."

He chuckled and returned her hug. "Maybe we can try pizza or burgers next time."

She eased back, all smiles now. "Extra cheese on my pizza."

"Of course."

If only all of the hurts of the world could be erased with such a simple fix.

Chapter Five

"So how's everything going?"

Marie Horton's sweet voice filled the empty salon. Her dear friend from Sacramento had called to check in while Jenn was decorating the front windows. The cell lay on a station closest to the front and Jenn decided to take a break and have a seat in the salon chair while chatting on speaker. Jenn glanced around the place, pleased with the progress she'd made so far.

Baby steps in the new business and in life seemed to be the common thread holding her together.

"Some parts have been better than I expected and some haven't gone quite the way I'd hoped," she admitted.

Marie had been the one solid anchor in Jenn's life when she'd settled in a new town after leaving Rosewood Valley. As the preacher's wife, Marie had welcomed Jenn with loving, open arms and their connection quickly turned into a friendship. God knew just what Jenn had needed at that time and she'd forever be grateful to Marie for her compassion and listening ear.

She'd created a good life for herself in Sacramento. She'd got her cosmetology license, joined a Bible study group and made friends. Her work with the church and her experience growing up on a farm had even led to a successful series of farm-to-table church dinners she'd coordinated with Marie. That had been such a huge leap for their church and quite the fundraiser. Jenn couldn't help but feel like she'd made a difference during her time away from home.

"Have you seen your family yet?" Marie asked. "Or gone by the farm?"

"I've been to the farm and I've seen my youngest sister and my parents."

That had been three days ago. She hadn't heard from her father. Jenn had texted her other sisters, Rachel and Violet, after she'd gone to the farm, but neither had messaged her back. Her mother had texted a few times, asking Jenn to come for dinner, but Jenn didn't think now was the time to jump back into something so special and meaningful. She had to give everyone, including herself, time to acclimate to this change.

"Oh, wow. That's great progress," Marie replied. "Were those good meetings?"

Jenn crossed her legs and stared out the front window. She had a great view of the park across the street so she didn't want to obstruct that with her window decor. She'd gone for simplicity and hung vibrant flowers of various sizes and colors from the wooden ceiling and draped some thin white lights. Once she got her window clings with her salon name on the front glass, the entrance would be complete.

She wished everything was so easy to tidy up and make new. But none of this new life could be rushed. She had to cling to the patience her parents had instilled in her. Getting angry and frustrated is what got her into this mess in the first place. She'd learned so much since she left and she had to prove with her actions that she was a different person now.

"Chatting with Erin went well," Jenn replied. "My mom welcomed me with a hug I desperately needed and invited me to church this Sunday. I'm not sure I'm ready to face the entire town or the church just yet."

Nearly everyone in town went to the white chapel on the hillside and she knew she couldn't hide from them forever, and she wasn't, but seeing them all at once in one place left her feeling a little insecure and unsure of herself. Not to mention, it was the same church she and Cole had been married in. So, no, she simply wasn't mentally prepared to step back inside those doors.

"Give yourself some time," Marie told her.

"And how about seeing your father? How did that go?"

"We haven't spoken." Jenn swallowed the lump of remorse and guilt in her throat. "I saw him in the barn, but he didn't come to talk to me."

"And you didn't go to him?"

"I thought about it, but I don't want to push just yet. I know him and he needs to process the fact I'm back."

Silence filled the salon and Jenn glanced to her cell on the yellow chipped countertop that made up the front station.

"Are you making an excuse?" Marie asked after a yawning pause.

"Maybe," Jenn admitted. No need to lie or ignore the truth. "I'm still scared and I guess I just wanted him to take that first step. Literally."

She'd gone home, taking the biggest leap of faith in the past three years. Now she needed her father to be ready to talk.

"He will," Marie assured her. "Obviously I don't know him, but he's your father and I have no doubt he loves you. There's damage that can't be undone. But sometimes the strongest people and relationships come from the toughest times."

"I know and that's what I'm holding out hope for." Jenn sighed and turned in the salon chair to grab her phone. "I plan on going back tomorrow. I'm tired after working in the shop all day trying to get it ready to open."

"How's that going?"

"Once I eliminated the old musty smell and did a thorough cleaning, the place has shaped up nicely. I made some posts on social media and already have a few appointments scheduled for the end of the week. So, I'm hoping my state inspector passes me when she comes in, but I have everything up and running so there should be no problem."

Each positive step forward gave her a new level of hope. Jenn's goal was to add a little more each day and put one proverbial foot in front of the other to rebuild her life. She wanted to stay in Rosewood Valley, but the deciding factor would be how she was received. Not just by her family, though they were definitely a huge part of her journey, but also by the town. Did people still chatter about her running away and deserting her family? Did they trust her coming back with only the purest of intentions? Only time would tell.

"This is great news!" Marie exclaimed. "Good for you. Just keep moving forward and please know I'm here for anything you need. Day or night. I'm always a call or text away."

"I know you are and I appreciate you being in my corner."

"I'm not the only one in that corner. You've got a family that's there, too. Believe it or not."

Jenn smiled, loving how her friend could lift her spirits with her soothing words and calm tone. Just a quick call had Jenn optimistic for a future here in her hometown and encouraged that better days were ahead. She couldn't let herself believe anything else.

Once she disconnected the call, she came to her feet and slid her cell into the pocket of her jeans. She turned to find Cookie sleeping beneath the shampoo bowl again. Apparently that's where she felt the most comfortable, but she couldn't stay there. If the state inspector came in and saw a dog in the salon, Jenn would get fined and that was the last thing she needed. Once she opened, she'd have to keep the dog upstairs in her apartment and schedule a break somewhere in her day to take her out to the potty…which was across the street at the park. Not convenient, but that would have to do until the owner was found.

Jenn had a sinking feeling she was the owner.

Erin didn't have a bad idea about taking the pup to the farm. There would be plenty of space to run free and thrive. Jenn didn't think now was the time to show up with a drop-off, though.

Besides, she'd gotten used to her new roommate and didn't feel quite so lonely. Maybe God knew she needed a companion, one who couldn't judge and had unconditional love. The dog was lost and she couldn't ignore the parallel life they seemed to have. They were both just trying to find a place to fit in and be safe and loved.

"Ready to go upstairs?" she asked.

At the sound of her voice, the pup lifted her head and gave a quick wiggle of her tail. A small one, but still. Slowly the dog seemed to be showing signs of trust and happiness.

"Let's go, girl."

Jenn turned off the lights and led the way toward the back staircase leading up to her apartment. The old creaky steps and dated floral wallpaper leading to the second floor were just another reminder that none of this was her style. Of course taking wallpaper down was free, so she could put her restless efforts toward that endeavor. Maybe peeling and scraping would be a good outlet for her frustrations. The open loft apartment wasn't much better with the old, scarred hardwood floors and more random wallpaper. At least Jenn had her own furniture, which helped the place feel a little more homey.

If she did indeed end up staying in town, she'd definitely talk with Luke about eventually upgrading the place and maybe even see about buying the building from him. Of course those were long-term goals as her savings had taken a hit to come back and put down rent and deposits and get the start-ups for her salon. She didn't think Luke would mind if she decided to change out the decor of the apartment.

Her thoughts drifted back to the handsome vet. She'd been so thankful he'd been around when Cookie got into that hair color. And that she'd seen him before she'd faced her mother. It had calmed her. But if she let herself think too much about him, she'd remember how her heart felt a little flutter the moment her eyes locked with his. She'd remember the way he seemed in a panic about his daughter with the gum and her birthday pictures. She'd remember his soothing voice when she'd been frightened about the dog.

She'd remember another man who'd made her heart flutter and the promise he'd made to her to love her forever. But their forever had been cut short.

Jenn massaged the back of her neck as she made her way to the bathroom. Maybe soaking in a nice hot bubble bath would relieve today's soreness and ease her mind a bit. Her fingers slid over the pitcher charm on her necklace. She'd never forgotten her mother's motto of pouring into yourself before you could pour into others. That saying had helped Jenn through life. And while sometimes she felt guilty for taking time for herself, she also knew she would be of no use to others if she didn't recharge every now and then.

Her phone vibrated, breaking into her thoughts. For a moment she considered ignoring it, but she should at least glance at the screen.

The moment her eyes landed on the sender, her heart clenched once again.

Her oldest sister, Rachel.

With a lump in her throat and her heart thumping at a rapid rate, Jenn grabbed her cell and opened the message.

We need to talk.

Jenn's thumbs hovered above the keys as she contemplated her reply. She wanted to see her sisters so badly. No matter the outcome or how they received her, Jenn had to take this step toward repairing each and every relationship. And even though Rachel had taken a few days to respond, Jenn eagerly typed out her reply.

I'm in the new salon across from the park on Sycamore St. I'll be here all day tomorrow if you want to stop by.

She hesitated before sending one more quick message.

I'd love to see you.

She held her breath, waiting and watching as the three dots danced on the screen, showing her sister was typing. Could this reconnection with Rachel be as easy as with Erin and her mother? Was that why Rachel had taken a few days to reply? Maybe she was just gathering her thoughts.

But what about Violet? Would she reply soon?

I'll be there in the morning after I help dad.

Jenn didn't know whether to be relieved that Rachel had agreed, or afraid of the unknown and what was to come. A heavy dose of both settled in her gut as she replied.

Can't wait to see you. Love you.

As she stared once again, hoping for a reply, Jenn realized that was the end of their conversation. No more words from her sister to give hope that their meeting would be a joyous one. Out of all the Spencer girls, Rachel was most like their father. She lived and breathed farm life and wanted nothing else in this world than to take over Four Sisters and raise her own family there.

Jenn had no idea what tomorrow would bring, but at this point all she could do was relax in that promised bubble bath and say a prayer that everything would work out in God's time.

* * *

So much for that relaxing bath.

Jenn piled her hair up on top of her head the next morning. She hadn't been able to soak or even wash her hair because there was no hot water. Last night, she'd made a cup of honey lemon tea, popped it in the microwave to get hot, and grabbed a book that hadn't really held her interest until she'd finally given up and went to bed.

Waking up in a surly mood was not how she wanted to go into meeting her sister.

Jenn had fired off a text to Luke, telling him hot water was of the utmost importance. Her own hygiene aside, she couldn't have her state inspector come and check things out before her opening if there wasn't sufficient water. She wasn't sure what happened, considering she had hot water while cleaning and mopping yesterday morning.

He'd texted back almost immediately and claimed he would stop by at some point today in between his appointments. She sincerely hoped this was a simple fix because she still needed that bubble bath. Any type of self-care and a little pampering was necessary. She didn't think such things were selfish, not when her mother had always told her girls that they had to take care of themselves before they could take care of others.

Jenn hooked the leash onto Cookie's collar and

led her out the front door of the salon. The spring sun sent a surge of confidence through her. That boost of light and warmth lifted her spirit. She would go into this day and this meeting with Rachel full of optimism and with an open mind. She had to listen to what her sister needed to say. As difficult as this might be, Jenn had to let each family member share their side. They deserved nothing less, and if that meant being angry or saying harsh words, then so be it. Jenn would do anything to mend this family back into one solid unit.

As soon as Cookie did her business, she crossed the street and headed back toward her salon. But a familiar woman stared across the open distance.

Violet stood on the sidewalk just outside the shop door. Jenn didn't have time to be worried or react to the rapid beat of her heart and the gnawing nerves in her belly. She stepped off the street and shortened Cookie's leash so the pup would stick close to her side.

"I didn't expect to see you," Jenn stated, wincing at how that could be perceived as rude and unwelcoming. "I mean, I'm glad you're here. I just…when I didn't hear from you, I wasn't sure you wanted to see me."

"Of course I want to see you," Violet said.

"You're still my sister, no matter what. I just had to process everything."

That familiar voice Jenn hadn't heard in years calmed the turmoil within. Violet had always been a little bit of the rebel. Jenn was glad to see her sister still loved changing up her hair color. Today offered a bright red, but her younger sister always looked gorgeous and could pull off any shade or style she wanted.

"I wasn't sure when you didn't respond to my text," Jenn offered.

"I didn't quite know what to say," Vi explained with a subtle shrug. "I still don't, but I couldn't let more time pass without coming."

Jenn nodded, completely understanding. She wasn't sure what to say, either, but the fact her sister had come here of her own accord set Jenn's mind on an even better path than before. So far two of her sisters had come to her, and her mother had literally welcomed her with open arms. This homecoming already had so many positives, which was what Jenn needed to focus on. She couldn't let her mind go into any type of negative space. Homing in on anything dark was certainly not the direction she needed to go. Light and love and all of that…that was what Jenn needed to thrive.

"How did you know where to find me?" Jenn asked.

"Well, Rosewood Valley is a small town with tons of chatter, but Rachel told me."

Of course they'd talked. Very likely there was a family group chat without Jenn. Hurtful, but understandable considering she'd been gone so long. Now they all knew she was back in town and they all were dealing with this news in their own way.

"Are you coming in?" Jenn asked.

Violet turned and glanced toward the salon, then back, her eyes drifting toward Cookie.

"Your dog is adorable."

Violet bent down and extended her hand, but Cookie wasn't having any part of the stranger. Even though Vi was a vet, the dog had no clue of her sister's love for animals. And Jenn hadn't gone to her sister's clinic the other day because, well…she'd been afraid of how she'd be received. Not to mention Luke's office was closer to the salon.

"She's a stray," Jenn explained. "I'm still trying to find the owner."

Cookie scooted closer to Jenn's leg and Violet smiled as she came back to her full height.

"Looks like you're the new owner. Dogs are smart with good instincts and she knows she's safe with you."

Yeah, Jenn was fully aware she'd become the chosen one, but there had to be someone wanting their pet back. In a town this small, someone could come forward at any time.

"So, you coming in?"

Vi's attention came back to Jenn. She realized she was holding her breath, wondering what her sister would say once they pushed past the small talk. The nerves in her belly curled but Jenn had to let her sister take the lead here. Whatever made Violet comfortable, Jenn would follow.

After a moment, Violet nodded and stepped forward. She pulled one of the double wooden doors open and gestured for Jenn and Cookie to follow.

"Your window displays look nice," Violet commented.

Jenn smiled as she stepped inside. "Thanks. I just finished them. Still waiting on my salon decal for the front glass, but that should be ready this afternoon."

She bent down and unhooked Cookie. The dog immediately went to the back, beneath the shampoo bowl. Poor girl was still scared, but at least she wasn't skittish with Jenn anymore.

"So, I assume you didn't stop by to discuss my windows or the dog." Jenn turned to face her sister once again. "Did you want to dive right into the past or keep our conversation casual for now?"

Violet shrugged as she glanced around the

shop. She moved to one of the two stations against the wall, turned the chair around, then sank into it. With one foot propped on the footrest, she kept her other on the floor and slowly pivoted the seat back and forth. A stall tactic.

Considering Jenn had been absent from this town and Violet's life for the past three years, taking another few minutes to collect the right words seemed appropriate.

Jenn didn't have those magical words that would erase the fear and anger. She didn't have the ability to make her family understand her actions, but she hoped in time, and with her coming back, they would listen to her side. But she was fully aware she'd have to extend the same courtesy and listen to them as well. No, not just listen, but understand and live in their point of view for a time. The only way to bridge their differences and hurts was to cross to the other side of the scenario and put herself in their place.

"I'm not sure what to say," Violet finally said, bringing her chair to a stop. "I've rolled this conversation over and over in my mind for so long and now that you're here, no words are coming to me."

Jenn nodded. "Well, I can start by saying I'm sorry." The most difficult words to say, yet usually the most important. "I needed to get away, but I could have gone about things a better way and not stayed gone so long."

"You're right. You could have handled things better." Violet rested her elbows on the black leather arms of the chair and laced her fingers together. "When you lost Cole, we all knew you were hurting. But shutting everyone out and placing the blame directly on Dad was wrong."

That heavy, dark moment in her life came rushing back. The harsh words, the tears, the unbearable heartbreak. Cole had been a hard worker, helping tend the family farm, and he could never say no to her father. That fateful day Will Spencer had asked him to go out into the fields when he wasn't well had been the worst of her life. Her beloved husband had never come back.

Channeling those feelings was the only way to help her now.

"I can admit I was wrong," Jenn agreed. "I'm here now because I want you all to know how much I care. I know I haven't shown it recently, but you all are my life. There wasn't a day that went by that I didn't want to reach out, but I just didn't know how."

"You're back because the farm is in trouble."

Jenn nodded. "That's the part that gave me the final push I needed."

"Would you have ever come back if everything was just as it was before?" Violet asked.

Jenn made her way to the other station next to her sister and took a seat. She had to be completely transparent here if she had any intention of moving forward in a positive direction.

"I like to think I would have," she admitted. "I had made a new life, but nothing ever felt permanent. I got my cosmetologist license and was working for a wonderful lady. I had a Bible study I attended once a week at a local coffee shop and I have a good friend from the church I'd been attending. She's been urging me to reach out and come home. Then when Erin texted me, I knew that was a sign that the time had come, and I couldn't run anymore."

"And what were you running from exactly?" Vi asked, tilting her head to the side. "From the family that loved you and mourned Cole's loss as well? Or were you running from your own guilt over how you treated our father?"

Now pain fueled her sister's words. Jenn expected this and her sister deserved to let all of those pent-up emotions and words out so they could deal with everything.

Violet opened her mouth and lifted her hand to say something just as the front door opened and the bell chimed. She'd still not taken that annoying thing down.

When Jenn turned to see who the new visitor was, her breath caught in her throat as she stared back at her oldest sister, Rachel. Looked like she'd get her entire family reunion wrapped up right here. Nothing like jumping straight into it.

Chapter Six

Jenn came to her feet, unsure if she should cross and attempt to hug her sister or remain still and see how Rachel responded. These next few moments were crucial in their repairing process.

The oldest of the Spencer sisters hadn't changed much in the past three years. She still embraced that whole cowgirl lifestyle. With her signature side braid, button-up shirt, faded jeans and her well-worn dusty boots, Rachel had no doubt come straight from the farm.

Rachel's eyes darted to Violet then landed firmly back on Jenn. No smile, no arms wide-open for an embrace. That open wound in Jenn's heart seemed to crack even wider, but she couldn't focus on the pain. She had to focus on the hope that she could mend these broken fences.

"Should I go?" Vi asked.

"No need," Rachel said, her gaze still locked on Jenn. "We're all in this together."

Maybe that was a good sign? Jenn didn't know whether that meant they were all one big family or they were all in the same mess but on opposite sides.

"I'm glad you stopped by," Jenn told her sister. "You look really good, Rach."

"Thanks."

The dry reply had a new wave of discomfort and awkward awareness pumping through her. At least she'd discovered her biggest hurdles—her father and Rachel. Erin and her mother were going to be Jenn's support system and apparently Violet wanted to be in the neutral zone. Jenn didn't want any of them to be on different ends of the playing field. She wanted them all on the same side, together, as one united family…just like they used to be.

Jenn figured she might as well just start things off and break through this unwanted tension.

"I'm sorry," she said simply, then realized the words might sound empty and meaningless. "I know that can't be a blanket statement that covers all that has happened between us, but I am truly sorry for not reaching out over all this time. I know words probably don't mean anything to you right now but—"

"They don't."

Rachel's curt reply had Jenn cringing. Violet's echoing gasp was proof that this situation had gone too far for too long. Rachel had deep wounds...wounds that Jenn had caused. And as much as Jenn wanted to pull out her own defense on her reasons why, she didn't want to stand here and make excuses for the years' long gap of her absence.

"I understand you're angry," Jenn started again. She crossed her arms over her chest and realized that stance might look confrontational, so she dropped her arms to her side once again. "I also know I can't fix everything from the past with a few words or a quick visit. I'm here for as long as it takes."

"And then what?" Rachel asked. "You'll leave again?"

Jenn shrugged, still holding on to the honest approach. "I'm not sure what the future will bring. I'd like to stay. I'd like to try to find my way back to my family. If I'm not welcome here, then I'm not sure I could remain in a town where I would run into everyone but not be accepted. So only time will tell."

Her sister stared, lips thinned, as if trying to think of a reply or gather her thoughts.

The front door chimed once again and Jenn glanced around Rachel just as Luke stepped through. He took in the sight of the three women and stilled.

"Apologies." He held up a hand and offered

a smile. "I didn't mean to interrupt. I can come back later."

"Come on in," Violet told him as she stood. "I need to get back to the clinic and I think Rachel has to get back to the farm."

"Actually, I don't—"

Violet smacked her sister's arm. "Dad needs help, remember?"

Rachel blew out a sigh but had manners enough to paste on a smile a she addressed Luke. "I've been here long enough."

Long enough? More like ten minutes.

But maybe that time frame was already more than she'd counted on. Jenn's nerves ramped up even higher. She and Rachel had settled nothing, if anything, Jenn knew full well where she stood with her oldest sibling. Ground zero. She'd have an uphill battle to fight, but Jenn wasn't letting that deter her from making the climb. Life was full of valleys and mountains, and standing in the valley now, she had nowhere else to go but up.

"I'm glad you two came by," Jenn told her sisters as they made their way toward the door.

Luke eased aside and held the door open. "Hope I didn't run you guys off."

"Not at all," Violet assured him. "I have appointments in a little bit anyway. Just wanted to see my sister."

"Maybe we can get together at the farm," Jenn called, hopeful.

They both glanced her way, but only Violet replied.

"Yeah. Maybe."

Once they were both gone, Jenn's heart sank just a little more. Definitely not the homecoming she'd been hoping for. Actually, she wasn't sure if things could have gone worse. Only moments ago she'd been full of hope and a little excitement, but that had diminished fast and left her with the harsh reality that the hurdles she had to jump were higher than she'd expected.

Their meeting was brief and painful, so Jenn still didn't have any more direction than she did before Rachel arrived.

Luke closed the door behind the women and turned to her. A shroud of concern covered his handsome face. Those piercing eyes held her in place with a level of care and worry she hadn't seen from him before. She didn't necessarily like having her private life on display for anyone, let alone Luke, but with this small town there was no way to hide everything. She had no doubt he'd already heard rumors about her and her family.

"I'm sorry," he started with a sigh. "I didn't mean to interrupt."

Jenn tipped her head and attempted a smile

she didn't feel. "Don't be sorry. I'm not sure you were interrupting. Maybe more like saving me."

Luke took a step toward her and she realized for the first time he didn't have Paisley. They seemed to be a strong duo and other than the brief encounter at the farm, she'd only seen them together. Likely she was in school, but being here alone with Luke seemed odd. She found him too appealing and much too distracting.

"I won't pretend I know what's going on," he said, "but I can listen if you need to talk."

Shocked by his generosity, Jenn smiled. "I appreciate that, but nobody wants to get mixed up in my family's drama. Drama that I caused, by the way. I take full blame, but this is such a delicate situation and I'm afraid I'm not handling it very well."

Luke slid his hands into his pockets as he took another step closer. That striking gaze continued to hold her in place and she wondered what thoughts, or even judgment, rolled through his mind. He seemed to genuinely care and want to help, but she wasn't so sure there was anything anyone could do at this point. Everything from here on out solely rested on her shoulders. A heavy load to bear, but unavoidable.

"You're communicating with your family, so I'd say that's a step in the right direction."

Luke's calming words eased some of that

heavy weight off her shoulders. Just having someone from the outside and detached from the situation give any type of advice seemed to calm some of her nerves. Or perhaps that shift in emotions stemmed from her unwanted pull to her new landlord. Regardless, she appreciated the fact he took the time to comfort her.

"I assume you're here to check out the water heater and not listen to my problems."

Luke shrugged, clearly in no hurry to move along his visit. She couldn't help but compare that subtle fact about Luke to Cole. Her late husband was all work all the time. Rushing from one project to the next. Luke had a laid-back attitude that calmed Jenn in a way she didn't even know she needed.

"No reason I can't do both," he informed her.

Another rapid wave of warmth spread through her. She wasn't looking for attraction or anything else. Family first. That had to be her motto now until her relationships were all restored.

"That's sweet, but just getting hot water by tomorrow is all I can ask for," she joked as she turned toward the back of the salon. "My inspector is coming at noon to give the okay for me to open, which I need because I've already scheduled several appointments for Friday."

His footsteps echoed behind her as she led the way to the utility room. She glanced at the sleeping dog, thankful she'd calmed down after the visitors. At least one of them had calm nerves.

"Looks like Cookie is liking her new home," Luke commented. "I've still not heard of anyone looking for their lost dog. Violet would be a good one to ask, too."

Jenn cringed. "I didn't even think to ask her to check around. I was just so shocked to see her show up unannounced, I guess nothing else crossed my mind."

Violet had followed her dreams of becoming a vet. Jenn had kept up with her sisters via social media and knew her sister's love of animals had turned into the perfect career. Jenn also hadn't thought how Violet and Luke would very likely know each other, considering they were both in the same line of work. Even though Luke focused on farm and livestock, while Violet did smaller animals, they had to run into each other or even call on each other every now and then.

Jenn couldn't help but wonder if Luke knew more about their family situation than she'd initially thought. In a town as small as Rosewood Valley, there weren't many secrets...especially when a prodigal daughter returned to the fold. She didn't like the idea of being the center of the gossip mill, but that was out of her control and she couldn't worry about what anyone other than her family thought of her.

When they reached the small utility room, Jenn stepped aside to let Luke assess the situation. If he knew about her family's history and drama, he was gentlemanly enough to not say a word. Did he know their farm was in trouble? No, she highly doubted her proud father would ever say anything to anyone about struggling. Her father would go down on a sinking ship before asking for a life jacket.

Luke stood with his hands on his hips and stared at the water heater.

"I have no clue about these things, so I'm hoping you do," she stated, breaking through the silence. "And I'm hoping this isn't too costly of a fix."

Jenn watched as he glanced around and muttered under his breath. She crossed her arms and tried not to compare Luke and Cole once again, but the memory slammed into her with no warning. Cole had always been a hands-on guy and one that always knew how to fix things. Busted pipes in their little rental on the edge of town had been no problem. They'd laughed in the midst of the chaos of shooting water, a flooded bathroom and soaked clothing. Cole had made everything in her life an adventure right up until his final day.

"Jenn."

Blinking, she pulled herself from her thoughts

and directed her attention back to Luke. He faced her now, the crease between his brows growing deeper at his apparent concern.

"Sorry," she said, dropping her arms to her side. "You caught me daydreaming."

"I said we're going to have to replace this. I can go buy one today, but I might not be able to install it until later tonight. I'm due at the Millers' farm in an hour and it's a county over."

"I wonder who else could install it," she murmured, trying to think of anyone she used to know who did repairs or maintenance. "I can ask around. I don't want to stress you or cause a long day. I'm sure you're busy with Paisley this evening."

Luke slid his thumbs through his belt loops and widened his stance. "She can come with me. I'm sure she'd love to see Cookie if it's not too late since it's a school night. Shouldn't take but a couple hours to install so long as there's no complications."

"Well, if it gets too late, I can always take Paisley back to your house and get her in bed," Jenn offered. "If that's okay with you. But I also don't mind calling around to see who else can install. I'm sure the hardware store has a list of contractors."

Luke shook his head. "No need to pay someone when I know how."

"I didn't even think you might have help already with Paisley," she amended, embarrassed that she'd just assumed. "I just didn't want you to go out of your way if she needed you."

"I don't have evening help," he replied. "If I get called out on an emergency, she just has to go with me. It's only happened a couple of times since I've been in town."

Jenn paused and thought for a second. "How long have you been in town?"

"About six months."

Jenn realized she didn't know much about him at all other than he was a single father, livestock vet and now a fairly new resident. She shouldn't ask more questions. Luke's personal life certainly wasn't any of her concern, but she couldn't help the curiosity that got the best of her.

"Where did you move from?" she asked.

"Small town in Oregon where I grew up."

"So you're used to small towns. You must feel right at home here in Rosewood Valley."

Another casual shrug as his gaze darted away for the briefest of seconds before returning back to her.

"I've visited plenty over the years, but it's still quite an adjustment," he told her. "Paisley loves it here and this is home to her, so this is where I'll be. She's all that matters."

Confused, Jenn blinked and tucked her hair

behind her ears. "Paisley has always lived here? But you just got here?"

Luke stared for a moment before he offered a slight smile. "Yeah. I guess I just thought you would've heard my backstory by now. You know, being a small town and all."

"It's not like I talk to many people," she muttered.

Luke blew out a sigh. "I'm Paisley's uncle and now permanent guardian. The rest is probably a story for another time."

The hesitancy and tenderness in his tone told Jenn that whatever Luke had been through, or was still going through, had hurt him on a deeper level. If he wanted to disclose more, he would. But men were stubborn creatures. Her father, her late husband, both hardheaded and full of pride. As much as she wanted to know more about Luke, she also had enough issues without digging into anyone else's. Besides, if he wanted to open that door wider to let her in, he would.

"We all have those painful parts of our past we don't want rising to the surface." She figured they already had that much in common. "You'll hear quite a bit about me, no doubt, considering you do work with my dad and other ranches and farms. I'm sure the gossip mill is all abuzz with the prodigal daughter coming home."

His brows drew in slightly as he tipped his

head back. The wave of worry emanating off him calmed something within her and she had no clue how he managed to do that with little to no effort.

"I'm not one for gossip," he replied in that firm yet soft tone. "I try my best to stick to my own business and try not to get caught up in others'."

"That's good to know."

"I should get going."

Luke started toward the doorway and Jenn eased aside to let him through, but he stopped just in front of her. She had to draw her eyes up to look at him and another wave of awareness sent warmth through her belly.

"For what it's worth—" Luke began "—and just from the little I know about your family, they are amazing people and I'm sure everything will work out."

Something about his reassuring words soothed her once again. She didn't know how a virtual stranger and outsider knew exactly what to say, but he managed to give her a sense of peace for the time being. No, he'd actually been bringing her peace since she met him. That fast, hard pull toward him should worry her, but there wasn't one worry in her mind where Luke was concerned.

"I pray that's the case," she replied. "I just

want it to be easy and I know that's not going to be how this will work."

"Nothing in life is easy, but it's our actions and reactions that can change any course."

Yeah, and she'd derailed three years ago, so her actions would have to be drastically different than before. And her reactions couldn't go into that default mode of anger. She'd had time and therapy to help process what happened, and to understand that her father hadn't caused Cole's death.

"If you're going to cry, can you give me a heads-up?" He bent down slightly to meet her gaze. "I'm not the best at handling tears and I tend to get awkward."

Jenn couldn't help but laugh at his crooked grin framed by his dark, cropped beard and she knew she'd given him the exact reaction he wanted. How did this man who didn't even know her somehow figure out how to make her smile when her heart was breaking? Not to mention when he was dealing with his own turmoil.

"I'll save the tears for private," she promised. "I'm just frustrated and worried more than anything. I wish I could see into the future and know everything will be okay."

That intense stare of his held her in place. She wondered what he was thinking, found herself caring more than she wanted to admit. Not only was he an extremely handsome man, he also seemed to have a giving, compassionate heart. How could he not capture her attention? How could she not return that same type of grace and empathy?

"We're not guaranteed easy, are we?" he asked. "But I am a firm believer that things work out the way they should."

"I used to feel that way," she admitted. "I don't know anymore."

He opened his mouth to say something else, then closed it. With a brief nod, he eased past her and started toward the front of the salon. Jenn followed behind, wondering if he found her to be a negative person. She didn't mean to be, but she also couldn't help how she felt or her true feelings.

"I'll let you know what time I'll be back later," he told her as he reached for the front door. "Hopefully I won't be too long at the Millers'."

"I'm not going anywhere," she assured him.

Once he was gone, Jenn turned just as Cookie came out from beneath the shampoo bowl. She stared at Jenn like she was looking for some guidance or waiting for her to do something. Right now, she wasn't sure what to do or where to go. Every part of her wanted to head back to the farm and see her dad. She'd give anything to help him in the barns again. To work alongside him like she'd done as a young girl. Her parents had taught her to be well-rounded and independent.

So much changed on that fateful day. But Jenn figured the only thing she could do was try again. She'd have to keep going back, keep proving that she wanted to mend their relationship. Not only did she need to fix what she'd broken, she had to make sure the farm and her childhood home were saved. She couldn't even fathom how worried her parents must be, but Jenn had to find out exactly what was going on before she could figure out a solution.

The drought had taken its toll on the crops last year and her mother's canned goods for the farmer's market would've been affected. Not to mention all the baked goods she sold to the local bakery and most of that was done from ingredients from their crops as well. Selling some of their livestock had to have been one of the most difficult decisions her father had ever made... and she hadn't been here to help or support them during that stressful period.

Cookie sat in front of her and pawed at her leg. Jenn suddenly had an epiphany. Maybe she could incorporate a little of her experience from her time away and bring that into Rosewood Valley. It certainly wouldn't hurt to discuss the idea with her mother or sisters.

The farm-to-table events she'd set up at her church just months ago had been a big hit and a great moneymaker for their youth programs.

What if they could do the same at the farm? Would the people of the town embrace such a new, fresh idea for this area? Would her family think she was crazy for proposing this scheme? First they'd have to trust her again and they'd have to work as a team to pull everything off.

She shot off a text to her sisters that she'd like to talk with them if they had the time to stop by her shop.

Maybe, just maybe, she could salvage her relationships and the farm with one master plan.

Chapter Seven

"They're all good to go."

Luke squatted down to his bag and reorganized his supplies. After all the vaccines he'd given this week, he needed to double-check his inventory back at the clinic and make sure he was well stocked. He'd gotten sidetracked the other day with Jenn and Cookie. Plus, still being the new vet in town, he had a reputation to uphold. Not only that, Luke didn't want to disappoint any of Charles's old clients. Taking over this clinic had been a blessing and perfect timing for the events of Luke's life.

"I appreciate you taking the time to come all the way out here," Allen Miller stated, rocking back on his booted heels. "It's not just anyone who would have kept on all the farms in this county."

"I love my job." Luke came to his feet and hoisted his medical bag at his side. "I'm happy to have the work and the opportunity. I should be thanking you all for giving a new vet a try."

"You had big shoes to fill. You've done really well. I know some were concerned with you being younger, but you've proven your worth."

Luke didn't know he'd been the topic of conversation or that his age had been in question, but he was glad to know he had the approval of so many farmers in the area. Without them, he wouldn't be employed or be able to care for Paisley.

And now he could add more attorney fees on top of everything else if he had to head to court for a custody dispute. He'd put every dollar he had to keep his niece where she belonged. While he was told the process would likely move slow, his attorney had been texting him and keeping him updated every step of the way. Even when there was nothing to report, she reassured him not to worry and she had everything under control. She had more confidence than he did that any judge would see Paisley was best with Luke, especially considering that was how Paisley's parents wanted her raised. While they might be gone, the intent of their will was as plain as black and white.

Hopefully the case wouldn't even make it to court and Paisley would never have to know anything happened. Of course if there was family who wanted to see her, Luke would meet with them in person and supervise. He had to be protective of Paisley regarding everyone he brought into her life. He'd never had a more important job.

"I'm glad you're all pleased." Luke's boots scuffed over the sprinkling of hay on the concrete barn floor as he made his way toward the wide-open door. "Don't hesitate to call if any of your swine have reactions to their vaccines, but they should be fine."

"Will do." The farmer nodded. "Be safe traveling back. Supposed to storm soon."

The sun had disappeared behind the dark gray clouds and his first thought was how Paisley would love putting on her rain boots and dancing in puddles so long as there was no thunder and lightning. Maybe he could get the water heater installed and get Paisley to the puddles before bedtime.

Luke waved bye to Allen and climbed into the truck. Just as he sat his supply bag on the passenger seat, his cell vibrated in his pocket. He fished the device out and stared at the screen. His lawyer. He didn't know if he should be scared or excited, considering the past few exchanges had merely been a text. He hoped with each interaction that he'd find out Talia's cousin was dropping her custody battle. Wouldn't that be the best-case scenario?

He swiped the screen and put the phone on speaker as he put the truck into gear.

"Autumn," he answered, circling the drive to head out. "Please tell me you have good news and we can put this all behind us."

"I'm afraid that's not the case. Beacon Law Firm claims their client wants to move forward and, I'm sorry, but you're not going to like this next part."

He gripped the wheel and held his breath. "What is it?"

"Carol is requesting to meet Paisley in person as well."

A ball of fear coiled tight in his gut as he pulled down the tree-lined drive leading toward the county road. He attempted to relax his breathing, something he'd learned from his therapist, and tried to get control of his emotions before he spoke. He had to stay in control here, of his words and his actions.

"Do I have to let her see Paisley?" Luke asked. "I don't even know this woman so I'm not sure that's the best move. I'm not just going to subject my niece to a stranger who will try to sway her to come live with her."

"I understand your position and no, we do not have to make the two meet. For now," Autumn quickly added. "If the judge orders a meeting, then we won't have a choice, but we can definitely put this off and I think that's for the best as well."

A wave of relief slid through him. One hurdle dodged. But how many more did he have to go? That whole fear of the unknown had him clinging to his faith and selfishly praying a little harder than before.

"Could I maybe talk with Carol on my own?" he asked. "I understand her wanting to see her family, but at the same time, she would have to understand the situation. Paisley knows me, we're in the only home she's ever known, and this is what Scott and Talia wanted."

"I would advise you not to reach out to her," Autumn warned. "That's not a great move and, like you said, we don't know her. She could twist your words, and we don't want anything going against you. You have to look like the solid foundation for Paisley. You moving to her hometown is a great step. You already had that in place so it doesn't look like you're making moves just to impress a judge. How's the land coming for the home and the new clinic?"

Luke sighed as he made another turn to get onto the highway to take him back to Rosewood Valley.

"Slower than I'd hoped," he replied.

And by *slower*, he meant at a standstill. But he had hope. The Spencers hadn't come out and told him no, so that meant there was a chance. He had a surge of guilt, though. As he got to know Jenn a bit more and listen to her touch on her fears and worries, he'd been keeping this secret that he wanted her family's land to provide a more stable environment for Paisley. They needed a fresh start, something that could be just for them. Having a home and clinic in one place just made sense.

Still, his growing attraction for his new tenant, coupled with the fact she trusted him and had started confiding in him, did not sit well with his conscience.

"Keep working on that." Autumn's stern voice echoed through his truck. "We want to show not only stability but progress, and that you're putting all of Paisley's needs first just like her parents intended."

Paisley had been blessed with the very best parents. Luke worried time and again that he wasn't near their level, but he'd try harder and harder each day to show Paisley how much he loved her.

"I'm not doing all of this to impress some judge I don't even know," Luke grumbled, more than frustrated. "I'm doing this because it's the right thing to do and because I love Paisley like my own."

"I know this, but nobody else does. I'm well aware you have your niece's best interest at heart. I also know you are taking your duties seriously in carrying out the wishes of your brother. I promise, I'm in your corner here and doing everything possible to make sure Paisley stays right where she belongs."

Any other outcome terrified him. He'd never been this scared of anything in his entire life, not even when he'd been left at the altar with nothing but unopened wedding gifts and a broken heart.

Sylvia had done a number on him and it had taken quite some time for him to realize that they weren't meant to be and that she'd done him a favor by leaving.

But he couldn't let his mind travel to that unsettling place of his past or the unpredictable future. He had to hold on to his faith and be optimistic. He had to keep going with his life like he and Paisley would be a team forever. He'd gotten used to his little wing-woman and there was nobody else he wanted in his life right now.

"So what are the next steps?" he asked.

"Well, I'm going to go back and tell them that we are not bringing Paisley to the first meeting. You will have to fly to Washington when the magistrate sets the date. The system is pretty backlogged, so I don't imagine this will be fast or soon."

Wonderful. Just what he wanted, for this whole ordeal to drag out. One more thing to stress about. Relying on faith had gotten him through so much in life. Vet school, his breakup with his fiancée, the loss of his brother and sister-in-law, this move. He knew God guided every step of the way and had a plan, but Luke truly wished he knew Paisley would stay with him. That's all he wanted. Maybe he wasn't the best father figure—he had no clue what he was doing—but he and Paisley were finding their footing together. They were growing as their own family unit and they shared that deep bond from the loss of two very important people.

"I guess you didn't deliver terrible news, considering," he told her. "I appreciate all the work you're doing. Sorry if I'm cranky at times."

"Like I said, it's understandable. Nobody wants their world rocked like this and not to come to Carol's defense, but I think she just wants a piece of her family, too."

That was what terrified Luke. If the judge saw this woman—a married veteran with a stable life—would that trump everything in the will?

"I'll let you know as soon as I hear anything," Autumn added. "Don't lose hope. We've got this."

Luke thanked her and disconnected the call. As he continued down the highway in silence, he tried to push aside all the thoughts clouding his mind, but he couldn't. All his failures and reasons why he wouldn't make a good guardian ran through his head.

Would the judge see that he'd never had a committed relationship? Would he come across as unstable because he was still single and had just moved?

More than ever, he needed to acquire that land from the Spencers. Setting roots had to count for something, right? He had to prove he was the right choice, aside from the obvious will. Luke needed to make sure a solid plan was in place before any meeting with the judge or before this case progressed any further.

All he could do was press Will a bit more. But making the elderly man understand this was the best option for everyone, and a solid step to save his farm, was the only way to go into this. Luke couldn't push too far or too hard or all of this could be lost and he'd be starting over.

Paisley couldn't go live with anyone else. He refused to even think of his life without her.

"Come on, Cookie."

Jenn stood outside of her car holding the back door open and snapping her fingers at the pup. She smacked her legs, whistled and tried to coerce the dog from the back seat. But Cookie merely backed up with her butt against the opposite door. Jenn wasn't sure what other tips or tricks or mind games to play to get the dog comfortable enough to get out of the car.

The sky grew darker and a rumble of thunder sounded in the distance. She really wanted to get into the barn or even the house before the rain cut loose.

"Jenn."

Her father's voice boomed from behind her. That familiar, stern tone had her straightening as the ball of tension grew in her belly. She hadn't heard his voice in three years, let alone heard her name pass through his lips. She wanted to cry over that sweet sound. She wanted to run into his arms and get one of those strong bear hugs he was always so good at.

But time and tragedy had changed everything and robbed her of the life she'd always envisioned.

Slowly, Jenn turned and shoved her hair from her face. Her father stood several feet away, his thumbs hooked in those signature red suspenders. He stared across the gravel drive from beneath the wide brim of his worn brown hat.

"Hi, Dad."

"Your mother went into church to set up for a dinner. Should be back around five."

Jenn laced her fingers in front of her, not sure what to do and never believing in a million years she'd ever feel uncomfortable around the man who'd raised her and loved her unconditionally. But he was talking to her, so she wasn't going to back away.

"I'm here to see you, actually."

"That so?" His hands dropped to his sides, but he remained still.

Jenn dipped her chin. She recognized his stubborn side and she also realized that his pride and heart had taken a hard hit because of her.

"Yes," she confirmed. "I have a pet now and thought she could use the yard to run around but she won't get out of the car."

"A pet? Does that mean you're staying in town?"

Will Spencer started taking a few steps toward her and she noted the slower pace than what he'd once had. Farming wasn't an easy life and he'd been doing this for decades. She wondered what else had changed about her father since she'd last been here. How was his health? Was there anything else within the family she should worry about? Or was the farm the most pressing issue now?

"I'm renting a building in town from Luke," she explained. "The one on Sycamore."

Her father's steps halted as a crease formed between his thick, silver brows.

"Luke? My vet?"

Jenn nodded.

Another flash of hesitation moved over his face, but Jenn had no idea why the mention of Luke's name gave her dad pause. Was there an issue between the two men? Luke never mentioned a thing and he knew full well who her father was. Surely there wasn't any tension. She couldn't imagine either man at odds with the other. And wouldn't her sisters have said something?

A nudge on the back of her thigh pulled Jenn's attention back to the car. Cookie stood right behind her now as if trying to see if there was actually a threat outside the safety of the vehicle.

"What's your dog's name?" her father asked.

"Cookie." Jenn shrugged and focused back on her father. "It's a long story. She's not actually mine. She was a stray that ended up at the shop and I can't find the owner."

"Then you're the owner."

Jenn sighed. "That's what Violet said."

His eyes narrowed slightly, enhancing the crow's-feet around the corners. Yeah, he'd definitely aged over the past three years. Jenn couldn't help but wonder how her actions had affected his health.

"You saw your sister?" he asked.

Jenn nodded. "I've seen everyone now."

"Rachel?"

Once again, she nodded.

"So, you really are here to see me?" he asked.

Jenn reached back, needing to find solace in her new furry friend. Cookie turned into her hand, clearly wanting the comfort as well. Maybe they were the best team as they waded through this uncertain period together.

"I think it's past time," she replied. "Don't you?"

He continued to stare at her, and nothing but the low thunder overhead filled the silence. A slight breeze kicked up and Jenn tucked her hair behind her ears. She could grab a clip from her purse, but she didn't want to break this moment.

Her father continued to simply stand there, saying nothing. Everything about him from his weathered hands to those signature suspenders only reminded her how much she'd missed him. Missed working in the barns or in the field, missed spending quiet time or getting sound advice. So much had changed on that fateful day when she'd lost her world and placed the blame directly at her father's feet.

The fact that he hadn't turned his back on her like last time seemed promising...at least that's how she was interpreting the situation. Jenn couldn't help but wonder if her mother said something after Jenn had left the other day. Had they discussed Jenn being back in town? Had her parents talked about how her father hadn't spoken one word? While her mother might be calm, soft-spoken and at times passive, there was no way she would have just bit her tongue over the way Will Spencer had treated his daughter that day.

And this was precisely why she'd brought Cookie. Having a buffer and something else to break this inevitable tension had been a must.

Jenn turned and reached into the car, carefully hoisting the dog up in her arms. Maybe she'd realize this was the best place to visit. A nice wide-open area to run and be free for a bit. Jenn would keep an eye on her so she didn't venture too far into the fields and get in with the cattle, but she didn't believe Cookie would, timid as she'd been acting. Maybe she didn't like storms.

"Are you leaving her here?" her dad asked.

"I figure it was good for her to be out of the apartment, so we both came for a visit."

She set the dog down, but she remained right by her side. Jenn hadn't even considered that Cookie might be afraid of the storm rolling in as they'd left home. Jenn didn't want her terrified, so maybe they should at least get into the barns.

"You needed the support of a dog to visit me?"

Will Spencer had always been a keen man with a sharp mind. Time might have aged his face but nothing had touched his ability to know her inside and out. No other man in this world knew her like her father. No matter the differences or the wedge between them, nothing could erase their bond. She had to cling to that bond now and trust their solid foundation would see them through.

"After my last visit, I wasn't sure how I'd be received."

Once again, her father's thumbs slid into his suspenders as he ran his hands up and down in that memorable way. The man seemed to do his best thinking while wearing out those red straps.

A fat drop hit her arm and Jenn glanced to the darkening sky as the clouds rolled in with a bit more intensity.

"Spring storms are unpredictable," her father muttered as another drop hit her. "You staying or going?"

Jenn pulled her attention back to him. "I guess that depends on you."

"You're still my daughter."

He turned and started toward the back of the house, and Jenn figured that was the only invitation she was going to get to follow along. She snapped her fingers at Cookie and fell into step behind her dad. Thankfully the dog did as well and by the time they hit the back porch, the skies opened and sheets of rain pelted right where they had been.

She never thought she would have to wait for

an offer to go inside the house she grew up in. And maybe she could walk right in, but Jenn wanted to be respectful. She'd left, not had any contact due to shame and embarrassment, so she couldn't expect to just pretend nothing happened. She needed to face her past before she could confront the issue with the farm and how to help.

Honestly, Jenn didn't know what area to address first—the blame for Cole's death or the long absence. One thing was certain, this storm raging outside was nothing compared to the turmoil rolling through her family.

"Get on in the house," he grumbled. "I need to go finish working on the stalls."

Jenn knew an excuse when she heard one, and years ago she would've called him out on it. Now...well, he was at least talking to her, so she'd give him his space. Besides, no storm would keep Will Spencer from a task. If anything required repairs, he'd always had the mentality that everything needed doing right that minute.

"Do you need help?" she offered, always remembering her manners and because she genuinely cared. "It's getting nasty out there."

"I've got it."

Without another word, he headed back out into the storm, leaving her on the covered porch with her pup. He rushed toward the barn and out of sight. He hadn't asked her to leave, but he also didn't want to accept her offering of help. He needed time to himself and she respected that.

Baby steps, right? Hope wasn't lost, she'd just have to be patient.

Chapter Eight

The place smelled the same. Like yeast and love.

Jenn had always found the kitchen of her childhood home to be like a big, cozy hug. Her mother loved to bake and always had something amazing in the oven or on the counter ready for any unexpected guest who might stop by. She'd instilled that trait into each of her girls and still to this day, Jenn loved to get creative in the kitchen. Her mother's biscuit recipe was hands down Jenn's favorite. She'd made them a few times for church events over the past three years. Each time they'd been a huge hit and Jenn thought of her mother with every compliment from the parishioners.

Cookie remained right beside her as Jenn took in her familiar surroundings. The long island in the center of the kitchen still seemed to be the hub of the room. A basket of fruit sat in the middle, along with a pile of mail, a folded dish towel, a forgotten cup of coffee that made her smile. Clearly her father still had that afternoon cup like always. The temps could be thirty degrees or ninety. The man insisted on an afternoon jolt of caffeine.

On the counter next to the sink sat a plate with a glass dome lid. No surprise a platter of cookies was ready for any guest or family that stopped by. Her mother had always been the gracious hostess.

Obviously some things never changed, which soothed her soul and relaxed her a bit more. Jenn didn't know what she expected when she stepped back into her old home. She honestly hadn't given the space much thought since she'd been focused on the people and not the things. But seeing the same floral wallpaper, the same framed sign with her mother's favorite scripture above the breakfast table, and the yellow apron hanging by the pantry, eased even more of those jumbled nerves inside Jenn. Maybe she needed this familiarity to help with her transition. And perhaps being alone for this next step was for the best. This way she could take her time and walk through, like reacquainting herself with an old friend.

Rain pelted the windows and she moved through the house, taking advantage of her privacy. She tried to practice potential conversations she'd have once her father came in. Would he want to listen to her first or get his own thoughts off his chest? She'd let him take the lead and go from there. She had no way of knowing how things would go or how this day would end, but she held tight to the fact she'd jumped a few hurdles just to be here and she had to keep up this positive momentum.

Jenn started to pass through the dining room, but paused at the table and chairs. This wasn't the same set that had been in her family for generations. Where had they gone? Jenn had always thought those pieces would go to her once she built a house with her husband. Or at least, she'd assumed as much since she'd been the first one to get married.

That gut reaction of recognizing her loss hit her once again. Coming back home stirred up too many memories, but thanks to a long string of counseling over the years, she had learned to not only cope with her grief but live with it. She and Cole had been ready to build their dream house back on the family land when the accident happened. They'd started off in a small rental in town, then to save money, they'd moved into the loft apartment over one of the barns on the farm until they could save enough to break ground.

Jenn hadn't ventured to that part of the property yet, and she honestly didn't know if she'd be ready for that monumental step anytime soon.

Moving beyond the new furniture and into

the living room, she smiled when she saw her father's old recliner. She couldn't believe that thing was still standing. She'd been a little girl when he'd bought that big ugly leather thing. Her mother had tried to protest that it was too large and an eyesore for their small living room, but then she'd realized that Will Spencer worked hard in the fields and barns and just wanted one thing in this house. He never cared about decor or anything else and never asked for anything of his own. He'd just wanted a comfortable chair to relax in at the end of a hard day's work.

Jenn turned toward the fireplace and spotted the row of various frames and photographs. Pictures had always been so important to her mother. The woman was always snapping every event to lock in the precious memories. As her eyes traveled over the different pictures, Jenn was pleased to see that several were from her childhood. She'd never been omitted from the family, even though she'd removed herself for a short time. Her mother's love never wavered.

And for that, Jenn knew she'd carry this guilt forever. Now she just had to learn how to live with it and overcome, to be a stronger daughter, sister, friend and Christian.

Swallowing the lump in her throat and straightening her shoulders, Jenn pulled in a deep breath. As difficult as this part of her journey was, she had to push the past and the nega-tive thoughts to the back of her mind. When she turned again, she laughed at the sight of Cookie, who had taken up residence in the corner of the worn, plaid sofa.

"We're not moving in," she told the pup. "Don't get too comfortable."

The dog curled tighter into a ball and nes-tled deeper into her position. Jenn had no idea what made this animal so comfortable around the Spencer clan. Maybe she knew good people. Jenn had always heard dogs were keen to per-sonalities.

The screen door opened and slammed shut. Jenn assumed her father had returned from the stalls, so she turned to head toward the back of the house once more. Maybe they could talk a little more in depth now…she hoped.

"That man is going to be the death of me."

Jenn chewed the inside of her cheek to keep from laughing at her mother's muttering filter-ing in from the kitchen. Sarah had grumbled that same statement beneath her breath Jenn's en-tire life. As frustrated as she'd get with her hus-band, Sarah Spencer loved Will with her whole heart. Those two had an unbreakable bond. Jenn looked up to them and wanted a love like theirs. She'd *had* a love like theirs, so the question now was, would she ever find that again? Were people blessed enough to fall twice?

Jenn truly wanted to believe that she deserved a second chance and that one day, she would recognize when the right person came along. Somebody worthy of her opening her heart once again. But the risk of it being shattered scared her, and that was a fact she couldn't deny. But did she want to live the rest of her life in fear?

"Jenn," her mother called just as Jenn stepped from the dining room into the kitchen.

"Hey, Mom."

Her mother rested her purse on the center island and opened her arms just like she'd done the other day. "Oh, honey. You don't know how happy I am to see you in here."

Just as Jenn stepped forward to accept her mother's love, her mom dropped her arms and shook her head.

"No, wait. I'm all wet," her mom complained. "It is crazy out there and your father is insistent on repairing those broken stalls. I don't know why he won't just come in."

"Because I stopped by and he's still processing," Jenn stated simply. "And I don't care if you're wet, Mom."

Jenn closed the distance between them and embraced her mother, inhaling that familiar lavender perfume. Her petite mom always gave the strongest hugs. Jenn held on a bit longer than she used to, but she had time to make up for.

"Has he seen you or talked to you?" her mom asked as she eased back.

Jenn nodded. "I was trying to get Cookie from the car when he came up to me."

"Cookie?"

"My dog. Well, she's not *my* dog, but mine until I find the owner."

Her mom glanced around. "Did your dog stay out in the storm?"

Jenn released her mother and laughed. "Oh, no. She made herself at home on your couch."

A wide smile spread across Sarah's face. "Good for her. I hope you both make yourselves at home here."

Jenn started to reply, but her phone vibrated. She pulled it out and glanced at the screen.

I'm here with the new heater. P came with me.

"Oh, shoot." Jenn noted the time and groaned. "I don't know how I lost track of time."

"What's wrong, honey?"

"Just a minor setback at the salon," she explained. "My landlord is there now to fix it, I hope. Can I get a rain check on my visit?"

"Darling, don't you dare insult me by asking if you're allowed to come back. This is your home."

Her home. No matter what had taken place in the past or what the future held, nothing would change the fact that all her core memories and her family belonged here. Having her mother state that so adamantly smoothed out another wrinkle on Jenn's path.

She nodded. "I promise to be back. Not sure how full my schedule is tomorrow, but soon."

Jenn called for Cookie, who took her time coming in from the front of the house. Her little paws clicked on the hardwood as she came to stand obediently next to Jenn.

"Are you sure you want to go out in this storm?" her mother asked.

"I'll be fine," she assured her.

Her mother gave her one last hug, just as tight as the first.

"I love you, Jenn. Be careful."

"Love you, Mama."

That transition back into her mother's love and affection seemed too easy. She knew her mom had unconditional love and knew she was forgiven, but Jenn also recognized that she'd have to address the past to fully heal all wounds—hers and those of the people she loved.

"But when will they be here?"

Paisley swiveled around in one of the two

salon chairs and asked the same question she'd asked since they arrived twenty minutes ago.

"Honey, I already told you she's on her way." Luke smiled gently. "It's rainy and she was visiting her parents."

Paisley brought the chair to a stop and adjusted her glasses as she stared out the front window. Luke knew what had to be rolling through his niece's mind. Apprehension and alarm. But he couldn't dwell on the bad weather and the accident that had robbed them of his brother and sister-in-law. He had to put on a brave front; he had to show Paisley that not every worry resulted in a disaster or tragedy.

"Everything is fine," he assured her. "How about you come help me in the back while we wait?"

That way they'd be away from windows and Paisley didn't have to see anything going on outside. He was slowly learning that distraction was sometimes the best option for a child. Anything to keep her mind on moving forward and overcoming the pain.

"I don't know anything about tools or fixing things," she told him, still staring toward the main street.

Luke crossed the salon and spun her chair so she faced him. He braced his hands on the armrests and smiled again.

"Well, I didn't know anything about hair bows or little girls, but I'm learning. Maybe we can teach each other as we go."

Her lips quirked into a half smile. "You haven't done *too* bad with me, I guess. You did get those purple boots I love."

If only life's problems could be fixed with purple boots...

"So, what do you say?" he asked. "You up for handing me some tools when I need them?"

She nodded and Luke took a step back to allow her space to hop down from the chair. She marched toward the back, in those purple boots she so loved, and he noted her hair seemed to be falling from the style he'd tried this morning before school. He never knew there were so many videos to watch about doing hair. He felt ridiculous saving so many to his phone, but he knew Paisley loved all things girly and her mother had been a master at making her look adorable. Maybe Jenn could show him a few things because hands on might be a better way for him to learn.

Granted Jenn was busy trying to get things open and her new business started, so he'd casually mention it if she had the time. Paisley would probably love if he learned how to step up his game. And perhaps selfishly he just wanted so spend more time with the one woman who had captured his attention since his failed engagement. The timing wasn't great for him to even entertain a relationship, but God had a plan and maybe part of His plan was Jenn. Only time and his heart would tell.

"Okay, first we have to get this big thing out." He patted the side of the water heater. "You're going to help me unhook it and then I'll have Jenn help me get it out the door while you and Cookie play. Sound like a plan?"

Paisley gave two thumbs-up. "I'm ready."

Luke opened his tool bag and pointed to various objects, educating Paisley on what each one was and its purpose. After that quick Contractor 101 course on an eight-year-old level, he got to work shutting off the water. Just as he was figuring out the best way to get the old contraption out from such a tight space, the back door opened and a flurry of activity ensued.

Cookie came rushing in with a clatter, her wet paws trying to find traction on the old wood floors. She shook her whole body, sending water flying around them. Paisley's squeal of delight as she raced toward the dog had Luke chuckling. Then Jenn stepped through the door and she apparently didn't find anything amusing if her scowl was any indication. Her hair hung in ropelike strands around her shoulders and her shoes squeaked as she took another step inside.

"Still raining, I see."

The joke just slipped out, but she apparently had a sense of humor because a smile flirted around her mouth as her gaze cut to his.

"Just a mere sprinkle," she replied with a soft smile. "I'm sorry I lost track of time, but I really need to dry off before I can help."

"Not a problem." He pointed toward Paisley, who was petting and holding a very wet dog. "I've put my best girl on the assistant job for now, so take your time."

Jenn turned to Paisley. "Honey, there are towels in the cabinet by the shampoo sink. Would you want to get some and dry off Cookie for me?"

She glanced at Luke. "I'm supposed to help Toot."

"Go on ahead," he told her. "Then you can come back and help me. I promise there will still be work to do. Cookie is dripping everywhere."

She nodded and patted her thigh, calling for Cookie to follow her toward the front of the shop.

"I really am sorry," Jenn repeated, lowering her voice and scrunching up her nose like she'd done something wrong. "Have you been waiting long?"

"Not at all and there's no need to apologize. I already drained the water from the tank and just need your help getting it out. No rush on my end."

She offered him another one of her sweet smiles before heading up the back stairs to the loft apartment. Luke released a sigh and tried not to think about how gorgeous she'd looked with her hair in disarray and her minimal makeup smeared from the rain...

And he shouldn't be thinking anything about how cute she was—makeup or no makeup. Yet he couldn't help where his thoughts went—he was human.

"Get it together," he muttered to himself, turning back to the task he should actually be worried about.

While he scolded himself, he couldn't discount that their innocent meeting might just be Divine intervention. He really wished he knew because that gaping wound from Sylvia had taken a long time to heal. Only someone truly special could slide into his heart once again.

Taking a risk at this time in his life terrified him, but he couldn't ignore his feelings so he'd have to take all of this day by day. He just didn't know how strong he was to open up again, especially after the damage to his heart with the loss of not only his only sibling, but his sister-in-law.

There were so many factors working against these unexpected feelings he had toward Jenn, he really wasn't sure how everything would pan out.

Once Jenn discovered that he wanted her family's land, she likely wouldn't be friendly toward him and would probably find him deceitful, so his worries of opening his heart again might be a moot point. But he'd promised Will and Sarah that he'd keep this under wraps and he'd always been a man of his word. He still felt like he was lying every time he talked to Jenn, knowing this secret lived inside him.

Had she come back home because the farm was in trouble? Or had she come back for another reason? Did she have some grand plan to save her family homestead? Luke never wanted to see anyone fail and he hoped the Four Sisters thrived...he just wanted a portion of their space so he could start building a solid life.

He had to move forward with his plan. It was the home he wanted for Paisley. The country location was perfect because Scott and Talia were planning on building in the country, so Luke knew he could continue to fulfill their wishes. And it would show the courts he was the right fit, the *only* fit for his niece. Proving stability and a solid family homelife was the only way he could fight this ridiculous custody battle that never should've become an issue to begin with.

While he didn't have to have this exact piece of property, it made the most sense for several reasons. The Spencers were in a bit of a bind and any large income could make or break them in keeping the rest of their land and their home. Plus, having an already established barn that he could use, and having an office on-site, would be better than the setup he had now.

He'd already started this process and hoped to be making momentum. It wasn't like there was a ton of real estate available that would fit his and Paisley's needs.

His niece's laughter filtered through from the salon. She'd been asking for a dog for some time now. Apparently Scott and Talia had promised her one with the land they were going to build on, but Luke wasn't in a position to take on anything else at this point. Cookie came into their lives, sort of, at exactly the right time. She could get her dog fix to hold her over until the time came for them to choose the right one...just as soon as they found a place to live first. The lease was coming to an end, but Luke knew the landlord would work with him, considering the special circumstances.

Luke managed to get the water heater un-hooked and pulled away from the wall. Now all he had to do was wrestle this thing outside and get the new one in. Doing this in the middle of a storm wasn't the smartest, but if her inspection was tomorrow, they had no other choice. He'd at least wrapped the new water heater box with a large tarp, so it was safe from the elements. Once the lightning stopped, they could get everything swapped out. He just hoped it didn't last into the night. Paisley had to be at school by eight and he liked to get her in bed before nine.

It wasn't too long ago that schedules meant nothing to him if it didn't involve his job. Now everything he did centered around one little girl...and he was perfectly fine with that. A year ago he'd never believe he'd be in a new town starting a new life in a parent role. He never would have dreamed his brother and precious sister-in-law would be gone, leaving their child an orphan. Life literally changed in a split second.

"Okay, how can I help?"

Luke blinked and glanced around the water heater to see a refreshed Jenn. She'd pulled her hair up into some knot on top of her head, scrubbed her face clean of the makeup mess, and had pulled on an oversize T-shirt and a pair of sweatpants. Definitely different from any woman he was used to...and much too lovely for his sanity.

"Why are you looking at me like that?" Her brows drew inward as she stared back. "Please don't tell me there's another issue."

He blinked and scolded himself. He wasn't some teen with a silly crush. He was a grown man with responsibilities, and that didn't include flirting with his tenant.

"No, no. I was just lost in thought." He patted

the old heater. "This needs to get outside and I'll need your help getting the new one in, but we might have to wait for the storm to pass."

Jenn pursed her lips and glanced around the corner wall toward the front of the salon. "I hate for you to take up your whole evening and I know Paisley has school in the morning. How about I call and reschedule my inspection?"

"Absolutely not. I know what it's like being self-employed. Each day not working is a hard blow. We'll get this taken care of, but I'm not sure Paisley will want to go back home in this weather."

Jenn tipped her head. "Is she afraid of storms?"

Luke swallowed. "Yeah. Um…my brother and his wife were killed in an accident on a stormy night. She was actually worried when you weren't here yet."

Jenn's mouth dropped as her hand went to her chest. "Oh, that sweet girl. I had no idea, Luke. I'm sorry. I seem to be saying that quite a bit to you lately."

"And you have no reason to," he replied. "So maybe she could go upstairs with Cookie? If she gets tired she can crash on your couch or something."

"If it starts getting too late, you guys go on home. I assume she'll feel safe with you driving her rather than me?"

"I'm really not sure on that one. This is the first big storm she's been outside of the house in since the passing of her parents. I'm pretty much taking this evening minute by minute."

"Gotcha."

"Actually, each day is minute by minute," he countered with a sigh. "Some days I feel like I'm nailing this parenting thing, and others…well, she eats dog treats as you saw."

Jenn scoffed. "Stop that right now. Do not question yourself. I'm obviously not a parent, but you were put into a delicate situation that not just anyone would step into. Give yourself some grace."

"That's what Pastor Dane spoke about last Sunday," Luke told her. "Grace. It hit me, and I'm trying, but there are times where this new life is difficult."

Jenn reached out and gave his arm a reassuring squeeze. "Paisley loves you and trusts you. She feels safe and happy in your care. You're all the family she has right now, so that's already an unbreakable bond."

Luke nodded, knowing every point she made was valid. He had also been telling himself the same things. Only now, someone else threatened to sever that bond. He couldn't let that happen. He'd fight with all the love inside him to keep Paisley right where she belonged.

"Which church do you go to?" she asked.

When he told her, Jenn's brows rose as she dropped her arm. "No way. That's the church I grew up in."

"Your parents still go there," Luke tacked on. "I've seen your sisters there, too."

"So you know my whole family?"

Luke had to tread carefully here, but he also had to be honest. "I haven't spoken much to your sisters. Well, Vi just a few times because of our similar fields, and Rachel a couple times at the farm. I don't really know your other sister."

"Erin."

Luke nodded, not sure what else to say here. Maybe circling back to the work would be best because he didn't want to venture too far into her family life.

"Hopefully this storm passes soon so we can get that new heater in and Paisley can get to bed on time."

Jenn tapped her finger against her chin, clearly in thought. Her short, painted pink nails captured his attention and he found himself wondering what was rolling through her mind.

"Since we can't do much with the storm, we could all just go upstairs," Jenn suggested. "Paisley and I can bake some cookies or something to distract her and keep her busy. Plus we can eat cookies, so…a win-win in my book."

Luke couldn't help but smile as so many thoughts raced through his mind. Her main concern right now was Paisley, not her pressing issue to get her business open. And she didn't mind opening up her home—or loft—to them so they could be comfortable.

If he wasn't careful, he'd start falling for this woman. Could he trust his heart? After what he'd experienced with his fiancée and then the loss he'd just gone through, was he still too vulnerable and not ready for anything more than a good friend?

"If you're sure," he replied.

Her stunning smile spread wider. "I wouldn't have offered if I wasn't."

Chapter Nine

"Now crack two eggs."

Paisley looked at the egg in Jenn's hand, then darted her gaze back up. The little girl sat up on the island with her legs crossed, looking too adorable and giving flashes of a life Jenn could have had. But this wasn't her daughter, Luke wasn't her husband and this familial setting wasn't hers to own. She was merely helping a friend, nothing more.

"What if I mess it up?" Paisley asked, wrinkling her nose.

Jenn scoffed. "Everyone messes up one time or another. That's how we all learn. I trust that you're going to make the best cookies we've ever had."

Paisley pushed her glasses up her nose and grabbed an egg. With her teeth worrying her bottom lip, she tapped the shell on the edge of the bowl.

"My mom always did it like this," she murmured. "Why isn't mine breaking?"

"Tap a little harder."

Paisley smacked the egg against the side of the bowl once more and the entire thing spilled onto the counter, with some of the shell dropping over the edge and into the bowl.

"Ugh. I knew I couldn't do this right."

Jenn grabbed the roll of paper towels and pulled off several. "Nothing wrong here," Jenn insisted as she wiped off Paisley's sticky hands. "There are more eggs and I'll get this cleaned up. Confidence is key in everything. Remember that. Next time, you'll get it. And if not, you'll get it after that. Why? Because you're going to have confidence in yourself. Right?"

Paisley gave a slight shrug as Jenn shifted to clean the counter. Luke moved from the window facing the street to cross the open loft apartment. He came to stand beside the island and slid his hands into the pockets of his jeans. He said nothing, but his gaze met Jenn's and that soft smile that flirted around his mouth had her heart doing a little dance.

None of this was real. This wasn't some second chance she'd been given. She barely knew the man, honestly. Just because she found him attractive and adored his niece didn't mean they could strike up a relationship.

She hadn't come back to town in the hopes of that coveted second chance. She wasn't sure they even existed for everyone, but she certainly had more pressing matters to focus her mind on. Getting sidetracked by Luke's handsome features and his giving heart wouldn't help her mend fences with her family or figure out just how dire their situation was with the family land.

Making these cookies gave her another idea for the farm to table. She wanted to incorporate some of her mother's amazing desserts like rhubarb pie or warm apple turnovers. She'd add that to her growing list of recipes she'd started. Once she had all her thoughts and a well-laid out plan, she'd approach her family. She was still waiting to see if her sisters would respond to her text.

Jenn turned back to Paisley and handed her another egg. "Now, let's try this again. You've got it."

The sweet girl tapped and tapped, finally cracking the egg and carefully plopping it into the bowl with the dry ingredients. Only one small piece of the shell fell in.

"Now we get that little piece out and move on," Jenn told her. "Well done. I drop shell all the time, so you're practically a pro."

Paisley beamed as she glanced to Luke, then to Jenn. "I had confidence just like you said."

"See? We knew you could do it, you just had to believe it yourself."

Paisley sighed. "I wish I would've had that advice for my last spelling test," she muttered.

"You did perfectly fine on that," Luke chimed in. He placed a hand on Paisley's shoulder for reassurance. "Some of those were difficult and you only missed two."

"But I didn't get the bonus points right," she told him. "I just want you proud of me."

Luke wrapped his arms around her. "Honey, I couldn't be more proud of you. I don't expect perfect. I just expect you to try and now that you have Jenn's advice, there's nothing you can't do."

Jenn's heart clenched at the tender exchange, but a piece of her hurt knowing Paisley only wanted to do everything right for Luke. That in and of itself spoke volumes about their bond and their love. And while Jenn didn't know them well, she knew enough to know that Paisley could do no wrong in Luke's eyes.

Luke released her and tapped his fingertip to the end of her nose. "Now, let's get going on these cookies I was promised."

She giggled, which Jenn assumed was the exact response he'd been going for.

In no time, they had chocolate chip cookie dough on the pan and in the oven. Jenn grabbed some disinfectant and cleaned the area of the egg spills while Paisley washed her hands. The aroma of cookies soon filled the open space,

pushing Jenn's childhood memories to the fore-
front of her mind. Nearly all of her recollections
revolved around the kitchen and her mother and
sisters. So many stories and laughter and life les-
sons were shared during those times. And perhaps a little life lesson had been shared here as
well with Paisley.

"How about a movie while we wait?" Jenn
suggested.

Paisley nodded. "But not a baby movie because I just had a birthday and I'm older now."

"Of course," Jenn insisted. "I never once
thought you a baby. I only let big girls help in
the kitchen."

Luke gestured toward the sofa. "Have a seat,
kiddo. And if you get sleepy, you can fall asleep.
I'll get you home and tucked in as soon as I'm
done downstairs. Okay?"

Jenn still felt guilty for having him stay, but
he'd insisted, and considering this was his building, she couldn't really argue.

Once the movie was playing on the television,
Paisley cuddled deeper into the old sofa with a
pile of pillows and a blanket from Jenn's bed,
which was at the other end of the loft.

Luke went back to the window as Jenn pulled
the pan of hot cookies from the oven and placed
it on the stovetop.

"Rain letting up any?" she asked, reaching to turn the oven off.

"Looks like it. Would you want to help me get that new one inside or do you want to wait until it's not raining at all?"

"I won't melt," she told him with a smile.

Luke came to stand in front of the sofa, looking down at Paisley and blocking the view of the movie.

"Jenn and I are going down to work on the water heater," he told her. "Do not touch the pan of cookies. It's still hot. If you need anything at all, we're right downstairs. Okay?"

"Can I get a cookie before you go?" she asked.

"Coming right up." Jenn was already on it, scooping two onto a plate and grabbing a small glass of milk. "I'd let them cool a bit, but here they are."

She delivered the snack to the sofa where Cookie seemed to be waiting for her own.

"None for you," Jenn told the pup.

"Make sure the dog doesn't get any," Luke stated firmly. "Dogs cannot have chocolate."

Paisley held her plate and cup. "I'm not sharing cookies. These are all for me."

"You worked hard on those," Jenn replied. "You deserve it."

"But no more," Luke added. "School tomorrow. We don't need you hyped up on sugar before bed."

"Can I take one for my teacher tomorrow?"

"Of course," Luke told her. "Now be good and remember we're just downstairs."

Jenn led the way to the first floor and propped the back door open at the base of the steps that led outside. An old broken cinder block clearly had been the makeshift doorstop, so she sat it in place. Just a fine mist of rain fell now, and a very distant rumble of thunder was all that was left from the spring storm.

"Thank you."

She turned at Luke's statement, finding him on the bottom step.

"For what?" she asked.

He rested his hand on the end of the rail. "For making Paisley feel confident. She's been struggling lately."

"Because she wants to prove something to you."

"Yeah, I know." He let out a sigh and shook his head. "I don't know why. I've never told her I expect anything from her. We're just going day by day, you know?"

"I never thought for a second you were pressing her for anything."

Jenn took a step toward him just as he came down off the step. That worried look all over his face had Jenn wishing they knew each other better. The guy looked like he could use a friendly hug, but would that be weird or awkward?

"May I say something as an outsider looking in?" she asked, trying for a non-touching approach.

"Please. I'm struggling as well."

"It's not so much that the two of you are struggling, it's that you still haven't found your footing. You have to push aside that doubt and focus on each other. Nothing else matters. Nothing else *can* matter."

Luke continued to hold her gaze as he pulled in a deep breath. She hoped she hadn't overstepped and she hoped he understood she had his best interest at heart.

"You and Paisley have come to mean a lot to me," she added, hoping again she wasn't going too far. "I just have to be honest and tell you what I see because you both love each other and, in the end, that's all you need."

"You're right," he replied. "Nothing matters but Paisley, which is why I'll do everything I can to keep her."

Jenn blinked. "Keep her?"

Luke raked a hand through his hair and sighed. "Apparently my sister-in-law has a cousin that is asking for guardianship. I just found out about all of this and it's stressful."

How worrying for him. Jenn figured he wouldn't have opened up to her about something so important and personal and unguarded if he didn't trust her. That fact humbled her and in some odd way, helped her in her own journey. She felt as if she'd just stepped deeper into a new level of coming home and watering those roots she'd had planted for so long. Yes, she knew plenty of people in this town, but making new friends was part of the fresh start she needed.

"First of all, thank you for opening up and trusting me," she started. "I want you to know I'm here for you and I'm always a safe place. I can't imagine the stress you're under."

Jenn had so many questions swirling around in her head, and she needed to pinpoint the right ones and try to help.

"Where was this cousin when they first passed away?" Jenn asked. "I mean, why is she just now coming forward? Sorry, I have so many questions that are absolutely none of my business."

"No, it's fine," he said. "I had the same questions and this actually feels good to talk about. I haven't spoken to anyone except my attorney. Carol was Talia's cousin and away overseas in the military until recently. I guess when she came back, she realized what had happened and wants custody of her cousin's child. But Paisley doesn't know this woman, so I haven't said a word to her."

"No, I don't blame you. This is certainly quite a bit to take in."

Luke nodded, resting his shoulder against the doorframe of the back door. "She's married with a stable life so I have that working against me."

Jenn's brows drew in. "Is this a happy marriage? Is she still active in the military and going to be gone again? Don't sell yourself short, here. Weren't you the one in your brother's will who he wanted as custodian? That has to speak volumes to any judge."

"That's what I'm praying for."

Jenn stared back into those mesmerizing eyes and wished more than anything she could make his worry and pain disappear.

"Now I should be the one apologizing," he stated. "You have enough going on and I just unloaded my issues."

His bold words startled her and she shook her head as she crossed her arms. "Hey, that's what friends are for, right?"

Friends. That's what they were and she wanted to lay that out there. Maybe he was interested, maybe she was, but no matter what else happened or didn't happen, she knew this was a man who could be trusted. And she valued their short time together already.

When he said nothing, she did start to worry she'd gone too far.

"At least, I like to think we're friends," she amended, dropping her arms to her sides.

"Absolutely," he confirmed. "But none of my friends have ever made me cookies so you might just get elevated to best friend status."

Best friend. Her last best friend had been Cole…but surprisingly the idea of letting Luke into that role didn't terrify her.

Chapter Ten

"Good morning."

Jenn greeted her next client on this gorgeous sunshiny morning. The water heater was put in without any more issues, she'd passed her inspection and she'd already gotten her first official day under her belt as a salon owner.

"Morning," Mary Major replied as she shut the door behind her. "What a beautiful spring day."

Jenn clutched the purple shampoo cape and nodded. "That it is."

"I'm so glad you opened this place back up." Mary hung her purse on the row of hooks near Jenn's station. "My last stylist never could get the cut just right."

Jenn remembered Mary from living here before. The woman had strong opinions, knew every single person in Rosewood Valley and never hesitated to give her unsolicited advice.

But she'd also run the local large livestock veterinary clinic with her late husband like a champ. Mary knew her stuff and there wasn't a thing she wouldn't do for anyone in town.

The woman eased into the salon chair and faced the mirror. "I have a confession," she stated. "While I do need a haircut, I really couldn't resist seeing you again. I can't believe you're back after all this time."

Jenn smiled, though inside she winced. She had a feeling that was why her book had suddenly gotten full. Word had spread that not only was she back, she was ready for business and social time. Some townsfolk probably did legitimately care about her and how she was doing, while others were just being nosy and ready to spread gossip. Well, she would hold her head high and focus on herself and being the best businesswoman possible. She couldn't control what others thought or what they said, but she could protect her heart and that was what she'd have to do.

"It was time for me to come home," Jenn said. Might as well just be truthful. "I need to do some repairing and I needed employment, so this was the perfect setup for me."

"And renting from Luke. You got a great landlord."

Jenn slid the cape over Mary and fastened the closure. "He's been so helpful in this transition back home. I don't know what I would've done without him."

"He's one of the good ones," Mary agreed. "I worried who would fill the shoes of my Charles, but Luke has done an exceptional job. Not to mention having to take custody of his darling niece. Such a tragedy the way that poor girl lost her parents."

Jenn didn't bother replying. Though the entire situation was indeed a tragedy, Jenn had a feeling that Mary just wanted to talk. That had been an early lesson in standing behind the chair. Know the clients and get a feel for their day. Mary loved chatting and even if Jenn chimed in every now and then, Mary wouldn't slow down.

"The Lord has His hand on all of this, though," she went on. "My Charles hadn't been gone but a month when Luke came to town. Having him take over the clinic was certainly a blessing, and the old farmers really seem to love him."

Of course they did. Jenn couldn't imagine anything about Luke that someone could find fault in. After the way he'd opened up to her the other evening, she had a better understanding of what all he was dealing with. New town, new position in his career and personal life, and now a custody dispute. That definitely had to remain in Jenn's head. No way would she repeat any of what Luke had shared, especially to the town's busybody.

"And Paisley is such a doll," Mary crooned.

"I love when she comes into the office. I always give her little chores because she is like a sponge. She just absorbs all the information and wants to work and feel useful. It's tough with Mother's Day coming up."

Jenn had completely forgotten about Mother's Day. She made a mental note to do something special for her mom, but she truly had no idea what.

"Apparently there's a Mother's Day breakfast at school on Monday," Mary added. "Paisley was at the office the other day and asked if I'd go with her. Poor thing. This has to be so traumatic for such a young one."

At thirty-one years old, Jenn couldn't imagine losing her mother at this age, let alone as a young child.

"That's sweet of you to step in," Jenn told her. "I'm sure that day will be difficult."

Jenn wondered why Luke wouldn't just keep her home on that day, but she also assumed that Luke wasn't one to run away from feelings or hard times. He'd want to face them head-on and not dodge the issue. Unlike her, who ran at the hardest moment in her life and pushed aside everyone she loved for as long as possible.

"So tell me about your absence," Mary chirped. "What did you do all of those years you were gone?"

The change in subject left Jenn a bit winded. "Well, I got my cosmetology license and worked in the same salon for two years."

Jenn rested her hands on the back of the chair, already thankful she'd blocked out more time for Mary's appointment. This wouldn't be a quick trim.

"I had a great church family and friends," Jenn went on. "And even started a farm-to-table program at the church for fundraising for their youth program." Could something so simple and fun work here?

"Well, it sounds like you had quite the life there." Mary beamed. "What made you come home to stay and not just visit?"

She didn't want to get into the text Erin had sent, proclaiming the struggles with the farm. That had to stay within the family. Jenn had no idea what people in town knew, but her father had always been a prideful man and there was no way Jenn would discuss it.

"Rosewood Valley has always been home," she replied simply. "It's nice to be back and see how some things are exactly how I remember and some things have changed."

"Well, I'm glad you're home and I'm sure your family is happy to see you again." The woman's expression softened. "You all went through so much when Cole passed. So tragic."

Yes, it was, but Jenn didn't want to focus on the pain or the loss. When she thought of Cole, she tried to remember their good times and the love they shared.

"You know, that's something you and Luke have in common," Mary tacked on with a smile. "He's experienced a devastating loss, too. Not to mention he's single and one of the most genuine people I've ever met."

Oh, no. No, no, no. There would be no matchmaking. The only matchmaker Jenn trusted was the good Lord Himself.

Jenn laughed, trying to act like she thought Mary was joking, though she knew the woman was quite serious.

"Good thing I'm not looking for a boyfriend." Jenn slid her hands through Mary's hair and shifted the conversation. "So how are we cutting today?"

Mary smirked, but thankfully moved on and explained how she'd like her new style. Jenn tried to focus, but all she could think was how much she'd been drawn to Luke lately. Not just Luke, but his darling niece. But was she drawn to him because of the picture in her mind of the life she'd always wanted or was there more?

Could she have that second chance she'd only read about?

Thankfully Mary was easily distracted by

whatever topic Jenn threw at her, and once Mary had the perfect cut and was on her way to lunch with friends, Jenn started cleaning up her mess.

The door chimed and Jenn gripped the handle of her broom as she met her sister's gaze. Rachel stopped, as if unsure if she should enter or not.

"You're always welcome," Jenn told her. "Are you here to talk or for a cut?"

Rachel grabbed her signature braid and shrugged. "I probably could use a cut, but I don't have time today. I ran to the feedstore for Dad and saw your text about having something to tell us."

Jenn nodded and propped her broom on the wall beside her station. "I do. You're the first one to take me up on that."

Rachel blinked. "Seriously?"

"I'm just as surprised as you are." Jenn laughed, hoping to break the tension. "I'm glad you're here."

Rachel shut the door but didn't move any farther into the space. That was fine. At least she'd come by.

"I'll be quick," Jenn started. "And I don't need an answer or anything right now. It's an idea that I'd like the family to think about."

Rachel crossed her arms and stared across the distance.

Jenn couldn't believe she had her oldest sister's undivided attention, and she wasn't about to waste this moment. "I'm sure you know I'm back because Erin texted me. I mean, it was past time for me to come home, but that text about the farm being in trouble was all the nudge I needed."

Jenn took a step forward, but before she could continue, Rachel chimed in. "I sold my house about a year ago to help offset some costs."

Jenn jerked back. "What?" she whispered. "Rachel, you loved your house."

"I love Four Sisters Ranch more and now I can live in the loft above one of the barns on the property. It all worked out, but even with my house funds, we just had to sell too much livestock so our production is low."

Jenn's heart ached for her sister. She'd had no idea just how dire the circumstances had gotten. Her idea might just make a difference.

"I started a program back in Sacramento." Jenn smoothed her hair behind her shoulders. "It was a farm-to-table event we hosted once a month to raise funds for our youth program at church. I would make mom's biscuits for church dinners and those were a hit, then I did some jellies. One thing led to another, and an idea blossomed to try a full meal and charge per plate. It was such a success, and I don't think we have anything like that here in Rosewood Valley."

Rachel blinked a few times but remained silent. That sliver of hope narrowed.

"You hate the idea," Jenn murmured.

Rachel held her hands up. "I'm just processing it. Rosewood Valley doesn't have anything like that. The concept sounds interesting, but we have to dig into the logistics before we jump in headfirst."

Jenn nodded as joy rushed through her. But Rachel dropped her hands as she continued.

"Are you staying to help?" her sister asked.

Jenn pulled in a deep breath. "I suppose that's a legitimate concern for you and the rest of the family, but yes. I have intentions of staying. There's nothing I want more than to help and prove how sorry I am."

Rachel gave a quick nod and moved back toward the door. "Well, time will tell and so will actions. I certainly hope you're here for good. We all need to heal."

She turned and opened the door but threw one last glance over her shoulder.

"Great idea by the way. I'm curious to see what the family thinks."

Then she was gone. Well, that made two of them. But once she had the details laid out in front of the whole family, Jenn was confident they'd embrace it and be one step closer to getting their farm back to the glory it once was.

* * *

"Sweetheart, we have a slight issue."

Paisley slid her purple boots on and stared up at Luke as he curled his fingers around his first cup of coffee on Monday morning.

"Mary is sick and cannot do the breakfast today," he explained, hating to have to tell Paisley. This day was already difficult enough, and now the fill-in mother figure couldn't attend.

His niece's face fell as she looked down to the floor. He wished he could snap his fingers and be done with this day and the Mother's Day holiday coming up this weekend. Unfortunately, facing battles was the only way to get stronger. He wondered if he was being too harsh for a child, but that was the only way he knew how to cope.

"You can stay home," he offered. "Nobody would think anything of it. I don't have appointments until eleven, so I can take you to breakfast in town first."

Paisley brought her gaze back to him. "Can you call Jenn?"

He jerked. "Jenn?"

"I bet she'd come with me. Will you call her?"

A whole array of feelings spread through him. Sure, he could call her, but would she feel put on the spot? Would she feel obligated? Not to mention how last-minute this was.

"Please, Toot?" Paisley wrinkled her nose. "Or do you think she'd say no?"

Luke had every ounce of confidence that if Jenn was free, she'd be there.

"You go on and brush your teeth and I'll see what I can do," he assured her.

Once she scrambled from the room and down the hallway, Luke set his mug on the coffee table. He pulled his cell from his pocket and thought about texting, but a call would be faster. He only hoped she was a morning person and he didn't wake her.

He tapped her name and waited for her to pick up.

"Good morning," she answered on the second ring. "Is everything okay?"

Of course she would answer sweetly and ask about his needs.

"Not really," he replied. "But before I ask the biggest favor from my new best friend, I want to preface this by saying you don't have to say yes if you are busy or not comfortable."

"Well, now you've got my attention."

Luke kept his eye on the hallway as he lowered his voice. "Paisley has a Mother's Day breakfast at school this morning and Mary was going to go with her, but she's sick. Is there any way—"

"I'd love to."

Luke chuckled and shook his head as relief spread through him. "I had a feeling that's what you'd say, but it's last-minute and I'm not sure of your schedule."

"I'm always off on Sunday and Monday. The timing is perfect. Should I pick her up? I don't even know where you live."

Paisley came back down the hallway, her eyes locked on his as she silently asked for the answer. Luke nodded, then laughed as she gave a fist pump in the air.

Luke gave Jenn the details and said they'd meet her at the school. He wasn't so sure how this amazing woman had dropped into his life in such a fast yet effective way, but he'd have to say something to Will. Luke didn't like keeping this secret. Not to mention, he really needed to peg the man down for some type of answer. He had to get things moving in a more stable direction. His rental agreement here was almost up, the custody issue had put yet another strain on the timeline and Luke really wanted to start a solid life with Paisley. He wanted a forever place to call theirs with a yard she could run around in, a dog chasing her, maybe a tire swing. A family life that she deserved and had been robbed of.

Paisley came bouncing back in with her backpack. "I'm ready to go!"

"Do you need to take the project in?" he asked.

"Not until Wednesday and I want to add more glitter to it if we can tonight."

Of course. Because there wasn't enough glitter on the posterboard covered in pictures of Talia. This girl definitely wanted her mother to shine so he'd live with glitter particles all over the kitchen floor.

"Did Jenn sound happy, too?" Paisley asked as they headed toward the garage.

Luke couldn't get Jenn's elated tone out of his head. She had been thrilled and her excitement warmed his heart in areas that hadn't been touched in so long.

Paisley climbed into his truck and reached for her seat belt, but stopped short as she faced him. "Don't tell Mary, but I'm kinda glad that Jenn gets to be there today."

Luke tapped the tip of her nose. "It's our little secret."

Because secretly, he was glad Jenn was going, too, and now he'd have to figure out what to do with his growing attraction and strong feelings for the sweetest woman he'd been deceiving. When Sylvia had hurt him, he'd vowed to never blindside or deceive anyone like that. Yet here he was, holding in a secret. He had no clue what Will and Sarah Spencer would ultimately decide, so until then, he had to keep this burden to himself.

Chapter Eleven

"Jenn Spencer. I heard you were back in town."

With a cringe, Jenn turned to face a familiar voice. She'd barely taken two steps inside her old elementary school and met up with a smiling Paisley when she was called out. She hadn't taken into account seeing other people and facing her past. All she'd known was that when Luke called with panic in his tone, she couldn't say no.

"Good morning, Carla," Jenn greeted with a forced smile.

"I had no idea you'd be here today," Carla stated glancing at Paisley. "And who is this?"

"I'm Paisley," the girl said. "Jenn is my best friend."

Jenn's heart swelled and she didn't think it possible to be so affected by being here and having this sweet child at her side, hand in hand.

"Oh, you're Luke's niece." Carla's eyes widened as they shifted back to Jenn. "Are you and Luke…"

"Friends," Jenn confirmed. "It was great seeing you again."

She held on to Paisley's hand as she turned and headed toward the cafeteria. The crowd seemed to move quickly through the old hallway and Jenn focused on the students' adorable artwork lining the walls from each class instead of her rapid heartbeat.

She didn't even think people would assume she and Luke were an item. She hadn't had time to think at all, actually. She'd only known Paisley needed someone and Jenn didn't have plans for the day.

"That lady seemed nosy," Paisley whispered as they found a table.

Jenn couldn't help the slight snort that escaped her. "People like to talk, especially when they don't know the full story. They just want all the information."

"But you didn't lie." Paisley took a seat on the bench and looked up at Jenn. "You and Toot are friends. I'm glad he found you. Or maybe you found him. I don't know what happened first, but I'm glad it did."

Yeah, Jenn couldn't deny she was pretty pleased, too. She always believed people came into lives at precisely the right time. She wasn't sure who found whom, but she had a feeling she'd found another piece of a solid foundation in her life. A building block seemed to just slide into place where Luke was concerned. Part of her felt like he'd been part of her life for much longer than just a couple weeks. The support he'd instantly offered spoke volumes of the type of solid friendship he provided.

"Jenn?"

At the familiar voice, Jenn turned to see Erin coming toward them.

"What are you doing here?" her sister asked, her bright green eyes wide with confusion and glee.

Jenn stood back up and smiled, pleased to see a familiar, friendly face.

"Paisley asked if I'd join her this morning. This is Luke's niece."

"I know Miss Paisley." Erin beamed down at Paisley. "I'm so glad you brought my sister."

Paisley's eyes widened as she looked between Jenn and Erin. "Wait a minute," she said, holding her little hands up as she turned around on the seat. "You didn't tell me you were related to Miss Spencer."

Jenn laughed. "I didn't think about it."

"Is she your teacher?" Jenn asked.

"No," Erin replied. "I'm second grade now. I moved up from kindergarten a couple years ago. Paisley is in first grade, but I'll have her next year and can't wait." She winked at the child. "I hear what a smart student she is and how she's always helpful around class. I definitely need good helpers."

Erin had made a career move. Just another reminder of how some things had changed and she'd missed out and had no clue. Not only did Jenn want to work on repairing her family, she wanted to get to know them all over again.

"I can't believe Toot's best friend and Miss Spencer are sisters." Paisley's focus continued to shift between the two, then she narrowed her eyes. "You guys even have the same necklace. That's cool."

Instinctively, Jenn's hand went to the pitcher charm hanging from the chain.

"Our mother bought all of us one of these," Erin explained. "There are four of us sisters."

Paisley adjusted her glasses as her eyes got even wider. "Four sisters? I don't have any. That would be amazing. Are you all, like, best friends?"

Jenn met her sister's gaze as they both continued to smile, but the tension seemed to settle between them. Yes, they were the closest of the four, but they'd still not resolved the past few years.

"We better get ready to start," Erin stated in her teacher tone. "We can talk later."

Jenn didn't know if she was relieved that the topic was dropped or crushed that her sister hadn't said how close they were. But this was not the time or the place to get into the past.

Jenn eased back down next to Paisley as the principal introduced herself and started with a few remarks about mothers and the importance of women as role models. Paisley reached over and took Jenn's hand in hers and every bit of Jenn's resolve threatened to crumble. She could not break down in tears here. She was here to support Paisley and to have fun, not to reflect on what she needed to rebuild with her own family.

The principal continued to talk, recognizing the strong teachers who were often mother figures within the school. Happiness welled up within Jenn at the praise regarding her sister. She'd always been a natural nurturer.

When the cafeteria workers brought around the breakfast, Paisley wrinkled her nose and leaned toward Jenn.

"You want my pears?" she whispered.

"I was going to ask you the same," Jenn murmured in reply. "I don't like them, either."

Paisley's bright eyes came up to meet Jenn's. "So what do we do with them?"

Jenn glanced to the rest of the tray with a fresh blueberry muffin, a bowl of what looked like strawberry yogurt and the fresh pear slices. She pursed her lips and focused on Paisley, who waited on an answer.

"I say we eat what we like and politely lay our napkin over the tray when we're done. Then nobody will know what we left."

Paisley's delicate mouth split into a grin that offered a view of the recently lost tooth.

"I knew you'd have the answer," she said. "And I knew you'd be nice about it. You're the nicest person I know, except Toot. You guys are kinda the same."

"The same?"

Paisley nodded and reached for her blueberry muffin. "Yeah. Always trying to make sure other people are happy. That's why I like you so much. You and Toot make me happier than I've been."

Those words from the most precious little girl had Jenn's heart taking a tumble. Paisley unwrapped her muffin like her statement hadn't just made a monumental impact on Jenn's life. Knowing that something as simple as a life lesson that stemmed from a dislike of pears had Jenn smiling. She was so glad she came, that she could help make Paisley's life a little brighter.

Paisley held her muffin in one hand and reached for Jenn's hand with the other. "Thanks for coming today."

Jenn swallowed the lump of emotion and nodded. This darling girl holding her hand was all that mattered in this moment. "I wouldn't want to be anywhere else."

* * *

Luke had just finished up at another local ranch. Springtime brought all the babies on the farms and new life always gave him a burst of happiness. He glanced to the passenger seat and wondered if his attempt at a thank-you gift was too much or ridiculous. He felt he owed Jenn something for jumping in at the very last minute to assist with Paisley. That selfless act couldn't go unnoticed.

Since he had time to spare between his last appointment and when he had to get his niece from school, he felt this was the perfect time to swing by the shop…even if he did feel silly with his gift.

Luke pulled into an open spot about two shops down from the building he now owned. There was no discreet way to get his thank-you gift inside without being obvious. Perhaps he should've parked around back.

No. There was nothing wrong with bringing a present to a friend, especially one who had done something so sweet. And perhaps this generosity also stemmed from that level of guilt over the farm. Luke had called to set up a meeting with Will Spencer but hadn't heard back. Luke not only wanted to move forward with the possibility of purchasing some land, but he also wanted to fill Jenn in on the situation. If Will and Sarah wanted to be the ones to tell their daughter, that was perfectly fine with Luke, but the woman deserved to know. For all the joy and smiles she'd brought into his life and Paisley's she shouldn't be kept in the dark.

Luke moved down the sidewalk, clutching the gift at his side, with his shoulders back like this was perfectly normal. He didn't see anyone around, but in a small town, someone was always looking.

As he stepped into the nook leading to the double doors of the salon, he spotted the closed sign. He knew she was closed today, but would she have the shop locked? He hadn't thought of that. Of course he had a key, but he respected her privacy and days off.

He gripped the antique brass knob and smiled when the fixture turned beneath his palm. The moment he stepped in, the strong scent of chemicals or whatever she used for her clients filled the space. He figured that was better than the stuffy air the old building had before she came along.

Luke closed the door behind him and glanced around. He wondered if she was upstairs or in the back. Now he felt silly because he should've called first or at least texted.

"Jenn?"

No answer. He reached into his pocket for his cell when a noise from the back caught his attention. Cookie came out and didn't get too close to him, but she did give him a glance before turning and going back to where she'd come from. Clearly just making sure there wasn't a threat. The dog might be leery, but she was smart and protective of Jenn.

Luke looked back to his phone to make the call when he heard the sniffle.

"Jenn?"

Another sniffle.

"Just a minute."

Her voice drifted out from the room she called the dispensary. Confused at the sadness in her tone, he wondered if she was back there crying. Should he turn around and leave? Of all the times to drop in unannounced.

"I have something for you," he stated, moving toward one of the stations. "It's no big deal. I can just leave them out here and—"

Jenn came from the back room and dabbed at her red-rimmed eyes with a tissue. His heart clenched at the sight and he dropped the bundle of tulips on the stylist chair and closed the distance between them in about two strides.

"What is it? Are you hurt? Is it your family?"

Without thinking, he gripped her arms as a level of fear mixed with concern seemed to take over.

"No, no. My family is fine," she assured him

with another slight sniff. "It's just been an emotional morning. You happened to come in at the wrong time."

"Or maybe I came at the right time," he countered with a gentle squeeze. "What can I do to help?"

Watery eyes came up to meet his and an overwhelming sense of that need to protect and shield her from harm consumed him. He hadn't been kidding when he'd told her he didn't do well with tears. But right now, the urge to console her overrode any awkwardness.

"Nothing you can do." She dabbed the tip of her red nose. "Just going to the school and seeing so many people I used to know, having Paisley hold my hand like she was thrilled I was a stand-in, and seeing all of those happy moms and daughters...it hit me all at once. And Paisley and I...we—we had a moment over pears." Luke had no clue what that meant, but clearly that was the icing on the cake for her emotions. More tears spilled and she brought her hands up over her face in some attempt to hide her vulnerability.

Luke slid his hands up and down her arms to offer some sort of solace. He'd never once thought of how she'd feel or how her past might come into account when he called her this morning.

"I'm sorry," he offered. "When I called earlier

it was out of desperation for Paisley. If I'd known anything would trigger such strong emotions, I never would have pulled you in."

"Oh, I loved going with her."

Jenn dropped her hands then attempted one of her signature smiles, but he knew a forced gesture when he saw one.

"I'm glad I could be there for such a special day, so she didn't have to go alone," Jenn added. "No matter what my issues are, I would do it again to see that smile on Paisley's face."

The kindness that lived in this woman never ceased to amaze him. Luke realized he was still holding on to her and slowly eased back. God had His hand on every situation, there wasn't a doubt in Luke's mind. He just wished he knew how to handle everything going on within his own life so he didn't cause Jenn more heartache down the road.

"Selfishly I'm glad you were there for her, too," he admitted. "Paisley really admires you."

Jenn's grin widened, more genuine this time. "I adore that darling girl and I was wondering something."

Luke rested his hands on his hips, completely resisting the urge to envelop her in a comforting hug. He'd give anything to take away this pain she struggled with.

"I know Paisley has gone to work with you,

but do you think she'd like going to my family's farm to see some of the horses?" Jenn asked. "I haven't ridden in so long and that always calmed me. I thought she might like something like that if we can't get our schedules together."

"She'd love that," Luke replied. "With this fast move here, and dealing with my brother's insurance, and now the custody case, I'm afraid I haven't scheduled time for the fun things."

"You're moving?" she asked.

Luke nodded. "The house my brother lived in was a rental until he and Talia could build. There's only a short time left and I'm running out of options."

Actually the only option he had was still up in the air. Too many emotions settled deep into his gut, but he couldn't exactly let them all out now.

She dabbed once more at her eyes and fisted her tissue. "Do you have anything in the works?"

And there went that familiar, unwanted, heavy dose of guilt. He wanted to open up completely to her, but he'd made a promise to her father. Luke had always been a man of his word and valued honesty and integrity. He'd staked his reputation for his career on those exact qualities.

Now he was faced with doing the right thing, but for whom? The right thing for Will? For Jenn? For himself?

"I have something I hope will work out," he

admitted. "I just don't know yet and I promised the owner I wouldn't say a word."

"Well, I pray everything falls into place for you and Paisley," she told him. "I'm sorry I was so upset when you got here. Had I known you were coming, I would have composed myself sooner."

"Don't apologize for being human and having authentic feelings."

He certainly couldn't take her apology, not with this deceit hovering inside him.

Jenn pulled in a deep breath and sighed. "So, what did you need before you had to console me?"

"I wanted to say thanks for this morning." He moved toward the chair where he'd dropped the bouquet. "I thought these would look nice in here and that you deserved something for your kind gesture to Paisley."

Jenn's eyes widened at the sight of the flowers. Then moisture gathered once more and she had that soft yet sad smile. Right now, he wasn't sure if this was a good or bad thing he'd done.

"I wasn't sure what type of flower you liked, but tulips seem to be the flower of the season," he tacked on, more because he wanted to fill the awkward silence.

"Tulips are my favorite flower," she whispered. "My late husband always brought them for me in the spring. This is just… Wow. A really nice memory and touching gesture all rolled into one."

A spear of relief hit him. He'd chosen the right gift and made her smile with a pleasant memory at the same time. He hadn't realized he'd been holding his breath for her reaction, but he made a mental note that tulips were another key to unlocking deeper layers to this amazing woman.

"You didn't have to bring me anything," she told him, bringing the buds to her face for a quick sniff. "But I won't turn down fresh flowers."

"I did and you deserve them," he replied. "And to answer your question, Paisley would love to see the horses. Are you and your family on better terms now? Have you had a chance to sit down with them?"

Jenn pursed her lips. "Not really. Mom will always welcome me and Dad is talking to me, but nothing has been resolved. I have apologized to each of them, but you know, that's just a small step on this journey. I have to keep proving to them that I'm here for whatever they need. I know there are some issues with my family that brought me back home, but I can't get into that and I just hope they let me help. I need them to understand I want to make things okay again, if that's even possible."

He knew of the ordeal she couldn't speak of, but he had to pretend he didn't. He had to remain an outsider when it came to the business of the farm. Whatever else they wanted to do with the land was up to them. He prayed Will would sell just that front portion with the barn for Luke to have his practice and his future home. He just had to make Will see that selling that fraction of property would be best for all parties. They would essentially be helping each other out.

"I'm sure your family will see how much you care," he replied. "I don't know everything that happened, but you're back and trying. That counts for something, and like you said, you can keep showing them how much you love them by being there over and over. They'll see that you are serious."

Jenn dipped her head as a corner of her mouth kicked up. "You ever think about becoming a therapist? You know, if the animal gig doesn't work out."

Luke shook his head. "Oh, no. I'm definitely not the one to be dishing out advice. I'm simply telling you what I see from my point of view."

"It's nice to be able to talk about this to someone," she admitted. "Especially an outsider. You probably have a better view than me since I've been stuck in this cycle for the past three years."

Don't pry, don't pry, don't pry. This isn't your place and you can't fix her problems.

"Can I ask what made you leave to begin with?"

So much for that quick self pep talk.

Jenn glanced to the flowers and he wondered if he'd overstepped his bounds. She deserved her privacy and to keep her pain to herself. Maybe bringing those bad memories to the surface wasn't the best way to handle this situation.

"Forget I asked," he amended with a wave of his hand. "It's not my business."

"No, you're fine."

She clutched the flowers and moved to the chair at the shampoo bowl. She sank down and pulled in a deep breath. Luke had a feeling she wanted to talk, so he waited while she gathered her thoughts. He crossed to the stylist chair and spun it around before he took a seat as well. Jenn ran a fingertip over the yellow ribbon on the stems as Cookie sauntered back in and made herself comfortable at Jenn's feet.

"My husband passed away on the farm," she began. "We had only been married a short time, a few months, actually. We lived in a loft above one of the barns and had plans to build on the property. I even still had wedding gifts in boxes that hadn't been opened. I wanted to save the good stuff for our new place."

A sad smile formed on her lips as she stared down at the multicolored buds. Luke wished he could erase her pain and sadness. But he'd learned over these past several months that talking and getting those emotions out in the open only aided in healing. He wasn't sure if Jenn had spoken to anyone over all this time or how her process was going. He did know grief had no time limit.

"Cole and Dad worked flawlessly together," she went on, now bringing her attention to Luke. "They were both workaholics and one day my dad asked Cole to get some cattle in from the pasture. Cole had been up all night sick and I told Dad to have Rachel do it, but Cole insisted. He was gone longer than we all thought he should've been. When Dad rode out to see what was going on, he found Cole on the ground with his horse beside him. We thought Cole had fallen and hit his head or something, but it turned out he'd had a heart attack."

Jenn paused as she chewed on her bottom lip for just a moment before continuing.

"He didn't make it to the hospital," she finished.

There was nothing like that crushing blow. That single moment in time when someone made that devastating statement that your loved one was no longer living. Nothing could prepare a person for that life-altering time. It was something everyone experienced at some point or another in their lives, but it was also something that not many people shared. Having Jenn open up to him turned something inside his heart… that same heart that had taken a beating more and more over these past couple of years seemed to be healing. And not just healing, but *feeling* once again.

Luke had no clue what to say or how to console her. Maybe only listening was all she needed. Still, he should say something so she didn't feel alone, so she knew he cared…and he certainly cared more than he should. Much more than a friend. These growing feelings and his attraction were becoming impossible to ignore. He suddenly found himself wanting to uncover every layer until he knew everything about Jenn Spencer.

"There's no words I can say to make your pain go away," he started. "I appreciate you trusting me with your feelings and just like you told me the other night, you're safe with me. I'm always here to listen or give advice if you need any."

She offered a soft smile that melted his heart.

"I haven't even told you why I left," she added. "You might not find me so nice."

"There's nothing you could say that would change my opinion of you."

Jenn crossed her legs and shook her head. "Don't form your opinions just yet. I said some pretty harsh things to my family, specifically to my father, before I left. I let anger and pain drive my actions and my words. I became selfish and ran from my heartache instead of staying with the people who love me the most. I'm not proud of how I handled myself, but I'm back now to make amends. My family is struggling a bit, so they're more vulnerable than before. I'll always carry that guilt, but all I can do now is try. That's actually one of the reasons I came back was to help them with this hardship. They're proud, so I won't go into details, but I have to be here now for them."

Jenn had a heart of gold and a giving nature. He truly didn't believe there was a selfish bone in her body and he knew her well enough to understand how she would always feel guilty for leaving, but coming back and facing that past spoke volumes on her character.

And him keeping this secret from her spoke volumes on his, especially since she didn't want to divulge her family's issues. He already knew enough, but he couldn't say a word. And now he had confirmation on why she was back—because the farm was in trouble. He'd suspected as much, but her confirming it took his guilt to a new level.

"You're brave for tackling your flaws head-on," he told her. "Not many people would do that, so don't beat yourself up too much. Just understand your family is hurting, too, and you guys can help each other heal."

Her brows drew in as she tilted her head. "You sure you aren't a therapist?" She laughed.

"Trust me, I'm much better handling animals than people."

"Oh, I'm not so sure about that," she countered as she came to her feet, clutching the flowers. "You've listened to me go on and on about my problems and you've given solid advice that makes me feel like I'm not such a bad person."

Luke also rose and hooked his thumbs through his belt loops. He'd have to leave soon to get Paisley from school, but he wasn't quite ready to go. Not only did he value adult time, but he also valued this time with Jenn.

His cell vibrated in his pocket, but he'd let it go to voice mail and check it in a moment. He didn't want to break this connection.

"Nobody could ever think you're a bad person," he assured her.

That megawatt smile widened and he was so glad they'd gone from tears to happiness. He wanted to continue to do that for her—to be the one to make her smile and see the sunshine in life again.

"I'm really glad you ended up as my landlord." She took a step toward him and placed a hand on his arm. "And I'm grateful for the listening ear and flowers. You really made my day."

He wanted to ask her on a date. A real date with dinner, maybe take her hand to lead her down the street under the moonlight. But he couldn't do a single thing for a variety of reasons. The private conversations with her father and the fact she might not be ready for such a large step. After hearing so much about her late husband... Clearly they'd had a special love and bond. Was she ready for someone else to come into her life and try to start a relationship? Was he ready himself?

Maybe they'd met at this point in their lives so they could help each other heal. He wondered if that was the case, but until he knew for sure and had some direction from above, he'd have to bide his time.

Luke could wait because someone like Jenn would be worth everything.

Chapter Twelve

Luke drove beneath the arch to Four Sisters Ranch as his heart beat a little faster. He gripped the wheel and prayed this meeting would go according to God's will. Luke had to hold tight to the faith that everything would work out exactly the way it should for the best interest of not only his future, but also Paisley's.

He'd left Jenn's salon and checked his phone to find the missed call had been from Will and the guy wanted to meet to discuss the sale. Luke had picked up Paisley from school and taken her back to his office where Mary thankfully offered to watch her for a bit.

This meeting would be a pivotal point, no matter the outcome.

The gravel crunched beneath his truck tires as he pulled up near the horse barn and killed his engine. The afternoon sun shone down on the property and the bright warmth instantly gave him hope for today. After coming away from

Jenn and feeling even closer, he had to believe his life was going in the right direction.

Luke stepped from his truck, pocketed his cell and headed into the open bay of the barn. He might as well go ahead and check on the livestock while he was here and make sure the influenza hadn't taken hold of any other animal. Even if the Spencers decided not to sell, Luke would still tend to their needs and care for their stock just like before.

Will stepped from the small office in the rear of the barn and adjusted his worn hat.

"Thanks for coming," the old rancher greeted. "Want to come on back?"

"Absolutely."

With each step he took toward that tiny office, Luke's nerves skyrocketed and his heart quickened. He'd waited for this moment for months and had to respect whatever decision Will delivered. But that didn't mean Luke couldn't plead his case before Will started talking.

"I appreciate you meeting with me," Luke stated as he stepped into the narrow space.

A small desk, two chairs and a narrow floor-to-ceiling shelving unit on the wall were all that made up the simple area. Life on farms were simple for the most part. It was all the grunt work that made everything run smoothly and that people didn't often see or appreciate.

"I'd like to say something first, if you don't mind," Luke requested.

Will eased his large frame down into the squeaky old leather chair and nodded. "Go ahead."

This was it. His last chance to plead his case.

"I know this situation isn't ideal or even comfortable for you and your family," Luke began. "I respect whatever decision you and your wife have come to, but I also have to reiterate the fact that selling a portion of your land to me is a smart move. It's no secret that I'm in a bind and need a place to go for my home practice. But I know you're in a bind, too, and deeding off a section of your land is better than potentially losing it all later. I value family, as I know you do, so please know that everything I'm doing is to provide for mine and for yours."

Luke remained literally on the edge of his seat as he finished his speech. He hadn't even thought about what he wanted to say, he just went with the words on his heart. Will Spencer had never been an easy man to read. The stoic, stern look on his face provided no indication as to his thoughts or how he'd reply.

"You are right this is difficult for the family," Will began. "Sarah and I have discussed this in great detail and weighed all of our options. We are willing to sell you a portion of the land with the front barn. We feel this is the best move so we can still retain the bulk of the land, plus the home that my grandfather built."

Luke didn't know what to say because this reply actually stunned him. He had wondered once it came down to a decision that Will would actually be able to let go of any part of his property, but Luke wasn't about to second-guess this decision. He wondered how the rest of the family had taken this.

"I can't thank you enough," Luke stated. "I promise to care for my part just like you have."

"I know you will, son, and that's why I'm comfortable with this transaction. Now, as far as the price, we discussed a range and Sarah and I are pretty firm on what we need to get our farm back up and running and to get some of our cattle back. It won't be perfect, but we're trying to be fair and still take care of our own."

Luke nodded. "I understand."

When Will shared the price, it was a bit more than Luke wanted to spend, but he'd make it work. He wasn't about to turn down an opportunity like this, not when he'd prayed for so long. Finally, a door had opened.

Now, if he could erase that custody dispute, he and Paisley would be just fine.

One life hurdle at a time.

"How did your girls take this news?" Luke asked.

He'd just seen Jenn and she hadn't said one word. Did she even know? Now that a verbal deal was done, there would be no reason to keep this from her any longer.

Will let out a deep sigh and rocked back in the creaky chair. "We haven't told them yet. We know they might be upset at first, but they'll see this was best in the long run. We plan on having a family meeting soon."

And then Jenn would know. He didn't want to keep this from her any longer. He wanted to have a blank slate to start fresh. She deserved nothing but honesty, especially after she'd poured her heart out to him. Would she feel betrayed? Like he'd deceived her or tried to get close to her on purpose?

"Will, I have a favor." Luke shifted in his seat, more than uncomfortable with this situation. "Jenn and I have become pretty good friends and I feel like I'm lying to her by keeping this secret."

The old guy rocked forward in his seat and grunted. "Is that so? Jenn's renting from you, isn't she?"

Luke nodded, suddenly feeling like he was trying to impress his crush's dad.

"She's a strong woman," Luke went on. "I

know she'd understand the situation, but keeping this from her doesn't seem right."

Will's green eyes stared across the antique desk. That same emerald color he'd seen in all the sisters could be piercing or mesmerizing, depending on the situation.

"Sarah and I will tell the girls when we feel the time is right." Will came to his feet, a silent indicator this meeting was about to come to an end. "I'd appreciate you keeping all of this to yourself for the time being. Things are...shaky within the family right now, so the timing isn't the best. I've put off making a concrete decision about this farm long enough and with that late frost a few weeks ago, we lost some of the produce we could've used to sell at the markets, and I don't want to have to sell off any more heads of cattle."

While Luke didn't like that the family had fallen on hard times, he was taking this blessing and using this chance to make everything right and good. Will and Sarah would bounce back from this. They were strong people with decades of farming experience, not to mention they were a solid family unit. They had a support system.

They had Jenn.

"I can't keep lying to her," Luke stated, rising to his feet as he held Will's intense stare. "I'd never tell you how to handle your own family, but I'd appreciate you talking to her soon. I want her to continue to trust me and not think I've been deceiving her."

"My Jenn won't think that," he confirmed. "She's got a big heart and loves with everything in her. Although her emotions do get the best of her at times and she leads with that instead of common sense. She's a bit like me, I guess. We can be hardheaded, but definitely know a good person, and she knows you're genuine."

The sad undertone of such a robust man caught Luke off guard. He'd never heard Will speak in such a remorseful way. Clearly this man harbored the same pain Jenn did. Luke prayed they'd come to peace soon.

Coming into this meeting, Luke said he'd trust and respect whatever decision Will made and that included figuring out what was best for his family. If he wasn't ready to disclose the sale, then Luke just had to be patient. And he hoped Jenn understood his actions when the time came.

Jenn finished sweeping the floor after her last client of the day had left. Her favorite soft classical music filtered through the shop and she hummed along to the familiar melody. She turned to dump the dustpan and caught sight of the classy white tulips on the table in the waiting area between two pink velvet chairs she'd found online. Little by little this place was becoming her own and settling in felt good.

Between the steady work, her pup that she might as well just embrace as her own, and the connection with Luke and Paisley, she nearly had the perfect fresh start. She'd only been in town a few weeks but did wish her family progress would move faster.

She'd been working on a spreadsheet regarding the farm-to-table idea. She'd also been researching recipes and trying to figure what would go best for the crops her family typically could have on hand during various seasons. She wanted something solid to take to them when she met up with the entire crew and was pretty confident she had a well-thought-out plan. She wondered how much time they'd need to process her return or if they'd ultimately open their arms once again, but hopefully with this plan to help breathe new life into the barn and help boost their finances, they'd see just how serious she was about sticking around and proving herself.

Jenn tapped her foot on the trash can pedal near her workstation and dumped the contents of the dustpan. In the midst of working at night on her spreadsheet, she'd completely forgotten her dispensary was running low on a few items. She needed to place an online order for more hair color and retail merchandise. She hadn't realized how fast those products would fly off the shelves, but she was thrilled her hometown had embraced her little shop.

The front door opened with a soft, pleasant chime, since she'd finally replaced that horrid bell, and Jenn shifted her attention to the entrance.

"I have a surprise!"

Paisley came skipping in with a small purple gift bag in her hand and an adorably wide smile on her face. Could there be a sweeter child? Considering all she'd been through, Luke had to be doing something extremely right.

"A surprise?" Jenn asked, propping her broom on the wall. "I love surprises."

"Well, it's not really for you." Paisley came to a stop and wrinkled her nose. "It's for Cookie."

"Oh, that is so nice," Jenn told her, then glanced up when the door opened once more and Luke sauntered in. "I was wondering how she got here."

That crooked grin he offered certainly did not help the fact she was trying to ignore her attraction. She hadn't felt a pull toward anyone since Cole passed and coming home with all of her emotional baggage wasn't the best time to try to see if she was ready for anything.

What if she took that leap of faith with Luke? What if she wasn't ready and she ended up hurting him? Or perhaps he wasn't even interested in her in that way.

He had brought her flowers, though. Yes, he'd said as a thank-you, but flowers implied more in her opinion. Still, guys had a different mindset, and she wished she didn't put so much thought into this, but she couldn't help herself. This whole scenario was unfamiliar to her. She'd dated Cole through high school and then they'd gotten married. The courtship had been flawless, like God had designed them for each other. Jenn didn't have experience in dating or how to even go about asking someone out.

Goodness. Was she already at that stage? Did she want to take that leap? Just the idea of getting close with another man sent her heart racing. She'd never even held another man's hand. Mercy, she didn't know if she could do this.

"Jenn?"

Paisley's tender voice pulled Jenn from her worrisome thoughts.

"You okay?" Luke asked.

Shaking her head, Jenn laughed. "Sorry. You caught me daydreaming. So, should I go get Cookie for this surprise? I'm sure she's upstairs sleeping on my couch."

"Go get her." Paisley bounced up and down. "I want to give this to her and Toot brought some of my birthday pictures for you if you want one."

"If I want one?" Jenn asked, placing a hand on her chest. "Of course I want a birthday picture of my very best friend."

Paisley smiled wider and Jenn gasped. "Wait a minute," she murmured, leaning down. Jenn took her chin between her finger and thumb and tipped her head. "Did you lose another tooth?"

"Yep. And the Tooth Fairy brought me a note that said she'd been so busy, she ran out of money but she'd get me tonight."

Jenn pursed her lips as her gaze caught Luke's. He merely shrugged as he held a small envelope.

"Well, I'm sure she'll return and leave even extra since you had to wait."

Jenn shot a wink to Luke and he merely chuckled as he shook his head.

"Can I go get Cookie?" Paisley asked.

Jenn straightened. "Absolutely."

Paisley ran toward the back of the shop and raced up the back steps. The floors creaked overhead and the sound of giggling filtered through the old building.

Jenn crossed her arms over her chest as she met Luke's piercing blue gaze. "No cash, huh?"

"I almost texted you, but I feel like you've bailed me out enough."

"I would've brought over something in a heartbeat. Now you just have to give more."

Luke narrowed those beautiful eyes. "I think you should pitch in after that promise you made."

"How much does a tooth go for these days?" She reached into her pocket and pulled out a twenty. "This cover it?"

Luke's brows rose as he held up a hand. "Um…that's a bit much for this fairy. I can't be dropping bills like that. Do you know how many teeth kids have?"

The horror and shock on his face had Jenn laughing once again. He seemed to do that for her. Make her smile for no reason, give her a bright spot in her day, and make her fall straight into believing that second chances truly did exist.

"I have some ones, if that will help," she offered as she slid the twenty back into her pocket.

"You're not paying," he said. "I've got it covered now. When they lose teeth late at night, there's a slight panic that kicks in."

"Well, now you know to keep something on hand. Was this her first tooth?"

"Second, but the first one she lost at school so I had a little time to prepare before bed."

Jenn couldn't imagine the fun of such simple things like playing Tooth Fairy. There were so many tasks like that that she wondered if she'd ever get to experience. She was still young, but not as young as she'd been when she and Cole had planned their family together.

The pounding of footsteps on the stairs and paws on the hardwood pulled Jenn's attention to the back of the salon. Cookie raced in with Paisley and the two looked like the perfect team.

"Do you like it?" Paisley beamed. "We got her a new collar. It's purple to match my boots."

Jenn looked closer at Cookie and noticed the purple sparkly collar peering beneath the fur. "Oh, that's so cute. You guys did not have to get her anything."

"P insisted," Luke explained. "We were picking up some supplies over at the feedstore and she found this."

"Well, I think it's perfect," Jenn gushed.

"Can we take her for a walk in the park?" Paisley asked. "I got my chores done at home and I don't have any homework."

"Honey, she might have plans this evening," Luke murmured.

"Actually, I'm free," Jenn told them. "But first I want to see those gorgeous birthday pictures."

"You haven't even seen them." Paisley took the envelope from Luke and pulled out the pictures. "How do you know they're gorgeous?"

Jenn shrugged. "I know what you look like and you're gorgeous, so I know your pictures will be, too."

"I didn't know what you'd want so I had Toot get you four."

Paisley handed over the images and Jenn's heart clenched at the sweetest face staring back. One picture she was sitting on an old wooden fence in a field. The wind blew her hair away from her face. The next she had her head thrown back laughing as she clutched several daisies. One picture she seemed to be in motion on a tire swing beneath an old oak tree. She knew that tree was in the field beside the church on the hill on the edge of town. She'd been on that tire swing many times herself.

But it was the last image that truly captured her heart. Luke and Paisley hand-in-hand, walking away from the camera with the sunset in the back, but the two were looking at each other. The perfect moment locked in time of the family they were creating together.

"Are you crying?" Paisley asked. "Do you hate them?"

"What?" Jenn blinked and realized a tear had escaped. "No, no. I love them. I'm just so happy that you wanted to give these to me. May I keep all of them?"

"Of course," Luke told her. "Do you have a leash for Cookie?"

"Hanging by the back door."

While Jenn propped the photos on her work-

station, Luke grabbed the leash. The moment
he came back, Cookie started doing circles and
prancing toward the front door. Jenn swiped her
keys from the top drawer of her station and gestured.

"Let's go," she told them.

Luke held on to the leash with one hand and
took Paisley's in the other as they neared the
crosswalk on the corner. Jenn locked up and met
up with them, then they strolled over to the park
entrance together. This place had always been
so special to her. Her family would come here
for walks or pictures. Their Sunday school pic-
nics were always in the center of the park with
the gazebo, the old stone bridge arching over the
creek, and a small pond with a fountain nearby.
Proms, weddings, really any special occasion,
called for a trip to the Rosewood Valley park.

As they entered the wrought iron gates leading through the main entrance, Paisley stopped
and turned to Luke.

"Can I hold the leash?" she asked. "I promise
to be careful."

Luke hesitated and glanced to Jenn.

"I'm fine with it," she told him. "Cookie has
never pulled me before. She's too obedient to
try to get away."

"Please, Toot?"

Luke handed over the leash. "Stay with us,

though. If there's an issue, I want to be able to step in."

"She'll do just fine," Jenn murmured.

Paisley started just a bit ahead of them, skipping alongside the pup. Her lopsided ponytails bounced against her shoulders and Jenn made another mental note to show Luke some easy styles. She just hadn't had time.

"I worry too much sometimes and others I don't think I worry enough because my mind is preoccupied with everything else going on."

Luke's words tugged at her heart. "She knows you're trying. That's all you can do. And the fact you're worried only proves how much you care. Give yourself some grace."

"You've said that before."

"That's because you need reminding."

They curved with the paved path and Jenn caught the eye of a group of women doing yoga beneath the tall maple trees. One woman in particular seemed to be zeroing in on Jenn.

Carla. But of course. No doubt she'd take this sighting and run with it. Jenn didn't care if people wanted to gossip about her and her life now. She was happy and working on starting over. She couldn't prevent others from talking and she simply had to focus on her own life.

The park seemed busier than usual, but that's what happened once the weather started turning from winter to spring. Every warm day a cause for celebration.

And she wasn't naive or oblivious to what this looked like. A little girl and a dog walking ahead of a single man and single woman. This was an image that had been in her head for so long, and now here she was right in the middle of her own dream…but this wasn't how she'd designed her life to be. This wasn't her family, though she was growing more and more used to this duo with each passing day. The touching gift from Paisley for Cookie had pulled Jenn into their little world a bit more.

But she needed to make things right with her own family before trying to push ahead and see if there was more between her and Luke beyond a friendship. She had to discuss her idea for helping the farm and find out if they were ready to forgive her.

For this moment, though, Jenn intended to enjoy her evening walk with a man she might just be falling for.

Chapter Thirteen

This whole domestic scenario was certainly not lost on Luke. Years ago this was exactly how he'd envisioned his life, but his fiancée hadn't shared the same outlook. Looking back at the heartache he'd endured after she left, he could see now that God's hand had been on that situation and she hadn't been the one for him.

And everything he felt for Jenn seemed different in every single way. She brought a sense of hope and light, she wasn't afraid to expose her heart and be vulnerable, and she adored Paisley. He honestly didn't know what else he could ask for, other than a chance at happiness with her on a deeper level.

She'd come back to Rosewood Valley to heal her family so he had to believe she wanted a fresh start.

The subtle ringtone from her cell pulled her from her thoughts.

"Oh." Jenn paused and reached into her pocket.

Luke waited while she read the text, but also kept his eye on Paisley and Cookie.

Jenn let out a little gasp that jerked his attention back to her.

"Something wrong?" he asked.

"No, I'm just surprised and now a little nervous," she admitted, sliding the cell back into the pocket of her red cardigan. "My mom is calling a family meeting and that was a group text with all of us on there. It's tomorrow at four."

Those expressive green eyes came up to his and his heart kicked up. Not only because of the level of worry on her face, but because he wondered what that meeting would bring. Were Will and Sarah going to finally disclose the sale? No matter what the meeting was about, this was another step Jenn needed to complete in order to continue on her journey toward healing.

They started walking once again and he had no doubt thoughts were racing through her mind.

"Nothing to worry about," he assured her. "Your mother obviously wants to mend things."

"She's always been one to take action. She doesn't like conflict. When we were younger, and my sisters and I would argue, she'd make us stop talking and hug for two whole minutes. She set a timer and those seconds felt like forever."

Jenn's soft laugh flittered on the wind and seemed to wrap around him like the sweetest embrace he'd ever had. Her hand accidentally brushed his as they walked side by side along the path. Luke didn't allow himself the time to think or talk himself out of his actions. He reached for her hand like it was the most natural gesture in the world.

And when her fingers slid through his and she gave a gentle squeeze, Luke released that breath he'd been holding. Maybe they were on the same page here…he just prayed they remained that way once she uncovered the truth.

A scream cut through the tender moment, and Luke jerked his focus to Paisley. Cookie darted off toward a ball that bounced by, Paisley held the leash, but got pulled down to the sidewalk before ultimately letting go.

Both he and Jenn took off running, her for the dog and him for Paisley. He crouched next to her and raked his gaze up and down, looking for any injuries. A tear in the knee of her jeans revealed a scraped knee, but she sat up cradling her arm with tears streaming down her face.

"It hurts," she cried. "Where's Cookie? She saw a ball and pulled me. I couldn't keep up."

"She's right here." Jenn came back holding on to the leash as she squatted down as well. "What's hurt, honey?"

"My arm." Paisley sniffed as more tears fell. "I can't move it."

Luke knew just by the way she was holding herself that the arm was likely broken. A wave of nausea overcame him at the thought of her hurting in any way. While he'd been daydreaming and holding hands with Jenn, his niece had gotten hurt.

He scooped her up into his arms and came to his feet.

"I'll meet you at your truck," Jenn told him. "I'm putting Cookie in and we'll take Paisley to the ER."

"No need for you to come," he told her as they rushed back to the main entrance. "I can handle this."

"But you don't have to alone."

He couldn't think right now, didn't know how to fix this right this second as Paisley sobbed against his chest. He should've been paying attention. He shouldn't have let his selfish thoughts cloud his parental judgment.

"I want her there," Paisley murmured.

Then it was settled. He just had to get himself together and be strong for her. He couldn't get swept up in his own guilt and remorse right now. His little girl needed him and he was almost positive this was her first broken bone, so no doubt she was scared in addition to the pain.

Once they were on their way to the hospital, Luke might have run a few yellow lights that teetered on being red. He'd risk the ticket at this point. Jenn, with her calming voice of reason, offered soothing words to a still crying Paisley. Just having Jenn here helped his nerves as well, but none of this would have happened had he been watching his niece.

"The doctors will fix you right up and when we get done, I'll get you some ice cream if Luke doesn't care," Jenn stated. "Whatever kind you want."

"Chocolate chip," she sniffed as she leaned against Jenn.

"Two scoops of chocolate chip, it is."

He pulled into the ER entrance and raced around to help Paisley out. Once again, he carried her and tried to control his movements so he didn't jerk her around too much.

A flurry of activity seemed to happen at once. Thankfully the waiting area wasn't busy and a nurse ushered them back to a room. X-rays confirmed the break and Paisley cried even harder while Jenn cradled her and rocked her in one of the hard plastic chairs. Luke gave insurance info and couldn't bring himself to take a seat. His nerves were still on edge and figured Jenn was doing the best job of consoling Paisley at this point. He was glad she'd come and offered to be by their side. She certainly didn't have to, but again, her selflessness spoke volumes for her character.

In no time, they were back on the road with a newly wrapped arm with a purple cast…because what else would she choose?

And apparently they were stopping for ice cream. He'd do anything to make her smile and take her mind off the pain and the worry of the upcoming weeks trying to maneuver with one arm.

He owed both of them an apology—Paisley for losing track of his responsibility and Jenn for taking her hand and just assuming that's what she'd want. He hadn't asked and they hadn't had time to discuss that turning point in their relationship. He needed to tell her how he felt before she learned of the sale. He didn't want her believing the worst in him and when the time came, he needed her to understand his actions. If they had a firm foundation before that time, he thought they might just have a chance.

But between the sale and then the custody hearing, there was a possibility he could lose it all and lose any future with a woman he'd come to truly care for…just like before.

Now that the pain meds had kicked in and the ice cream helped dry up the tears, Paisley had asked to go back to Jenn's apartment so she could make sure Cookie was okay. Paisley sat in the corner of Jenn's sofa and Cookie rested at her side as P toyed with one floppy ear, lulling the pup back to sleep.

"Well, this was quite an eventful day." Jenn sighed as she rested on one of her barstools.

Luke leaned against the island and faced Jenn. He'd never gotten that worried look from his eyes or the creases between his brows to diminish since the accident. She reached for his hand and curled her fingers around his.

"She's okay," Jenn assured him. "Kids break bones all the time and they bounce right back. She's already excited about who all can sign her cast at school. She really is one special girl to always look on the bright side of things."

"She wouldn't have to do any of that had I been paying attention," he muttered.

"Then if you're at fault, I am, too," she countered. "I had no idea Cookie would take off after a ball. She's never done anything like that with me or I would not have let Paisley hold the leash. I'll take the blame."

He jerked and shook his head. "Absolutely not. She's my responsibility." Luke leaned in and lowered his voice. "How is this going to look to the courts?" he asked. "I still don't have a permanent living arrangement lined up, I also let her break her arm."

"Hold up. You didn't *let* her do anything. Accidents happen, right?"

Luke quirked a brow. "Is that why you've come to realize since being gone? That Cole's death was an accident?"

Jenn stared back, shocked that he'd made that correlation, but his tone wasn't malicious or judgmental. His question came across as totally legit.

"I'm sorry." He blew out a sigh and flattened his palms on the stained countertop as he dropped his head between his shoulders. "I shouldn't have said that or compared the two situations. Clearly they're not the same and I didn't mean to be insensitive."

"You're not insensitive and maybe the situations aren't the same, but that doesn't mean we aren't experiencing parallel moments."

Luke raked a hand through his hair and moved around her to take a seat on the other stool. Jenn turned to face him, finding herself closer than she thought she'd be. His broad shoulders and stubbled jaw screamed rugged and tough, but this man was a big softy and had a giving heart.

"I can't ignore what's happening here."

Luke's low words after a long pause of silence had her breath catching in her throat. She waited for him to elaborate because this was one area she definitely wanted him to take the lead on.

"I'm attracted to you," he told her, glancing over her shoulder to check on Paisley before shifting that cobalt gaze back to her. "I've tried to tell myself this is a bad idea, but the more I say that, the more I want to spend time with you and learn everything."

Jenn's heartbeat quickened and she honestly couldn't believe this was happening. She never thought she'd find love again and honestly hadn't been looking for it.

If God was giving her a second chance with her family and with a man He chose, who was she to second-guess?

"I think I'm ready to move on," she told him. "This is hard and scary and I have so many emotions, but I feel the same. I want to know everything about you and Paisley. You both just make me happier and I've smiled more in the past few weeks than in the past three years."

A grin lifted the corners of his mouth. "I haven't seen Paisley this happy since her parents passed."

A burst of hope consumed her, warming her throughout. She didn't believe in coincidences. She believed in God's timing and she'd had to restore her faith since Cole's passing. Coming home had been the riskiest move, but she was starting to see why her journey had led her back at this precise moment.

"I should be honest as well and tell you that I might just find you attractive, too."

Luke's wide smile framed by that dark, close beard had her stomach in knots. She'd finally put her thoughts out in the open, and knowing Luke reciprocated her feelings sent a burst of warmth and hope through her. She'd wondered if she'd ever get such a reaction from anyone ever again.

Luke reached for her hand and laced their fingers together. The gesture still seemed right and comfortable. Nothing forced or awkward. Luke put her at ease with so many aspects of her life and she couldn't wait to see where they went from here now that they'd opened up. Would he ask her on an actual date soon? She hadn't been on a real date in so long, but the nerves in her belly weren't from fear or apprehension, but rather excitement at the new chance she'd been given.

"I should probably get Paisley home and settled in for bed."

But he didn't move. He continued to stroke the back of her hand with the pad of his thumb and hold her gaze with those beautiful blue eyes. She could lose track of time with this man and she knew without a doubt she was falling for him. The idea of falling in love again used to seem foreign, even scary, but she felt safe with Luke. He had a stellar reputation, an unwavering faith like hers, and had gone through heartache only to come out stronger on the other side. They already had so much in common.

"Please let me know if she needs anything," Jenn told him. "I hate this for her and for you, but we'll get through this."

Luke came to his feet, tugging her along with him as he continued to hold her hand.

"I like the sound of the 'we' part," he stated, and if possible his grin widened. "And thanks for being there for us tonight. This was really my first emergency and I didn't handle it well."

"You did just fine," she assured him. "And don't worry about anything with the courts. She's safe, she's where your brother wanted her, and she's one of the happiest little girls. You're doing a great job."

Luke's arms came around her and Jenn wasn't sure who needed this comforting embrace more. Perhaps leaning on each other was what forged their bond so quickly and perfectly.

"Why do you always know the right things to say?" he asked.

Jenn chuckled as she leaned her head against his chest. "I'm a beautician. We're also therapists, because our clients tell us everything and need advice."

Luke eased back and laid his hands on her shoulders. "You should charge more."

"Only if my landlord raises my rent," she joked.

"I have a feeling he won't do that."

When he stepped away, Jenn didn't like the loss of contact. She knew he had responsibilities, and that was one of the reasons she was so drawn to him. But at the same time, she wanted him to stay. She wanted to curl up on the sofa and watch a movie, pop popcorn and snuggle with a blanket.

"We don't have to go yet, do we?" Paisley pouted as she continued to pet the sleeping dog.

"Afraid so," Luke told her. "The doctor wrote you off school tomorrow, but you still have a bedtime and I have to work. So you can come with me or hang at the office with Mary."

"You can stay here if you want," Jenn suggested to the little girl. "I don't have a full day, but I'll be downstairs."

She looked to Luke and shrugged. "I mean, if you're okay with that. I just thought Paisley might be more comfortable."

"Can I?" Paisley asked, staring up at Luke with her wide eyes.

"I'm fine with that. But we need to get you home and in bed." He faced Jenn once more. "I'll need to head out about ten in the morning so I'll bring her by around then. That work?"

"Absolutely. I just have that family meeting at four."

"I'll be back by three at the latest."

Jenn shot Paisley a wink and the little girl giggled. Not only was she falling for the man, she was falling for the most precious child. Now she just needed to sew up the unraveled hems with her family and this new chapter in her life would be on the perfect path.

Chapter Fourteen

Luke maneuvered his truck away from his last stop of the day and headed down Sycamore Street toward Jenn's shop. While yesterday had been an awful day with the broken arm, he couldn't help but look to the silver lining. And that lining surrounded Jenn in all her beauty, both inside and out. She seemed to be that missing piece in his life, like she'd been designed to fit flawlessly into the void he'd had for so long.

The way she'd handled Paisley had been nothing short of nurturing and motherly. Not that anyone could ever replace Talia, but Paisley needed a female role model in her life. Someone she could trust and look up to as a good example. Jenn had all the qualities Luke had ever wanted, and some he didn't even realize he was looking for.

He'd just pulled into a parking spot in front of the salon when his cell vibrated on the console. Luke put the truck in Park before answering.

"This is Luke."

"Hey, Luke."

Autumn's voice penetrated the space and instantly put him on alert.

"The initial date has been moved and closer than I'd thought. I'm hoping you can meet in Washington in three days."

"Three days?" he repeated. "So soon?"

"I know, it's much sooner than we'd anticipated, but the judge had an opening and we might as well not put off the inevitable."

Luke pinched the bridge of his nose and closed his eyes. The hum of his engine and the traffic around him filled the silent space. His thoughts were all cramming against each other in his head and he honestly didn't know what to say.

"I know you're worried," Autumn added. "But I'm right there with you and we have your brother's will on our side. I truly believe this will go in your favor."

"What if it doesn't?"

That niggle of doubt pounded in his mind and on his heart. How would he tell Paisley? At seven years old, her world had already crumbled once. She'd just found her new normal and was getting somewhat back on track. So if this judge, who knew no parties involved, decided that a married couple with a stable life was the better option, there wouldn't be a thing Luke could do to stop that ruling.

"We're not going to think like that," Autumn

firmly stated. "I'll email you all of the documents you will need to bring, along with the address to the courthouse. This will be in the judge's office, so not an actual courtroom."

"I don't have to bring Paisley, do I?" he questioned.

"No. This will just be adults. But there might not be a decision made that day, so prepare yourself. And there could also come a time when the judge does want to meet Paisley and maybe get her opinion or see how she interacts with Carol."

"She doesn't even know the woman, to my knowledge."

"Just another advantage in your favor," Autumn reminded him. "There are far more boxes checked for you than Carol."

Luke blew out a sigh as he stared into the wide window of the salon. Jenn passed by every now and then, broom in her hand. He didn't believe this woman had come into his and Paisley's lives at this exact moment only for Paisley to be ripped from his care.

"Just send me all the information and I'll be there," he assured her. "And thanks."

"We'll get through this."

Luke disconnected the call and all he could think was that if he had to tell Paisley she wouldn't be living with him, wouldn't see Jenn, wouldn't see Cookie or her friends at school…

The whole life she'd had here would cease to exist, and Luke refused to believe anyone would be that heartless to remove a child from a stable life.

But her arm was broken, the sale wasn't even under contract for the new land, the rental lease would be up soon. He could play this mind game all day with himself, but in the end, he knew he had no control here. And maybe that's what irked him the most. For so long he'd lived alone, doing his own thing, controlling his own outcome…or so he'd thought.

Losing his brother and raising Paisley were all serious indicators that he controlled absolutely nothing. God had the ultimate say and Luke just needed to be still and listen. But that was the hard part. He was human and flawed and just wanted answers.

Right now, though, he had to get Paisley and give Jenn the break she needed to go to her family's meeting—which was just another area that gave him worry. He had to trust that everything would work out just the way it was supposed to.

Jenn took a deep breath before knocking on the back door. She felt silly knocking, but she still wasn't sure if she should just walk right in.

"Why did you knock?"

She turned to see Rachel at the base of the

back porch steps. She only had one braid over her shoulder and she clutched her well-worn brown hat in her hands.

Jenn hadn't spoken or even texted with Rachel since the other day at the salon. She wondered if her sister had given any more thought to the farm-to-table idea.

"I didn't know what to do, really," Jenn admitted.

"You know Mom won't want you knocking." Rachel mounted the steps and came to stand directly in front of Jenn. "And this is a family meeting. Family just walks on in."

Rachel held the door open and gestured Jenn inside.

"Let's see what Mom has in store for us," Rachel murmured. "I hope we don't have to hug for two minutes."

Jenn chewed the inside of her cheek to keep from laughing. This was the one and only time in her life, she wished for just that. She could use a good two-minute hug, especially now that she and Rachel seemed to have turned some type of corner.

But the moment she stepped inside and eyed all the contents on the long island and her mother's smiling face, she knew this was no regular meeting.

"Surprise!" Her mother beamed. "We're canning beets."

Jenn knew this familiar assembly line setup. They'd canned her entire life, though typically more in the summer and fall. Spring was a rarity, but apparently this was the only way her mother knew to get all of them in one place for a good amount of time.

This was about to get interesting.

"Your father will be in shortly," Sarah told them. "He's still working on those stalls in the barn."

Erin and Violet stepped in from the living room. Erin with her wide smile and Violet with her vibrant hair. Her sisters appearing just like she remembered here in the family home had Jenn's heart swelling. And if emotions were overwhelming to her, she couldn't imagine how her mother felt.

"What about the hugs?" Rachel asked. "Wouldn't that be quicker than canning?"

Their mother went to the hooks on the wall next to the pantry and plucked off a variety of aprons. She handed one to each girl, then slid her favorite yellow one over her head.

"I'm all for hugs," she told them. "But I also need to get these beets canned and we're done dancing around Jenn being back. There's too much that needs to be said and not over a text or a phone call."

"I couldn't agree more," Jenn chimed in.

"I'm sorry I didn't stop by after your last text," Violet chimed in. "I've been swamped at the clinic."

Erin winced. "And I've been so busy at the school. I'm sorry."

Jenn shrugged. "No worries, really."

Erin nodded, then gestured at the canning supplies. "Before we dive into this, can we address the rumors in town about Jenn and a certain vet dating?"

Jenn jerked as all eyes immediately turned to her.

"Who's saying that?" she countered, not denying the statement, though they hadn't gone on a date. Yet.

"I heard it, too, but didn't want to bring it up," Violet added.

"Girls, no gossip." Their mother had that stern tone, just like when they'd been kids. "We're not here to discuss Jenn and who she might or might not be dating."

Jenn hadn't even thought of the impact her relationship with Luke would have on the family.

"Would it bother anyone if I did date Luke?" she asked, glancing around the room.

Silence filled the space until her mother piped

up. "It's been three years, honey. You don't need to ask us how we feel. It matters how you feel."

"But I want to know," she insisted, her eyes moving to her sisters. "There seems to be so much up in the air right now and tension between us. I guess we can start there."

"Mom is right." Erin nodded. "If this is something you're ready for, then I definitely support you. I'm thrilled, actually. No matter how things are between all of us, you still deserve to find love and happiness."

Of course Erin would be in her corner, and their mother. Jenn expected nothing less. But she turned her attention to Violet and Rachel as she held her breath. The girls stared back at her, but instead of seeing bitterness or resentment in their eyes, they had a new look. Something akin to compassion.

"It's not up to us," Vi told her. "And Luke is a great guy who took on a huge responsibility when his brother passed away. That act alone says a great deal about his character. Not to mention, he's got a stellar reputation with farmers. I've never heard one negative word about him."

Jenn would imagine finding anything negative with Luke would be quite difficult.

When Jenn met Rachel's gaze, her oldest sister simply shrugged. "You'll have no complaints from me. He's been nothing but amazing here on the farm. He's had to bring Paisley a few times."

"Oh, that dear girl of his loves our tire swing," her mother added. "I looked out my window one day and the image of her there took me back to when you all were little. It was nice having those memories come to life."

Jenn could instantly see Paisley in that swing hanging from the old oak in the front yard. Her hair probably lopsided, her purple boots on, not a care in the world. Innocence could be so precious, and Jenn loved that Paisley had felt at home here.

"Let's talk and work." Her mother moved to the island and pointed. "Come on, girls. These beets won't can themselves."

Jenn smiled as she went to the end of the island where there was a box of lids for the jars. The jars were all lined along the countertop, spread out on either side of the sink. Beets sat in large pots ready to be boiled and chopped.

"I'll cut," Violet volunteered. "Rach, you're too aggressive with the knife, so why don't you help Jenn?"

Rachel rolled her eyes as she pulled her apron over her head and flopped her braid out. "I had one mishap when we were teens."

"And we don't want another," Erin added.

"Oh, I love the sound of my girls bickering in

the kitchen." Sarah clasped her hands together and smiled. "I won't even make you hug. I'm just happy you're all here. It's been too long and that's why I called this meeting. We need to stop dancing around the subject of Jenn being back and all this anger and pain that has filled us for the past three years."

Jenn knew that was her cue to pick up the conversation and either apologize again or begin her defense. Probably best to do both.

"That's why I'm back." Jenn pulled in a deep breath and flattened her palms against the island. "I stayed gone too long, I'm well aware of how that impacted you guys. Unfortunately, I can't turn back time or change my actions. All I can do is apologize and show you all that I'm here to stay if you'll welcome me back. I don't expect us to be perfect overnight, but I pray that we can find our way back to each other."

"I think the person you should be apologizing to is Dad," Rachel stated.

Jenn glanced at her sister and started to reply when the back screen door creaked, pulling all of their attention to the man in question.

"I don't need an apology." Her father remained in the doorway as he hooked his thumbs in his suspenders and kept his focus on Jenn. "All I've ever wanted was for you to come home so I could tell you how sorry I am. I never meant any harm to Cole. Working hard is all I know and he thrived on that same work ethic."

Jenn nodded. "You two were perfect together. I can see now that nothing that happened that day was your fault. That realization came from a great deal of therapy and prayer. I hurt so bad back then and I wanted someone to blame his death on. You never should have been the target."

Saying those words out loud for the first time to her father immediately lifted that heavy weight she'd dragged around with her for so long.

Her mother shifted and came up beside her. "Will, tell her everything. It's time."

Jenn blinked toward her mom and then back to her father. "Everything? What is she talking about?"

Her father sighed and shook his head. "It's about Cole's death."

Jenn's heart clenched as her mom took hold of her hand. What were they keeping from her that her parents both had those prominent lines between their brows. The worry on their faces did nothing to help her nerves.

"We learned after you'd gone that he had an underlying heart condition he'd been born with." Her dad took a step toward her. "There was nothing anyone could have done. There was no way of knowing he had this problem. Nothing he did on the farm that day caused his death. His heart attack was just a product of his illness. The coroner's report was mailed here with your name on it, so we kept it for a while. Then when we didn't hear from, we opened it and learned the truth."

Jenn tried to wrap her mind around what she'd just heard. None of this made sense. How did she not know about this? And why hadn't anyone told her before now? If she'd known, that could have changed everything. Why hadn't she tried to reach out sooner? Or why hadn't they?

She swallowed the emotions clogging her throat and tried to focus.

"We knew you were upset," her mother told her in that soft, caring tone. "We wanted to give you the space and time to heal. I always knew in my heart you'd come back, but it had to be on your terms and not because of anything else."

"I don't even know what to say," Jenn muttered.

"Maybe there's nothing left to say," her father told her. "Maybe the fact that you're home, that we're all ready to mend this broken family is all that we need."

The stinging in her eyes and throat had Jenn swallowing hard, but she knew that battling tears away wasn't the answer. She was human, surrounded by people who loved her, and they all just wanted to move forward in a more positive direction.

"I thought…" Jenn closed her eyes as a tear slid down her cheek and tried to speak again. "I thought I'd ruined everything with my harsh words that I didn't mean. I wanted to return so many times, but then I let fear take hold of me. The longer I stayed away, the easier it was to ignore the problem."

Rachel inched closer to her side and slid her fingers through Jenn's free hand.

"I'm still angry you ran away," she admitted. "Angry we were all hurting and none of us other than Mom reached out. But I see the pain you're in and I don't want that. I want us to all be one unit again. Now more than ever."

Jenn turned to look at her beautiful sister who also had tears in her eyes.

"That's all I've ever wanted. And I know there are problems with the farm, so I want to help."

Her mom squeezed her hand tighter before releasing. She moved back around the island and started busying herself with the beginning process of canning the beets.

"That's another thing we all need to discuss," Sarah told them as she pulled out just the right utensils and laid them on the counter. "The farm."

Jenn released her sister's hand and dabbed at

her damp cheeks. Will Spencer came on into the kitchen to stand next to his wife. Jenn caught Rachel's worried look before turning to face her parents.

"Should we have a seat for this?" Erin asked.

"Not unless you want to," their father replied. "We've been thinking of ways to generate more income here on the property. Nothing has come to us and as you know we had to sell a few head of cattle to offset some unexpected expenses."

"We can't sell the house," Violet inserted. "Just make sure things don't come to that. We'll find a way to get more money."

"I've been working on something since I got back and wanted to wait until we were all together to discuss."

Jenn glanced down the island to the pot of beets. The last time she'd done anything with beets was with Marie for a farm-to-table dinner at their church.

She had all eyes on her now. Maybe this was grasping at straws and nothing would come from her plan, but perhaps this would spark something that might take hold and grow roots. She had to try and she had to show what she'd been working on.

"At the church I attended, we were raising money to build up the youth program," she started. "I did some canning and would give

Their mother's eyes shifted to their father and he let out a sigh.

"We're not tearing it down," he confirmed. "But we are selling it."

Jenn blinked, confused at that statement. "You're selling the barn? How is that even possible? It's on our property."

He nodded in agreement. "We're selling that piece of the land with it as well."

"What?" Erin exclaimed.

"No," Rachel said at the same time.

Jenn didn't take her attention off her dad. She wanted to know why he'd come to this conclusion and if it was too late to stop the sale. Hadn't she just presented a great plan? Did they need to do something so drastic like break up their land?

"Have you signed papers?" she asked.

"Not yet. We have a verbal agreement."

Jenn shrugged. "Then call it off. There are other ways to fix this without selling off pieces."

"Maybe so, but this is going to be a good move for all parties involved," her dad added. "Your mother and I have thought long and hard about this. We've been praying for a couple months now on this decision and feel this is the right path for us."

Jenn shouldn't get worked up or agitated without hearing all of the information, but she couldn't deny the sharp edge of annoyance that speared her.

"And who has talked you into selling?" she asked. "Because I don't think you would have thought of this on your own."

His eyes met hers. She didn't like that look. She'd seen it before when he didn't want to reveal a truth to her. She'd seen it the day he'd come to tell her that Cole was unconscious in the field.

"Dad?"

"Luke Bennett is purchasing the land."

Jenn felt her lungs constrict, and she struggled to take a breath. The dream of a second chance she'd been hoping for suddenly vanished.

Chapter Fifteen

Luke checked his cell once again. He'd asked Jenn earlier to see if she could keep Paisley while he was out of town for a couple days for the custody dispute and she'd happily agreed. But he hadn't heard anything from her since the family meeting. The fact that there hadn't been one single bit of communication from her end had a sickening pit forming in his gut.

He stepped onto the front porch with a mason jar of sweet tea in one hand and his phone in the other. Paisley had gone to her room to color a picture for Jenn to hang on her refrigerator in her apartment. Paisley had said Jenn needed more color in that place, and Luke loved that his niece was so fond of someone this special.

But had he messed things up by going with her father's wishes? His loyalties had been torn and no matter what he'd done, he would have betrayed someone he cared about.

Luke padded barefoot over to the porch swing as a new set of worries rolled around in his mind.

If she had indeed found out, was she talking her parents out of the deal? And not just her, but what did the other sisters think? Will and Sarah valued family just as much as he did so their opinions would certainly hold weight. What if the girls convinced their parents that the sale was a mistake? Then where would he be?

He'd be at the mercy of a judge and have to admit that Paisley had a broken arm and soon they wouldn't have a house.

Luke set the tea on the porch railing and raked a hand over the back of his neck. Until he heard from Jenn, he wouldn't be able to relax. He'd told Paisley she'd be staying with Jenn for a couple days and his niece had squealed with excitement. But if Jenn changed her mind because of the family meeting, he'd have to ask Mary. He didn't have many options.

Tires crunching over gravel yanked his attention from his troublesome thoughts. Seeing Jenn's car pull up the long drive had Luke coming to his feet. She'd never been here before, but the town was small and clearly she had no trouble getting his address.

He took a sip of his tea before setting the jar back on the rail, but he remained on the porch as she came to a stop just behind his truck.

Her eyes met his through the windshield and he saw the truth all over her face.

She knew.

There was no way around this confrontation and he'd known this whole time the talk was inevitable. Had known at some point they'd have to face this reality. He just wished there had been a better way...but that hadn't been his call.

Jenn broke eye contact as she exited her car. With slow, careful steps, she came around and made her way up the stone path toward the porch. Luke leaned against the white post and crossed his arms over his chest. He tried to force a casualness he certainly did not feel.

Those vibrant green eyes met his as she remained at the bottom of the steps and rested her hand on the rail.

"Did you use me?"

Her accusation caught him off guard. "What?"

"For the land," she tossed back. "Did you use me to get closer to my father? Maybe to see what I knew about how dire things were? Or perhaps to try to get me in your corner?"

Luke willed himself to have patience here. She was hurting and had just discovered this business deal. He'd had months to process the possibility and very little time to come to terms with the fact the deal would go through...unless Will and Sarah changed their minds after speaking with their girls.

"I had already talked to your father well before you came to town," he defended. "I've never used anyone for anything, let alone a woman I've come to care about."

"You lied to me."

Luke shook his head. "I never lied. I made a promise to your father that I wouldn't say a word until he and your mother decided what to do."

"You listened to me talk about my family problems," Jenn went on, the hurt lacing her voice couldn't be ignored. "You knew who I was the moment we met, but I had no idea there was already some plan in place to steal part of my family's property."

Luke straightened. "I've never once tried to steal anything. I respect your parents and I saw there was a need and I was in a bind myself. I thought this was the most logical solution."

Jenn crossed her arms and widened her stance as her chin tipped up and she leveled him with her stare.

"I don't like being deceived," she volleyed back. "I opened my heart to you and all this time you were trying to take a piece of my family's livelihood. You knew I came back to help them and still kept this to yourself. I know what my dad told you, but I thought we had something special. I thought we trusted each other and could lean on each other."

"We do and we can," he countered. "I've

opened up more to you than anyone. Nothing has changed between us. Or nothing has to change. Don't let this ruin what we've built."

All could not be lost, not when he was so close to having the most amazing woman in his life. She'd admitted she had feelings for him. She couldn't just turn that switch off…could she?

She eyed him fiercely. "But what we built wasn't on a truthful foundation."

The front door opened and closed, and Luke tensed as Paisley came out to stand beside him.

"Jenn. I didn't know you were coming." Her little voice had so much happiness and excitement. "I just finished something for you."

Luke glanced down to see Paisley holding up a picture she'd colored of a house. In front of it stood a dog and three people. His heart ached at the sight and he didn't have to guess who those people were. Paisley wanted a family like she'd had. She wanted that happiness and stability… and he thought he'd found all of that for her… and himself.

"You drew that all by yourself?" Jenn asked, starting up the steps. "That is so beautiful, Paisley. You are a true artist."

"I need to work on my dogs," Paisley stated. "I don't think this looks like Cookie."

Jenn glanced to the paper and nodded. "I think it's exactly like Cookie. I can't wait to put this in my apartment. I do need more artwork if you'd like to make anything else."

"Really? Maybe when I come stay with you, I can bring all my stuff and you can tell me where you want new things."

Jenn's smile faltered for the briefest of moments, but enough that Luke caught it. Her eyes darted to his, then back to Paisley's. "I would love that. Maybe you can show me how to draw a house like this. I was never good at art."

"This is going to be the best sleepover ever," Paisley exclaimed. "Would it be okay if we made a blanket fort and watched a movie, too? Me and Mommy always did that."

Luke's heart clenched. Just another piece she'd been missing from her life that he hadn't known. He'd give absolutely anything to erase that pain she held inside. Unfortunately, that wasn't how life worked and all he could do was his absolute best and pray that was enough.

"Of course we can," Jenn replied. "My sisters and I used to do that all the time. I'm an expert builder. We're going to have so much fun."

That compassionate, loving nature of Jenn's had Luke swallowing a lump of guilt. Even though he'd hurt her, she still found it in her heart to love on his niece like nothing had happened. He honestly didn't expect her to just deny Paisley or turn her away, but Jenn continued to prove over and over just how special she was. He couldn't lose her and he had every intention of fighting for everything he wanted.

Jenn, Paisley, the land. He wanted it all and he didn't think that selfish to acknowledge. He had to get a solid foundation to secure his future. There wasn't a doubt in his mind that he was on the right track. He just needed to hold tight to his faith that everything would work out the way it was meant to.

"Honey, can you go inside for a minute so Jenn and I can talk?" Luke said.

Paisley glanced to him, then to Jenn, then back to him. "Is something wrong?"

"Not at all." There he went lying again, but he had to shield his niece. "Just boring adult conversation."

"Okay, then. See you in a couple days, Jenn." She skipped back inside, not a care in the world.

The moment the door closed behind her, Luke shoved his hands in his pockets and glanced to Jenn, who now stood just one step below him. Close enough to touch. And he wanted nothing more than to reach out and comfort her, but considering he was the one who'd caused her pain, he kept to himself.

"There's nothing I can do to change what happened," he started. "I never once intended to hurt you or deceive you. I'm sure that's what this looks like from your angle, but you know me, Jenn. You know that's not my character."

Jenn held his gaze for a moment before glancing away toward the setting sun. He studied her profile, not at all surprised how her natural beauty still captivated him. This woman had a strong personality, a loving heart, and those qualities made her passionate about those she cared for. Those were also the same qualities that had him falling for her in such a short time. He valued everything she brought into his life and hadn't even realized what he'd been missing until those traits were thrust in his face.

"I don't know what to believe anymore," she murmured. "I know I need time and I'm not sure about us."

She turned back to face him with unshed tears in her eyes.

"I think you need to handle this custody issue out of town and give me some space," she went on. "I need to focus on my family and what this new chapter will look like for us now that we're moving forward."

"Are you shutting me out?" he asked.

"I'm letting you go take care of you, and I need to take care of me," she amended. "There's no point in going over this again when I can't trust you right now."

She was letting him go. Fine. He could give

her space, but he wasn't going anywhere. They were made for each other.

"I'm sorry, Jenn. I can't tell you how much, but I'll earn your trust back," he vowed. "I'm not giving up on us. You deserve someone who puts you first, who values you, and who won't leave you to do this life on your own."

A lone tear slid down her porcelain cheek and Luke didn't even try to resist anymore. He swiped the moisture with the pad of his thumb, then dropped his hand to his side.

"Thank you for keeping Paisley while I'm gone. No matter what is going on between us, she loves you."

And so do I.

The revelation hit him hard, but he shouldn't be surprised. Those feelings had been below the surface, but he hadn't faced them. He'd been too afraid to face them. But having Jenn stand before him in tears over his actions put everything into perspective.

"I'd do anything for that girl," Jenn whispered.

Then she turned and descended the steps. She stopped at the bottom and tossed a glance over her shoulder. "Make sure to text me her school schedule and anything else I need to know while you're away. I'll be praying for you."

And then she was gone, leaving him on the porch with his jumbled up feelings and his remorse. Yes, she was upset with him but still put his situation in her prayers.

Jenn Spencer was definitely a woman he wanted—no, *needed*—to have in his life. Just as soon as this custody hearing was over, he'd set out to prove he could be the man she needed.

Jenn pulled on the reins to bring Starlight to a stop. Getting back on the old mare she'd ridden years ago felt like another piece falling right back into place.

And now, as she glanced up at the barn where she and Cole had lived during their short marriage, she waited on all the feelings to rush over her. Surprisingly, a sense of peace overcame her and she smiled up at the sunshine.

The warm sun seemed to beam right down on her. She'd taken the morning off, needing to gather her thoughts. She hadn't been on a horse in years and knew now was the time. She'd always been able to get a clearer head with fresh air and a ride through the property.

She'd needed to come here. To see the place she and Cole had made into a home. They'd only been married a few months before tragedy struck. They hadn't built their dream house on the land and they'd barely just started their lives together.

The level of peace that settled so deep within her had to have come from God. Oh, sure therapy and a break from this place had all helped her heal emotionally, but that deeper level of healing only came from the One above. And nothing would erase that darkness in her life. No amount of prayer or counseling could take away what she'd experienced, but she could learn and grow. She *had* learned and grown, or she wouldn't be here. Coming back to Rosewood Valley at this precise time was exactly where she needed to be.

She just wished she could get a better bead on all of her emotions surrounding the sale and Luke's part in everything. Try as he might to explain his side of things, Jenn couldn't help but feel betrayed. Had he used her to get closer to the family? Yes, she fully believed he'd approached her parents before she came back into town, but hadn't she just made a convenient landing into his life? Could she trust her feelings right now? Between being back and facing her past, and feeling the first spark of a connection with a man for the first time since Cole, maybe she was in a vulnerable position and needed to slow down.

She'd always led with her heart, so she didn't really know another way.

"Morning."

Jenn startled as she glanced to the side of the barn where her sister stood. Rachel adjusted her hat against the morning sun, but remained by the entrance to the grain barn.

"Hey," Jenn greeted. "I just needed to ride and clear my head."

"About Luke?"

Jenn nodded. "And everything going on with us as a family."

"We're on the right track." Rachel slid her hands into the pockets of her jeans as she started toward Jenn. "Being trapped canning beets for hours will do that."

Jenn laughed and nodded in agreement. "I hate beets."

"None of us likes them." Rachel chuckled as she reached to stroke Starlight's nose. "But they'll be good to go for the farmers market next month and if we're going to move ahead with the farm-to-table idea you had, we'll use them. That was brilliant thinking, by the way."

That three-year-old wound on Jenn's heart started to mend. Simple words, well-meaning words, could provide a balm like nothing else.

"Thanks for your support," Jenn told her sister. "I really think this can be as big or as small as we want to make it. We can keep the events to a minimum or really grow it to be something weekly."

"Endless possibilities."

Starlight shifted and Jenn tightened her grip on the reins. "Just like our family now that I'm back... I hope."

"I'm glad you're back," Rachel told her, moving

closer to her side and taking her hat off to meet her gaze. "I was angry for so long and felt you took the easy way out by running away, but I can see now that you handled the pain the only way you knew how. I don't want to be angry anymore."

Jenn gripped the horn of her saddle and swung a leg off to dismount. With a tight hand on the straps, she reached for her sister with the other. Rachel opened her arms and fully embraced her. The strength and love emanating from her filled Jenn with another layer of hope and joy.

"I love you," Rachel murmured before she eased back.

"Love you, too, sis."

Rachel adjusted her hat and took a step away. "I'm not sure what's going on with you and Luke, but I can tell you that from everything I know of him, he's a great guy. It's not his fault that our farm is in trouble and he happened to have a logical solution to fit his life and ours."

"No, it's not his fault," Jenn agreed. "But he kept that from me even when I poured my heart out to him, worried over how to help and even if you all would let me back in."

"I understand why you're confused and frustrated," Rachel told her. "And we both are well aware you're always fast to make decisions with your big heart and not your head sometimes."

"I feel like that's not a compliment."

Rachel smiled. "It's you, and we love you regardless. All I'm saying is that if you stop and think, especially from Luke's point of view, you might have a different outlook."

"So you're in his corner?" Jenn joked.

"I'm in the corner that brings you happiness and peace, and I think he could be good for you."

"I'm scared."

Admitting that out loud had to be a new level of recovery. She should be proud of herself, and she was, but she also still had a legitimate fear of giving her heart away again.

"It's okay to be scared," Rachel said. "It's when you let that fear hold you back and you look for reasons to run away from the fear that gets you in trouble. What if you ran toward the fear this time instead of away from it?"

Jenn pulled in a deep breath and glanced down to her old sneakers. So many worries and doubts had kept her from living her life these past few years. She had to start living and honoring her late husband instead of letting the pain and shame take over.

She couldn't be angry with Luke for trying to provide for his family, but that didn't soothe the bruise he'd left on her heart by omitting his intentions. Even with that harsh reality, she did understand he was in a tough spot. Luke didn't have a malicious bone in his body and Rachel might be onto something. If Jenn ran toward her fear, clinging to her faith with both hands, maybe something spectacular would happen. If she just let go and let God...

"Cole would want you to move on and be happy," Rachel added.

Jenn smiled as she met her sister's beautiful eyes once again. "He would."

"And I think Luke makes you happy."

Jenn nodded in agreement as a new outlook spread out before her. She didn't have to find a problem here and she had to give this second chance a second chance.

With a new vision for her future, but still one more thing left to do, Jenn mounted Starlight once again.

"Thanks for the chat." She glanced down to her sister and pulled back on the reins to get Starlight moving. "I need to head down to the main barn to see Dad."

"Maybe you can come to church with us on Sunday?" Rachel asked. "For Mother's Day?"

Jenn nodded. "I'll be there."

As she rode away, an overwhelming peace seemed to wrap its loving arms around her. Coping with all her unsettling emotions might be difficult, but she knew she had a whole host of people who loved her and cared for her, and she wouldn't have to take those next steps alone.

Chapter Sixteen

Jenn finished putting the saddle and blanket back in the tack room, then wiped her hands on her jeans. When she turned, her father was standing in the doorway, leaning against the frame.

"Starlight has missed you."

Jenn nodded. "I missed her, too."

"Where'd you ride?"

"All around." Jenn lifted a hip on one of the tack boxes and relaxed. "Had to see where Cole and I lived. I hadn't been back there for so long. Had a nice talk with Rachel."

"Good." Will Spencer stepped into the room and took off his hat then hung it by the door. "You look good being back here, Jenn. I used to dream of you here. The dreams were so real that I'd wake and think I'd walk down and find you saddling up your horse."

Jenn eased farther onto the tack box, crossing her legs like she used to as a kid while her father talked. She missed these talks. Missed his wisdom and guidance. Missed just the sound of his voice.

But this talk would be the most important stepping stone to their fresh start. With no one around, they could get back to their basics.

"Your mother kept asking me to reach out to you," he went on, looping those thumbs in his suspenders as he rocked back in his worn boots. "I told her you had to mend in your own way and all we could do was pray you'd return. I knew you would, deep in my heart, I knew it. But I was starting to worry."

"I never meant to hurt anyone," she told him. "I know my actions proved otherwise, but I hope you can see that I do love you guys and I know I was wrong to just go like that."

"You weren't wrong to go," he countered. "Nobody can say what's right or wrong when it comes to grief. I certainly don't like how you shut us all out, and for so long, but you're back and I know you want to be here. You couldn't have come before."

"Shame kept me gone longer than necessary," she admitted, toying with the ties on her sneakers. "I would think about reaching out and then I'd let so much time pass, I didn't know if I'd done too much damage."

"There's no such thing between a parent and a child." He took another step forward and took her hands in his rough, strong ones. "You could've come back in ten years, and I might still be bitter about you being gone, but I would've come around and welcomed you back just like I did this time. I had to push aside my pride and remember you're one of mine and no matter what happens, there's nothing that can break that bond."

She squeezed his hands, loving that familiar warm feel of the man who'd raised her. Those hands had done so much in over sixty years. They'd covered scrapes with bandages, they'd assisted in learning to ride bikes, they'd steered cattle from one pasture to the next, and every bit of those actions were done in love. While she hated that she'd been gone so long, she was here now and forever and that's what mattered.

"You know I love you and I really am sorry for blaming you." Jenn had said it before, but she couldn't stress enough her remorse. "I want you to know that I don't blame you. I never did, I just wanted to be angry with someone."

"I know, honey. And honestly, I blamed myself for a long time until we uncovered the truth."

Jenn wrapped her arms around her father, beyond thankful he'd welcomed her back home. When his arms banded around her in that bear hug she'd always sank into, she smiled against his shoulder.

"I have something for you." Her dad eased

back, placing his hands on her shoulders. "Or I should say, I saved something for you."

Jenn wouldn't have a clue what he'd saved, but she waited and watched while he moved toward the storage cabinet in the corner. He opened the double doors and reached on the top shelf and pulled down boots.

No. Not just any boots. *Her* boots. The ones she'd left behind in this very room. She'd not put on a pair of cowgirl boots since leaving Rosewood Valley and never thought she would again. But this familiar pair in her father's hands brought tears to her eyes.

"I told you that I knew you'd be back." He set the boots on the tack box next to her. "No cowgirl can ride in sneakers."

He gestured toward her old shoes and laughed.

Jenn unfolded her legs and toed off her shoes, immediately reaching for her well-worn brown boots. Sliding back into them felt like just another hug from a familiar friend. She hopped off the box and stared down at her feet, loving how this looked exactly right.

"Much better," she agreed, glancing up to her father. "I can't believe you held on to these."

"What else would I do with them? You were going to need a pair when you returned and these are already broken in."

Jenn smiled as she stepped forward and

wrapped her arms around his thick frame once again. She had years' worth of hugs to make up for.

Will Spencer enveloped her in his strong embrace. "We're going to be alright, Jenn. Nothing time and love can't fix."

She blinked away the tears and held on just a moment longer before she eased back.

"But we need to talk about this sale," he added. "I know you're not happy with it. None of you girls are thrilled. But your mother and I made the best decision for the family and honestly, for Luke and Paisley."

The logical side of her could see that point, but the emotional side still hurt over the secrets both men had kept from her.

"Luke is a great guy," her father went on. "I wouldn't have agreed to this otherwise. He values family just as much as we do and all he's doing is trying to get a firm foundation in place for his new life."

"I just wished he would've told me all those times I opened up to him," Jenn explained. She took a step away, leaned against the box once again and held her father's worried stare. "We were building something more than a friendship, but it's so new, I'm worried if I can truly trust my emotions. Rachel told me to run toward the fear instead of away from it."

"She's always been wise with her words."

"But still…"

"You're scared." Her father grunted. "If you let fear run your life and make all your decisions, you'll be miserable. I think it's time for you to be happy again, don't you?"

Her father's immediate response, so firm and so confident, had Jenn jerking back just a bit.

"Yeah, I do," she readily admitted.

There went those thumbs in the suspenders again as he sighed. "I know you, and I know that someone as kindhearted as Luke would scare you because you're afraid to trust your emotions. He's come into your life at a time when you need it most and you don't want to get hurt again."

Again.

The word hovered in the air between them. She knew he spoke the truth, but could she be strong enough to run toward this second chance without abandon?

"You can do what you want as far as your heart is concerned," her father continued. "But don't be upset with him because I asked him to keep the sale to himself. You wouldn't want to be with a man who couldn't keep his word, would you?"

That logical question had her mind racing. No, she wanted a man who kept his word, who could be trusted and was honorable. Luke possessed all of those qualities and more…which was why she knew she'd be welcoming him back into her life. She truly prayed this whole ordeal hadn't ruined something that could be beautiful.

It was time to fully come back, to embrace her family and her faith, and let the Lord guide her. She had to listen to Him.

"I've seen that look on your face," her father murmured. "You're working on a plan."

Jenn smiled. "Maybe I am. Maybe my eyes are opening to new possibilities for the first time in a long time."

"You deserve all the happiness, sweetheart. And Cole would want you to live your life."

Jenn nodded. "He would, I know."

"So you'll talk to Luke?"

Jenn nodded once again. But she was still anxious about what he'd be facing when he went to the custody hearing. She wished she could be there for him and offer all her support. Knowing he faced his worries and this unknown alone broke her heart. What would happen to him if Paisley was taken away? How would he recover from that? He'd upended his entire life to come here and had made so many plans to push into their new life together.

She leaned in for one last, tight hug before exiting the barn. She pulled her cell from her pocket and stared at the string of text messages.

Her thumbs hovered over the keys and she ultimately knew she needed to reach out. She had to take this step and maybe this would help alleviate his stress even if just a little.

Praying for your hearing. Once you're home, we should talk.

She waited a moment, then added one more line.

You're forgiven and I understand your actions.

With a deep breath, she crossed the drive to her vehicle. Jenn could only pray for the future with her and Luke because from here on out, she was going to put her worries on God and focus on the happiness she could finally see and embrace.

Luke's nerves rolled through his stomach. There was only one outcome where his world would be right. He adjusted his tie and came to his feet. He couldn't sit on that hard bench in the sterile hallway anymore. The judge was running late and each minute that ticked by only added to Luke's anxiety.

The text from Jenn gave him hope that once he got back, they were going to be on the right path. She'd reached out with her prayers and words of forgiveness and encouragement. As much as he wanted to dwell in that happy moment, he had to focus on today and his Sweet P.

"Shouldn't be too much longer," Autumn assured him just as he turned to pace. "Try to relax."

Luke shoved his hands into the pockets of his dress pants and tried to focus on her soothing tone and not the woman sitting just down the hall who was ready to take Paisley from him.

He hadn't even looked at Carol or her attorney since they'd arrived. Her husband must be the other guy, but Luke couldn't concentrate on that right now. He had nothing to say to them and was saving all his energy for the judge. He tapped the file of documents against his thigh, stared at the door to the judge's chamber and willed it to open.

"Excuse me."

Luke turned, shocked as Carol stood before him. She stared back at him with wide dark eyes. Her inky black hair framed her petite face.

"Would it be alright if we spoke alone before we go in?" she asked.

Luke glanced to his attorney, who had one brow lifted and eyes on Carol.

"I'm not sure that's best," Autumn stated.

Carol offered a smile that seemed genuine, but

Luke didn't know this woman and could only trust his instincts.

"I promise, I'm not doing anything malicious," Carol assured them. "And he doesn't have to say anything. I just want to say something to him in private."

Autumn ultimately glanced to Luke and nodded. "It's your call."

"It's fine." Luke gestured for Carol to follow him toward the other end of the hallway.

Their shoes clicked on the marble floors of the courthouse, echoing throughout. He made his way to the narrow window and eased one hand in his pocket, while clutching his folder in the other.

"I'm sure this is difficult for you," Carol began immediately. "Talia and I weren't just cousins— we were best friends growing up. We lost touch somewhat when I left for the military. Long story short, when I returned home from my final deployment, I heard of her passing. I was devastated, as I'm sure you are. I'm sorry for your loss as well."

"Thank you."

Carol tucked her dark curls behind her ears and continued speaking. "Other than my husband, I've never been close to anyone like I was with Talia. So I wanted to know that I could still be part of her family, and she mine." Her eyes glistened for a moment. "Paisley is all I have left of my best friend."

Her voice caught on those final two words and Luke's heart ached for her. They were both mourning.

"And all I have of my brother," Luke retorted, needing her to also understand his point of view.

Carol offered that gentle smile again. "I know. I didn't think of the will or Paisley when I filed for custody. To be honest, my grief made me a little selfish."

Luke listened, taking in her point of view. He wasn't a heartless person and he understood her position, he just wished she could understand his.

"I know the will stated that Paisley should be with you," she went on. "Going against what Scott and Talia wanted isn't my intent. I want Paisley to be happy because at the end of the day, she's the only one that matters."

"I agree."

A new spark of joy surrounded him. He didn't want to jump to any conclusions, but he thought Carol might be pulling back from this fight.

"I don't want to fight with anyone," she told him. "I'm hoping you and I can maybe come to some agreement without getting the courts involved."

Frustration spiked in him. "And why didn't

you call me before I traveled here if that's what you thought?" He shook his head and sighed. "I apologize. I didn't mean for that to come out harsh. It's a stressful time for all of us."

"It is," she agreed. "I'm sure I didn't help your grieving process, and I could have called you. But I wanted to meet you in person and talk to you face-to-face."

"Understandable." He leaned against the windowsill and figured he could take a little bit of the control now. "So what are you thinking now?"

"I just want to be able to see her." Carol's eyes welled up again with unshed tears and she forced a smile. "I know she doesn't know me, but if I could meet her and maybe visit sometimes. I don't think that's too much to ask."

Visits? In lieu of having Paisley taken from him and moved to another state? No, this certainly wasn't too much to ask.

"Anyone who loves Paisley and is an extension of either of her parents would be beneficial to her upbringing," he replied. "I'm sure she'd love another female in her life, and visits would be a good thing."

"I would really love that. My husband told me that I should talk to you first before going in and that I should think of Paisley and that uprooting her from the life she's known probably wasn't the best, considering all she's been through."

"I couldn't agree with him more."

Carol dabbed at her damp eyes and turned toward the other end of the hallway. She waved her husband over and the tall, broad man joined them.

"Hi. I'm Dylan." Carol's husband extended his hand to Luke. "Nice to meet you."

"Luke." He shook the man's hand and nodded a greeting. "I think we've established a reasonable solution for now."

Carol slid her arm through her husband's and glanced up at Dylan. "I know that Paisley is best in the home she knows and with a school and friends she's familiar with. I've asked for visits, maybe we can even start with a phone call or video chat or something first."

"It's a good plan," Dylan agreed.

"Does she know anything about this?" Carol asked Luke.

He shook his head. "No. I wanted to see what happened today before I said anything to her."

"I'll give you my number and—"

The door opened down the hall, stopping Carol. An elderly lady stepped out and glanced to the few of them out here waiting.

"The judge is ready for you all."

Luke met Carol's eyes and she smiled before turning her attention back to the woman.

"I think we won't be coming in today."

Finally, this worry over losing Paisley was over. Now he could get back to Rosewood Valley and pick up that conversation Jenn wanted to have. For the first time in months, he didn't have the heavy burden of regret or guilt weighing on him. He could move on, with the two most important ladies in his life.

Chapter Seventeen

❧

"Did Toot say why he'd be late?"

Jenn settled beneath the blanket fort—which was rather impressive, if she did say so herself—and plopped the big bowl of extra butter popcorn between them. Paisley had already stayed one night and Luke had texted and asked if Paisley could stay for the evening as he'd be later than he'd first thought. Maybe his flight was delayed or something, but she couldn't believe he'd said nothing about the custody arrangement. She wanted to ask, but the way they'd left things before he'd gone out of town didn't really give her that luxury.

"I'm not sure, honey."

Jenn grabbed the remote and pointed it toward the television. The fort was high and wide and open just on the side facing the TV. Paisley had been so impressed with how they'd set this up yesterday, Jenn had just left it. Good thing since Paisley had rode the bus here right after school and would be staying.

"Are you ready for another movie night?" Jenn asked, scrolling through the selection.

"And there's no school tomorrow," Paisley added. "I bet I can stay up late."

Jenn clicked on one of her favorites from her own childhood and eased back against the mound of pillows.

"I'm not making that call," Jenn told her. "I'm sure Luke will be back before bedtime and then he can say yes or no."

She hoped. Because if it was up to her, she'd pull an all-nighter, old-school slumber party and watch all the movies Paisley wanted. Of course the little one would likely fall asleep, but it would let her feel like a big kid. But Jenn wasn't her mother or even her guardian, so she wasn't going to decide.

"I really like staying here." Paisley grabbed a small handful of popcorn. "I don't know what we're going to do when we have to leave my house."

Jenn's ears perked up and she glanced to Paisley. "What do you mean?"

She had no clue what the little girl did or didn't know about the housing situation or the move to the farm or even the interim between leaving the rental and building on her family's property.

"I know that where we live now won't be ours

forever," Paisley explained around a mouthful of popcorn. "I heard Toot and the landlord talking about how the end of the month is some date, but the guy told Toot he understood if we need a little longer."

Well, that was at least something. Jenn wasn't quite sure of his plan or vision. She'd been so upset, she hadn't allowed that part of his life to enter into hers. But now she wanted to know. She wanted to see the mental image he'd created and she wondered if there was room for one more.

As the movie played on, the chime from the back door echoed up the steps and into the loft apartment. Jenn eased her head from the blanket as footsteps grew louder up the staircase. The door swung open and Luke stood there filling the space. His eyes landed on hers and her heart kicked up. She wasn't sure what she was more nervous about, the talk she intended to have with him or how the custody hearing went.

No, that wasn't true. She was a nervous wreck about knowing the future for Paisley. She couldn't imagine not having this darling girl in her life. She couldn't imagine either one of them not in her world.

"Who's hiding in that big fort?" Luke called out.

Jenn smiled as Paisley snickered. "No boys allowed."

He quirked a brow at Jenn and she merely shrugged. "It's true. We made a pact."

"Then I guess there's no surprises for anyone."

The blankets were immediately demolished as Paisley used her purple cast to thrust them aside and then ran toward Luke. His low laugh filled the space as Paisley grabbed hold of his arm with her uninjured one and started pulling.

"You're allowed," she said, "just give us the surprises."

This commotion pulled Cookie from her slumber on the ottoman, which they'd shoved over to the other side of the loft. The pup jumped down and did a series of stretches before making her way over to Luke.

He scratched the top of her head and leaned down to whisper something to Paisley. The secret seemed to last a while and Jenn had no clue what on earth he could be saying. But he finally straightened and smiled down at his niece at the same time she squealed and jumped up and down.

"What's your surprise?" Jenn asked as she came to her feet and stepped over the chaos.

Paisley turned to face her and shoved her staticky hair away from her face. "It's a surprise for you! Toot just needs my help."

Jenn glanced to Luke who had a smile on his face. "I had a great trip that turned out even better than I thought."

A wave of relief swept over her. "I can't wait to hear all about it. I'd actually like to talk to you privately if that's possible."

Luke's smile faltered, his brows drew in. "Am I going to like what you have to say?"

Jenn took a step forward and clasped her hands in front of her. She hadn't expected to get into this right here and now, but he seemed happy and she didn't like how they'd left things.

"I think you will," she told him.

"Then I think Paisley should stay, if you don't mind."

Jenn opened her mouth, but before she could say anything, Luke held up a hand.

"I think our talks might go together, but I'd really like to go first."

Because Jenn still had that sliver of fear from moving forward with her strong emotions for him, she gestured for him to go ahead.

"Absolutely."

He reached into his pocket and pulled something out, but kept it clutched in his hand.

Jenn eyed his fist, then brought her attention back to his. Was he about to propose? Was she ready for that big step? She'd already envisioned Luke and Paisley in her life and her future, but what exactly would that look like?

"I know there was a lot that went on without your knowledge," Luke started. "I hope you know that I can wait for you and whatever you need for me to do to show you that I'm here for the long haul. The more I think about our situations, which led us to this point, the more I think that it's been your default to run from what is hurting you. To shut it out. And I'm not saying you're wrong, but I am saying I don't want you to run anymore. If something is hurting you, I want to shoulder it. If your heart aches, I want to heal it. I want a chance to show you that I have fallen in love with you and that I want more. I want everything."

Jenn's breath caught in her throat. She wasn't sure what to say, but she couldn't just remain silent.

"You're right," she murmured. "Our talks do go together."

His smile widened as he eased around Cookie to take a step toward Jenn. "Is that so?"

"I know you're an honorable man, one that's true to his word. I value that about you and I can see now that you were in a tough position. I don't think for one second that you used me and I'm sorry for saying that."

Luke shrugged. "People say things in the moment when their emotions get the best of them."

"You still deserve an apology. And you were right about another thing," she added. "I have been eager to run away when I'm hurting. I try to get far away, but that's not the answer. While you on the other hand, you run toward the heartache because you're ready to fix everything. I need to be more like that. I need to be more like you because you can bring out the best of me."

She held her breath while she waited for him to say something, but he turned his back to her and squatted down to Paisley. Then he passed her whatever had been in his hand, and Paisley took Cookie over to the corner. Jenn tried to see what was going on, but these two were being quite sneaky.

"What are you guys up to?" she asked.

Luke turned back to face her and had that wide, handsome smile she'd come to love.

Yes, she loved him. She couldn't deny her feelings another minute and she wanted him to know, but she had to see what on earth these two were planning.

"I know how important your family's land is to you," Luke started. "And I want you to know it's important to me, too. I see my future there with Paisley and my practice."

He took a step forward, reaching for her hands. Jenn's heart beat faster as she stared into those mesmerizing eyes. She could get lost in the gaze of this man who so clearly loved her, too.

"And I see a future there with you," he added.

Those strong hands holding on to her coupled

with his bold statement sent a jolt of courage and hope through her. Like a switch had been turned on and for the first time in years, she had that light shining once again. Jenn knew Luke was the right one to make her live again, because he'd come into her life in a way that she hadn't expected and hadn't been looking for and he'd made her whole again.

"I love you." She blurted the words out with no lead-up or finesse, then laughed. "I guess I should have said something beautiful like you just did, but that's all I can think when you're holding me and looking at me."

"That's going to work out really well since I love you, too." He leaned in and pressed his lips to hers for the briefest of moments, so sweet and tender, then eased back. "Paisley has something to show you."

Jenn glanced at the little girl who'd come up beside them with Cookie. The dog wiggled her tail and panted with her mouth open, as if smiling herself.

"You know I kept telling you that Cookie needed a new collar?" Luke asked. "Paisley just put one on if you'd like to see it."

Paisley bounced on her tiptoes and squealed as Jenn bent down to check out the new accessory.

"Read it out loud," Paisley exclaimed.

Jenn moved the curly fur out of the way and gripped the gold circle charm.

"Will you marry us?"

Jenn straightened immediately and jerked her attention to Luke. If possible, his smile had gotten wider and Paisley reached up to take his hand. Now Jenn had the duo staring at her, waiting on an answer.

"I know this is crazy," he started. "But when something is right, it's just right. And I'm not saying we have to marry next week. I'll wait for whenever you're ready."

"You're going to say yes, right, Jenn?" Paisley asked, her eyes wide and full of hope.

A swell of tears filled Jenn's eyes as she laughed. "Am I going to say yes? Of course I am. Who wouldn't want to spend a lifetime with the most perfect people?"

"She said yes, Toot! That means I'm going to have a mom and dad again and a dog. That's all I've ever wanted."

Paisley launched herself at Jenn, who burst into tears. "I'm so happy," she sniffed, holding the girl. "I don't know why I'm crying like a baby."

Jenn eased Paisley down and pushed hair from the child's face. "You're definitely not a baby and sometimes we have so much happiness inside, we can't hold it all in and it leaks out."

"I just really love you," Paisley added.

"Aw, sweet girl. I love you."

"Can we have more slumber parties and forts when you and Toot get married?"

Jenn tapped the tip of Paisley's nose. "Absolutely, but are we letting boys in?"

Paisley pursed her lips and glanced up to Luke.

He merely shrugged. "Don't let me infringe on girl time."

"Maybe sometimes," Paisley replied.

Jenn came back to her feet with her arm around Paisley. She wanted to hold this moment forever. She wanted to lock away these overwhelming precious emotions and always remember how it felt to fall in love for a second time. Another chance at the life she'd always dreamed of with a man who had a heart of gold.

"I know why I'm back at this moment," she told Luke. "To find you."

"I think we all found each other," he amended, then glanced down to Cookie. "I guess this means you're claiming the dog as yours, right?"

Jenn laughed and reached for him so they all embraced in a long overdue group hug. "I'm claiming all of you."

Epilogue

"Are you ready for this?"

Jenn stared up at the white church nestled against the hillside. Instead of a feeling of dread or loss, she still had that hope that Luke had brought into her life.

She turned to him as she held his hand on one side and Paisley's on the other. With a smile and a burst of joy for this new, fresh start, she nodded.

"More than ready," she told him. "I need this."

Her first service back in over three years. The progress she'd made had her feeling like she could accomplish anything with her faith and this man by her side.

"Jenn?"

She released their hands and spun around at the sound of her mother's voice. There, walking toward her, was her entire family. Her parents, Rachel, Violet and Erin. All of them as one unit approaching her with smiles on their faces and love in their eyes.

"Oh, honey, I didn't know you were coming today," her mother cried as she drew closer. "And on Mother's Day. My heart is so full."

"It's time," Jenn replied. "Luke convinced me that our fresh start should be right here."

Her mother's focus shifted to Luke. "Then I have you to thank for giving my daughter that spark of light back."

"No thanks necessary." Luke grinned. "I'd do anything for her."

"I suppose since we're all here, I have some news to share." Jenn reached for Luke and Paisley's hands once again. "I'm getting married."

Her sisters squealed, her mother clasped her hands, and her father gave a nod of approval. Jenn expected nothing less from this crew she loved with her whole heart.

"Oh, darling." Her mother wrapped her arms around Jenn, then Luke, then Paisley. "This is absolutely the very best news."

"God has His hand on all of this and each of us," Jenn explained. "We don't have a date and we plan to build on the land that Luke is buying. For now I'll stay in the apartment and his landlord has agreed to extend the lease for as long as he needs while we build."

"There was always a plan," her father chimed in. "I couldn't be happier for you guys."

"Does this mean I get to swing on that tire

swing all the time when we move there?" Paisley asked.

"Absolutely," Sarah stated. "You can come swing on it now all the time if you'd like. My house is your house now."

Paisley glanced up to Jenn and drew her brows in as if confused.

"What is it, honey?" Jenn asked.

"Will this make your mom and dad, like, my grandparents? Or what should I call them? I've never had this many people in my family."

Jenn's heart couldn't swell with love any more for this beautiful girl. "I bet you can call them anything you'd like," she replied.

"You bet," Will Spencer declared. "I've never had a granddaughter before, so what should we call you?"

Paisley smiled and shrugged. "I'm just Paisley, but you should be Gramps or something like that. You look like a Gramps."

Her father chuckled as people maneuvered around them to get into the church. Jenn didn't miss that mist in his eyes as he glanced away. The sun shone bright, as if beaming down from the heavens directly onto their family and casting that warmth only the Lord could provide.

"I'm almost afraid to ask what I look like," Jenn's mother replied with a grin.

"Hmm…" Paisley thought for a minute. "I think you look like a Nana. Is that okay?"

"Nana it is."

"We should get inside before we're late and have to sit in the back," her father chimed in.

"Because you know he hates sitting in the back," Rachel muttered, which had her sisters snickering.

"We're going to take up two pews," Violet stated as they all started up the steps.

"I hope as our family grows, we can take up even more," Sarah added.

Jenn hoped for that very same thing. Nothing was more important than family and she couldn't wait to start this next chapter of her life.

* * * * *

Dear Reader,

The Love Inspired family is a warm, loving community that has welcomed me with open arms, so thank you! In the Four Sisters Ranch series, I knew I wanted to submerge the Spencer family in forgiveness and a deeper bond of love that only time and love can provide.

Up first, young widow Jenn Spencer. The prodigal daughter returns with fear in her heart, but she's still hopeful she can mend the tattered fabric of her relationships. What she isn't ready for is the unexpected help from her new landlord and his adorable niece. Luke takes custody of his precious niece when his brother and sister-in-law pass suddenly. While he's navigating the waters of fatherhood, he's also trying to find his own footing in a new town.

Luke, Jenn, Paisley, and an adorable stray pup find they balance each other and make quite a remarkable team on this journey of life. What these four don't know is they need each other to lean on during these difficult times.

I truly hope you fall in love with these characters just as I did. I also hope you know there is always hope to make amends. Yes, the journey might be difficult, but you have no better guide than the One who created you. Trust Him.

Be Blessed,
Julia

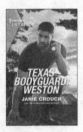

Me and Brenda

Me and Brenda

Philip Israel

AVON BOOKS ◢◣ NEW YORK

AVON BOOKS
A division of
The Hearst Corporation
1350 Avenue of the Americas
New York, New York 10019

Copyright © 1990 by Philip Israel
Cover illustration by Terry Widener
Inside cover author photograph by Lenore Israel
Published by arrangement with W.W. Norton and Company, Inc.
Library of Congress Catalog Card Number: 89-29477
ISBN: 0-380-71537-6

First Avon Books Trade Printing: January 1992

AVON TRADEMARK REG. U.S. PAT. OFF. AND IN OTHER COUNTRIES, MARCA REGISTRADA, HECHO EN U.S.A.

Printed in the U.S.A.

OPM   10   9   8   7   6   5   4   3   2   1

For Lenore

Me and Brenda

1

ONE DAY I GET A CALL TO PICK UP A CUSTOMER IN
front of the Green Leaf Tavern in Woodside. I pull up there, the guy gets in the back
seat but instead of telling me where he
wants to go he leans over to the front, puts
out his hand, and says to me, "Croppe. Al
Croppe. C-r-o-p-p-e."

Now I'm in that cab to make money, not
tell people if they're acting strange or not, so
I shake his hand and tell him it's a pleasure
to have him in my car. He gives me an address in Manhattan and I start heading for
the Queensborough Bridge. He turns out to
be a talker. He goes on and on but I'm

hardly paying attention. While we're on the bridge he says, "Sid General wants me to do the sheets." At that time I never heard of Sid General and for all I knew he was talking about laundry. He says, "It's a lot of work when I do the sheets but I pick winners nine out of ten times. You know anybody who can pick winners nine out of ten times?"

I say, "No sir! Nine out of ten! That's amazing!"

I get a lot of passengers who know how to pick winners but none of them are dressed too good.

A couple of days later, after my shift, I'm sitting in the Green Leaf Tavern and a guy comes up to me and says, "Rabbit Ears." I look at him like he's nuts. He says, "Third race. Aqueduct. I did the sheets today."

When I finished eating I walked over to the OTB office which is only two doors down from the Green Leaf Tavern. I put five dollars on Rabbit Ears to win. I'm not a gambler but I don't ignore a tip that drops on me from out of nowhere like that. The next day Rabbit Ears paid me fifty-five dollars.

Subsequently, Max, the afternoon bartender at the Green Leaf, told me something about this guy Croppe. There's a twenty-four-hour-a-day, seven-day-a-week poker game at Sid General's apartment, which is somewhere in the neighborhood, and this guy Croppe plays once a week, usually on Friday. He'll start at two or three in the morning and play till afternoon, twelve hours at a time, then he'll come into the Green Leaf for breakfast.

Now, I spend some time in the Green Leaf myself, and I happen to be the type of person who gets along with all kinds of people. So, you sit in the Green Leaf, you have a

few beers and people get to talking. If you sit long enough
you hear everything, and you hear everybody's version of it.

The Green Leaf is located in Woodside, at the intersection
of Roosevelt and Broadway. I call this area Woodside but
some people say it's Jackson Heights. There's no official
boundary so you can call it what you want. But I'll admit
one thing—Woodside is the wrong type of name for this
area. There are no woods around here. It is not, as they say
out west, Big Sky country. What we got here are buildings.
Not like in Manhattan but still pretty big. You could say
that this area is a city in its own right. We got thousands of
houses, dozens, maybe hundreds, of ten- to twenty-story
apartment buildings, stores, restaurants, law offices, gas stations, you name it. We got a big hospital, Elmhurst General,
a few blocks down. And there are all kinds of people living
around here—Irish, Hungarians, Jewish, Korean, Chinese,
Indian, Colombian—you name it, we got it. We also got the
IRT subway running overhead on Roosevelt Avenue. We
got the IND subway running under Broadway. We got a
station overhead for the IRT which is built right over the
street with stairs going up and down and more stairs to the
IND which has a station underground. So it's a very active
place. We got more cars, trucks, buses, and people—more
action crossing the intersection of Roosevelt and Broadway—than they got in the whole states of Wyoming,
Colorado, and Montana put together.

I don't claim that this is the cleanest or the quietest place
in the world. With all those steel girders from the Els we got
plenty of pigeons overhead. I don't have to tell you what

that means if you're walking underneath. But even so, this is a very nice place. In fact, if you take the time to look at it—and not many people do—but if you do, it's very impressive.

One day, about ten years ago, we had a blizzard. The wind was blowing and it snowed so hard you couldn't see five feet in front of you. I didn't work that day. I got up at five o'clock, which I always do, and it wasn't snowing yet. But I listened to the weather forecast, which was a lot different that morning than what I heard the night before. The night before they were saying, "No snow." It was supposed to snow south of here in Baltimore, Washington, maybe Philly, but not here. But at 5 A.M. they were saying it was going to be a big storm—twelve to fourteen inches. When I heard that I went back to bed. I was not going to get in a car and get stuck out on some side street or up on a bridge somewhere. One four-dollar ride could hang you up all day. A lot of people stayed home. The Green Leaf Tavern was open because Max and Genelli came in. They had no customers. All day long Max was wiping the bar, wiping the glasses, and looking out the window, which is not a bad way to earn a day's pay. Genelli, the cook, was sitting at a table in the back reading yesterday's paper, which is another good day's pay. Then, around two o'clock in the afternoon, Dave Winger came in.

Dave Winger first came to the Green Leaf about three or four months before that blizzard. When I saw him in there— and I'm not talking about the day of the blizzard now, because I wasn't there that day, I'm talking about the time three or four months before that, when I first laid eyes on him—I could see that he looked out of place. He was a young guy, twenty-three or twenty-four years old, and he didn't fit in. So naturally I went over and talked to him and after that we got friendly. But I'll get to his story later. Right now I'm talking about the day of the blizzard. At that time Dave was working all around this whole area—Woodside, Elmhurst, Maspeth, Jackson Heights—and when he got paid he'd walk over to the Green Leaf.

On the day of the blizzard he walked over from Elmhurst. He looked like a snowman when he came in. He orders a beer and he's about to order a plate of manicotti when all of a sudden the door blows open and in comes another snowman. This snowman slams the door shut and starts stamping his feet. He's wearing a fur coat and a fur hat and a big scarf, which he takes off and hangs up. This is Al Croppe. He's dressed like a college professor—tweed jacket with elbow patches, blue shirt, and a striped tie. And he starts right in. He says, "Max, we should work for the post office. Snow, sleet, nor rain will keep these harbingers from their appointed rounds. Gimme a hot drink, Max. Coffee Royale. This is a day that will live in infamy. It's gonna be remembered like the Blizzard of '88. You remember the old-timers talking about the Blizzard of '88? That's what we got here. A day that reminds me of poetry. I'm serious. Did I ever tell you that once upon a time I wanted to be a poet? If things were different, a little change of circumstances here or there, I could be in a loft in Soho right now writing poetry. You remember *Snowbound*? James Whitcomb Riley. When I was a kid I memorized that poem. They had a two-day snowstorm and this kid wakes up and looks out the window and he says—

> "And when the second morning shone,
> We looked upon a world unknown.

"That line used to give me the chills. A world unknown. Take a look out the window. Does that describe it or not? A world unknown. You remember Miss Martin? We had her in eleventh grade. Red eyes like she was always crying. *Thanatopsis* by Walt Whitman:

> "Yet a few days,
> And the all-beholding sun
> Shall no more see thy corpse."

Then all of a sudden, in the middle of this, he turns around to Winger and says, "Hey, guy, how about this snow, huh? Al Croppe. C-r-o-p-p-e. Croppe." And he puts out his hand.

Winger shakes hands and tells him his name.

Croppe says, "Whatta you drinkin'? Beer? It's eighteen degrees Fahrenheit out there. This is no day for beer. You got pipes inside. Intestines. That's like plumbing. It'll freeze on a day like this. Give the man a hot drink, Max. Coffee Royale for Mr. Winger and another one for me."

Dave says, "No thanks," but Max puts two cups up on the bar, puts a big shot of booze in each one, and fills them with hot coffee.

Croppe says, "To your health," and he takes a nice long sip. "Ahhhhhhh!" he says. "That's good! Feel that inside? Max, I been up all night. Real estate deal. Twenty-four million dollars. Lawyers from five firms sitting at the table. So much money on the line you couldn't blink an eye. Everybody figuring percentages. One fraction of a percent comes to hundreds of thousands of dollars. Lawyers like vultures. Agents. Salesmen. Each man for himself. You can't trust anybody. You can't blink an eye, Max."

Max is nodding. He's wiping the bar. He don't blink an eye. But he don't miss a word either. I know that because he's the one who told me what happened that day. First I got the story from Max and later I heard it from Dave.

Croppe says to Dave, "You look like a businessman yourself. Let me take a guess. I say you're a plumber. Am I right? You know why I guess that? Because every plumber I know dresses like he got his clothes in the Salvation Army. That's not an insult. Don't be insulted. To me, clothes mean nothing. I look in a guy's eyes. I look in his face. His phisonogomy. I'm looking at you right now and I say you have a very impressive face. I mean it. You're a guy that could command troops. I'm not kidding. I know people and I say you are a young man who could be very successful. You make a decision and you stick to it come hell or high water. Am I right? You're not taking me serious but I mean it. Max, tell him. I'm a businessman, Mr. Winger. I'm what is called an entrepen-ewer. My livelihood depends on knowing people. And I don't mean making their acquaintance. I mean judging them. Knowing what they're made of. I look at you and I see a young guy with potential. I look at you and I like what I see. Max, what's Mr. Winger's line of work? Plumbing?"

Max says, "He does everything. Plumbing, electrical, you name it. He's got a big reputation. I take his calls. You got a call from a lady in Maspeth today, Dave. Name is Dellawood. I got the number here. This guy has customers all over."

Al says, "Did I say it? I said it just from looking at his face."

Max says, "Some of these people think he's a saint."

"A saint?" Croppe says. "What's he do that makes him a saint?"

"He does good work," Max says.

Croppe looks from Max to Dave and back to Max. He doesn't believe this. He says, "Come on! Why is this guy a saint?"

Max says, "I didn't say he's a saint. They say it. One lady said it."

Croppe says, "You said he's a saint. You said, 'The man is a saint.' "

Max says, "Dave, tell him."

Dave is not going to get into this. He's got nothing to say.

So Max says, "He's a nice guy, he gives good prices, he treats people nice, he does extras for them, so they like him. Some of the people around here—you know the old people around here—the last time they had work done was twenty years ago. They call in somebody for an estimate and they can't believe what they hear so when they ask Dave he sounds cheap. And they all tell me he does beautiful work. So they love him."

Croppe says, "So the man is a saint because he gives a discount. Is that it? Okay. That's all right. I appreciate that. I understand it. As a matter of fact, I think it's good. There's a profit in that. But I don't understand why you get your calls here. Don't you have a phone?"

Dave doesn't answer.

Al says, "Max, doesn't he have a phone?"

Max says, "I guess not."

Al says, "He can't afford a phone?" Nobody answers. Al says, "That's okay. Nothing to be ashamed of. A lot of people can't afford phones. Listen, Dave, maybe we can help each other out. Tell me exactly what you do. You do painting?"

Dave nods.

"Carpenter? You also a carpenter?"

Dave nods.

"Electrical? You do electrical?"

He nods again. But he's not enjoying this.

Croppe says, "Jack-of-all-trades and you don't charge."

Dave says, "Of course I charge."

Croppe says, "But you work cheap. That's why you can't afford a phone. That's why you buy your clothes in the Salvation Army."

Dave says, "I don't buy my clothes in the Salvation Army."

Croppe says, "I know you don't. I just say that because it looks that way. Tell me, how do people hear about you?"

Dave says, "I don't know."

Croppe looks at Max. Max shrugs. He wants out of this

too. But Al says, "Max, how come they call here? How come
you get so many phone calls?"

Max says, "I don't know. Word of mouth."

Croppe says, "Word of mouth? They call a bar? Would
you hire a guy to fix your house by calling a bar?"

Max says, "Why not? The lady from Maspeth, the one I
just said about, she heard from the lady in Elmhurst where
he's workin' this week, Mrs. Blitnis."

Croppe says, "What's he doing for Mrs. Blitnis in Elmhurst?"

Max says, "Paintin' an apartment. And she heard about
him from somebody else."

Croppe says, "Dave, I like what I hear. I got a proposition
for you. Wait a minute! Let me talk. You haven't heard what
I'm going to say."

Dave says, "I don't need to."

Croppe says, "I'm going to set you up in business—full
backing—money to advertise, hire help, whatever you need.
'David Winger Home Repair.' How's that sound? And it's
your business. You're in charge, not me. You price the jobs,
you supervise the work, you hire the secretary. All I do is
back you. Don't shake your head. I know what I'm talking
about. Max, tell him. I'm a businessman. I'm what is called
an entrepen-ewer. I put up the cash, you put up the know-
how. That's all it takes. You start small but you grow big.
You understand?" He takes out his checkbook and he waves
it at Winger. "I got the cash right here," he says.

Dave says, "Forget it."

Croppe says, "Whatever you need. Just give me the number and I write it. Fifty thou? A hundred thou? You got it. Take the money, rent an office, hire a secretary, hire guys to do the work, and start advertising. 'Need a paint job? House look shabby? Call David Winger. David Winger will personally come to your house and discuss the job. No obligation. He'll make your house the showplace of the neighborhood.' We put it on billboards, newspapers, radio talk shows. The next thing you know people start to call. The secretary makes an appointment and you go see the job. You dress like an engineer. Safari outfit—pith helmet, khaki pants, khaki shirt, loops and pockets all over. You got stuff hanging from every loop. Measuring tape, pens, pencils, flashlight, clipboard. You name it. You rent a jeep. You drive to the house. 'Hi, I'm David Winger'—the Boss himself— 'We'll take care of everything. No problem.' And everybody gets a discount. That's what people want. Something for nothing. You take out your calculator. You figure you need two thousand dollars for this job. You put two thousand on the calculator and add maybe twenty-five percent. What's that come to? Twenty-five hundred. Am I right? Then you give 'em a discount. You split the difference. You say, 'That job would normally cost twenty-five hundred dollars but the price to you, with my Senior Citizen discount, is twenty-two fifty.' If they're not senior citizens, you've got a New Homeowners discount. If they're not new homeowners, you got a Washington's Birthday discount. If it's not Washington's Birthday, you got a Veteran's Day discount. You got a Spring Cleaning discount, a Fall Clearance discount, a Winter Snowball discount, a Summer Vacation discount. You got a discount for everything and everybody. On top of that you got freebies. You look over the job and you say, 'We're doing so much for you here, why don't we really finish it up. We're going to carpet those stairs for you for free. My gift to you.' That's how you do business. You give things away. You understand me? Now, you want to know why I'm doing this. What's in it for me? Why am I being so generous? Well I'm going to lay it on the line. I'm not being generous. I'm an investor. I am what is called an entrepen-ewer. I look for deals like this. I do deals like this every day. Tell him, Max. Every day. The way it works, the standard form is, I get you started, you cut me in on forty-nine percent and after the business becomes successful you buy me out. We agree on a price ahead of time. It's all put in writing. Legal. Black and white. You're covered. I'm covered. And that's it. That's the whole story. All I need from you is a figure." And he's waving his checkbook. "Name a figure and I make out the check right now."

Dave says, "Max, who is this guy?"

Al says, "You don't like it? Is that right? Maybe you think forty-nine percent is too much. Maybe you don't want me for a partner. I'm too vulgar. I'm not a Fifth Avenue personality. All right. I'll tell you what. I'll buy your name."

Winger starts to laugh. "Hey, man," he says, "what is this? A comedy routine?"

"Come on," Al says, "what's your price?"

Dave says, "What're you talking about? You can't buy my name."

"Why not?" Al says. "I buy your name, I rent a store, open

the business, and call myself David Winger Home Repair. I get myself a manager, I buy him the safari outfit, he goes around with a clipboard and says he's from David Winger. He looks at a job, gives a price, and subcontracts out the work. The customer pays me because I'm David Winger Home Repair. All I do is advertise and rake in the money."

Dave says, "If you believe that, you can do it without my name."

"No, I can't," Al says. "If I say Albert T. Croppe Home Repair, nobody knows me. Nobody ever heard of me painting, doing electrical, roofing. I can't do that stuff. So I need a name with a reputation. A name like that is gold. All you gotta do is gimme a price."

By that time Al's food is ready. He ordered his usual, which is ham and eggs, scrambled, with french fries, toast, and a Coffee Royale. Genelli brings it out and sets it on the bar. Al sits down and starts to salt his eggs and put ketchup on the fries. Max pours him another Coffee Royale. He looks over at Dave, who's sitting there with just a beer and the Coffee Royale which he hasn't touched, and says to Max, "Give Mr. Winger some eggs. On my tab."

Dave says, "It's okay. Thanks anyway but I already ordered."

Al says, "You already ordered. You know what? I like you. You're an independent bastard. You stand on your own two feet. Nobody's gonna do nothin' for you. Am I right? There's only one problem. You know what the problem is? The problem is that you're not a businessman. Don't get mad. I'm not trying to insult you. I'm speaking frankly be-

cause I like you and I wanna give you a break. I'm gonna
teach you a few things. Dave, in business a name is gold. It's
your most valuable asset. I'll give you the check here and
now and we go to a lawyer and sign the papers. Then I own
your name. I go into business and I'm David Winger Home
Repair. If you want to go into business later, you use some
other name."

Dave says, "I'd be pretty stupid to do that."

Al says, "No, you wouldn't. You can make a lot of money
that way. It happens all the time. You think every business is
owned by the guy who started it? The guy's name is still on
it but he sold out long ago. You sell your business and part of
the price is the name. That's what accountants call 'Good
Will' and, believe me, it goes for a high price because it's
valuable. If you sell me your name I go to the bank tomorrow and I'll get fifty thousand dollars to start a business. I
can see you don't understand that because you don't understand how business works. That's what I'm tryin' to teach
you. In business, the hardest thing to come by is a good
reputation and you got that already. If you got that you are a
guaranteed money-maker. The banks are looking for guys
like you. You're a safe investment. You know, I can't believe
I'm talking like this. I'm trying to convince you! I'm drooling
here and you can't see it. I don't understand. Listen, I'm so
sure that you are a winner that I'll work out any kind of
partnership you want. I say we need fifty thousand to start.
That's my estimate. You got a better one and I'll be glad to
hear it, but I say fifty thousand and I got my twenty-five

thousand right here." And he's waving his checkbook. "Just name it and we're in business," he says.

Dave says, "Well, I don't have twenty-five thousand and there's no way I'm ever going to have it so forget it."

"Listen, man," Al says, "if you don't want to do it, that's okay, but don't talk stupid. Don't say you can't get the money because it's not true. All you gotta do is walk into a bank and it's yours. Let's be serious. Let's talk like grown men. Let's understand the finances of this thing. You are a man who is sitting on a fortune. What you are doing is like owning oil leases and deciding just to pay the taxes and not develop them. Suppose you owned a vacant lot and somebody told you there's oil under it but you need fifty thousand dollars to get the oil out. What would you say to him? 'There's no way I'm ever gonna get that money.' Would you say that? Be honest."

Dave says, "If you have oil you can get money."

Al says, "That's just what I'm telling you! You got a reputation and in business that's better than oil. That's gold. A reputation is gold, Dave. Your name is gold around here. I heard where you're talking about. Woodside, Jackson Heights, Sunnyside, Maspeth. You're talking about half a million people, maybe a million people. The banks are looking for somebody like you. You ought to be rich right now. You got so much going for you, you ought to make up some excuse for not being rich. It's embarrassing. You come to the bank with me on Monday morning and in ten minutes you'll walk out of there with twenty-five thousand dollars. I got my twenty-five thousand right here and we're in business. I know people there. I know them all. It's no problem, Dave."

Genelli comes out of the kitchen again and now he's got a plate of manicotti. He puts it down in front of Winger and Winger orders another beer.

Croppe says, "You orderin' beer again? Beer with manicotti? That's Italian food. You don't drink beer with Italian food. You drink red wine. Max, give him a glass of red wine. I'm going to show you the ropes, kid. You start dealing with bankers and businessmen and you got to know about things like wine. When to drink red, when to drink white. This is the kind of thing that goes with money. When you get rich you act rich. Max, red wine! And put everything on my tab."

"I'll have beer," Dave says. "And I got my own money. Take it out of this, Max." He pulls out a wad of tens that he just got from Mrs. Blitnis, peels off two, and lays them on the bar.

Al says, "Max, that's Confederate money. It's no good. Your money's no good here, Dave. Put it away. I'm makin' an investment. You are a gold mine and I'm investing in you. This is my treat. Monday morning you come to the bank with me and I'll show you what I can do for you. And just to show my good faith, I give my pledge right now. Max, gimme a pen!" Max hands him a pen from behind the bar and Al makes out a check. "This is made out to you, David Winger, for twenty-five thousand dollars." He tears it off and tries to hand it to Winger. Winger won't take it. "What's your problem?" Al says. "I don't understand you. Come on. Talk straight. What is the problem?"

Winger says, "Max, do you know this guy?"

Max says, "He's a regular customer."

Al says, "You know, I'm a patient man. Nobody ever calls me a saint but I like to think that I have certain virtues and one of them is patience. In fact I'm more than patient. I am a long-suffering individual. I put up with a lot. But I've never been insulted like this. You've been insulting me since I walked in here and I've got to tell you that I think you're a rude person. All I want to do is hand you this check as an article of faith. All I want to do the whole time I been talking to you is take you in on a serious business deal. I've got Max's word as your reference, and you're not denying what he says, and on just that I'm willing to put up a lot of money. I'm not doing this out of charity. I'm doing it for business. But I am showing good faith. I'm showing faith in you. And what you've been doing the whole time since I came in is making fun of me."

Dave is not the kind of person who makes fun of people. He doesn't insult people. The whole reason he came to New York is to be a nice person—which is something I'll explain later. So this upsets him. He says, "I'm sorry. I never meant to insult you."

Al says, "Then what did you mean?"

Dave says, "I didn't mean anything. But you walk in here and offer to buy my name. I don't know you. I don't know where you come from. I don't know anything about you. The whole thing is very strange."

Al says, "I know it sounds strange to you. To you, working five, six days a week and making just enough money to

buy clothes that look like they come from the Salvation
Army, that sounds normal. That's why you can't afford a
phone. You get your business calls in a bar, for Chrissakes.
That's normal to you. That's why any real business deal
would sound strange. Look, man, I talk straight. I don't play
games." He picks up the two tens Winger laid on the bar.
"You worked hard for this money. Am I right?" He tears the
bills in half and drops them on the floor. Winger is so surprised he doesn't know what to do. He's just staring at the
guy. Al says, "That's what that money is worth. It's nothing,
man. I'm talking big money. Max, give him credit for that
money. Put it on my tab. Put everything on my tab."

2

I NEVER PERSONALLY SPOKE TO SID GENERAL. I USED to see him around the neighborhood, but I didn't know who he was until Max told me. He's a big fat guy who wears white suits all the time. I used to see him carrying a white suit in a plastic bag from the French cleaner—which is owned by a Korean. It used to be owned by a Hungarian Jew. Which is how this neighborhood goes. Sid does all his own shopping so I also used to see him with bags of groceries from the supermarket, which he buys to feed his poker game. Max tells me he also does odd jobs. Not odd jobs like cleaning somebody's basement. He's got a big Lincoln Continental and he chauffeurs people around in it for a fee. There are stories around that he's also an enforcer. I'm told he'll do it for whoever pays his price. But I don't know if that's true. What I do know is that his main job is the poker game, which is a twenty-four-hour-a-day, seven-day-a-week operation in his apartment. He sits on a high stool and takes something out of every pot. I've heard it's a dollar, I heard it's five, I heard it's ten, but I don't know which it is.

His face is all bags. People say he never sleeps more than three or four hours a day. Most of the time he sleeps in his car because he's got no furniture in his apartment except stuff for the poker game. He'll drive out to some place like Flushing Meadow Park or a quiet street in Douglaston or College Point and doze off behind the wheel. It's not a healthy way to live if you worry about cholesterol but Sid is more worried about not letting people know ahead of time where he's going to be.

I've been told that it's not unusual for a guy to drop five to ten thousand in one night at that poker game. And this kind of game is cash on the line. You can't get in there without showing three or four thousand. Since Al Croppe is a regular, that tells you something about his financial situation.

Nobody gets into that game unless they have Sid General's personal approval. Now since everybody has Sid's approval, even if the players don't know each other or don't like each other, nobody accuses anybody else of cheating because that would be an insult to Sid. But it just so happens that on the day of the blizzard Al Croppe had the feeling

that somebody was cheating. Al had three aces, two of them
showing, and a young guy who'd never been there before,
who was wearing a white cap which he didn't take off all
night and which really bothered Al, was raising him by fifty
dollars with only a pair of sevens showing. Al couldn't help
thinking that the guy was cheating because otherwise why
would he raise him with only a pair of sevens? But he
couldn't say anything. Al had those three aces, two showing,
and behind that, in the hole, he also had two fives. From the
way Al was betting the guy had to know he had more than
the two aces. So why was he raising with only those two
sevens? Naturally he had a third seven in the hole. Maybe he
had a full house. But there is no full house that will beat an
aces-high full house, which is what Al had and what this
guy should have been figuring Al had. So why wasn't he?
He's got that dumb-looking white cap on, which he's been
wearing all night when it's so hot in that apartment you
could sit in your underwear, and if he wasn't cheating, Al
figured, he had to be stupid. So Al is hesitating about
whether to raise him or not and at the same time, the pot is
getting so big and it's costing him so much money and the
guy is raising and raising so much that Al is worried. But
he's not going to drop out with an aces-high full house. So
he's sitting there and thinking. Should he raise or not? After
a while Sid says, "It'll cost you fifty to see him," which is
Sid's way of telling him that he's holding up the game. Al
does not like that. He's not an amateur, he's not a new guy,
and he's not an idiot like Joe—who's sitting behind him on
the couch—who loses early and then hangs around. But he

still can't figure out what's going on. So he's looking at the guy's sevens.

"You in or out?" Sid says.

"I'm thinkin'," Al says.

"Hey, Al, you ain't got enough brains to think for that long," Joe yells over from the couch.

"He sits back there so he can smell my farts," Al says. He picks up a fifty—which is his last fifty—two twenties, and a ten and puts them in the pot. "I see you and I raise you fifty," he says.

The new guy touches his cap. Maybe it's a good luck charm. He nods his head a couple of times and Al would like to stick his fist in the guy's teeth but naturally he keeps a poker face. The guy picks up a fifty and drops it in the pot.

Al is relieved that all this raising and raising, one on top of the other, is going to end.

"I see you," the guy says, "and I raise you," and he drops in another fifty.

Al would like to spit in the guy's face. What the hell can he have? He's got to have a full house. The guy has a full house and figures Al has three aces and figures he's gonna beat those three aces. Al picks up two twenties and a ten and drops them in the pot. "What've you got?" he says.

"Four of 'em," the guy says and he turns over two more sevens.

"Shit!" Al says and throws down his cards. Now he knows the guy didn't cheat because the guy's an idiot, because only an idiot would stay waiting for a fourth seven when Al already had two aces showing and was betting so big that he drove everybody else out.

He gets up from the table and says, "What time is it?" Sid tells him it's three o'clock.

He says, "A.M. or P.M., for Chrissake?" because the shades are down and he can't tell.

"How long you think you been here?" Sid says.

Al says, "That's it for me," and he goes to the bathroom.

This apartment looks like somebody just moved out because there's no furniture. There's a bunch of coats on the floor in the bedroom, a roll of toilet paper in the bathroom, and the kitchen is full of grocery bags that Sid uses for garbage which Joe takes down to the incinerator every once in a while. Meanwhile, until he does, the bags are sitting there full of empty beer cans, pizza crusts, cheese, and whatnot. It's roach heaven. There's a big coffee pot in there, powdered cream and sugar, and a stack of paper cups. Then there's food, like maybe cheese or doughnuts, and beer in the refrigerator.

Al's in the bathroom and he's mad. "Sevens!" he's yelling, "four sevens!" and they can hear him even while the toilet's flushing. He comes out and gets his fur coat from the pile on the floor in the bedroom. Joe's sitting on the couch with his coat on and he says to him, "Where you goin'?"

Al says, "I'm goin' for breakfast."

"We got stuff here," Sid says.

"Dried-up cheese and beer ain't my idea of breakfast," Al says. "Eggs is breakfast."

Joe says, "I'll keep you company."

Al says, "No thanks. I gotta make a stop."

You got to realize that the shades are down and nobody has bothered to look outside so they don't know it's snowing.

Joe says, "I ain't doin' nothin'. I got all day. I'll wait for you."

"You can't come," Al says. "I'm stopping at the Yoga Institute. I'm doing meditation for the rest of the afternoon."

"Come on, Al," Joe says. "Is he kidding about that yogi stuff or what?" But the guys are into another hand and they don't hear him.

Al goes out and gets the elevator. He went to the poker game after midnight and there was no sign of snow. The forecast didn't mention snow. They said it was going to snow south of here, in Washington and Baltimore, maybe Philly, but not here. Maybe a few flurries or something like that. Now he gets out of the elevator and the first thing he sees through the glass door in the lobby is the blizzard. It's a foot deep and blowing like crazy. This amazes him. He never suspected it for a minute the whole time he was in there. This is why I consider poker players stupid. They go in there, pull down the shades, stay twelve, twenty-four hours, and don't know what's going on outside. They don't know if it's day or night. The world could come to an end and if it didn't make any noise they wouldn't know about it.

Al goes to the Green Leaf Tavern and that's where he meets Winger.

3

DAVE WINGER DID NOT START OUT IN LIFE TO BE A
plumber or a house painter. And I can tell
you that he won't end up that way either. I
used to sit and drink beer with Dave
Winger in the Green Leaf Tavern and we
had some long talks. He comes from a col-
lege-educated family in Ohio which makes
good money and is not used to doing the
kind of work Dave is doing here. I believe
this was a case of a kid rebelling against his
family. His father teaches college. His
brother is a lawyer and his sister is married
to some big executive. Dave tells me he gets
his know-how about electricity and work-

ing with his hands from a grandfather who made a fortune
as an inventor for things they use on farms. He also had an
uncle who was an artist. So you can see that although he's
working with his hands, he's not doing it because he has to.
He's doing it for an idea. A theory. He says to me he wants to
know what life is all about. He says that sitting in an office
and making money isn't his idea of life. I said to him, "What,
in your opinion, is your idea of life?" He says, "I'm not sure
but right now I think the best a person can do is if other
people say, 'My life is better because of him.' "

Well that's very nice and I have no objection to it. But if
you think about it, you'll see that it's the kind of thing only
rich people can do—people who have the time and money to
do what they want. To me that's like playing. As far as the
rest of us are concerned, we don't have time to find out what
life is all about because we have to make a living. In fact, if I
did find out what life is all about it wouldn't make any difference to me because I'd still have to make a living. So as far
as I'm concerned, even though he lives here, works just as
hard as anybody else, and drinks beer with me in the Green
Leaf, Dave Winger is still living a different kind of life and is
a different kind of person.

For instance, one night we're sitting and talking and I
asked him why he quit college. He says to me that college
wasn't teaching him anything real. He wanted to get out in
the real world, meet real people and see real life. Now we're
sitting in the Green Leaf and talking. This is what he chose
to do. So what does that mean? I've got to assume that sitting here and talking is what he means by real life and I'm

the real people he's talking about. I don't know how to take that. Is it a compliment or an insult or what? And what is real life? If sitting and talking in a bar is real life then everything must be real life. So what is he talking about?

I resented that kind of talk. I don't have a college education to throw away for deep ideas and I don't do saintly work because I have to support a family. I work twelve-hour shifts five days a week and I don't have the time or strength for anything else. But let's put that aside. Let's talk about him. I have to admit that he was not a hypocrite. At least he tried not to be a hypocrite. He came out here, got a cheap place to live, and took odd jobs. Mostly he worked for old people and he didn't charge them much. So he had what you might call a special clientele because this area has a lot of old people and they passed his name around from one to the next. Most of them don't have a lot of money. And I can tell you they're not big tippers either. When they have a problem with their houses they let it go because it's too expensive to fix. But now here comes Dave Winger and he works cheap and does a beautiful job. Once word of that got around the man had more business than he could handle. Then he had a reputation and he could have worked anywhere and charged anything. But he didn't. I give him credit. He kept working for the same kind of people as before and not charging much. But don't get the wrong impression. These are not all poor people. They're not starving. They don't have it easy and they live close to the vest but some of them own houses. In fact, I wouldn't be surprised if some of them had plenty of money socked away. I said that to Dave

but he didn't care. That kind of stuff didn't bother him because he liked working for these people. He liked the people,
all of them—crackpots, cheapskates, senile, the whole
works. And once the people got to know him, when he spent
a few days working in their houses, they liked him. They
loved him. You have to see some of these old people. I get
them in my cab. They're slow, maybe they got arthritis,
maybe they're hard of hearing or they don't see too well, and
everybody takes advantage of them. But not Winger. And
they appreciate that. They love him. They think he's a saint.

Let me tell you how he operates. I once went with him to
give an estimate. The way that happened has to do with the
way Queens is laid out. This area, central Queens—I'm talking about Elmhurst, Maspeth, Jackson Heights, Woodside,
Astoria—in this whole area nothing is straight except the
main avenues like Queens Boulevard, Northern Boulevard,
and Broadway. Everything else is broken up. You're on a
street and all of a sudden it ends. Then it picks up again
someplace else which you can't find. The buses aren't going
to go on that kind of street. They stick to the main routes.
The subways go to Manhattan so they're no help. The only
way to get around here is to walk or take a cab or a car
service like the one I work for. That is expensive for the
average person. With the tip you can't get away for less than
five dollars on the cheapest ride. When Winger goes to price
a job he'll walk or take a bus but sometimes he just can't and
he winds up in a cab. One day, by coincidence, I got the call.
I took him to a place on a side street off Calamus Avenue and
he says to me, "Do you want to come in?" I radioed in that I

was getting off the seat, which you're allowed to do for a few minutes as long as you're in the area, and I went with him.

He rings the bell and through the window we can see his customer coming. She's holding on to one of these aluminum walkers and moving so slow that it takes forever. She's got a bottle of nitro pills in her hand like she's expecting a heart attack any minute. To open the door she has to open two locks and two chains and push back a bolt. It took her so long and was so hard that I didn't think she could do it. But she managed and she lets us into the living room. The place is full of old pictures. Nothing's been moved since her husband died, which was probably back when Eisenhower was president. It smells like his coffin is still in the dining room. She says to Winger she wants a paint job, no extras. He looks around and gives her a price on the low side because he feels sorry for her. She heard he's cheap so she's expecting he'll give her a price that would have been cheap twenty years ago and she thinks this price is high so she's not happy. But she figures she's not going to do better and he comes highly recommended so she says okay. After we leave I said to him, "You're not going to make a living with prices that low."

A couple of days later he comes to work. He looks around and decides he can't paint yet. He's got to take off the old moldings and buy new ones because the old ones had so many coats of paint on them that they'll chip in a few weeks if he paints over them and he can't work that way. Then he looks at the electric outlets and decides they're so old they might cause a fire and he can't let an old lady live in that condition. So he replaces them. Then he spackles, sands, and caulks, even though it wasn't part of the deal. Then he washes the walls so he doesn't have to paint over dirt and grease. Finally he paints. All those extras make the job last a day, maybe two days longer and cost him more in materials than he figured on but he says to himself that he can't charge her for any of it because he already gave her the price.

Now this is all very nice and these people really are better off because of him. So he has his wish. But let's face it. He couldn't do this if he really had to make a living. That is why, from the very beginning, from the first time he told me his story, I always believed that one day Winger would either go back home or change the way he does business.

But that's all right. I don't hold that against him. I look at it this way. I hope that when I get old there's another kid like him around, trying to do good, who'll fix up my place for me.

4

ON THE DAY OF THE BLIZZARD WINGER WAS WORK-
ing at the Blitnises' apartment on Ketchem
Street. The Blitnises loved him. Mrs. Blitnis
was always running down to the bakery,
buying cake and putting it on the kitchen
table for him. She kept a pot of coffee hot
and she was always telling him, "Mr.
Winger, take a break. You work too hard."
Of course she's not paying him by the hour
so if the job takes longer it costs him money,
not her. But he enjoys it and she means
well. They sit in the kitchen and talk and
the Blitnises can't get enough of him. These
are lonely people. Nobody visits them. The

children are in California or Texas or maybe they're only in
Manhattan but I know they're never on Ketchem Street. So
having Winger there is big stuff and they don't want to miss
a second. Mr. Blitnis is a guy who reads all day, he's got
glasses as thick as window panes, but as soon as Winger
comes into the kitchen for a break he shuts his book and
comes in to talk. He's a philosopher. Mrs. Blitnis said to me,
"If he wasn't such a philosopher we'd have enough money
to retire in Florida. We had a grocery store for thirty-seven
years. I did all the work and he read books. If he sold philosophy and made some money I'd say, 'All right,' but he never
sold any philosophy. All he did was read."

Mr. Blitnis doesn't pay attention to this. All he's interested in is books and he's always talking about what he's
reading. He tells Winger there was a Greek philosopher who
said you shouldn't eat beans. Another philosopher, Aristotle, spoke from cards. I don't know what that means but I
suppose this kind of information is educational.

Mrs. Blitnis serves Winger on her good dishes, like he's a
guest of honor. Winger tells her not to because he has paint
on his hands. She says, "Don't worry. They're old. I bought
this set in Washington, D.C., on my honeymoon when
Franklin Delano Roosevelt was president." And they look it.
But it was a nice thing for her to do.

When he's halfway through the job and they can see how
nice it's going to be, Mrs. Blitnis sits him down and says to
him, "Mr. Winger, I want to tell you something. You're a
nice man. You talk nice and you're respectful. You don't
cheat people. You do good work and you're conscientious of
the senior citizen."

He could do worse than go through life with that to remember. Sometimes a memory like that makes you more willing to be decent in later years. Of course there's also the people who do one decent thing in life and from then on figure they got a license to be a bastard.

The Friday of the blizzard Winger got an early start because he knew he was going to finish the job that day and he wanted to finish early. When he walked to Ketchem Street the snow was just starting. He got to work, skipped lunch, and around one or two o'clock he's finished. He packs up his tools in a big canvas bag which he made himself and he's ready to leave. Mrs. Blitnis is all choked up. She can't believe she's never going to see him again. Mr. Blitnis isn't reading. He's hanging around like he wants to say something but doesn't know what. Mrs. Blitnis says, "Come up and visit us. Take a look at your work. You should have pride and enjoy it." He says he'll try. She goes to the bedroom and gets his money out of a drawer. This is a straight cash business. Nothing written down. She went to the bank when it opened that morning and got the money, all in tens.

She says, "Here's your money, Mr. Winger. You earned it. You did a beautiful job and I'm well satisfied. Let me count it over so I'm sure I'm not cheating you." And she starts to put the bills down one at a time on the kitchen table. "Ten, twenty, thirty, forty, fifty . . . You'll get some business on account of me," she says. "I already told some people about you."

He says, "Thank you."

She says, "It's the least I can do. I wish I had a mansion for you to paint. Now where was I? Maybe I better start over."

And she **picks up the bills** and starts over. "Ten, twenty, thirty, forty, fifty, sixty, seventy . . . The only thing is you should get a phone. It makes a bad impression to leave a message at a bar. Some people will think you're a drinker or something like that. I know it's not true but people get the wrong idea."

He says, "You're right. I should."

She says, "Where did I leave off?"

He says, "Seventy."

She says, "Are you sure?" She looks at the tens on the table and she's trying to see if it looks like seven but she can't tell. She wants to show him that she takes his word but she can't do it. So she fiddles around and stalls and finally she picks up the money and starts over. "Ten, twenty, thirty, forty, fifty . . ." and this time she gets it all counted. But she still doesn't hand it to him. She says, "You know, Mr. Winger, I'm so pleased with this job that I'm going to give you a tip."

He says, "That's very nice of you, Mrs. Blitnis, but you don't have to."

She says, "Melody Watson in the first race Tuesday. I got inside information." Then she gives him the money.

Winger never played the tip. Can you believe that? I'm not a gambler but the lady said she had inside information. For five dollars you take a chance.

He puts the wad of tens in his pocket and goes out. And he's surprised by the snow too. By then it's over his ankles and it's coming down in this terrific wind. He doesn't know what to do. In that blizzard it could take an hour to walk to the Green Leaf. And when he gets there the place could be closed. He could freeze to death in that time. But if he doesn't go to the Green Leaf he'll just go back to his room and hole up there with all that money in his pocket and eat tuna fish, which he doesn't want to do. It's a longer walk to his room than it is to the Green Leaf and in that weather there's going to be no buses, cabs, or anything. He could go someplace else, there's a million places, but that doesn't occur to him. He starts walking to Broadway. By the way, whenever I mention Broadway here I'm talking about Broadway in Queens, not the famous one in Manhattan. This is a very different street. I don't even know why they call it Broadway. He goes to Broadway, past Elmhurst Hospital, and keeps heading toward Roosevelt. It's not a long walk but in the snow he can't even make out the El. After a couple of blocks he's got ice on the bottoms of his pants, his shoes and socks are soaked through, and his feet are frozen. His face feels like ice and he's covered with snow.

Most of the stores are closed. Nobody's doing business. The storekeepers who stayed open are looking out their windows with their hands behind their backs. He passes a shoe store which is still open and he goes in. He buys shoes and socks and puts his old wet stuff in the canvas bag which is frozen stiff by now. Then he asks for a pair of rubbers.

I happen to know this salesman. I bought shoes there myself. He's an obnoxious person. He says to Winger, "Rubbers won't do you any good out there. The weather report is for twelve to fourteen inches. You need boots on a day like this."

Winger says, "It must be that high now. I didn't even know it was supposed to snow."

The guy says, "Last night I heard three different weather forecasts and not one of 'em said it would snow. Can you believe that? These guys make half a million dollars a year. They have fan clubs. And they can't forecast the weather. They don't know anything about the weather. They can't forecast the weather. All they do is read it off a card. You or I could do the same thing. But they get away with it. You know why? Because the public is stupid. You deal with the public every day like I do and you'll see what I mean. Listen, you don't want rubbers. I got something for you in boots. A waterproof boot that will last you ten years."

He brings out an old box which looks like it's been in the basement and pulls out a pair of orange rubber boots with a blue line around the tops and says, "I can give you a good price on these."

Winger takes a look and says, "I don't think so." He can't say no straight out, not to a guy like this, a guy who comes in to work on the worst day of the year and must be desperate for a sale. But these boots are ugly.

The guy says, "Try 'em on. In snow like this it's the only thing that'll keep you dry. They're not the fashion but what do you care what the fairies in Manhattan are wearing? You want a boot that'll keep you dry."

Winger doesn't want these boots but ten minutes later he comes into the Green Leaf Tavern and he's wearing them.

5

SO IN ALL THAT SNOW HE GOES TO THE GREEN LEAF
and that's where he meets Croppe. Croppe
gives him the song and dance about David
Winger Home Repair and to tell you the
truth I have no idea if he's serious or not.
Maybe Croppe himself doesn't know. The
man talks. It's like he puts out a hundred
lines with bait on them and if he catches
something, okay, if not, that's okay too.
Maybe if Dave took him up at that moment,
when he wrote the check, everything would
have come out different. It's one of those
things nobody'll ever know.

Dave is sitting there eating his manicotti,

drinking beer, not touching the red wine or the Coffee Royale, and he's looking at the slip of paper which Max gave him. He's got three hundred fifty dollars in his pocket from Mrs. Blitnis. When I first met him, if he had cash like that in his pocket he wouldn't bother with another big job. He'd give himself a couple of days off. But this time he goes out, right in the middle of the blizzard, someplace Croppe can't hear him, and makes the call. I think he was getting a little tired of not having money so he was ready to go for two big jobs in a row. So he leaves the bar and he has no more to say to Croppe and Croppe has no more to say to him.

He calls the number on the slip and the lady is surprised to hear from him in the middle of a blizzard. But she says to come over the next day, which is Saturday, and give her an estimate. He goes over there, gives the estimate, she says okay and tells him to start Monday. It's a big job which will take him a week. And it's in Maspeth which would be two or three buses for him. That is a lot of money so Monday morning he decides to walk. Most of the sidewalks are shoveled by then but it's bitter cold. There's no straight route from his place to hers. He's got to get over dead ends and under the railroad. In places like that the snow is piled high. When he finally gets there he's wet and he feels like he already put in a day's work. And right from the start the lady is nasty. She happens to be a very ugly person also. There's no coffee and cake on this job.

He's supposed to paint the whole downstairs—a kitchen, bathroom, dining room, living room, plus a foyer or vestibule, a little space by the front door for hanging up coats.

First off, he looks around to see how he's going to go about the job. She's right there with him, watching like a hawk, like he's going to steal something. He says to her, "I think I'll start in the living room."

She says, "Why the living room? Start in the kitchen."

If he said he was going to start in the kitchen she'd say, "Start in the living room." He should have said to her, "Look, lady, I do it my way or else get yourself a different painter." But Winger is not like that. He knows he could walk out and get a different job for the same money but he feels sorry for her—an ugly old lady who lives alone in a filthy place. That's how he is with these people. Like he owes them something. So he explains to her why he wants to start in the living room and finally she says okay. That doesn't mean she's happy. She's the type of person who's never going to be happy. But he figures that when he gets a few rooms done and she sees how the place looks she'll feel better and she'll be nicer. When he told me the story I said to him if that's all it took to make people nice they wouldn't put criminals in jails, they'd put them in fancy apartments. He says to me that in Scandinavia they do. I don't know about Scandinavia and I don't know if that's true so I dropped the subject.

He starts out by washing her living room walls. The walls are so filthy that just washing them gets them so much cleaner that she's already thinking they don't need a paint job. She has a devious mind so naturally she figures everybody else is just as devious and she figures that if the walls don't need a paint job he's not going to paint them. He's going to fake it. He'll tell her the water is paint, or something like that. So she starts another argument. It's so ridiculous that he doesn't know what she's talking about. Finally he says to her, "Mrs. Dellawood, if you want me to paint over the grease and dirt, I'll do that. I usually wash it off but if it bothers you, I'll just paint right over it."

She backs off but she keeps watching him like a hawk to make sure he uses paint after he washes.

By late in the afternoon he's ready to paint. Mrs. Della-wood is in the kitchen. She's got her TV on, she's watching quiz shows and drinking coffee. Naturally she doesn't offer him any. He's up on the ladder and he starts the ceiling. He's working away up there when all of a sudden the doorbell rings. She goes to the foyer and opens the door. Winger hears a girl's voice, which surprises him. He figured this nasty old lady wouldn't know anybody. The girl and the old lady start to make a big fuss over each other out there and he hears the young one calling Mrs. Dellawood "Aunt Dell." They come into the living room and Winger can't believe his eyes. This is a beautiful girl. She's about Winger's age, very sexy and dressed very nice. He can't figure how an ugly old lady like Mrs. Dellawood gets to have a beautiful niece like this. The girl could be an actress. He says, "Hello," and she answers polite enough but she doesn't really pay attention to him. He can't take his eyes off her. He's painting but he keeps trying to look at her. But she doesn't know he's there. It's like he's part of the ladder. The two of them, the aunt and the niece, who is named Kathy, go into the kitchen and have coffee and talk. He's up on the ladder painting but he's listening to them. He's dying for her to come out and talk to him. He figures she's got to come out sooner or later. But she doesn't. She sits in the kitchen with Aunt Dell talking about her job. He's taking in every word. She's a commercial artist in an advertising agency. She's telling stories about ad campaigns and conferences, and everything is for big money. Aunt Dell is going tsk, tsk over everything the girl says.

He finishes for the day and they're still in the kitchen. He cleans up, packs his stuff, and goes in to talk to her. But he can't get a conversation going because she's not interested. He hangs out in the doorway trying to get her to pay attention to him but she won't.

The next day he can't wait to see if the girl comes back. Sure enough, around four o'clock the doorbell rings and there she is again. Now I believe that what's happening here—the reason for these visits—is that the old lady has money. Why else would this girl run out there every day? What she's doing is trying to make sure she's in the will. Naturally Winger doesn't think of that. He takes a look at this girl and he can't think straight.

She's a little friendlier this time because she saw him before but she's still not interested. She looks at what he's done and then goes into the kitchen with Aunt Dell and they sit there and talk again. This time the conversation is about promotions. The girl got a raise three months ago and now she wants another one. She's talking about other people's salaries and it's all big numbers. This one is getting a six-figure salary and that one got a twenty-five-thousand-dollar raise last month. They're telling her she's got to wait at least six months before they'll consider giving her another raise but she's on the fast track and she doesn't want to be slowed down so she's thinking of changing jobs.

Winger is doing his usual beautiful work. The girl even says to her aunt, "It's beautiful." Winger is standing right there but she doesn't say it to him. It's like she doesn't see him. Every day that week she comes to visit Aunt Dell. She's always discussing promotions, raises, big money, and Winger is taking in every word. This is a beautiful girl and it's driving him nuts. Even when he's not on the job he's thinking about her. He can't imagine why she won't look at him. Every day he's thinking of what he can say to her to get her attention but nothing works.

Now you would think, if he's not interested in money, that the way she talks about money would turn him off. But it doesn't. Which to me is suspicious. But I have to admit there are also other things going on here. First of all, this is a very beautiful girl. Second of all, he's a young guy, in his twenties, and he's lonely. He's got no money and he's not traveling in the kind of circles he's used to so he's not meeting the more educated type of girl he's used to. I suspect that when it comes to sex and female companionship, he's probably getting desperate. When he sees this girl he's so anxious he forgets the ideals he likes to tell me about and just goes after her. His problem is that he's so anxious that he doesn't understand why she's not interested in him.

Finally it's his last day on the job. Mrs. Dellawood is as happy as she's ever going to be. Her place never looked so good. She knows he's not going to cheat her. She's probably thinking of how to cheat him. But all he's thinking about is the girl and for this last day, he's got a plan. He's going to tell her about his uncle who was an artist. Since the girl is a commercial artist he figures she'll be interested enough to get a conversation going.

He's already putting on the last touches when she comes in. She comes over to look at what he's doing and he says to her—but cool, like he hasn't been thinking about this all last night and all day today—"Hi. I couldn't help overhearing what you've been telling your aunt. I heard you say you're an artist. My uncle was an artist. He painted landscapes."

She says, "That's nice."

He says, "Out in Ohio. He had exhibitions at some of the colleges. He sold a lot of paintings." She doesn't say anything to that. He says, "This room is finished. The whole job is done. I guess that's it." He's letting her know that she's got to speak up if she wants to get anywhere with him. It's now or never. But the girl doesn't even know what he's talking about. He doesn't understand that because he wants this girl so bad. He starts talking about art and painting again, like that's really going to get her interested, but in the middle of what he's saying she walks away and starts talking to Aunt Dell. That's when it finally dawns on him. For some reason, all of a sudden, he realizes how he must look to her. When she looks at him she sees a house painter, a poor guy in old clothes. When he talked to me, he could imagine that that meant he was a real person. But this girl is not interested in that kind of real person. She's interested in six-figure salaries. So when Winger finally sees this he doesn't say another word. He doesn't look at her again. He picks up his tools and all he wants to do is get out of there.

Meanwhile, the two of them, the old lady and the niece, are walking around looking at the job. They're looking for defects. They don't find any so the old lady comes out and gives him his money in an envelope. It's all cash, no receipt, no record, but he doesn't count it. He just shoves it in his pocket. He's so disgusted he doesn't care. And this is serious because if she didn't put in the full amount, once he walks out the door there's nothing he can do about it.

He's ready to go but all of a sudden the niece, Kathy, calls her aunt. She found a defect. The old lady calls him back and tells him to fix it. He doesn't argue. He unpacks his tools and takes care of it. Meanwhile they keep walking around, looking for more defects. He finishes and he's ready to go again. The girl is in the room watching him. All of a sudden, without thinking about anything, he says to her, "Next week I'm opening my own business."

She doesn't say anything. She's still looking for defects. But then, like she's being polite, she says, "What kind of business?"

He says, "I'm calling it David Winger Home Repair. I won't do this work myself any more. I'm hiring other people to do it."

She nods but she doesn't say anything.

He says, "Your aunt is lucky. After this my prices will go up. This is just kind of a training program I'm giving myself. I don't want to be in a position where I send people out to do work that I haven't done myself."

She looks at him. She says, "Really? That's interesting."

He says, "You'll probably be seeing my ads."

She says, "Who's doing them?"

He says, "I haven't decided yet. I've been concentrating on this part first—getting the experience. You can't run a business unless you've done the work yourself."

She says, "You mean you do all this painting and housework just for experience?"

He says, "Yes, of course. Otherwise I wouldn't do it."

She says, "You mean you don't have to do it?"

He says, "No, I'm just trying to learn the business."

She says, "But how do you make a living? Do you make enough from this kind of work?"

He says, "Oh, no. Not if you're doing just one job like this. There's no money in it this way."

She says, "Then how do you make a living?"

He says, "I have money."

She says, "Really? Then I have to give you credit—I mean to go out and do this kind of work. But you're very smart to do it. It's the only way to learn a business. But it takes a lot of nerve, I mean to go out as a house painter when you don't have to. But I hope you realize how much money it takes to start a business. If you're going to do it on a big scale."

He says, "Oh, sure. If I don't do it on a big scale it's not worth it. I've got the money. All I needed was the experience."

She says, "You'll need advertising, bookkeeping, payroll help, legal advice. It can cost thousands. Are you sure you can raise that much money?"

He says, "It's no problem. I have the money."

She says, "Do you have backers?"

He says, "No. I'm using my own money."

She says, "That's wonderful. And you certainly have the

right attitude. You're out there learning the nitty-gritty. Meeting the public. A lot of businesses fail because people don't know who they're selling to. It's very exciting to start something new. All on your own. How much do you think it will cost to start up?"

He says, "I figure I'll have to put in between fifty and a hundred thousand dollars before I turn a profit."

She says, "Have you thought of what will happen if you don't succeed? That's a lot of money. I'm sure you'll succeed, but anything can happen. Even if it's not your own fault. That's a lot of money. What will you do if you lose it?"

He says, "I'll try something else. Money is no problem. I'm not worried about that."

She pulls up a chair, sits down, and offers him a cup of coffee. She's got more questions. He doesn't tell her he lives in a furnished room in Jackson Heights and that he dropped out of college to meet real people. They talk about business. They talk about banks. They talk about advertising. He talks about growing up in a small college town in Ohio. He tells stories about his uncle, the black sheep of the family, and she laughs. He mentions that his brother's a lawyer and his father's a college professor. She can't get over him. She can't get over how he has the guts to go out on his own and work with his hands. What she doesn't say but what she can't get over most of all is that money is no problem to him.

He walks out of there about an hour later and he's got her name and phone number on a piece of paper that smells from perfume.

SATURDAY AFTERNOON, A WEEK AFTER THE BLIZ-
zard, I'm sitting in the Green Leaf talking to
Max. Max works six days, 2 P.M. to 10 P.M. I
would not work that schedule for anything.
That's the worst shift I ever heard of. But
that's what he does and I understand it's his
choice.

I'm usually in the Green Leaf on Saturday
afternoon because I don't work Saturdays.
Saturday is not a good day to drive a cab.
What you get on Saturday is women going
to the hairdresser or taking their kids shopping, which puts the kids and the women in
a bad mood and isn't worth the trouble.

They don't tip good either. And you get long periods of time when there're no customers at all. So Saturday is my free day. I go out with my wife on Saturday night but the afternoon is mine. I don't do much. Maybe I go for a walk or see a movie at matinee prices or I go to the Green Leaf—but it's my time. Brenda never asks me what I do Saturday afternoon and I never tell her. I make it a point not to tell her. Not that I do anything I need to keep secret but if some day I do something she doesn't have to know about, it's better that I've been keeping things to myself all along than if I have to start suddenly.

While I'm talking to Max, Dave Winger comes in. He's flush with money because he finished the Dellawood job and he's still got money left from Mrs. Blitnis. Now he's dealing in twenties instead of tens. He lays a twenty on the bar and orders a beer. Max gives him a couple of slips of paper with his calls. He draws the beer and pushes back the twenty and says, "You're covered."

Dave says, "What are you talking about?"

Max says, "It's on Al Croppe's tab. He owes you twenty."

Dave says, "Did he tell you to do that?"

Max says, "You heard him."

Dave says, "I didn't believe him."

Max says, "He said it so he meant it."

Dave says, "Has he been in today?"

Max says, "I didn't notice." Of course that doesn't mean anything. Max is a nice guy but he is not going to give out information about Al Croppe. If anything, he'll give information to Al Croppe. Al is a big tipper. That buys him a lot

of eyes and ears and some very closed mouths. So if you're
dealing with Al Croppe you got to be careful who you talk to
and what you say.

Dave says, "You think he'll be in?"

Max says, "I can't predict Al Croppe."

Dave says, "I'd like to talk to him."

Now I'm listening to this and I'm thinking it's very
strange. First of all, I didn't even know Dave knew Al
Croppe. At that point nobody told me yet that they had that
long conversation on the day of the blizzard. So I'd like to
know why he's looking for Al Croppe. He should stay away
from people like Al Croppe. And he should know that without me telling him.

But he says, "If you see him, would you tell him I was
looking for him?"

Max says, "Sure."

A customer down at the other end of the bar calls for a
drink so Max goes down there. As soon as he goes away I say
to Dave, "Why are you looking for Al Croppe?" But Dave
doesn't want to talk. He's looking in his beer. He shrugs.
This surprises me. I say, "I wouldn't mess with a guy like
that."

He says, "Why not?"

Now that is a stupid question. Dave Winger is supposed
to be smart. He's got high ideals. He's got a college education—at least part of one. He knows about jails in Scandinavia. He talks philosophy with Mr. Blitnis. But here he is
asking for a con man who does nothing all day, twenty-four
hours a day, three hundred sixty-five days a year, except go

around conning people out of their money. So I say to him—
and, believe me, it's so obvious I feel foolish saying it—I say,
"If you know anything about Al Croppe you should know
that Al Croppe is not a guy for you to mess with." But he
doesn't want to talk about it. And that annoyed me. I'm only
a cabdriver so I'm not supposed to be smart. But if he's such
a big thinker how come I have to teach him not to piss in the
sink? I get up and say, "Brenda is expecting me to take her to
the movies. I gotta go." And I'm mad.

A couple of days go by and late one night Dave is up in his
room and he hears the doorbell. There's a separate doorbell
in that house for each of the roomers. There're three of
them, and they're all sharing one bathroom. Very high class.
This is the first time anybody rung his bell so he's not sure
what it is. At first he thinks it's a fire. He goes downstairs
and opens the door and it's Al Croppe.

"I'm just passing your street," Al says, "so I rang your bell.
I only got a minute. I hear you want to talk to me."

Dave says, "I wanted to talk about the business deal you
mentioned."

Al says, "It's eleven o'clock at night. I can't talk business
now." And he's looking at his watch.

Dave says, "When can we talk?"

Al says, "What's it about?"

Dave says, "I'm interested in what you said. You remember? In the Green Leaf."

Al's making faces like he's in a big hurry and he says, "I'll
tell you what. I'm keeping some people waiting but you're a

good kid so I'm going to give you a few minutes. What's your proposition?"

Winger brings him up to his room, which is furnished with landlord-type furniture. An old tan linoleum with blue flowers on the floor. They sit down and Winger says to him, "I decided I'd like to hear about that business proposition— what we were talking about in the Green Leaf."

Croppe says, "Oh, yeah? What made you decide that?"

Dave says, "I thought it over."

Croppe says, "You thought it over? That's a problem. You took too long. That was a one-day special."

Winger can't tell if the guy is serious or not. So he's already uncomfortable. Maybe he's also sorry he started this. His brain got a little cloudy because of the girl but once he talks to Croppe, gets him in his room and sees him up close like that, reality sets in and he cools off. But Croppe doesn't get up to go. He sits there. If the offer is closed, why is he sitting there? The trouble is that Dave doesn't understand a guy like Croppe. What Croppe is doing is waiting to hear what Dave really wants. He figures Dave has a deal to offer him. Otherwise why would he want to see him? But Dave is not in Croppe's league. So nothing happens. Finally Croppe says, "If you got an idea, lay it out for me."

Dave says, "I'm just talking about what you said that day in the Green Leaf."

Croppe says, "Is that all?"

Dave says, "That's what I said."

Croppe says, "All right, let me tell you what the situation

is. You're talking about that day we had a blizzard. Am I right? The Green Leaf was warm and the two of us were trapped in there. So I made you an offer. I made a very generous offer. It was too generous. I'm not going to make an offer like that again. I'm a serious businessman. Now I don't have a lot of time so don't play games. If you got a proposition, I'll listen. I'm always ready to hear a proposition."

Dave says, "I was just thinking of what you said at the Green Leaf. I wanted to do what you said. You said I would put up the reputation and the know-how and you'd put up the money."

Croppe says, "You think that's a reasonable thing for me to do?"

Dave says, "It was your suggestion."

Croppe says, "And how much do you think your reputation and know-how are worth?"

Dave says, "I don't know. What do you think?"

Croppe says, "I don't think they're worth shit."

Al himself told him that his reputation was gold. Now Al turns around and tells him the opposite. So Dave is shocked. He's insulted. Maybe he's embarrassed. He sits there like his head was cut off.

Al says, "How many people around here know you?"

Dave says, "I don't know."

Al says, "I never heard of you. There are maybe a thousand, maybe ten thousand handymen around here. How are you different?"

Dave is quiet.

"You see what I'm saying?" Al says. "Let's be realistic.

You're putting up shit and you want me to put up fifty thousand dollars."

"I don't think it would take that much," Dave says.

Al says, "You don't know what you're talking about. You ask me for money but you don't have enough experience to know how much it costs to get a business started. You need fifty thousand dollars and not a penny less. But I'll tell you what I'll do. I'll put up half. If you can raise twenty-five thousand I'll put in the other twenty-five thousand. And I'm only doing it for one reason. I like your nerve. That's what you got going for you. There's not two guys in a million who'd have the nerve to call me in here and do what you just did. You were nasty to me that day. You were rude. Like my money wasn't real. And now you ask me for fifty thousand dollars. And you got nothing to offer in return. That takes a lot of nerve. But I give you credit because nerve is what you need in business. So I'm going to take a chance on you. You come up with twenty-five thousand and I'll put in twenty-five thousand." And he's looking at his watch like he's in a hurry.

Dave says, "Look, I'll tell you the truth. The whole point of my asking you was that I can't raise that kind of money. If I could I wouldn't need a partner."

Al looks at him like he's suspicious and says, "So whatever I say, it keeps coming back to the same thing. You want me to put up all the money. Do I have it right?"

Dave is embarrassed but he nods and says, "I guess so."

Al gives him a disgusted look. This makes Dave uncomfortable and he starts to talk, which is always a mistake, and he's stuttering and sputtering and he says, "Well, if you don't like it . . . it was just an idea . . . you mentioned it in the Green Leaf . . . ," and this, that, and the other.

Al puts up his hand. He says, "I don't like being played for a sucker."

Dave says, "I wasn't doing that."

Al says, "I'll tell you what I'm going to do. I think you are a sharp operator. But I am too. You're smart but you're not smarter than me. We're equals. The two of us. Okay? So I am going to go partners with you. Fifty-fifty. But I don't go into a partnership in which I take all the risks. You want to be in business, then you got to put up half. I want you to put up twenty-five thousand and I'm going to show you how to get it. We will go to the bank together tomorrow morning and you will take out a loan which they will give you on my say-so. My recommendation is all you need. How is that for a proposition?"

Now Dave hesitates. He did not expect to have to put himself on the line with a bank for that much money. I don't know what he expected. The truth is, he didn't know either because he wasn't thinking about it. He was thinking about the girl. He didn't expect things to happen so fast. Maybe, in the back of his mind, he figured they'd negotiate back and forth for a while and somehow that would help him get the girl into bed. Who knows what he thought? But if he was really smart he'd have backed out right then and there—as soon as Croppe made the offer. It would have been embarrassing and it would have made Croppe very mad but it would have saved him. But it's a funny thing about people.

They're more ready to go sign up with a bank for twenty-five thousand dollars and get into a lot of trouble than they are to let themselves be embarrassed in front of a con man.

So he thinks it over and says, "Sure. I'm ready for that. I'd rather have my money in it anyway. I just didn't think a bank would give me that kind of loan."

Croppe says, "Don't worry about the bank. If you're with me you can get any kind of a loan you want. But you got to understand some basics. With banks, looks is everything. You can't walk into a bank the way you dress. You got to look like a businessman. The first thing you need is a suit. Let me see your best suit."

Dave says, "I don't own a suit."

Al says, "Then we'll get you a suit."

Dave says, "I don't have money for a suit."

Al says, "When you're with me you don't need money. I'll take care of the money. Let's go."

Dave says, "It's after eleven. Nothing's open now."

Al says, "The people I deal with are open all night."

7

THEY GO DOWN TO A BAR ON NORTHERN BOULE-
vard and call a cab. By then it must be 11:30
and Winger keeps saying he can't believe a
clothing store will be open that late at night.
Croppe says, "Don't worry about it." The
cab takes them up Ditmars Boulevard in
Astoria to one of the streets in the Forties
near Steinway. By the time they get there
it's midnight. Winger is expecting a big
store all lit up with neon lights. He figures
it's got to be a flashy place if it's open all
night. But this is a dark street and it's dead
quiet. They get out in front of a big white
house with a screen porch next to a church.

Winger looks around and sees nothing. Al starts walking up the path to this big white house. The place is abandoned. The screens are still up in the middle of the winter. Nobody shoveled the walk and there're footprints all over the snow, like a lot of people were walking around in the yard. Al starts heading toward the house and his feet are going *crunch, crunch* in the snow. Dave yells, "Where're you going?" Al goes around the side of the house. Dave runs after him. It's pitch black in the back but he sees some steps going down to a basement door. Al is already down there. Dave is afraid of slipping on the ice but he goes down after him. Al rings a bell. Dave says to him, "What is it? What's going on?" But Al doesn't answer. The door opens and there's this big, tough-looking guy with a black beard. They can see a light inside. Al says, "Is Freddie here?"

The guy has this thick foreign accent. He says, "Who wans ta know?"

Al says, "I'm Al Croppe. C-r-o-p-p-e. Croppe. Sid General sent me."

The guy says, "Wha' chew wan'?"

Al says, "I wanna talk to Freddie. Is Freddie here?"

The guy hits himself on the chest like a gorilla and he says, "I Freddie. Wha' chew wan'?"

Al says, "My friend here needs some clothes."

Freddie looks at Dave. It's so dark he probably can't see him out there but he says, "Okay. You come in."

They go in the basement and there's not much light but they can see that the place is jammed to the walls with clothes hanging on long racks made of galvanized pipe. It looks like the biggest rummage sale in history. Except it's all new stuff. They got everything. The stuff is squeezed in so tight that if you pull something off a rack the stuff on either side of it comes off. There's piles of stuff in the corners— shoe boxes, shirts in plastic bags, underwear, socks, every- thing—it's piled chest high. Things all over the floor. You step on them when you walk. There's suits and ties on the floor between the racks and they just leave them there so when you go down the aisles you get them tangled up in your feet. The light is so bad you can't be sure what colors you're looking at. Al goes right to work pulling suits off the racks. "What size you take, Dave?" he says. "My friend here needs a couple of complete outfits," he says to Freddie. "He's gonna need a suitcase too. You got luggage?"

Freddie goes over and sits on a table and watches them. He says, "We got evrating."

Al picks out two suits, two sport jackets, and four pair of pants. "Grab some shirts off that pile," he says.

"Whad color you wan'?" Freddie says. "Here. Take. Take dis. How many you wan'?" And he starts tossing shirts onto a table. Every time he takes one off the pile some of the other shirts slide down to the floor.

"Ties," Al says.

Freddie says, "Ties, belts, socks. You need undawear? Take undawear."

Al picks out a big suitcase and says to Dave, "Pack all this shit up and I'll take care of the man here. How much you want for this shit."

Freddie says, "Two hawnert." And he holds up these two

fat fingers that look like white carrots with the dirt still on them.

Al laughs. He says, "Be serious, man. We're in a hurry."

"Two hawnert," Freddie says and he's waving his fat fingers.

Al says, "Is the boss in? I think you got me mixed up with somebody else. You're giving me the retail price."

"The boss ain 'ere," Freddie says. "I make da prize."

Al says, "Look, Freddie, the boss knows me. He's not gonna like you rippin' me off."

"Two hawnert," Freddie says.

Al says, "Listen, man, I gotta tell you something. I like you and I'm gonna be straight with you. I can see you're not the kind of guy that anybody pushes around. So I'm going to let you in on something. This place is known. You know what I mean? That's why they leave you here by yourself. One of these days this place is gonna get hit. Look at all this shit. You get caught with all this in here and you won't get any money. You'll get time. You understand me? You know what I'm talkin' about? They're settin' you up, man. Look, I'm talkin' to you straight because I like you. I like the way you handle yourself. You don't let nobody push you around. Now listen to me. I'm going to do something for you. I don't want to see you take a rap for somebody else. I got people in this business, the retail end, and I'm gonna send them down here to buy you out. The whole thing. They'll pay your price. You understand me? You get yours, the boss gets his. I'm gonna do that because I like you. I'll give you a phone number you can call to set it up. Now this stuff, what I got here, this is nothing. This is peanuts. Small potatoes in an operation like you're running. Am I right? One suitcase. You won't even notice it."

Freddie holds up his two fat fingers again and says, "Two hawnert. And don't give me bullshit."

Al says, "I'll tell you what I'll do. I'll give you twenty-five. That's for yourself because you're tough. You're a tough man, Freddie. I give you credit. You don't back down. I like that. I'll tell you what I'm gonna do for you. If you ever need a job, you look me up. Al Croppe. C-r-o-p-p-e."

"All righ'," Freddie says. "You big bullshit but I come down. One hawnert."

"For Chrissakes, man!" Al says. "What's the matter with you? I'm offering you twenty-five for yourself. Money in your pocket. The boss doesn't know if two suits are missing. He doesn't care. He expects you to make something for yourself. You want to lose his respect? You got to let people know you take care of yourself."

"One hawnert," Freddie says.

Al says, "One hawnert, your ass. I can get it retail at that price. I can go to Macy's and buy it for that. Let's be serious. Let's do business. You and me. You want to do business for your boss, then go get a job at Macy's. You work here, man, and you got to stand up for yourself. You understand me? You and your boss, that's oil and water. He's lookin' out for number one. That's what you got to do. I'll give you fifty dollars for yourself."

Freddie looks around. He gets down off the table and comes over to Al like he doesn't want anybody to hear and he says, "All righ'. Fifty dolla'. Take da stuff."

Al takes out a twenty-dollar bill and hands it to him and starts heading for the door. He says, "Dave, get the luggage and let's go."

Freddie says, "Hey! Wha' you doin'? Thirty dolla' more. You gimmie thirty dolla' more."

Al says, "Hey, Freddie, I'm bein' nice. What are you tryin' to pull on me? I'm a wholesale customer. I told you Sid General sent me. Why do you keep talking retail? Fifty dollars, that's retail. I put the wholesale price right in your hand. You got any complaints, talk to Sid. Let's go, Dave."

"You don' go nowhere," Freddie says. "You bullshit."

Al's disgusted now. He says, "Dave, you got thirty dollars on you? Give him thirty dollars and shut him up."

Winger's got plenty of money. He's got the mon€ ʳ from the Blitnis job and the Dellawood job but he doesn't want to give it away. But he's scared. He doesn't know who these guys are and he wants to get out of there so he gives Freddie thirty dollars and they leave.

When they're outside he says to Al, "Wha̠ ̣ind of place was that?"

Al says, "Immigrants. You know the kin ᴐf stuff they do. Hole-in-the-wall. In twenty years he'll ᴡn a department store. He'll drive Macy's out of busines᷍ . Those bastards are taking over the country."

Dave says, "That's no store."

Al says, "Hey, kid, you're smart. You're a college boy. So act it. If you don't know, don't ask."

They get a cab and Croppe takes him home. Dave doesn't

like this. Now he sees he made a mistake. But he doesn't know how to handle it.

He gets out of the cab with the suitcase and Al says to him, "Hey, don't look so sad. We got a good price for that stuff. The suitcase alone is worth fifty bucks. Don't worry about it. That's a good place to shop. We'll go back there one of these days and get you a whole wardrobe."

IF I HAD MY WISH, DAVE WOULD HAVE LEFT THAT suitcase in the cab with Al and said, "Forget it. I made a mistake." The man is a shark and Dave Winger was in no way prepared to deal with him. Dave was a naive kid, a babe in the woods. He should have apologized—just to get out of that car and get away from Al Croppe. "I'm sorry. I won't sign for a loan. I won't go to the bank. I'm out of this."

As much as I liked having him around here painting apartments for the senile population, I wish he went back to Ohio before he got involved with Al Croppe. The best thing would be if he had packed up that morning and I never saw or heard of him again. I knew what would happen once he went back to Ohio. Back there he's just like the rest of his kind. I wouldn't trust any one of them with a ten-foot pole. Once he's back in Ohio, I know what he's doing. He'll sit in the country club and tell stories about how he did charity work for the lower elements in Queens, New York. But what he says out in Ohio I don't hear. So I don't care.

And why should I care what Dave Winger does wherever he is? Why should I care and get involved if he's mixed up with a con artist like Al Croppe? It's no skin off my nose. Why should I even have an opinion? I'll tell you why. Because I liked Dave Winger. He was different. He wasn't always out for the buck. At least he wasn't back then. I know I was always knocking him and trying to show he was a hypocrite or that he was a rich boy playacting but I liked him for what he was doing. Even if it was an act, he was still helping people out and not trying to make money from them. He was not trying to squeeze anybody. He wasn't living for money.

I look around myself and what do I see? I'm in the Green Leaf and here's Max, the bartender. Now Max is a nice guy. He's a good bartender. I like him. You go in and talk to him and he'll give you a sympathetic ear. What you tell him will stay with him. He don't gossip. But on the other hand, I trust him only so far. If you're a good bartender you're friendly with everybody. But you're not everybody's friend. Say I got a problem with Al Croppe. I'm not going to discuss that with Max because I know that when Al Croppe comes to pay his tab he'll lay down an extra fifty dollars for Max. I leave a tip on the bar when I drink but it'll take a long time before my tips add up to fifty dollars. So as much as I like Max and as much as I trust him and no matter how friendly we are, I know what makes the world go round and I know which side Max's bread is buttered on.

But I don't have to talk about Max. I could talk about anybody. I could talk about myself. Do I eat shit for a two-dollar tip? I do. I smile at the customers and talk nice and carry suitcases and listen to all kinds of garbage and sympathize with everybody who sits in the back seat as if they were the best people in the world. And what do I get out of it? The difference between that fake smile and looking at people straight and telling them what I really think is maybe five dollars a day. Some days more, some days less. But that's twenty-five dollars a week and I can't afford to give it up just so I can enjoy myself by giving out honest opinions. When you deal with the public, you do not get bonuses for honesty. What you need is a smile.

But to get back to Dave Winger—once he went along with Al's deal, once he got involved in it, all that idealism went out the window for good. But I'll say this for him—he didn't throw it out just like that. He tried to get away from Al. The trouble was he was a baby. He was naive. Maybe he was weak. He was like a fly in a spider web. He knows he's got to get out of the web if he wants to survive but he just can't do it.

So the next morning, after they bought the clothes, when Al comes to take him to the bank Dave is not dressed in his new suit. **Dave** says to him, "I changed my mind. I can't go to the bank."

Al is dressed like a millionaire. His pants have creases so sharp they look like metal. He looks around. Winger's room is cheap. Old furniture. What people left out on the curb for the garbage pickup. Al sits down. He says, "Get dressed. I'll wait."

Dave says, "I don't like the way things are going."

Al says, "What things?"

Dave says, "Everything."

Al says, "For instance?"

Dave says, "I don't like that place last night. And I don't feel like I know what's going on."

Al says, "Nothing's going on. What do you want to know? Ask me. I got no secrets. We're partners."

Dave says, "I just don't like it. I don't feel comfortable with what's happening."

Al says, "You don't feel comfortable? What kind of talk is that? This is business, not a vacation. When you take a vacation you feel comfortable. In business you work. Work is not comfortable. It's a strain. You make commitments and you got to deliver. You gave me your word. I made commitments on that. I don't back out on my commitments. A man's word is his bond. It's a contract. It's a matter of honor."

Dave says, "I don't like what happened last night."

Al says, "Nothing happened last night."

Dave says, "I mean that guy Freddie. The whole deal. That place didn't look right."

Al says, "I'll tell you something, Dave. You're gonna run

into a lot of different people in business. Strange people. People with strange names. People who don't shave. People who don't take baths. But in business the only thing that counts is the dollar. A guy offers you a good price—you take it. You don't ask questions. It's a democracy. That scares a lot of people. They're not used to democracy. I'm lookin' at you now and I see a scared kid. Am I right?"

Dave says, "I'm not scared. I just think maybe I'm in over my head."

Al says, "You took the words out of my mouth. You feel like you're in over your head. That says it all. But that's why I'm here. I've been through all this. I'm your guide. We're on a boat and we're setting out on the sea of commerce. Sometimes the sea is rough but you don't get off the boat in the middle of the water. You'd drown. Then you'd definitely be in over your head. You stay on the boat until you come to dry land. Now, I would like to continue talking because you have a lot to learn and I feel it's my duty to teach you. But not right now because the first rule of business, Dave, is 'Time is money.' Just sitting here and talking is costing us money. I got a chauffeur and a limo downstairs and the man has to be paid by the hour so let's not sit here talking because it runs up the bill."

"You rented a limousine?" Dave says.

Al says, "When you go to the bank for a loan, what counts most is the impression you make. What they see. That's why when I go to the bank I travel first class."

Dave says, "How much does a limousine cost?"

Al says, "A thousand dollars an hour."

Dave almost has a heart attack. He's speechless. He doesn't know whether this guy is serious or joking. And he's afraid to ask who's paying for it.

Al says to him, "Relax. I'm not here to eat you up. I'm on your side. I know why you're nervous. Let's be honest. You're nervous because you don't understand me. Am I right? You haven't done business with entrepen-ewers before so you think I deal with shady people, like Freddie, and I rent limousines when you'd take a taxi or the bus. This is no good, Dave. You got to realize that I'm an experienced businessman and you're only a virgin. You're like a boy on his first visit to the whorehouse. Maybe you talked a little too big and now you're afraid to go. But we made an agreement and we're partners. We got to trust each other. If you don't trust me, that's very insulting. That means you're questioning my word, my experience, my knowledge—everything. I could take that as an insult. But I want you to know that I don't. I like you and I know, in your heart, that you are a nice kid and you don't mean to be insulting. You're just scared. You don't know banks. You don't have experience. But that's why I'm here. I'm here to protect your interests. My job is to make sure you don't get taken in. We're partners. What affects you affects me. We're in the same boat. If you get cheated, I get cheated. And you know me. I'm not going to get cheated. You understand?"

Dave is alone up there in his room with Al Croppe and he needs help but there is nobody who's going to help him. He sees he can't get out of this so he's desperate. When you get desperate like that sometimes your mind stops working right and you start to think you see a way out where there isn't one. Dave starts to figure that the bank will never give him a loan. He's got no collateral. The only thing he's got is Al Croppe's word and the bank is never going to take that. So he figures maybe it's safe to go. The bank will turn him down and that will be the end of the deal. And if by some crazy chance the bank does take Al's word, then that has to mean they know him and Al is telling the truth and he really is a legitimate businessman. If that's true, Dave has nothing to worry about. So either way he's okay.

So he gets dressed in a suit and tie and they go downstairs and there is Sid General and his limousine. He's wearing a gray suit like a chauffeur and a chauffeur's cap. I don't know if Al hired him, like he said to Dave, or if Sid is doing him a favor, or if they got some kind of percentage arrangement. Nobody knows what goes on between them and nobody will ever know.

Sid says to them, "Where you been? I'm waiting half an hour."

Al says, "The kid here is a careful dresser. Long time in front of the mirror."

Sid and Al laugh, which makes Dave feel uncomfortable, like they're making fun of him or they got some kind of joke behind his back.

It's a very plush car. There's a bar, a telephone, a little TV, and it rides smooth like a boat. Al turns on the TV to some game show and tells Dave to relax. Dave can't relax. He can't follow the program. Al is having a good time. He's yelling out the answers to the questions before the contestants can.

Sid drives up Queens Boulevard, stops in front of a bank, and parks at a hydrant. Al says, "Let's go," and he's out of the car, heading for the bank. Dave gets out and goes after him. He catches up to him inside just as Al is walking up to one of the people at the desks. He says, "I'm looking for Mr. Rollins," and he's pulling off his gloves, one finger at a time, like some European baron. The woman at the desk calls Mr. Rollins and a skinny guy with a mustache comes out and says, "Gentlemen, what can I do for you?"

Al says, "Mr. Rollins. Glad to meet you. Albert T. Croppe. C-r-o-p-p-e. Croppe. Jim Brooks told me you're the man in Queens to see. This is Mr. Winger. Mr. Winger, Mr. Rollins. Do you have an office where we can talk?"

Rollins looks like he's not sure what's happening but he leads them to the back where he's got a little office. Al sits down and makes himself comfortable. He says, "Did Jim call you?"

Rollins doesn't know what he's talking about. "Jim?" he says.

"Jim Brooks," Al says. "Am I in the right bank?" And he looks around like he's trying to see where he is. He says, "Jim Brooks. Chairman of the board."

"Oh! Oh, of course," Rollins says. "Mr. Brooks. Of course you're in the right bank."

Al says, "I was starting to wonder. Did he call you?"

Rollins says, "Mr. Brooks?"

Al says, "Yes, yes, Mr. Brooks. Jim Brooks. What's going on here? Dave, go out and tell Sidney we'll be longer than I expected. We're at a hydrant, Mr. Rollins. Can you see it from your window? Will I get a ticket there? I have a fetish about traffic tickets. I don't like to pay them, Mr. Rollins. It's a small thing but I don't like to pay them. Would you take a look out the window? The gray car." Rollins takes a look and sees the limo.

He says, "I don't think you'll get a ticket as long as your driver is in the car."

"All right," Al says. "David, tell Sidney we'll be a while."

Dave goes out. When he gets there Sid is sleeping. Sid is not the kind of guy you want to disturb or tap on the sleeve so Dave is calling him in this little voice, "Sid . . . Sid." But Sid is sound asleep. Finally he touches him on the arm and Sid jumps. Dave almost drops dead. He thought Sid was going to pull a gun and blow him away. By the time Dave recovers, Sid is smiling at him and he says, "What is it, kid?"

Dave says, "Al told me to tell you we'd be longer than he thought."

Sid says, "It's very thoughtful of you to come out and tell me that."

Dave has the feeling that Sid is laughing at him again but what can he do?

He goes back in and when he gets to Rollins's office Al is talking and Rollins looks very nervous. Al says, "Ah, here's David. David, we decided on a fifty-thousand-dollar loan. Mr. Rollins is going to get the papers now."

Dave wants to ask why fifty thousand. Al told him twenty-five. But he's afraid to talk in front of Rollins. When Rollins goes out to get the papers, Dave says, "What's going on?"

Al says, "Dave, we're in the bank and we're arranging for a loan to start our business, David Winger Home Repair. You know that. Mr. Rollins is getting the papers and writing us a check. We had a nice talk, Mr. Rollins and me. He's very interested that we should succeed. All these people want us to succeed. That should make you feel good."

Well this is not what Dave asked. What Dave really wants to know, what he can't believe, is why this banker is out there writing a check—for any amount of money. This whole deal is so strange that Dave can't believe he's doing it. But the explanation is very simple. It's Al Croppe. The man has an instinct. He knows people. He knows how to talk to people. In this case, he sent Dave out to see Sid General, so Dave don't hear what goes on at the crucial point. But look at the situation. He put the guy in a spot where he either gives them a check for fifty thousand dollars or else he's got to call the chairman of the board of the bank at home on a private number. And this is not the kind of guy who will do that. And Al knew it. I would bet Al never laid eyes on the guy before but he sized him up exactly just by talking to him for a few minutes. That's what I mean by instinct. It's not brains because Al is not all that smart. Of course it takes more than instinct to do this. It also takes a lot of nerve.

Now Dave, who is a lot smarter than Al, can't handle Al because he don't have that instinct or the nerve. So Al is running circles around him and Dave is so scared he can't think straight. He's trying. He's trying to figure out what's going on. He says to Al, "Who is this guy Brooks?"

Al is calm. He says, "Mr. Brooks is chairman of the board of the bank. Jim Brooks."

Dave says, "How do you know him?"

Al points to an air vent and he says, "Don't talk now. The place is wired."

So the two of them sit there for a couple of minutes. Dave knows the place isn't wired. He knows it's an air vent but he's so bamboozled he can't think straight. After a couple of minutes he gets a hold of himself and says, "What did you say to him when I was outside?"

Al says, "I gave him our sales pitch. You know the shpiel. Discounts. Golden reputation. Known all over. Jackson Heights, Woodside, Elmhurst. I'm talking you up, Dave. We're in it together. If you do good, I do good. Ah, here's Mr. Rollins. We're going to make Mr. Rollins very happy, aren't we, Dave?"

Rollins is carrying a bunch of papers and a check. He lays the papers down on the desk, one beside the other. Winger can't remember how many there are but it seems like a dozen, and he has to sign them all. Then Al picks up the check, which is made out to David Winger for fifty thousand dollars, and the next thing Winger knows they're back in the car and Sid is cruising on Queens Boulevard.

Dave has so many questions he can't get them arranged in his mind. He says, "What did you say to him when I was outside?"

Al says, "I told him I'm a friend of Sid General," and Sid and Al both start to laugh.

7

~~~~~~

THEY DROP HIM OFF AND WINGER GOES UP TO HIS room and lays down. It's the middle of the day but he's exhausted because he hardly slept the night before. Then, all of a sudden, he sits up in bed like a shot. He doesn't have the check! Croppe has it. He can't believe he's so stupid. He never even thought about that check. Fifty thousand dollars and he didn't pay attention to where it was. He gets up, changes into his regular clothes, and goes down to the Green Leaf. He tells Max he has to get in touch with Al Croppe. Max says he'll give him a message if he should happen to see him. Dave says, "I got to see him soon. It's very important."

Max shakes his head. He says, "If I see him, I'll tell him." Meanwhile Max gives him some slips of paper with names and phone numbers.

He puts the papers in his pocket and goes out. He can't think about making calls and giving estimates. All he can think about is that he just signed a bank note for fifty thousand dollars and gave away the check. He starts walking around the streets because he can't sit still. He goes down Roosevelt to Queens Boulevard, back up to Roosevelt, and then to Northern Boulevard. He's walking for hours. It's cold. There's still snow on the ground, but by now it's turned black.

All afternoon he feels like he's going nuts. Just for something to do he calls one of the numbers and walks over to give the people an estimate. He's so desperate from thinking about money by then that he gives them a high estimate. He gives such a high estimate that they look at him like he's crazy. They don't even complain. The guy laughs and says something about a misunderstanding.

It gets dark and he goes home. He never even ate lunch or supper because he's so upset he didn't get hungry. All of a sudden the doorbell rings. He goes downstairs, opens the door, and it's Al Croppe.

As soon as he sees Croppe he thinks he's saved. He was afraid Al took the fifty thousand and disappeared. He was afraid he'd never see him again. But here is Al coming to look for him. He's so relieved he feels like he loves the guy.

Al comes in laughing and acting buddy-buddy. "Hey, Dave," he says, "you're more trouble than you're worth. You never took the check. Do you know that?"

Does he know that? He's laughing now. He says, "I know. I forgot. I've been looking for you all afternoon."

Al says, "You're lucky you got me for a partner. I took care of everything. This could have been a real mess."

Dave says, "What happened? Do you have the check?"

Al says, "Listen to this. I went to see my lawyer, Donnie Grenlily. You ever hear of him? A very well-known lawyer. A top guy. Sharp, sharp, sharp. I wanted him to draw up our partnership papers. I figured you had the check and you'd take care of depositing it. So I call Donnie and Donnie's secretary tells me he's at the tennis club on Vernon Boulevard. I go over there and we sit down and have drinks and I'm telling him about the partnership and I reach into this pocket and what do I come out with but your check. You got no phone. It's two o'clock and there's no way I can contact you. The banks close in one hour. So what am I going to do? I'm not going to walk around with a fifty-thousand-dollar check in my pocket overnight. What if I lose it? So I say to Donnie, 'Donnie, what do I do?' He says, 'Al, you've got to deposit it.' I say, 'How can I? The check is made out to David Winger and he's got no account. I can't sign his name and put it into my account.' He says, 'Go in and open an account in his name.' I say, 'Donnie, I can't do that. They want all that information, Social Security, mother's maiden name.' He says, 'What's the alternative? You want to walk around all night with the kid's fifty thousand in your pocket? Somebody hits you on the head and it's gone. *Phffft.* Just like that. And who's on the line for it? Who's going to have to pay? Not you. That kid that's just trying to start out in life. Al, go in there and deposit that check. Sign David Winger and make up any information you need.' So that's what I did. So now you have a checking account for fifty thousand dollars. I had to make up a Social Security number, your mother's maiden name, and all that kind of stuff. But that doesn't matter. The only problem now is that it's in my handwriting. That means if you sign checks, they're no good. That's what we've got to straighten out."

Dave says, "Let's go down there tomorrow morning and tell them."

Al says, "Tell them what?"

Dave says, "Tell them it was an emergency and let's get the money out of there."

Al says, "You want me to go into a federal bank and tell them I opened an account, signed somebody else's name, gave false information, made up a fake Social Security number, and that now I want to take the money out? You must be kidding. I tell them that and they're not gonna give me money. They're gonna call the FBI. We can't do that."

Dave says, "Then what can we do?"

Al says, "That's just what I said to Grenlily. I said, 'Donnie, how am I gonna get the money out of there?' You see, when I came out of that bank I was so relieved to have the money in a safe place that at first I didn't realize what I did. But by the time I got back to the tennis club I was shaking. Let me tell you I was scared. I am not accustomed to lying to the authorities like that and, on top of that, putting it on paper. I interrupted his tennis game and I said, 'Donnie, you got me into this, how am I gonna get out of it?'

"Dave, I hope you realize that you can't go in there either. If I write a check to Dave Winger or to 'Cash' they'd ask you for ID. They won't cash a check like that without ID. If you show an ID that says David Winger with a different signature and different information all hell will break loose. You understand me? So I said to Donnie, 'You got to help me out.' Donnie looks at me and says, 'Why are you so excited?' He says, 'Don't worry. You think you're the only one this ever happened to? There's a standard procedure for this.' And he explains it to me. First of all, do you have a valid ID?''

Dave shows him some ID and Al says, "Good. Now we got to do what is called laundering the money. Sometimes this is done crookedly but what we're doing is honest. It's totally legal and aboveboard because we're not trying to hide this money or steal it from anybody. We're just trying to straighten out a misunderstanding. So here's what we have to do. First of all I'm gonna get Sid General to give you a lift to Atlantic City in his limousine. Now wait a minute! Let me finish. The reason for Atlantic City is because in Atlantic City fifty thousand dollars is peanuts and they won't make a fuss. Sid will take you to a hotel. Use your ID, take a room, sign for it. Everything just the way you would normally do. This is entirely on the up and up, straight and honest, so you don't have to hide anything. Sign for your room and tell them you want to establish fifty thousand dollars credit. Tell them you're staying five days and you need ten thousand a day. That sounds like a lot but, believe me, down there it's nothing. They'll look at your ID, fill out a form, and then they'll run a credit check. They ask your bank if you can cover fifty thousand. The bank will tell them yes because you've got the fifty thousand deposited in your name. So now everything is set. I write out checks before you go. I pre-date these checks and sign them with your name, in my handwriting, just the way I signed at the bank, so when the bank sees it, they'll accept it because that's the way they have your signature. You understand? What I'll do is write out check number two, number four, number six, number eight, and number ten. That's five checks, ten thousand dollars each, one a day. I'll leave the 'Pay To' line blank. When you go down to the cashier's window, you've got check number one on top. It's blank. Right? You fill it out. You leave the 'Pay To' line blank and say to the cashier, 'You got a stamp or shall I fill that out?' He says, 'I got a stamp.' So you leave it blank. And it's blank on check number two, the one I wrote. Now you fill out check number one right in front of him. He sees you do it. But you pick up the check-book and instead of tearing out number one, you tear out number two. You follow me? He can't see which one you're tearing out because you're holding the book up. You give him check number two, which I made out, he stamps the hotel's name on the 'Pay To' line, and asks you how you want the cash. You do this for five days and you got fifty thousand dollars. The hotel deposits the checks, the bank pays the hotel, and everybody's happy. The hotel does you a service and in exchange you stay there and pay for room and board for five days and gamble a little, which means they come out ahead. Everybody wins and we get out of a tight spot. Get yourself a safe deposit box in a bank down there and put the cash in it until you have it all. And that's it. What it amounts to is a nice vacation."

Dave says, "I don't like it."

Al says, "I knew you wouldn't. I said to myself, this sounds like fun. Dave won't like it. So if you got a different plan, I'll be glad to listen."

Dave says, "I don't know. But there has to be a better way. Can't you make out a check for fifty thousand dollars to somebody we trust, sign my name, and let him give us the money?"

Al says, "Look, you are now talking about big money, enough to set somebody up for a nice few years to live comfortably. I don't know anybody who can deposit a check like that and get cash right away. It'll have to sit there till it clears. That can take a week. There is nobody that I would give away fifty thousand to for a week on his word alone. It's too much. And nobody's going to sign an IOU because he doesn't know if the check is going to bounce."

Dave says, "We can make the IOU contingent on the check being good."

Al says, "Contingent! What is contingent? This is business. You don't do contingent in business. It's yes or no. You start with funny words and people don't trust you. Now look, this is the way my lawyer told me to do it. He said it's done all the time. The hotels know people do it and they like it. It's more rooms rented. It's gambling money. I got the checkbooks right here. You want them or not?"

Dave looks at the checks and says, "These have the wrong address."

Al says, "I told you I had to make up all that stuff. I couldn't remember your address and I couldn't stand there thinking about it when they asked me so I just said the first thing that came to mind."

Dave says, "How come you got them printed already?"

Al says, "They have a machine right there. I'll take you down there if you want to see it. Go down there yourself. It's on Vernon Boulevard near the tennis club."

Dave says, "Isn't there some other way we can do this?"

Al says, "Not if you want to do it legal."

So the next morning Sid picks him up and drives him to Atlantic City.

10

~~~~~~

I'VE BEEN TO ATLANTIC CITY. I TOOK MY WIFE. I couldn't picture Brenda in a gambling joint. I still can't. I picture Brenda at home, watching television. She was excited that day. I looked at her sitting next to me on the bus and I felt sorry for her. She had on this gray suit that must have been fifteen years old even at that time. I said to her, "Brenda, I don't feel like gambling. I'm just gonna find myself a seat and relax. Here's twenty dollars. See how you do."

I could see she was disappointed. She tried to get me to come with her but I wouldn't. So she went her way and I went mine. It didn't take her long to lose the twenty dollars and then she walked on the boardwalk and sat around by herself until it was time to get on the bus.

I went to a hotel, had lunch, a couple of beers, read the paper, relaxed, and watched the people. I don't need to gamble. I can take it or leave it because I know that gambling is all fixed. In a casino the odds are fixed in favor of the house. At the track, the horses are drugged. In sports, basketball teams shave points, in football they miss the spread, in baseball they throw games. The only way to win is if you have inside information. Otherwise you're throwing your money away.

Let me tell you what the psychology is in Atlantic City. First of all the games are fixed in favor of the house. They want you to gamble because the more you gamble, the more they win. So they arrange everything to put you in the mood. Everything is made of red, gold, and silver. Expensive colors. And everything is plush. They want you to feel like there's an ocean of money out there and all you got to do is guess the right number or put a quarter in the right slot and waves of dollar bills are going to break over your head. One bet will change your life. Maybe your next bet. So you got to keep betting. And all the time you're betting you feel that ocean of money rolling and rolling all around the casino.

In the limo on the way down Sid General says to Winger, "The only reason these hotels give you credit is so you can gamble. I guess Al explained that. You got to go in the casino every day and invest at least a thousand dollars. Even that's cutting it close for a guy they're giving ten thousand dollars' credit. You got to do at least a thousand a day in the casino or they'll stop cashing your checks."

Well, Dave doesn't want to gamble. Not a thousand a day. This is money he's got to pay back to the bank. But by now this is just one more thing. He feels like he's in quicksand and everything he does gets him in deeper.

It's a long trip to Atlantic City and Sid doesn't say much but every once in a while he opens up his mouth and gives Dave another piece of advice which makes things worse and makes Dave more nervous. He says to him, "When you cash the check, do it at the same time every day. That way you always see the same cashier. It'll save you trouble later on. And he won't bother you with questions."

Finally they get to Atlantic City and Sid drives him to a hotel. Who decided which hotel and how they decided, Dave has no idea. Sid is wearing his gray chauffeur's cap and a gray suit and naturally, with that limo, they make a good impression. Sid opens the door for him and takes his suitcases out of the trunk. He leaves the stuff on the sidewalk for the guys from the hotel and drives away. Winger is alone. He's standing there in the middle of the cold—don't forget it's winter—and he's out on the sidewalk, near the beach, and everything is bare and dead. He's stranded. He's even afraid to go in and register. But—surprise!—everything goes very nicely. No fuss. ID, registration, credit check, no problems. And in the morning they cash his check. Ten thousand dollars. He handles it like a pro. He walks a couple of blocks to a bank, gets a safe deposit box, puts in nine thousand dollars, and with the rest he's got plenty for eating, drinking, and gambling.

Let me tell you, you can get used to that situation. It's not hard to take. Two, three days go by and he's playing roulette and blowing his full quota, a thousand dollars a day, eating nicely, sleeping in a nice room, no problems. It's lucky he's a sensible kid because you could lose your head and blow everything you have. This kind of thing is like fever. That's why they have Gambler's Anonymous. He makes sure he puts that nine thousand in the safe deposit box first so he's not tempted to bet more than a thousand a day.

The third day he hits a hot streak at the roulette table and wins over three thousand dollars. But by then three thousand doesn't seem like so much. He works all week for three hundred fifty or at the most five hundred bucks, from which he has to take out his expenses, and here he is laying one thousand dollars' worth of chips on the table in one night, twenty dollars a chip, and a chip doesn't feel like anything. That's how fast you get used to it. And once you win you feel like you can always win. You feel like the next number you pick has got to be a winner. Then you have to bet because if you've got a number in your head—and you always have a number in your head—you think it's got to win so if you don't bet it you'll miss out. So Winger wins three thousand and keeps betting and before you know it he loses it all back plus the thousand he started with.

Another thing he gets used to very fast is the luxury, the respect, the people calling him sir. Waitresses bring him drinks on the house. The pit boss gives him a comp meal. He tosses a chip to the dealer and the guy calls him sir. It feels good. This is more like how he grew up. He didn't realize how much humiliation he was taking—not from other people but from himself, in his own mind, because he don't respect the work he's doing. He grew up respecting guys who work in suits with briefcases, professors, lawyers, businessmen, guys in suits, not guys who come home tired and dirty. The fourth day comes. He cashes his check. He puts nine thousand in the safe deposit box. He's got thirty-six thousand in there now. Enough to start a business. And that's what got him into this thing in the first place. But he hasn't been thinking about the business because he really got into this because of a girl, not because of a business. But now he's got the money and he realizes he better start to think about this business—David Winger Home Repair. He goes for a walk and tries to make plans in his head but he can't do it. First of all he doesn't really know what plans to make and second of all he doesn't even want to do it. When it comes down to it, he doesn't want to be in this kind of business. It's cold so he goes in and has lunch and then he buys some magazines and goes up to his room to relax.

He's up in his room and the phone rings. Right away this makes him nervous. He picks it up and it's Croppe. "Hey, Dave! How ya doin'?"

"What's wrong?" he says.

Al says, "What makes you think something's wrong?"

Dave says, "What are you calling about?"

Al says, "I want to see how you're doing. How is everything?"

Dave says, "It's fine. It's going according to plan."

Al says, "That's great. That's really great. I'm glad to hear it. I knew you'd be okay. I got a lot of faith in you. Listen,

Dave, can you do me a favor? Go out to a phone booth, out on the street somewhere, not in the hotel, and call this number." And he gives him a phone number. "Wait till three o'clock," he says. "That'll give you time."

Dave says, "What's this about?"

Al says, "You'll hear when you call."

Around 2:30 he gets a bunch of change and goes out and finds a phone booth. At three o'clock he dials the number. Al picks it up. Dave can hear street noises so he knows Al must also be in a phone booth out on a street and from the area code he knows Al is still in New York. Al says, "Listen, Dave, don't get nervous but we may have a little problem."

Naturally that makes him nervous right away. He says, "What's the matter?"

Al says, "Tomorrow morning go down and cash the check the way you always do and put the money in the safe deposit box. Then mail me the key. If you don't trust me, mail it to a friend or somebody you trust, but don't keep it and don't mail it to yourself. Then make sure you got nothing on you that could tell anybody that searches you or your room that you rented this box. Receipts, notes to yourself, anything—get rid of it. Then take all the checks you got left over and get rid of them too. Get rid of the pen. Everything you got that you used on the checks, get rid of it. And don't throw it in a wastebasket in your room or in the hotel. Throw it where nobody's ever going to find it, so nobody could ever tell you wrote those checks. You understand? Something happened up here and that stuff could be evidence against you. Get rid of it without any trace and you're

okay. Then just sit tight. I'm going to give you Donnie Grenlily's phone number. If there's any problem, call him right
away. But whatever you do, don't say anything to anybody.
You're in the clear as long as you don't say anything. We
might have a problem but we can handle it if you don't talk.
I'm going to be very straight with you. Your ass is on the line
and if you talk you may end up in jail. So let Donnie do the
talking. If anybody asks you anything, even if it's the police—especially the police—don't trust anybody. Nobody's
your friend down there except me and Donnie. Anybody
asks you anything, say, 'Talk to my lawyer.' "

You can imagine what this does to Dave. He says, "Al,
what happened? What's this all about?"

Al says, "It's very hard to explain over the phone. Just do
what I told you. Then, tomorrow morning, after you take
care of everything, after you put the cash in the box, mail the
key, get rid of the checkbook, the pen, and everything else,
call me at this number. I'll be here waiting for your call.
Ten-thirty tomorrow morning. There's no point in talking
before that."

Dave says, "You've got to tell me what's happening."

Al says, "Tomorrow morning, ten-thirty," and he hangs
up.

11

~~~~~~

SO NOW DAVE IS A WRECK. IT'S A LITTLE AFTER three and he's got to get through the afternoon and the night and then cash his check in the morning before he can call Croppe at 10:30 to find out what's going on. He eats dinner and goes to the casino to do his gambling. There's one thing about gambling—when you have money on the line it holds your attention. You forget all your other troubles. So when Winger plays roulette that night and starts to win he doesn't know what else is happening in the world. For a few hours he forgets Croppe. He has a lucky night and he's winning for a long time. But, as I say, the odds are in favor of the house and if you gamble long enough you lose. So eventually he loses what he won plus his thousand but it takes him almost three hours. Then he goes to a bar and has a few drinks. Between the liquor and the excitement he gets through the night. But he's scared. He's really scared.

In the morning he goes down to the cashier to cash the check. The cashier gives him the ten thousand but this time Winger thinks the guy is suspicious. Whether he is or not I don't know because Winger is my only source for this and he was so scared by then that he was a little crazy.

He puts nine thousand in the safe deposit box and keeps a thousand. He doesn't have to gamble any more but he keeps the extra thousand to pay the hotel bill and anything else that comes up.

He takes the checkbook and the pen and goes looking for a place to dump them. Atlantic City has a lot of vacant lots where they tore down buildings so there's a lot of old wood and stuff that can burn. In the winter bums use this stuff to start fires to keep warm. Winger finds a little fire in a vacant lot where nobody's around and he throws in the checkbook and the pen.

The next thing he's got to do is mail the key. He doesn't trust Croppe so he's not going to send it to him. He figures that could be the whole gimmick—to scare him, make him mail the key, and then Croppe takes the money and sticks him with the bank bill. But if he can't mail it to himself or Croppe, who can he mail it to? Guess who! He mails it to me. That was an expression of trust and friendship I could have done without. He doesn't explain anything. He just writes that I should hold on to this key and not tell anybody about it. He doesn't say what it is. But I take one look at it and I know it's the key to a safe deposit box. I see the postmark is Atlantic City and that's the first I knew he was down there. Maybe I don't know what's going on but it's easy enough to figure out that it's not something good. So I'm not happy. Without asking me, he pulls me into a deal which I don't know what it's about. And I'm supposed to take this risk for him without any compensation.

Back in Atlantic City, 10:30 A.M. comes, he finds a phone booth and dials the number. Al picks it up.

"It's all done," Dave says.

Al says, "Good. Then we're safe."

Dave says, "Safe from what? What's going on?"

Al says, "Here's the story. Sometime today, the bank up here is going to get the first check you wrote and they're going to bounce it."

Dave says, "Why?"

Al says, "I don't know. I think it's got something to do with the signature. I can't ask questions because they'll get suspicious. But right now we're okay. Let me ask you something else. Who saw you cash those checks?"

Dave says, "Just the cashier."

Al says, "Are you sure?"

Dave says, "Unless somebody was passing by at the time. But I don't think they'd pay attention if they were. Sid told me to do it at the same time every day so it was always the same cashier. He's the only one who saw me."

Al says, "That's good. That's very good. That means we're going to come out of this clean. We're going to smell like a rose. Those checks, every one of them, were made out by me. Am I right?"

Dave says, "Yes."

Al says, "And the only guy in the world who saw you cash them, the only guy who can say you cashed them is that cashier. Am I right?"

Dave says, "Yes."

Al says, "Then it's your word against his. But don't you say anything. Donnie will talk. He's gonna take care of it. He's gonna say you didn't cash those checks. He's gonna say you didn't make them out. And that's true because we know who did make them out. You follow me?"

Dave says, "I follow you but I don't understand why the bank would bounce the checks."

Al says, "I agree with you. That's why I say never trust a bank. That's my motto. The way I see it, they're giving us a hard time and that means we don't have to bend over backwards to help them. We're not gonna tell them who made out those checks because of the way they're acting. It wouldn't help you if they knew and right now all I care about is what helps you. All of us, Sid, Donnie, me, all we're interested in right now is you—not the bank, not the hotel— you. We want to make sure that you come out of this clean. So what we're gonna do is, we're gonna ask them—Donnie's gonna ask them, because he's your lawyer—he's gonna ask the hotel, the police, whoever bothers you, if you didn't make out those checks and you didn't cash them, what have they got against you? You understand me? They got one eyewitness that says you cashed them and that's all the evidence they got, and one eyewitness won't stand up in court. It's your word against his. That means you're off the hook. You're off the hook if you mailed the key. Did you mail the key?"

Dave says, "I mailed it."

Al says, "Good. Then they can't say you got the money. So they got no evidence at all. Who'd you mail it to?"

Dave says, "Russ. You know Russ. The cabdriver I'm always talking to in the Green Leaf."

That's me. My name is Russ. It's not my favorite name but that's what my mother put on my birth certificate—Russell—which I personally would not name a child. But I'm stuck with it and you can't blame anybody for his name.

Al says, "I know who you mean." But Al is annoyed. He don't want me involved. Maybe he thinks I'll mess up his plans. But he can't yell at Dave because he needs Dave to concentrate on what he's doing so he takes it out on me instead. He says some nasty things which Dave later tells me about. I won't repeat them here and I'm not going to be nasty myself. All I'll say is that I earn my money honestly, which Al Croppe never did.

Al says to him, "Dave, from what you're telling me, the news is good. You're home free. But you got to stay down there because if you leave it'll look bad. You leave and they'll put out a thirteen-state alarm. That'll turn it into a mess. So keep it simple. Stay there and give them a chance to accuse you. If they do, call Donnie. He'll take care of everything. Maybe it'll take an extra day or so more than we planned, but you'll come home with all the money and you'll be out of this."

What can Dave do? He's got to do what Croppe tells him. He went this far, he can't turn around now. They got him. He's their puppet. He's Pinocchio. Only he's dumber than Pinocchio. Pinocchio knew what he was doing. You remember the story? He goes to look for Gepetto. That's his own decision. Winger can't make a decision. All he can do is wait for them to tell him what to do next. He's plenty mad but he don't let Croppe know that because he needs Croppe. He's scared and he's got nobody else to turn to.

He goes in for lunch but he can't eat. He takes a walk. It's cold but he keeps walking. Finally, just to do something, he goes back to the casino.

He's got a thousand dollars in his pocket which he needs for the hotel bill. He's not supposed to gamble any more. All the checks are cashed so there's no point to it. But he starts looking around. He walks over to a roulette table and sees this fat lady in a yellow dress and a black raincoat. She looks like one of those gypsy people who sit in a store with a sign that says "Reader and Adviser." This lady has one chip in her hand and it's a hundred-dollar chip. The reason he notices her is because of the way she's acting. She's fidgeting around like she's really nervous. She shuts her eyes and then all of a sudden puts down her one chip on black without looking at what she's doing—as if she's got the evil eye and if she looks at it, it'll be jinxed. She turns around and walks across the aisle and stands there with her back to the roulette table, her eyes closed, and she's praying. Black wins. It's an even bet so they give her another hundred-dollar chip. Now she's got two of them. She puts one in this flea-bitten pocketbook and she watches a couple more spins. Same thing. She's all nerves, she prays and then, all of a sudden, without letting her eyes look down at the table, puts the chip on black again. She walks across the aisle like before and prays with her back to the roulette table. Black hits again. They lay down another hundred-dollar chip. She picks them both up, puts one in her pocketbook, and holds on to the other one. Then the same thing—and she wins again. That's three.

Meanwhile, he's also watching another lady at this table. This one isn't winning a hundred dollars every few spins. This one is playing every spin and she's winning big. This is a very different article. She's got on a ton of makeup and a million little lines on her face and the lipstick is sweating into the lines and looks disgusting. She's got orange hair, purple nails, and she's wearing this ugly blue suit. I think it's called electric blue. She looks like a witch but from the way they're treating her you'd think she was a beauty queen. The reason is, naturally, this lady has a big wall of chips in front of her and she's betting and laying out tips all over the place. She takes chips in each hand and spreads them around at different places on the board and she wins something on every spin. When you win on a roulette number you win a lot. It's thirty-five to one if you got the winning number, it's sixteen to one if you got it on the line between two numbers and one of them wins, and eight to one if it's on the corner of four numbers and one of the four wins. This lady is laying chips everywhere, putting two or three in some places, five or six in others, and she's hitting. Every chip she's got is worth at least twenty dollars. With five chips on a winning number she gets five times thirty-five. You figure it out. With twenty-, fifty-, a hundred-dollar chips, that comes to a lot of money. Every time the croupier shoves chips at her, she takes a twenty-dollar chip and tosses it back to him. When the waitress brings her a drink, she lays a twenty-dollar chip on the tray. When they bring her cigarettes, another twenty-dollar chip. They're falling all over this lady. She thinks she's the queen bee. She's only queen for a day, for as long as the chips last, but she knows that too. That's how gamblers are.

Winger is watching these two ladies rake in the chips and it looks to him like this is a day when everybody is a winner. It looks to him like the roulette wheel is saying, "Play me! Play me! I'm hot." And when it's hot, he who hesitates misses out. It won't stay hot forever. But the lady with the orange hair is betting too many chips for him to follow her. He's got to go with the fat lady in the yellow dress. She's laying down one chip at a time, always on black. He can handle that. Other people are doing it too and they're winning with her. Winger keeps watching and there she goes again, another chip on black, the same routine, and she wins again. He doesn't know how many times she won but he knows she hasn't lost. The lady is magic.

He's got ten hundred-dollar bills in a roll in his pocket. He pulls out the roll, peels off one bill, and lays it down on the table. The croupier says something to him and Winger wants to ask him what he said because he didn't hear it. The reason he didn't hear is because, just as the croupier was talking, somebody behind him yelled out, "Mr. Winger! Mr. Winger!"

The fat lady in the yellow dress is putting her hundred-dollar chip on black again. He wants to get a chip and bet with her but some lady behind him is yelling, "Mr. Winger!" and he's discombobulated by it because he's got so much fear in his mind from the thing with Croppe that he shoves his hundred-dollar bill back in his pocket. He turns around and sees the lady waving her pocketbook and yelling, "Mr. Winger! Mr. Winger! What a surprise!"

The croupier says, "No more bets."

The lady yells at him, "What are you doing in Atlantic City? How about that Melody Watson! Twenty-four to one. Did you ever have a tip like that in your life?"

The croupier says, "Number two is the winner. Black." The fat lady in the yellow dress is picking up another hundred-dollar chip.

The lady waving the pocketbook is still yelling at him. "I never expected you for a gambler. What is it? Melody Watson put you in the chips and you come here to parlay? I used to do that myself. I know a gambler when I see one. But it's not smart, Mr. Winger. Don't do it. You'll only lose. Especially at roulette. Come away from here. Come with me. You can't win at roulette," and she's grabbing his arm and pulling him. "Come on," she says. "Harry's here. It's a senior citizen trip. I want to show Harry who's here." She's pulling him and he's looking back at the table. The fat lady in the black raincoat is putting her money down again. Everybody at the table is betting with her. The other lady is pulling him to the doors. He's holding back. He hears the croupier say black is the winner. The other woman pulls him out of the casino into this fancy hallway that leads to the hotel. An old guy is sitting on a red velour seat reading a paper. Winger knows these people but they got him so discombobulated, especially with him expecting to be arrested any minute, that he can't think of who they are.

"Harry," she says. "Look who I found."

Harry looks up from his paper but he's a little slow and for a minute he can't figure out who Winger is. The lady says, "Mr. Winger, stay away from roulette. It's bad odds. It's worse than slot machines. Blackjack is the game. In black-jack we all got an equal chance. Come with me and I'll show you some ropes."

Winger says, "No, thanks. I'm just looking around."

She says, "Don't kid me. I saw you with your money on the table. If I didn't stop you, you'd already be losing money over there. Listen. I'm doing you a favor. I'll show you blackjack."

Harry says, "Don't listen to her. If you don't want to gamble don't do it. Stay with me. You can find plenty of enjoyment just looking around. People come here, they see the gambling, they spell caution to the wind, and they go home poor. I say, don't jump in unless you know the temperature of the water. Mr. Winger, this is not just a gambling mecca. This is a sightseer's paradise. You got fine stores here. Each and every hotel is a beautiful edifice worth looking at. Sitting here is like being in the finest shopping mall in America.

Even without gambling you can be lucky. Look at this. On the bus they give each of us a lunch ticket which I can't use because I'm under a doctor's care for gallbladder. For me, this lunch ticket is deadly poison. I'll give it to you for two-fifty. It's a five-dollar value."

Winger says, "No, thanks."

Blitnis says, "I can't eat fresh food. Only canned or stale. A five-dollar value, Mr. Winger. You can have it for two dollars."

Winger says, "No thanks. I've got to be going." But he doesn't move because he notices this big guy, maybe six-five or six-six, who looks like he weighs three hundred pounds, wearing a light suit, standing nearby and looking him over. Then he realizes there are four more like him. One comes over to him and says, "Mr. Winger, would you come with us?"

Mrs. Blitnis is very surprised. She says, "Mr. Winger, how come you know these people? You must come here a lot."

The men in suits surround him and start to walk. Winger is in the middle and he's got no choice. Either he walks or they carry him along.

Mrs. Blitnis yells after them, "Mr. Winger! Be in touch! Maybe we'll come down on an excursion together."

They lead him to a little office. Another guy comes in and he says, "Mr. Winger, your bank in New York returned your check," and he shows him the check. It's stamped "Account Closed." The guy says, "This is a lot of money, Mr. Winger, and you gave us four more like it. What are you going to do about it?"

Winger says, "I'd like to talk to my lawyer."

The guy looks at him like he knows what's happening and he says, "If that's what you want that's the way we'll do it. We'll call the police. You can call your lawyer from the police station after you're booked."

Winger's heart is beating like crazy. He's never been inside a police station, let alone arrested. It's a very scary thing. He says, "I want to talk to my lawyer."

The guy calls the police. He knows all the cops by first name, like they're friends. In a few minutes Winger is in handcuffs and they take him down to this new jail and courthouse they got in Atlantic City and they book him.

12

~~~~~~

I DON'T CLAIM TO KNOW ABOUT THE LAW OR THE police. What I know about cops I know from driving a cab. If a cop has not filled his ticket quota, he'll give you a ticket for nothing, for passing a yellow light, for not signaling, for making a left turn against a sign even if there's not another car in sight. You name it, he's there with the ticket—if he hasn't filled his quota. A ticket like that, a moving violation, costs me half a day's pay. I drive a twelve-hour shift. If I get a ticket, I'm driving six hours to pay for that ticket. That does not give me a warm feeling for cops. But if they already made their quota, it's a different story. If they made their quota you got nothing to worry about because then they don't give a damn what you do.

Winger's situation is not like getting a ticket. He's in jail. He's in jail for a gambling violation and down there gambling is religion. You get hauled in front of a judge for a gambling violation and they look at you like you're the scum of the earth.

I believe there's a reason for that. Atlantic City is one big gambling joint. Millions of dollars pass through those casinos every day. More money than anyone can imagine. When cash is flowing like that—no receipts, just cash going across the tables—everybody is going to want a piece of it. And who's dumb enough to say no to them? If you cut people in, they're your friend. I know what I'm willing to do for an extra buck. So with the amount of money they got down there they can get anybody to do anything, from top to bottom—fifty, a hundred, a thousand, something for everybody—and it won't add up to one day's intake. I got no proof that this is happening and I never heard that it's happening but I believe it is because it's human nature. It stands to reason. It's logical and it's good business. If everybody's covered, everybody's relying on the extra cash they get under the table and everybody's part of the action. If you come along and cheat a casino, you're messing with everybody's livelihood and everybody's mad at you.

Winger doesn't understand that. Maybe it would be worse for him if he did. I don't know how long he was in jail but finally they let him make a phone call and he calls this

Grenlily guy. Grenlily gets some local shyster to bail him out and a couple of hours later he's on a bus back to New York.

As soon as he gets back he's looking for me because I've got his key. He's also looking for Croppe. I'm a lot easier to find than Croppe is, so he finds me first. When he finds me it's Saturday afternoon and I'm in the Green Leaf. Winger comes in and the man looks bad. He looks scared, like somebody's after him. He sits down on the stool beside me at the bar and doesn't say anything. I say to Max, "Give this man a drink."

Winger says to me, "Do you have the key?"

I say, "I have it but not on me."

He says, "I don't know what I'm going to do."

I don't say anything because I don't know what's going on. All I knew was I got a key in an envelope postmarked Atlantic City. So I'm waiting for Winger to explain. If he wants sympathy he won't get it from me because he dragged me into something without asking my permission.

He's so nervous he can't sit still. He finishes his beer and says, "I've got to talk to you."

I say, "All right. Talk."

He says, "Let's go for a walk."

I say, "Which is it? You want to talk or you want to walk?"

But I can see the man needs help so I don't argue. I go out with him and we start walking on Roosevelt under the El. I don't like that. He's talking but I'm looking up at the tracks overhead. I've seen bolts fall off those tracks and I've heard stories about people getting hit on the head with them so I don't feel comfortable when I'm underneath. He starts telling me his story but I'm thinking about bolts so I cut him off. I say, "Listen, Dave, if you want to talk, let's go someplace and sit down and have a cup of coffee. I can't concentrate on what you're saying if I have to walk like this." So we go into a place and order coffee and pie. He starts at the beginning, with the blizzard, just the way I told it here. We were in this place for a long time and when he gets done he says to me, "What do I do? I have to get out of this."

I say, "What happened to Kathy Dellawood?"

He looks at me like I'm from another planet. He's not thinking of Kathy Dellawood. Then all of a sudden he says, "What's today?"

I tell him it's Saturday.

He says, "I have a date with her tonight. I've got to break it."

I say, "Why?"

He says, "I've got too much on my mind."

I say, "You got any money?"

He says, "I've got almost a thousand dollars. But I've got to pay it back to the bank. I've got to pay them fifty thousand dollars plus interest."

I say, "Listen to me. Go out with this girl. Blow some money on her. Show her a good time. Have some drinks, have dinner. You wake up in her bed Sunday morning and you'll feel a lot better. Believe me, that's what you need."

He says, "I've got to get out of this mess." Like he didn't hear a word I said.

I say, "I'll tell you the truth, Dave, I warned you. But you put yourself in that man's hands and he's got you. He's taking you for a ride. All you can do now is wait and see where he lets you out."

He says, "There's one thing I can do. I got forty-five thousand dollars in the bank in Atlantic City. I could pay all that back for starters. Then I'd only owe five thousand plus the interest."

I say, "Pay it back to who? The bank or the casino?"

He says, "I signed for it at the bank."

I say, "Either way, if you admit you got that money you're in trouble. They'll both want to collect—now you're talking about a hundred thousand—and it'll be evidence that you pulled a fraud in Atlantic City. You try to pay it back and you're going to be in worse trouble than you're in now."

He says, "What should I do?"

I said, "All you can do is wait and see what happens. You're in too deep to get out of it on your own. This is Croppe's scam. Your only chance is that Croppe is telling you the truth when he says you'll come out of it clean. So my advice, since you're so anxious for it, is don't do anything. Wait and see. That check the guy showed you was stamped 'Account Closed.' I've got to believe Croppe closed it and took the money. That means he's got fifty thousand out of this so far. He's got fifty and you got forty-five. He has to give the lawyer something. Maybe ten or twenty thousand to get you off. Maybe Croppe'll pay the lawyer out of that fifty thousand, give you five, six thousand to cover the bank with the interest, and still have twenty-five thousand for himself. You'd come out of it pretty clean then. If not, you're going to have to find yourself a lot of money. Don't ask me how. You're not going to make it painting. Just make sure that Croppe doesn't make you another offer that gets you into a worse mess. So all you can do now is wait and see. Get your mind off it the best way you can. Call up this Kathy Dellawood. That's my advice."

13

WELL, HE TOOK MY ADVICE AND THEN SOME. HE went crazy. I don't know what got into him. Maybe that week in Atlantic City turned his head. First he rented a white sports car. Then he gets dressed up in one of the outfits Croppe got him from Freddie and he goes over to Kathy Dellawood's place. She lives with a roommate somewhere in Sunnyside—two girls with a whole floor and two bedrooms. They drive to Manhattan, he pays maybe twenty dollars to park, picks up theater tickets, and they go to dinner. He spends big money on dinner and then they see the show. Champagne at intermission and after the show more drinks. Then he drives her home. She's very impressed with all this and she invites him in and just like I expected he wakes up Sunday morning in her bed.

But he's not happy. At least that's what he told me the next time I saw him. She's beautiful, she's impressed with him, but now that he got her into bed he doesn't like her. Why? Because the girl is only interested in money. But he knew that in the first place. He took Croppe's deal because of that. It just goes to show how confused he was in his own mind.

Sunday morning they're sitting in bed and he's telling her that money is not important. She agrees with him. She agrees with everything he says. She's no fool. She looks at it this way—she thinks the guy is rich, maybe a multimillion-aire, because she doesn't know that the sports car is rented and that there's no more money for shows and dinners and champagne. She figures he's a little bit crazy—working as a painter and saying that money is not important—and that fits right in with her idea of how a rich guy should act. And she's right. Rich people grow up with nothing to worry about and that makes them crazy. So they manufacture trouble for themselves. You read about it in the paper all the time. And she figures that's what he's doing and she thinks it's terrific. Her mistake is that she's too hot for the money. She's got herself so convinced he's rich she practically dragged him into bed, which is not cool.

When I saw him again I asked him how it was with her. He doesn't want to talk about it. But I'm very curious. So I'm annoyed. Sometimes we'll sit for an hour and he'll give me every detail of his problems and even if I don't want to hear it, I'm polite and I listen. But when I want to know something, that's different. Then it occurs to me that maybe he did something stupid. So I said to him, "Did you tell her the truth? Did you tell her anything about Atlantic City?"

He says, "No. I wanted to but I didn't get around to it."

I said, "Take my advice and don't."

A couple of nights later Winger is up in his room and his doorbell rings. It's over a week since he got back from Atlantic City and he still hasn't been able to find Croppe. This is driving him nuts. They're leaving him high and dry with the law and the bank. But when the doorbell rings he's relieved. He figures it's Croppe and that means Croppe has not skipped out on him. He goes downstairs, all excited, opens the door—and there's Kathy Dellawood. A girl like that rings the bell of any normal man in the middle of the night and he has to think to himself that even though things are bad, this makes up for a lot of it. But not Winger. His face falls. She says to him, "What's wrong?" She's probably thinking he's got another girl upstairs.

He says, "Nothing's wrong. I'm glad to see you." But he's upset, and not just because he wanted it to be Al Croppe. He's upset because now she's going to see where he lives. He may say he's disappointed because she's only interested in money but, meanwhile, he doesn't want to do anything that will give her the impression he doesn't have it. I don't know what she thinks when she sees the place. She has to be a little crazy herself to believe a millionaire would live in a cheap furnished room like that with an old tan linoleum with blue flowers. But that just goes to show you how people talk themselves into things. Wishful thinking. She wants him to be rich and she's so hot for the money that she'll believe anything. But she says to him, "How come you live in a place like this?"

He figures this is the time to tell her the truth. But he doesn't. I asked him what he said to her. He says, "I don't remember."

I said, "What do you mean, you don't remember? You remember everything else, how come you don't remember that?"

He says, "Just some bullshit," which isn't even the way he talks. So I know he's embarrassed by what he said. He probably gave her a song and dance about wanting to know how his workers were going to live, or to get an idea of what it meant to earn the kind of salary he'd be paying. Whatever it was, it served the purpose and made her keep thinking he's rich. Pretty soon they're in bed, which is what they both want and why she's visiting him at ten o'clock at night in the first place.

Afterwards she's talking to him about business. She loves to talk about business. They're lying there talking and it's eleven, eleven-thirty at night and the doorbell rings again. His doorbell didn't ring for six months, now all of a sudden it rings twice in one night. Now he's really upset. He knows it's Croppe and he's got to talk to Croppe. But what's he going to do with this girl in his bed? He'd like to get rid of her because he's had his action on that front for the night and what he's got to talk to Croppe about is more important to him than this girl, but he can't just throw her out.

She says to him, "Who is it?"

He says, "It's probably business."

She says, "At this time of night?"

The bell rings again.

He gets up and starts to put on his pants. He says, "You better get dressed. I'll try to keep him downstairs but he may want to come up."

He goes down and the second he opens the door Croppe says to him, "Dave, Dave, am I glad to see you! We have to talk. A lot is happening."

Dave says, "I've been looking for you. I want to talk to you."

Al says, "We got problems. It's that shyster, Grenlily."

A little while ago Grenlily was a top lawyer—sharp, sharp, sharp. Now, all of a sudden, he's a shyster.

Croppe says, "He gave me bad advice. Let's go upstairs and I'll explain it to you."

Dave starts to ask him questions right there, downstairs in the hallway. Croppe says, "Wait. Let's go upstairs. I'll tell you the whole story upstairs." But Dave is stalling. He says, "What happened to the money? Why did the bank stamp 'Account Closed' on the check?"

Al says, "I'll explain that."

Dave says, "Go on. Explain it. What's the story?"

Al says, "What is it with you? You want to stand out here so everybody can hear us? Let's go upstairs."

Dave turns around and goes up the stairs very slow. He fiddles with the door like he can't get it open, just to give her

more time to get dressed. Finally he opens the door and
there's Kathy sitting in his bed, wearing his shirt with the
top three or four buttons open and nothing else on. She's a
fantastic sight but it's not what he expected to see. She
didn't even try to get dressed. Winger doesn't understand
anything. This situation is what she dreams about. She
didn't want to get dressed. She thought this was the big
stuff—a secret middle-of-the-night business talk, and there
she is, a millionaire's mistress, in his bed, wearing his shirt,
in his hideaway, and they're going to talk big money. This
gets her hot. Power. Business. Secret meetings.

Croppe comes in, takes one look, and he's totally floored.
This is not his idea of David Winger. This is totally unexpected. And that's bad news for Al because his scam depends on him knowing how Winger thinks. So Croppe has
to reevaluate. He has to make sure Winger is not going to
mess up his plans. But one thing about Al Croppe—he does
not get rattled. I have to give him that. He does not so much
as blink an eye. He takes off his hat—he's wearing his fur
hat, fur coat, and maroon scarf—and he says, just like he
was expecting to see her there, "Miss, I'm sorry to barge in
on you at this ungodly hour of a winter night but David and
I have business that couldn't wait till morning. The name is
Croppe. Albert T. Croppe. C-r-o-p-p-e."

She says, "It's all right. Don't mind me. You go ahead and
talk business. I'll be quiet as a mouse."

Croppe says, "Excuse me again, but I have to ask you a
question. Who do you model for?"

She says, "What do you mean?"

He pulls out a business card and hands it to her. He says, "Do you have a portfolio?"

She says, "I don't know what you mean. I never modeled anything."

He says, "Does that mean you already have an agent and you're not interested in me?"

She says to Winger, "What's going on?"

Dave is mad. He says, "Don't believe him."

She shows him the card. It says "Albert T. Croppe. Modeling Agent."

Dave says, "Oh, no! He probably has all kinds of cards."

Croppe has this big friendly smile like he really likes them both. He says, "Dave, you're right. Listen to him, young lady. He knows. What he's saying to you is, 'Don't get into modeling.' It has ruined more nice girls than anything else. You know why? I'll tell you what happens. A girl like you is spotted and as soon as her portfolio gets around she finds herself on magazine covers. Just like that. Famous overnight. I know this business and I know what they're looking for. You'll be in ads, posters, everywhere. Everybody will want you. Before you know it you'll have the movie people offering you contracts. It happens so fast it takes your breath away. I've seen it. And you are the one it will happen to because you have what they want. All this probably sounds very glamorous. You're rich overnight, you're dating celebrities, royalty, but, believe me, I speak from experience, I have a list of successful models under contract to me and I've seen this happen—that kind of sudden wealth and fame is the most destructive thing you can imagine. I have seen more nice, sweet girls, like yourself, spoiled by it than by anything else. What Dave is saying is that he doesn't want that to happen to you."

Dave says, "Don't listen to him. He's not a modeling agent."

Al says, "That's right. Stick to your guns, Dave. And Miss—I didn't get your name—"

She says, "Katherine Dellawood."

He says, "Miss Dellawood, he's doing you a favor. Remember, I'm telling you myself. If you were to call the number on that card you might come to regret it. All those stories about big stars alone in their Hollywood castles are true. You could end up like that. Marilyn Monroe. Gloria Swanson. It's not a happy life. So don't let me lead you astray. Because I, personally, as a professional, would not talk you out of it. For me, having someone with your potential under contract is too great a temptation to pass up. I've been in this business a long time but I've never been struck so quickly— you, on the bed—the minute I walked in, you must have noticed my reaction, Miss Dellawood. The second I crossed the threshold I said to myself, This is the girl. You heard the expression, 'Her face is her fortune'? That's you. Do you read poetry? I'm a big fan of poetry. To me, it expresses the heart. When I need to say something from the heart I find that Shakespeare said it best. He said, 'Where your treasure is, there your heart is.' Keep it in mind. You're a wonderful girl, don't let your beauty ruin you. Now, if you'll forgive my intrusion on this cold winter night, Dave and I have business to talk about."

She says, "Please, don't apologize. You're very flattering. I'd like to talk to you when you have time."

Al says, "Thank you very much. My voice may sound emotional right now but it's because I'm holding myself back from telling you that you have only to sign a contract and your career is made. I won't do that. Stick with Dave here. Do what he tells you. Now, Dave, let's talk about our little problem. You know that once in a while a business gets a sudden cash drain. When that happens if you don't come up with the cash you have to sell something or borrow. I don't have to tell you that. You must understand that yourself, Miss Dellawood. It just so happens that in one of my ventures I was squeezed for cash last week. I needed fifty thousand dollars cash immediately. When you get in that position, the first thing you do, as you know, is you see your lawyer. So I went to Donnie Grenlily and told him the story. He said to me, 'If you need cash, if you need it in dollar bills right away, it's too late for a bank loan.' He said, 'You can't arrange a sale in that time either. Not for cash. So why don't you just take the fifty thousand you've got available to you.' I didn't know what he was talking about. I said, 'Donnie, what fifty thousand? I don't have any such thing.' He says, 'Yes you do. You got it in Dave Winger's account.'"

Al says, "Believe me, when I heard that I was shocked. I know Donnie Grenlily a long time and I never thought he'd give me a piece of advice like that. I said, 'Donnie, how can you think of such a thing? That boy's down in Atlantic City giving checks on that account. If I take the money out, those checks will bounce and that boy is in big trouble.' Now, to show you what lawyers are like in this day and age, he says to me, 'He's not in trouble. That's the beauty of the system I gave you for cashing those checks. If he did it just like I told you, nobody can say he cashed those checks. What do you think that whole setup was about?'

"This made my head spin. The man is such a conniver."

I'm a little surprised that Al Croppe talked like that in front of the girl. She's a stranger. She could go down to the hotel and give away the whole thing and become a second witness against Winger, which, from what Croppe says, is all the hotel needs. But maybe that's not the way things are done. I don't know. Or maybe he already smelled her out and that's what the whole modeling contract talk was about. The man has an instinct for people.

Al says to Dave, "I know what you're thinking and I agree with you. I don't like it either. I cursed him out. I said, 'You mean you set me up for this? Me and this boy?' He says, 'I didn't set you up. I did just the opposite. I gave you a system that protects you. You can take this money out of the bank and still be okay.' "

Al says, "I was in a real bind. I was squeezed. When people get you like that there is no mercy. I stood to lose a lot of money. I won't say how much but, believe me, when I say a lot I mean a lot. So I had no choice. I didn't like it but I did it. I saved the business and I thought, Well, I'm sorry it had to be this way but at least it's over with. But what I didn't know was that I was being naive because that's just where the problem started. Today Donnie calls me up and says, 'How much have you got in that safe deposit box?' I said, 'I personally have got nothing in there.' He says, 'Never mind

the games. How much is in the safe deposit box?' I say, 'I
don't know and I don't have the key. It's not mine and I can't
get it and I wouldn't get it if I could.' But he insists so I had
to tell him, 'I think it's forty-five thousand.' He says, 'That's
good because that happens to be my fee.' I say, 'Donnie, do
you know what you're saying? You're leaving that boy with
a bank bill of fifty thousand dollars plus interest. It was bad
enough before but now you're completely ruining him.' He
says, 'Did the hotel have him arrested?' I say, 'Yes.' He says,
'When they go to court are they going to have any evidence?' I say, 'No.' He says, 'Then it's a false arrest. They are
liable for that. We will sue them and collect a quarter of a
million dollars. That boy will pay off the bank and be sitting
pretty with two hundred thousand in his pants.' I say, 'Donnie, I don't know. I'll talk to him but he may not go for it.
He's a guy who will spend his whole life working off that
debt before he'd get rich that way.' He says, 'Nobody's such
an idiot.' I'm just telling you what he said. He says, 'Nobody's such an idiot. Go talk to him.' So that's why I'm here.
That's the story. Now it's up to you. You got the trial soon.
Donnie tells me the outcome is sure. He'll show them your
handwriting on your ID; they'll look at the handwriting on
the checks; they're completely different; and it's all over. So
he'll get you off but he wants all the money in the safe
deposit box. You got to decide what's the next step. You got
to pay the bank. You sue the hotel and you'll come out of it
clean and you'll be rich. A quarter of a million dollars. But
this is all up to you. I can't help you. Just tell me what you
want to do, Dave."

14

DRIVING OLD PEOPLE TO THE DOCTOR'S IS A BIG part of the business in any Queens car service. The next morning, after Al visited Dave and saw Kathy in his bed, that's what I happened to be doing. I was driving an old couple to the doctor's. At that time I didn't know what happened in Dave's apartment the night before. Now since I say that, maybe I ought to explain something else. I'm telling this story in the order it happened, not in the order I found out about it. I got a piece of it here, a piece of it there, from different people, and it was a long time before I had the whole thing. But it would not make sense to tell it that way, so I'm telling it the way it actually happened, although at the time it was happening I didn't know what was actually happening—if you follow me. And while I'm straightening that out, let me mention something else. You might have noticed that when I was talking about taking people to the doctor's I said car service when before this I was saying cab. Somebody explained to me that when I say cab I confuse people. I don't actually drive a cab. A cab has a meter and people stand on the street and wave it down. I drive for a car service. I don't have a meter and I don't stop for people waving at me on the street. The way you get a car service is you call on the phone and tell the dispatcher where you want to go and where to pick you up. In a cab you pay by the meter and they charge for time and mileage. With me, they give you a flat rate over the phone according to the distance and the price stays the same no matter how long it takes or what route I go by.

On this day I got a call to go to an address on Ketchem Street. I pick up the old couple on Ketchem and they're going to a doctor on Dry Harbor Road. I head down Broadway to Queens Boulevard and as we're passing the Georgia Diner and Macy's, which are across the street on the side going to Manhattan, the old lady points to the diner and says to the old man, "That's where we get it." She says to me, "If I want to get the bus to Atlantic City at eight o'clock tomorrow morning, what time do I have to call for a car?"

I say, "You can call any time. You can call right now. Just tell them to be there by quarter to eight. But don't call

later than seven-fifteen in the morning, maybe even seven
o'clock, because it's busy then."

She says, "We're going to Atlantic City. Last time I was a
big winner."

He says, "Some winner!"

She says, "I was ahead ninety-eight dollars and I was
ready to go home but when you go by bus you got to leave
when the bus wants to leave, not when you want to. While I
was waiting for the bus I lost the whole ninety-eight dollars."

He says, "This kind of thing is psychological. The gambler
is gambling from psychological necessity. That's why she's
never satisfied with what she wins. So she keeps playing till
she loses. Then she's really not satisfied. It's like the dog and
the manager. The dog doesn't eat the hay and neither does
the manager so nobody gets it. When I go to Atlantic City I
don't gamble. I study the psychology."

She says, "You think we'll see Mr. Winger again? I hate to
see a young man like that lose his shirt. Who would have
guessed him for a gambler?"

The old guy says, "It's not from gambling he'll lose his
shirt. It's those fellows who came for him. He better not
hang around with them."

She says, "I'm going to call him up and talk to him."

He says, "Why is that your responsibility? And, besides,
he doesn't have a phone."

She says, "A nice young man and he's going to get in
trouble."

They go on like that and I'm listening and wondering if I

should tell them I know Winger. It's a chancy business. It might seem like you'd get a bigger tip if you had a mutual acquaintance. But not necessarily. Sometimes people take you for a friend and you don't tip a friend. Sometimes they're afraid you overheard something they don't want you to. So you could wind up with nothing. Who knows what happened between Winger and these people? Maybe I don't want to get involved. My motto is, the less said the better. So I listen and say nothing and I don't hear anything I don't already know.

That night I get a phone call from Dave Winger. He's at the Green Leaf and he tells me he wants the key. I can tell from his voice that he's upset.

I get my coat and tell Brenda I'm going for a walk. She gives me a look because she knows I don't go out late at night. Not when I got to get up at five in the morning. And not when it's that cold outside. She says to me, "Is anything wrong?"

I say, "No."

She says, "How about we take a walk together? I'd like to get out too."

I say, "Not tonight."

When I get to the Green Leaf Dave is standing by the door. As soon as he sees me, before he says hello or anything else, he says, "Do you have the key?"

I say, "Sure."

He says, "Good. Let me have it."

I say, "Let's go dig it up."

He says, "What do you mean—'Dig it up'?"

I say, "I buried it."

He looks at me like I'm crazy. He says, "Are you serious?"

I say, "Yes, I'm serious. Why?"

He says, "I don't believe you."

I say, "So don't believe me."

He says, "You buried it? Russ! Did you put it in anything? Did you just stick it in the ground? How are we going to find it?"

I don't think it's such a bad idea and I don't like that he gets so upset. What did he expect me to do with it? Wear it around my neck? I didn't ask him for the key. If he doesn't like what I do he should have mailed it to somebody else.

I lead him over to 30th Avenue where it dead-ends up against the Brooklyn-Queens Expressway. There's what you might call a park there, but it's more like an empty lot. It's a cold night, the wind is blowing, the place is full of junk, and it's still got a lot of ice and snow. There's probably rats in there too. I stop and look around. I'm thinking. He hasn't told me about Al Croppe visiting him last night and saying that his lawyer wants the whole forty-five thousand, so I don't know about that yet. All I know is that the money's down there in Atlantic City, big piles of it in a box which I'm holding the key for.

He's looking at the lot and he says, "In here?"

I'm looking at the lot too. I say, "Somewhere in here."

He says, "What do you mean, 'somewhere'?"

I say, "We got to look."

He says, "For God's sake, Russ! What the hell is wrong with you? Don't you know where it is?"

I say, "Nothing is wrong with me, Dave."

He says, "What kind of thing is it to bury a key? We'll never find it in here."

I say, "Did you ever hear of Captain Kidd?"

He says, "What the hell are you talking about?"

I say, "What do you think Captain Kidd did with his treasure? Captain Kidd. Bluebeard. They all buried the stuff. It's the only safe way to hide anything."

He says, "If I didn't know you better I'd think you were trying to put something over on me."

I said to him, "Who asked you to send me the key? And what makes you think I got a better place to put it? Do I have a safe place in my apartment? Do I have a lot of room? Do I have privacy, for God's sakes? I got two kids and a wife in two little bedrooms. We're on top of each other. If my wife finds a safe deposit box key won't she ask me what it is? What do you think she'll say if I tell her I got the key to a box where somebody's hiding forty-five thousand dollars he got in a scam in Atlantic City? She's gonna say, 'What kind of an idiot are you to hold a key like that and get nothing out of it?' That's what she'll say. So I had to hide it someplace where she wouldn't see it. You sent it to me and I hid it—no complaints, no questions. I came out on a cold night and buried the fucking thing and now you're complaining because I can't find it! I don't need this, Dave. I didn't ask for it and I don't need it."

He says, "Okay, okay. Let's look."

We start to look. The whole situation is very unpleasant. It's cold, there's broken glass, and this is the kind of place where people go to .piss in the bushes. We're looking for maybe ten, twenty minutes but it seems like hours. Finally I say, "Maybe we should come back during the daytime."

He says, "Did you bury it during the day?"

I say, "No."

He says, "Then you're more likely to recognize the place at night. It won't look as familiar during the day. Do you think anybody saw you bury it?"

I say, "That's why I did it at night."

So we keep looking. He keeps asking, "Do you remember this rock? How about this bush? Or this bump? Or this pile of junk?" I'm never sure. I must have sounded like an idiot. We keep looking and looking and he keeps saying, "I can't believe this! I can't believe this!"

After a while he tells me what happened last night with Kathy and Al in his room. It comes out that he needs the forty-five thousand to stay out of jail. At that point I start to feel guilty. He doesn't tell me yet that he could sue for a quarter of a million.

The wind is blowing. The place is freezing. It's so cold that I've got tears in my eyes. Finally he says, "Let's leave it for tonight."

I say, "What are you going to do?"

He doesn't answer.

We walk back toward Roosevelt and I start trying to make him feel better. I say, "I'll come back tomorrow by myself and I'm sure I'll recognize the place and I'll find it." But he doesn't say a word. At Broadway we split. He goes his way and I go mine.

When I walked over to the Green Leaf that night to meet him I had no plan. I had no intention. I wasn't thinking of telling him anything but the truth. But when he asked me I just said, "I buried it," without thinking. I don't know why. I had the key in my pocket. I was holding it in my hand. I meant to give it to him. But it was forty-five thousand dollars. I just wasn't prepared in my mind to let it go so fast. But I wasn't going to steal it or keep it from him.

He used me without asking my permission and he didn't even appreciate that I was taking a risk for him for no reward. But I didn't want the key. I figured I'd give him the key the next day. I'd just tell him I remembered where it was and went back and dug it up.

15

THE NEXT DAY, AFTER MY SHIFT, I DROPPED IN AT the Green Leaf looking for him. I asked Max for a beer and I said to him, "Have you seen Dave Winger?"

He looks around, nods, and very quiet says, "He went to Atlantic City this afternoon. Rented a car."

I nod and act like it's no big deal but he stands there looking at me. I thought maybe Dave told him about the key and Max is too smart to believe I buried it so he's going to ask me where the key is and what I think I'm doing. He looks around a little more and then he says to me in a very quiet voice,

"Don't say I told you but Al Croppe and Sid General went down there after him in Sid's car."

I have one beer and get out of there. That whole night I can't sleep. The alarm goes off at 5 A.M. and it's still dark when I go to work. I sign out a car, get gas, and when I come out of the gas station I radio in that I'm ready. I get a call to Jackson Heights. A stewardess going to LaGuardia. You get this a lot at 6 A.M. Stewardesses on early-morning flights. They don't have fancy addresses either. I used to think stewardess was a glamour job and I expected them to live in fancy places and give wild parties but the ones I pick up live in two-, three-family brick houses which are nothing special, although I wouldn't mind if I could afford one. They're not big tippers either.

I drop her off and come out of LaGuardia but I don't call in like I'm supposed to. I head down 94th Street and before it turns into Junction Boulevard I cut back to Jackson Heights and go to Dave Winger's address. I get out of the car without radioing in what I'm doing and ring his bell. I got the key in my pocket. It's 6:30 in the morning, maybe a little later. I wait. No answer. I ring again. Nothing. I can't stand there for long because they may try to call me on the radio. I press the buzzer and hold it in. If he got back from Atlantic City very late last night he may be sound asleep. But he doesn't answer so I have to think that maybe he didn't get back at all. This makes me worry about Al and Sid following him down there. Who knows what happened?

A guy in a T-shirt with a beer belly comes to the door. He says to me, "Whadda ya want?"

I say, "I'm looking for Dave Winger."

He says, "He ain't in."

I say, "Did he go out this morning?"

He says, "He never came back last night."

I say, "Who are you?"

He says, "I'm the landlord."

I say, "Are you sure?"

He says, "Whatta you mean, 'Am I sure'? I gotta show you the deed? Who are you?"

I say, "I mean, are you sure he never came back."

He says, "You wanna go up and knock? Go up and knock."

I go up and knock. "Dave! Dave!" I say. Nothing.

I go down to the street and get into my car. I start the engine, the radio comes on, and right away I hear, "Car number one-forty-four, Russ, car number one-forty-four, Russ, where are you?"

I radio back, "Car number one-forty-four. I'm just coming out of LaGuardia."

He bawls me out for not answering the radio before. "Pay attention to the radio," he says. Then he gives me an address and tells me to get there fast. The place is up on Astoria Boulevard, near LaGuardia, which is where they think I am, so I start heading there. I pass a phone booth on a street corner and I put on the brakes, pull over, and get out. I ask information for Kathy Dellawood in Sunnyside. Luckily there's only one K. Dellawood in Sunnyside and the operator gives me the number. I call and get this sleepy girl's voice. I say, "Kathy?"

The girl is yawning. She says, "Who is this?"

I say, "You don't know me. I'm a friend of Dave Winger. I got to get in touch with him. It's an emergency."

She says, "He went to Atlantic City."

I say, "I know that but do you know where he went in Atlantic City or when he was planning to come back?"

She says, "Who is this?"

I say, "My name is Russ. You don't know me but Dave has told me a lot about you."

She says, "This isn't Kathy. Kathy went with Dave."

It takes me a second to straighten that out in my head, then I say to her, "Do you know where in Atlantic City they went?"

She says, "How do I know you're really a friend of his?"

I say, "Why else would I call and ask all these questions early in the morning. I was at his place and he wasn't there."

She says, "What's the deal with him? Is he rich and just fooling around as a painter or what? I don't like what's going on there."

I say, "The guy is loaded. He's a playboy. You know the deal."

She says, "Where does he get his money?"

I say, "From his parents."

She says, "I know that but where do they get it from?"

I say, "From business."

She gets annoyed. She says, "I know that. But what business are they in? Oil? Stocks? Real estate? What is it?"

I say, "It's family money. His father is in some kind of family business."

She says, "Why don't you give me a straight answer?"

I say, "I'm telling you what I know."

She says, "This doesn't smell right to me. Kathy's my friend and I'm not going to stand by and see her hurt."

I say, "Look, I'll be glad to call you back and give you any details you want but right now I got an emergency call from his bank and I got to get in touch with him."

She says, "It's seven o'clock in the morning. The banks aren't open yet."

I say, "It's his bank in Tokyo."

She says, "I don't like this. I don't like it at all."

I say, "Listen, miss, I got an emergency here. Tokyo is on the line and they want an answer. Where in Atlantic City is Dave Winger?"

She says, "Are you calling from a phone booth? I hear street noises."

I say, "I'm on a street in Ohio. I just got the call from Tokyo and my office isn't open yet. I'm on my way to work. I stopped off at a phone booth."

She says, "I don't trust you."

What can I say? The girl already must think I'm an idiot. I give up and it's quiet on the line for a few seconds and then she says, "I'll tell you what I know but I don't like it. All I know is he called her yesterday and asked if she wanted to go to Atlantic City. They rented a car and went down there. From the way she was talking it sounds like something fishy is going on."

I say, "Thank you for the information." That was a lot of trouble for nothing.

I drive the car back to the garage and radio the dispatcher. I say, "Car number one-forty-four. I'm just outside. I can't take that call. I got a family emergency. I need a ride to the Georgia Diner."

The dispatcher says, "What kind of emergency you got at the Georgia Diner?"

I say, "It's a family emergency."

He gives me a hard time. He wants to know how did I hear about it because nobody called in and I didn't say anything about getting off the seat to make a call myself. I give him a hard time right back. I don't care. They're not going to fire me. Good drivers are hard to find. Who wants to work for this kind of money? Maybe if they fired me I'd be better off. I'd go out and get a better job. I turn in the money I got for the ride to LaGuardia, except my share of it, which, with what I got in my pocket, gives me maybe twenty-five dollars. I get a ride to the Georgia, pay the driver, and tip him. No free rides from this company.

There's a little crowd waiting for the bus and I see the old couple I drove to the doctor's the day before yesterday. They don't recognize me but I see them look at me and then talk to each other like I look familiar but they can't figure out who I am. The woman is carrying a big bag with lunch or breakfast, probably both. She's already giving the guy an apple. He's got a book. The bus comes and by eight o'clock I'm on my way to Atlantic City.

Five minutes later we hit the Brooklyn-Queens Expressway and I'm already figuring this has to be the stupidest thing I ever did in my life. First of all, how am I going to find him? Second of all, he may be on his way back already. Third of all, I don't know what's going on. Maybe he just took off on a lark with his girlfriend. And, if not, if it's a bad situation like I'm thinking of, how am I going to rescue him from Al Croppe and Sid General? If I find them I'm going to get caught in the middle. And I don't even know what this is really all about. The best thing for me to do is what I always do—keep out of it. But here I am, heading for Atlantic City with my guilty conscience. If I just gave him the key instead of telling him about Bluebeard the Pirate I'd be driving my cab right now. It's the stupidest thing I can imagine.

We're out on the Gowanus Expressway and pretty soon I see the Verrazano Bridge. At least the ride won't cost me anything. They give you a voucher for lunch and they give you back what they charge for the ride because they figure everybody's going to lose it right back anyway. But I'm going to keep the money, have the free lunch, and come out ahead.

I try to sleep but I can't. I hear that old couple arguing. She's telling him she never loses at blackjack.

It's a long trip and it seems like all these people know each other, like it's a social club. We're cruising down the Garden State Parkway when for no reason I can see, this woman from the day before yesterday gets up and comes back to where I'm sitting. She says to me, "I know you from some-place."

I shake my head.

She says, "Don't I look familiar to you?"

I say, "No. I see a lot of faces and I got a bad memory for faces."

All of a sudden she yells, "You're the cabdriver! That's it! From the other day! Harry! It's the cabdriver! What's your name?"

"Russ," I say.

She says, "Russ, are you going to Atlantic City?"

Where else does she think the bus is going?

She says, "Don't make it a habit. You can lose your shirt in Atlantic City. Let me tell you some of the ropes. The first thing, lesson number one, stay away from slots and roulette. Crap maybe. But best is blackjack."

I say, "I don't plan to gamble."

She says, "Plan is one thing. Do is another. But if you don't want to gamble talk to my husband. Harry! I got a teetotaler here."

He turns around and says to me, "Good for you. I don't gamble either. There's plenty to do in Atlantic City without gambling."

He gets up, comes back to where I am, and sits next to me. The next thing I know, he starts lecturing me. He's talking into my ear like it's a hole and he's trying to fill it up. He won't leave me alone. He shows me his book, *The Carnegie Report on Education in America.* I don't even understand what the title means, for God's sakes, and he's lecturing me on that book and everything else. I can't get away from him. We're on a bus. Where can I go? It's like a cage.

I was stuck with him the whole way and he never stopped

talking. When I shut my eyes he said, "Are you listening?" I said, "I'm just resting my eyes."

But it's a funny thing. A guy sits there talking nonsense and you're not listening but something he says hits you and starts you thinking about something else entirely—if you follow what I mean.

Brenda tells me I should have more ambition. She tells me how smart I am and that I could be a success if I got a better job or went into business. I'll say this for Brenda. She respects me. And she's right. I should get out and do something different. But I don't like to be tied down. I don't like driving a cab but at least I'm out in the open. I'm on the streets. I'm getting around. I'm not tied to a desk or a store. But Brenda is right. I don't look ahead. I never say, "I'll do this for ten years," or, "In twenty years I'll be doing that." I take it one day at a time and that's no good. If you do that for your whole life, all of a sudden, one day, you wake up and it's gone, ten, twenty, fifty years and you're still driving a cab. I can see myself thirty years from now, when I'm seventy-five years old—if I should live that long—I'll still be driving a cab. I've got no retirement money. I'll drop dead behind the wheel and that'll be the end of it. My whole life. I'll have white hair and some young guy who's a little kid today will be the dispatcher and he'll yell at me, "Pay attention to the radio!"

I'm sitting there in the bus thinking of this and meanwhile the guy says to me, "Aristotle spoke from cards."

I wasn't listening to him and I don't know if that was part

of something else he was talking about or what. I only noticed he said that because I heard it before. I said to him, "Somebody else told me that. What does it mean?"

He says, "Lecture cards. The man was a lecturer. They have all the cards he used for his lectures preserved in the Library of Paris in France. That's how they know what he said. They make books out of those lectures."

I say, "How do you know that?"

He says, "I was in the grocery business for thirty-seven years. I speak seven languages. We had customers from all over the world. Rich and poor. Every nationality. That's an education in itself. When I retired I started to read books. People today don't read books. They watch television. On television everything has to be excitement—pictures, action, fighting. Everything is blown out of context. As a consequence people are ignorant. To me, ignorance is the biggest problem in the world today. Ignorance is hanging over the whole world like the Sword of Damascus."

He says that this book which he's got on his lap has a theory of education which is full of ignorance. He says, "With education the story is like the golden goose eggs. You try to get the golden goose eggs before they're ready and you kill the golden goose. Education today is the same thing. Children finish school too soon. They should go to school all year long until they're twenty-five years of age. That's the only way you build up an educated population."

I say, "If I had to support my kids until they're twenty-five, I'd starve to death."

He says, "Let the government do it."

I say, "That's a good idea. Let the government do it right now. Why wait till they're twenty-five?"

And we're talking like that the whole way. Anything that comes up, he's got an answer. But he wasn't so bad. It passed the time. Otherwise it's a four-hour ride.

16

~~~~~~

FINALLY WE GET TO ATLANTIC CITY AND THE BUS
drops us at a casino. Now the question is
how to find Winger. I go to the cashier to
trade in my voucher. They won't give me
bills. Chips or coins. I take rolls of quarters
and go to the casino so in case they're
watching it'll look like I'm here to gamble.
But I keep going through the casino, down
the corridor to the hotel. The safe deposit
box key is still in my pocket and it's got the
name of a bank on it. I ask the hotel cashier
how to get to this bank. He tells me the
nearest branch is on Pacific Street, which is
the first street in from the boardwalk. The

bank is a couple of blocks up Pacific from the street this hotel is on. I head for Pacific and then up Pacific to the bank. What I'm going to do when I get there I haven't figured out.

I get to the corner where the bank is and I'm about to cross the street when I notice this gray limousine with New York plates parked there. Limousines with New York plates are not rare in Atlantic City, so even though it's a shock I don't exactly drop dead. It could be anybody. But I did something stupid. I stood there trying to see who's inside. By the time I realized that it was Al Croppe, he's looking at me. Now I *am* ready to drop dead. I turn around and head back down Pacific as fast as I can go. I go one block and cut in to a street going toward the boardwalk. Sitting behind the wheel of a car all day does not put me in the best of shape so I'm already out of breath. I get to a hotel—all the hotels and casinos are on the boardwalk—and I look back. I don't see them coming so either they didn't see me and they're not chasing me or they're chasing me and they're about to come around that corner. Sid is fat so he has to be pretty slow and Croppe is probably in worse shape than I am. I know he drinks. Every time he has a cup of coffee there's a shot of booze in it. I'm out of breath but I have to believe I can move faster than they can. I don't wait to find out. I go into the hotel, through the casino, out to the boardwalk, and keep going. There's the Atlantic Ocean, right out there on my left but I don't have time to appreciate the sights. I go block after block, pass one casino, another, another, and finally I duck into one which has a row of white plaster statues of men wearing sheets and sandals like in the Roman Empire. I go through a revolving door and I'm inside.

It's not dark in there but it's not bright either. It's not crowded but it's not empty. It's not how I'd choose it but it's good enough so I can hide. I go to a section where they have slot machines and I take a machine way in the back, against the wall. If they come in here I'll see them before they see me. There's a lot of doors and I'm close enough to one of them so I can slip out. I take out a roll of quarters. I know that if I tear it open and let them all out I'll blow the whole thing. I peel back a little bit of paper so I can take out one quarter at a time. I put in the first one, pull the handle, and all of a sudden bells go off, lights start to blink, and the handle jams. The bells ring and ring and I'm dying. They're so loud that everybody's looking around to see who it is. I can't believe this. I'm the most conspicuous person in Atlantic City. They let them ring a long time because they want people to hear it. Finally a woman in a red and white striped suit comes over and says, "Congratulations! You hit the jackpot!"

I say, "How much?"

She says, "One thousand dollars!"

I say, "I don't believe it!"

She says, "It's true," and she turns off the bells and they give me a certificate for a thousand dollars and say, "Just take this to the cashier."

For once in my life, finally, I win something. But I can't stop to enjoy it because I got two guys chasing me. I go to the cashier and she says, "Would you like that in chips?" I say, "No, give me big bills." She looks at me like I'm a cheapskate or something, like I'm a bad sport, like I'm the kind of guy who quits when he's winning. But I don't care. This is no Wednesday night poker game with the boys. She starts to count, "One hundred, two hundred, three hundred, four hundred . . . ," and I'm looking around to see if they're after me. Everything looks normal but they could come through a door any second. I should be watching her count but I can't concentrate. I'm really discombobulated. She's counting and counting. This is a lot of money. I take out my wallet which, let me tell you, is skinny. This is a starving wallet. If I put those ten bills in my wallet it'll split the seams. So I roll them up and shove them in my pocket. Now I got three rolls of quarters on one side and a roll of ten hundred-dollar bills on the other. I feel like my pants are going to fall down. If I have to run now, I can't do it. I turn around and, believe me, at that point I forgot why I was there. All I wanted was to get back to New York with that thousand dollars. I could see myself laying five hundred dollars on the kitchen table and saying to Brenda, "Pay the grocery bill, pay the telephone bill, pay the electric bill, then take the rest and buy yourself some clothes." And I'll still have five hundred for myself. The problem is the bus doesn't leave until six o'clock. I've got to get through five more hours and there's nothing around here but gambling—slot machines, roulette, black-jack, craps, you name it. I don't even want to think about it. You see all that money and a thousand dollars is nothing. If I won a couple of bets in craps or roulette I could take home an even bigger pile. The only way to survive that temptation is to stay away from the casinos. But I also got Croppe and Sid General to worry about.

I got the five-dollar lunch voucher but it's only good at the hotel where the bus dropped us off. I go out to the board-walk and look around. The coast is clear. I'm walking back to the hotel and I'm like a madman. I'm laughing to myself. I got one hand in my pocket holding a thousand dollars, the other hand holding three rolls of quarters to keep them from bouncing. My eyes are popping out of my head and my head is going back and forth like a radar because I'm looking everywhere in case I see Croppe or Sid General. I get to the hotel. I buy a paper and I look for a place to eat. I find a cheap place, get a table, sit down, order lunch, and put the paper up in front of my face. I have no idea what I'm reading. All of a sudden I hear, "Russ, what are you doing here?" and I nearly drop dead. For a couple of beats my heart pumped so hard that I thought it damaged itself. I knew it wasn't Al Croppe. A second later I knew it was Dave Winger. I was scared anyway. I was so confused by running into Croppe, winning that thousand dollars, and everything else that I didn't know what I was doing or who I was hiding from or why I was hiding. I even forgot I came down there looking for Dave. I thought I was hiding from him too and when he said hello I felt like I was caught.

He says, "I saw you and I knew it was you but I didn't believe it. What are you doing here?"

I say, "I'm looking for you."

He says, "For me? How'd you know where I was?"

I say, "I found the key." I reach into my pocket to get the key but all I feel is that fat wad of hundreds. I know the key is in there but I can't take out the wad because I don't want anybody to know I have the money. We're talking and while we're talking I'm working around and around my pocket to get the key.

He's saying, "But I don't understand how you knew I was here."

I say, "I called your girlfriend and her roommate told me. I didn't know you'd be in this restaurant. As a matter of fact, when I was on the bus coming down here I was thinking it was a golden goose chase but I figured you really needed the key so it's worth taking a chance."

He says, "You took a day off from work?"

I say, "Anything for a friend." I was kidding but at the same time I wanted him to appreciate that I made a sacrifice for him. But I don't think he did appreciate it. He looked like he doubted me. I got the key out of my pocket and handed it to him.

He says, "Where did you find it?"

I say, "Right where I buried it."

He's looking at the key, feeling it, like it's missing something. He says, "So you did bury it."

I say, "I told you I buried it. Did you think I was lying?"

He says, "Did you put it in something or did you just stick it in the ground like this?"

I say, "It was in a little cardboard box."

He says, "Maybe that's why it didn't get rusty. But the cardboard must have rotted. Did it rot?"

I say, "What kind of test is this? Either you believe me or you don't. If you don't believe me, just say so."

He says, "You're a real character, Russ." And he's still feeling up the key. He says, "Come on over and meet Kathy."

I look over to where he's pointing and there she is. She's looking at us. And she is beautiful. Just like he said. Just like Croppe said. You'd think she's an actress. I go over to the table with him and we sit down. He introduces me but I don't like the way he does it. He says, "This is Russ. You remember I told you about Russ. The guy who thinks he's Captain Kidd."

She laughs.

I'm insulted and I'm very annoyed at Dave. Part of the reason I'm so mad, besides just that he's belittling me, is that this girl is so beautiful I want to make a good impression on her. I realize she's a twenty-three-, twenty-four-year-old girl, she's his girlfriend, she's a college graduate who is not in any way, shape, or form interested in me and never will be—and I'm not even dreaming of there being anything between us—but I want to make a good impression on her because she's so beautiful. I want her to like me. It's stupid and I know it but that's the way it is. Sometimes I think I don't care how Brenda feels about me. Brenda is not beautiful. But if you ask me, she's worth ten of this girl. I know that and even so I don't worry about Brenda but I want to make a good impression on this girl. But he introduces me in a way that makes me sound ridiculous. I feel like they're laughing at me. He tells her I found the key and she gets this funny smile. She says, "Then we can go right over and take out the money."

He says, "Let's finish lunch first." But I feel like something's wrong with the way they're talking. It annoys me so I decide to throw a little chill into them.

I say, "I don't know if this will have any effect on your plans but Al Croppe and Sid General are parked out in front of the bank in Sid's limousine."

She says, "When did you see them?"

I say, "About an hour ago. I think they saw me too."

They look at each other again. They don't say anything. The waiter brings my lunch and takes away their plates. They order dessert. Nobody's talking but I see them looking at each other. I start to eat. I'm eating and thinking and nobody's talking. All of a sudden I realize what's going on. I have the key. I told him I can't find the key. Then I come to Atlantic City with the key. I go to the bank where the money is—which I told them without realizing it when I said that Al and Sid were at the bank. I don't go in the bank because Al and Sid are out front. Then I come here and run into them without meaning to. What does that add up to? They believe I came to steal the money. He was suspicious as soon as I told him about burying the key and she must have given him an earful about that story. I don't know how smart she is but I think I've got her pegged. I know how greedy she is. Once they believe I lied about the key, even though I gave him the key, they're still suspicious of me. But I can't say anything because I don't want them to know that such things even occur to me. All I can do is act like nothing's wrong. They're having dessert but I don't feel like dessert. I'm already over the five dollars on the voucher.

The girl says, "If the three of us go over there together that might make too many people for them to try to bother us."

Dave says, "Three's not enough."

I say, "If you need people I can get two more."

He says, "Who?"

I say, "You remember that old couple, the Blitnises? You did their apartment over on Ketchem Street. They're here. They were on the bus with me."

He asks me how I know them, why they came down and everything else. He's very suspicious. I tell him the whole story about taking them to the doctor in my cab. He thinks it over. He's probably thinking that this is too much of a coincidence. But he says to the girl, "Five people would be safe. Especially with old people like that. They wouldn't try anything if there were five of us."

She says, "They can follow us back to New York."

He says, "They can follow us but if we stick together they can't do anything. As long as there are people around they can't do anything. There'd be too big a fuss. Five could do it. But I've got to tell the Blitnises something. I've got to give them an excuse for why I'm going to the bank and why they have to stay with me. I could say it has to do with gambling money. She's always saying I shouldn't gamble. I can tell her I want to quit while I'm ahead and take my winnings home and I'll feel safer with a lot of people around me."

I'm looking at him like this is a Dave Winger I never saw before. Mister Clean Conscience is all of a sudden Mister

Expert Liar. It shows you what happens when people get into a tight spot. Croppe and Grenlily use him and squeeze him and now, because of that, he doesn't trust me and he's ready to tell any lie to protect himself.

We go looking for the Blitnises and naturally we find Mrs. Blitnis at a blackjack table. She takes one look, gets up, picks up her money, and throws her arms around Dave. "Mr. Winger! Mr. Winger!" she says. "What a pleasure to see you!" She steps back and looks him over. "Were you gambling again?" she says to him.

He says, "That's what I want to talk to you about. Is your husband here?"

We go find Harry and Dave tells them his story about quitting and taking his winnings home. They eat it up. Mrs. Blitnis says, "Let's go. We'll stay with you the whole way back to New York."

17

SO THERE WE GO, ALL FIVE OF US, ME, DAVE, KATHY, and the Blitnises, marching across Pacific Street to the bank. The limousine is still there. Dave moseys right up to it like a hero. This is very hypocritical because I know that Dave is afraid of Al and Sid. I don't blame him for that because, for one thing, Sid has a reputation. But I do blame him for acting like he's not afraid just because he's got the four of us with him. Al rolls down the window. Dave says, "How long have you guys been here?"

Al says, "What is this? A delegation?"

Dave says, "They're my friends. They're coming to the bank with me."

Al gets out of the car and says, "Dave, I'm your friend. Ain't I your friend? Count me in. Where your friends go, I go." Then he looks at me. "Hey, Russ," he says, "why'd you run away?"

I say, "My hat blew off."

He says, "You need exercise, man. You look funny running like that. Driving that cab is making you a lard-ass."

I'm telling the story straight. I don't hide anything. I don't try to make myself look good. I'm an honest man, which these guys aren't.

Then he starts buttering up Kathy. He says, "Kathy, you are as beautiful in your coat here in Atlantic City as you were when I saw you in a lovelier costume, which I will not speak of here. I've been talking to people about you. People are interested. I'm ready to make appointments."

She says, "Who have you been talking to?"

He says, "Not now. We'll talk in private."

The man is a total, hundred percent liar but people believe him. I am believed less when I tell the truth than he is when he's lying.

Mrs. Blitnis is watching him and she says, "Who is this man?" Dave makes introductions all around. Now everybody knows everybody else's name but nobody knows anything about the people themselves that they didn't know before.

Al says, "Let's not stand around in the cold. We've got business. Let's go to the bank." But he doesn't go to the bank. He goes to the limo and gets an attaché case out of the back seat. Sid General watches all this from behind the wheel but he doesn't get out of the car.

We go to the bank. It's a very old place, very fancy but run down, left over from when Atlantic City was "The Playground of the World." In those days people came from all over for vacations here. The bank is marble—floors, walls, everything, all marble—but old and beat up, dirt washed into every vein and corner. Gold railings, gold bars on the tellers' windows, but the gold is wearing off and you can see the gray underneath. We go downstairs. A big, wide staircase made of white marble but it's so old that the steps have grooves in them from all the walking up and down. We go to the cage where they have the safe deposit boxes. Same thing—gold bars with the gold worn off. Old marble. An old lady is sitting in the cage and a guard is outside sitting at a table reading the paper. Dave signs so he can get his box. The old lady opens the gate and he's about to go in when Al says, "What are you going to put it in?"

Dave stops. He never thought of that. He's got forty-five thousand dollars in hundred-dollar bills. That's four hundred and fifty bills. It's not going to fit in his pockets. Al holds up the attaché case. Dave says, "Can I borrow that?"

Al says, "Borrow? I bought it for you. It's a gift. Come on. I'll show you how it works," and he goes into the cage ahead of Dave and says to the old lady, "We're together."

Dave doesn't want him in there but Al is already in. He's leading the way. We watch them go and then we stand there and wait.

Mrs. Blitnis says to me, "Were you gambling?"

I say, "No."

She says, "Good. Take my advice and don't gamble. Look at me. I have a system for blackjack but even I don't always win. My system needs time to work itself out. It can take all day. If I play all day, I win. But you came and interrupted me so I didn't have time. I don't know yet if the system worked or not."

Mr. Blitnis says, "What do you mean? If you have less money than you started with the system didn't work. If you have more it worked. What's the question?"

She says, "The system requires a full day. I can't judge from one hour's playing time."

He says, "Systems don't work." And they get into an argument.

I say to Kathy, "Did Dave decide what he's going to do about the lawyer?"

She looks at me like if she talked to me she'll get warts on her face. She turns around and walks away. Mr. Blitnis says to me, "That is some beauty. Is this Mr. Winger's girl-friend?"

Mrs. Blitnis says, "How long does Mr. Winger know her?"

I say, "A couple of weeks."

She says, "He'll be sorry for it. I'm not his mother. I can't warn him about everything. But if he likes this girl he's not as smart as I thought he was."

Kathy walks around the bank and we stand there talking about her. Finally Dave and Al come out. Dave is carrying the attaché case.

Al says, "All right, everybody. It's time for a celebration. I'm treating to dinner."

Dave says, "I'm sorry. We have to get back to New York."

Mr. Blitnis says, "We have time. The bus doesn't leave till six."

Dave says, "I got a car. I'll take you back in the car."

Mr. Blitnis says, "All the better. Then we don't have to worry about time. Let's join the man. Let's be festive. Eat, drink, and be merry. Then we'll drive back."

Al slaps Mr. Blitnis on the back. He says, "I like this man! 'Eat, drink, and be merry.' That's Shakespeare. Am I right? The Bard of London."

Blitnis says, "No, it's in the Declaration of Independence."

Al says, "You're right! I remember it now. My friend, we have a lot to talk about. I see you are also a lover of poetry."

Mr. Blitnis says, "I was in the grocery business for thirty-seven years."

Al says, "I want you to sit next to me. We'll talk about poetry. I'll give you some quotes and see if you can identify them. How's that? We'll have a contest. And I've got a great restaurant for it. A poetic restaurant."

Dave says, "Considering what I've got in this attaché case I don't think it's a good idea for me to go anyplace except right back to New York."

Meanwhile Kathy has come back to where we are. Al says to Kathy, "Kathy, help me out. I want everybody to get in the limo and come to the best restaurant in the world—my treat, in my limo, right now. How does that sound?"

She says, "It sounds great."

He says, "And we have something to talk about."

Dave says, "We have to get back to New York."

Al says, "Dave, it's safe. I guarantee it. Sid, my blood brother, will stand at the door of the restaurant and stop any dangerous characters."

Kathy thinks this is funny, but Dave is annoyed. Al says, "Listen, Dave, I'm serious. I understand why you're worried. But there won't be any trouble. I've got the ultimate guarantee. I don't like to mention this but Sid is armed. He's licensed and he knows how to use it. Believe me, with him protecting you, you are safe. If anybody acts suspicious, Sid will be there. I give you my personal guarantee that you will have that case and all its contents when you get back to New York."

Dave is not happy but Kathy is dying to go with Al. We all want to go. I also have money in my pocket, although nobody knows about it, but I want to go too. Whatever else you say about him, Al is a big spender. So why shouldn't I go? When else do I get a chance for a free meal in a first-class restaurant? Dave's the only one who doesn't want to go. He happens to be right but we're not interested in that so Dave has to give in.

We get in the limo, Kathy, Croppe, and Mrs. Blitnis in the back seat, Dave and me on the jump seats, and Mr. Blitnis up front with Sid. What Mr. Blitnis does up there I don't know. We start. Al takes out glasses, puts in ice from this little refrigerator, and pours whiskey-and-sodas for everybody. He says, "I propose a toast. Let's drink to what we're all here for—money."

Kathy laughs. "I'll drink to that," she says, and we all drink.

Al says, "But man does not live by bread alone. Let's toast to pleasure." And we all drink to pleasure.

Mrs. Blitnis is feeling it already. She says, "I also propose a toast. I propose a toast to Mr. Winger."

Al says, "I second that. To Dave Winger. A great guy." And we all drink to Dave Winger. "What else?" Al says.

Mrs. Blitnis says, "To life."

Al says, "To life!" And we all drink to life.

Dave says, "How far is it to this restaurant?"

Al says, "To the restaurant!" and we all drink to the restaurant.

Al pours more whiskey and soda. "Don't let the well run dry," he says.

Kathy says, "Let's make a night of it!"

Al says, "Yes, 'I burn a candle on both the ends.' That's Harriet Beecher Stowe. Let's drink to Harriet Beecher Stowe." We all drink to Harriet Beecher Stowe.

Al opens the glass partition to the front and yells up to Mr. Blitnis, "How about, 'I burn a candle on both the ends'? You know that one?" he says.

Mr. Blitnis says, "Of course I know it. It's a famous poem. William Butler Yeats. 'I burn a candle on both my ends.' Who doesn't know that poem?"

Al slams the partition shut. He says, "We are going to the best Italian restaurant in the United States of America."

Dave says, "Where is it?"

Al says, "Are you telling me you don't know where to find the best Italian restaurant in the United States of America? A restaurant written up in every guidebook? Internationally famous. People from all over the world lining up to get in. Where else would you look? There's only one place. And I am known personally to the owner. Luigi. I am going to order directly and personally from the owner. The meal of a lifetime. Twelve courses. Wine with every course. But we got time. We need another toast. Fill up the glasses!"

Mrs. Blitnis says, "No, thank you. I got plenty. It's a good thing Harry is up front. He's got a gallbladder and he shouldn't drink."

I look out the window. We're rolling down a highway. I can't tell how fast we're going because it's such a big, smooth-riding car but we're passing everything else on the road.

Dave says, "Where are you taking us, Al?"

Al says, "David, my friend, I want you to know that whatever I do I do out of love. That's why I do things in the City of Brotherly Love. You will love it there. The best Italian restaurants in the world are in South Philadelphia. A toast to brotherly love!"

Dave is upset and he's angry. Maybe he feels a little stupid because Al tricked him again. This is further than any of us expected to go. At first, when I heard it, I was upset too. But I figure, what's the difference? I got time. Dave's got a car to drive us back to New York. This is all on the house so why not enjoy it? I have another drink. I'm in a limo, I've got a thousand dollars in one pocket, three rolls of quarters in the other, and for once in my life I'm ahead of the game. I sit back and I'm feeling pretty good.

18

I EXPECTED A BIG, FANCY PLACE BUT IT WAS SO small we had to wait in line for a table. Croppe said it was world famous but it didn't look like much to me. There must be something to the place because the line waiting for tables kept getting longer. Normally, I will not stand in line for anything. Life is too short for long lines. I work twelve hours a day, five days a week. How much of my spare time do you think I'm willing to put in standing in line? But here I got no choice. We got to this restaurant at four o'clock in the afternoon, which is early for dinner, and there's already a line. But it's not as long as it gets later and we don't have a big wait.

Sid stays in the car. The man never gets out of the car. Dave holds on to the attaché case like he thinks everybody else is working on a plan to steal it. Al has Kathy off to the side and he's whispering to her and they're laughing. This makes Dave unhappy but he doesn't do anything about it.

Finally we get a table. Right away Croppe gets into this big discussion with the waiter. It's so involved that the waiter calls over two other guys. All these guys are wearing black jackets and black bow ties. I don't know if one of them's the owner or not and I don't care. Al can tell me any story he wants as long as he's picking up the tab. The four of them discuss what we're going to eat. They go into every detail—sauces, salads, dressings, cooked in oil, browned in butter, turned over once, turned over twice, details about food I never heard discussed before. Then they get to the wines. Red, white, heavy, light, aroma, and I don't know what else. They go on for twenty minutes. Croppe orders for all of us, which is fine with me.

The three guys in black jackets are not the ones who bring out the food. They got two other guys in brown jackets to do that. And the two guys in brown jackets don't take the dishes away after we finish. They got a guy in a white jacket to do that. It's like a union shop where everybody does a quarter of the job. It takes seven of them to wait on six of us.

The first thing they bring us is this little brown fritter with a white sauce. The waiter in the black coat comes over and announces what this is but I don't remember what he called it. We also get a white wine. When we finish, the guy in the white coat takes away the dishes and the guys in brown coats come back and bring us each a plate of salad with slices of cheese and salami and stuff like that with a lot of oil and vinegar. The waiter in black makes an announcement again about what it's called. He announces every dish like this is the ballet. We finish it and the guy in the white coat takes away the dishes and the guys in brown coats come back and bring us this little piece of cold fish. We eat the fish and then we get chicken livers and another wine. Then they bring out a hot dish of shrimp with a lot of garlic which looks to me like it's the main meal after a lot of little appetizers. The waiter in the black coat announces that this is "shrimp scampi del Greco." It tastes a lot better than it sounds. The guys in brown serve it and we also get a white wine. It's all been small portions but there was a lot of them and they were all good and there was garlic bread too so now I'm full. We're splitting each of these wine bottles six ways so we each get only one or two glasses but we're getting so many bottles that it adds up to a lot and I'm also pretty drunk. The guy in the white coat takes away the dishes and I'm ready for dessert but instead, here come the guys in brown coats and the waiter is announcing, "Baked Campagna capon stuffed with oyster del Torino and pasta side dish." This is another whole meal which I wasn't expecting. Croppe said twelve courses but I didn't pay attention because I don't believe anything Croppe says. I'm already full but I eat the chicken and wash it down with two glasses of white wine. Now I'm really stuffed like a pig. The guy in the white coat takes away the chicken and pretty soon the waiter is back

with the guys in brown coats and he announces, "Veal medallions in cream sauce with pearl onions." A medallion is
the metal thing they attach to the hood of a Yellow cab.
Naturally I realize this is something else entirely but I don't
know why they use the same word. This veal dish is another
full meal. When I finish it and the wine that comes with it
I'm filled to the gills. And by the way, each wine is also a
performance. Every time the guy brings out a bottle he
shows it to Al before he opens it. I don't know what Al
knows about wine but he acts like he's an expert. He reads
the label and gives the waiter a nod. The waiter pulls the
cork with his corkscrew and pours a little bit in Al's glass. Al
sniffs it, takes a sip, thinks about it, and says, *"Bellissimo!"* or
"Muy bien!" because you have to talk about wines in a foreign language. The waiter gets all excited every time Al ap-
proves, as if he never expected to get approval from such a
big expert like Al, and he gives him a big "Aha!" or *"Bellissimo!"* right back like this is the best news he's had in a long
time. Then he pours for everybody.

We finish the veal, they take away the dishes, and before
we know it they're back. "Beef à la Roma," the guy announces and they bring us this meat dish with vegetables,
another whole meal and another wine, this time red. I lost
track of what number course we're up to now but I'm hoping
we're near the end. I force this meat into my mouth but,
believe me, I don't enjoy it. It's just that you hate to leave it
over when you know that tomorrow, when you're very hungry and eating a hamburger someplace, you'll curse yourself

for not eating this when you had it in front of you for free. By the time I finish, the food has no taste. The place is starting to feel like a steam bath. I'm sweating. There's no air. I loosen my belt and the button on my pants. My stomach is so swollen I have to unzip my fly to make room. I even have to untie my shoelaces because my feet are swollen. When I bend to loosen my laces it feels like my stomach is going to bust open.

Now they're taking away the meat dishes and I'm praying it's all over. I look around and see Mr. Blitnis is sound asleep. Mrs. Blitnis has got the meat cut into tiny bits and she's still forcing food into her mouth with her pinky sticking out. Dave started with the attaché case on his lap but after a while he slipped it down out of sight under the table between his feet. He's young, he's got an appetite, but even he is finished. Kathy is leaning on his shoulder and smiling with her eyes shut like she's drunk. Sid is out in the car. They brought food out to him but I don't think he's eating like us.

Croppe gets up and walks around the table. "Everybody happy?" he says. "Anybody need anything?" He goes over to Blitnis and says, "Look at this guy! He's snoring! Hey, Mr. Blitnis! This is a feast. Let's have some poetry!" And he starts shaking him.

Blitnis wakes up but for a couple of seconds he doesn't know where he is.

Mrs. Blitnis says, "Let him sleep. This kind of meal is no good for him. He's got a gallbladder. Better he should sleep than eat this. He needs stale food. That's a doctor's orders."

Blitnis figures out where he is and says, "I'm under a doctor's orders."

Croppe says, "Gallbladder? Why don't you have it out?"

Blitnis says, "Not so fast. It's not a casual thing to cut open a stomach."

Croppe says, "Are you kidding me? They have a new operation for gallbladder. They do it in one day. In and out. I had both my gallbladders out and look at me. I can eat anything. Fit as a fiddle. Guess my age."

Mr. Blitnis says, "My doctor is one of the biggest surgeons on the east coast. He's taken out more gallbladders than all the other surgeons combined. He says, 'Diet first,' and if he says diet, I diet."

Croppe says, "Mr. Blitnis, gallbladder was cured in 1965. They got a simple operation. It's all done with computers. Your doctor doesn't know what he's talking about."

Blitnis says, "Mr. Croppe, my doctor is the biggest expert on gallbladder in the United States."

Croppe says, "Who told you that?"

Blitnis says, "Nobody told me that. I know for myself. I know doctors. You should hear how my doctor talks to his nurses—like they're dirt."

Croppe says, "Mr. Blitnis, I won't argue with you. I can see that you think for yourself. Just take my card in case you change your mind. I can make all the arrangements and you'll be in and out in one day. You won't even have a scar because they use a laser beam. And I'll tell you what else I can do. I'll get you a kickback on your Medicare. And it's all legal. But this is a feast so let's forget gallbladder. Let's have some poetry. You know any drinking poems? You know the one about, 'A bunch of verses beneath the bell—'?"

Mr. Blitnis says, "Of course I know it. It's a very famous poem. It's by an ancient Persian rugmaker, Omar Khayyám."

Croppe says, "Okay. Good. Let's hear it."

Blitnis says, "I don't have the memory I used to. I was in the grocery business thirty-seven years."

Croppe says, "In that case, let's have dessert."

They bring out pastry. I never saw pastry like that before. Every one of them looked delicious. But I couldn't eat anything. I couldn't take one bite. To this day it bothers me that I left all that pastry without tasting a single one of them.

19

WHILE CROPPE SETTLES THE BILL I GET UP AND GO
outside. It's dark out now. Sweat is pouring
off me. I stand out in the street and it's
maybe twenty degrees but it feels good.
Then they all come out. We get in the limo
and head back to Atlantic City. Everybody's
moaning and groaning about their stomachs
and their heads. The car is warm, the seat is
comfortable, and in no time I'm sound
asleep. I don't know anything, I don't see
anything, I don't hear anything, and I don't
know how long I been sleeping. All of a
sudden there's a big ruckus and I wake up.
Dave is arguing with Al. He's yelling, "I left

it there! I'm telling you I left it there! We have to go back!"

You know how when you go someplace to do something and you do everything but that? Or when you want to tell somebody something and you talk to them for two hours and tell them everything but what you meant to? The thing that's most on your mind is what you forget. It happens to everybody. So just imagine if you're dealing with an irresponsible kid like Dave Winger. It's his briefcase, it's got his money in it, but he leaves it there. And now he's half crazy and yelling and Al is talking calm to him, which is making him even crazier.

Al says, "Don't get excited. Getting excited won't help. Let's stop at a phone and call them."

Dave says, "I'll use this phone." Because there's a phone right in the car.

Al says, "You can't. It don't work."

Dave yells, "Then turn around! We have to go back!"

Al says, "Let's be sensible. You say you left it there and I believe you. You're the only one who touched it so you must know. You didn't want anybody else to lay a hand on it. But if you left it there, either they have it or they don't. Am I right? Whoever sat there after us either turned it in or they kept it. That's been done. It's decided. There's nothing you can do now. So stay calm. You can't change what already happened."

I thought Dave was going to start banging his head against the window. But I couldn't believe what he did. This is a boy who seems intelligent but he can't keep himself straight. He's always got to do something stupid. First he gets involved with this con man. Then, even after he realizes he's been used, he lets this same con man talk him into going to Philadelphia to eat dinner when he's carrying an attaché case with forty-five thousand dollars in it. He should have headed straight home with that money. Then he leaves it in the restaurant. Just like he let Al keep the check for fifty thousand in the first place. Where is his head? He's like a baby.

While they're talking I see the exit sign for Atlantic City. That means I must have slept for an hour. We pull off the highway and Sid stops at a phone. Dave jumps out, gets information, and calls Philly. He can hardly stand still. He gets the restaurant and asks if they saw a brown attaché case. He's so excited he has trouble explaining himself and they don't know what he's talking about. Finally he makes it clear and they say to hold on and they'll look for it. He holds on a while and they come back and tell him, "No briefcase." He goes nuts and goes through the whole thing again. He's yelling, "Not a briefcase. An attaché case." They tell him, "No case. No case of any kind."

He comes to the car and says, "We have to go back. We have to go back."

Believe me, the way I felt I didn't want to go back. I wanted to go home and get to bed. But we had to go back. So we turn around and we're on the road going in the opposite direction, back to Philly. Now nobody can sleep. Everybody's uncomfortable. We doze, wake up, doze, wake up again. Everybody has to go to the bathroom. The longer we're riding the worse it gets and the worse it gets the more awake and grouchier everybody gets. Pretty soon there are a lot of nasty things being said to Dave because it's his fault we're still in the car instead of in a clean bathroom in one of the casinos. Even Kathy is nasty to him. By this time she's figured out that he's not rich—although maybe she's wrong about that, we still can't be sure what his parents in Ohio are like. But she doesn't think about that. Probably all she's thinking about now is that Croppe is going to make her a world-famous model.

Finally we get to the restaurant and we all head for the bathroom—except Dave. He starts checking tables. He's like a nut, looking under tables and chairs, asking people if they saw a brown attaché case. The guys in black jackets are following him around, smiling at everybody with these stupid-looking smiles because they're helpless. They're apologizing all over the place, very embarrassed because they can't stop him and they don't know what he'll do next.

When I come out of the bathroom I feel better. It shows you what nature is. There's forty-five thousand dollars missing, Dave Winger, who's supposed to be my friend, is just about ruined, but all I know is that I'm mad at him because my bladder is full. When I come out of the bathroom, I'm a totally different person. I feel sorry for him again.

When I was in the bathroom alone I got a look at my thousand dollars, which I hadn't seen since they gave it to me. I knew it was in my pocket because I could feel it, but this was all so crazy that I was getting a little worried that I only imagined I won the money. When I pulled out that wad and saw the hundred-dollar bills I felt better.

By now Dave has looked everywhere, even the coat room and the kitchen, but he can't believe it. I help him look again. We look in places two and three times but it's not there. The money is gone.

So here he is in Philadelphia and everybody's looking at him like he's crazy. He came to New York with this idea of helping people. Instead, he winds up passing bad checks in Atlantic City. He owes a bank fifty thousand dollars plus interest. He had forty-five thousand in an attaché case that gave him a chance to pay it back but he left the money under the table in the restaurant. The man he trusted most, Al Croppe, is a crook. He's being charged with a crime, he's going on trial, and his lawyer is a crook. And he can't even pay this lawyer. He can't do anything.

We get back in the car and he looks like a dead man. Sid starts it up and we pull out. I shut my eyes and I don't say anything. Al is kidding with Kathy and she's laughing. I open my eyes and look at them. I see the three of them, Al, Dave, and Kathy, and you'd think any girl her age would go for Dave without a second thought. But she's cuddling up with Al who has to be at least twice her age and they're both laughing. Dave is alone, looking out the window.

Sid drives us to where Dave is parked in Atlantic City. Dave gets out and he expects Kathy to come with him but she says, "Dave, I think I'm going to ride back with Al."

Al says, "Listen, Dave, I don't want you to worry. You and I are friends and Al Croppe does not leave his friends high and dry. You're not lost yet. Get that chin up. Meet me at the Green Leaf tomorrow at six, we'll have dinner and we'll work something out. Meanwhile, you need a clear head. I'll take everybody home and you go by yourself so you can think."

Al slams the door, Kathy blows him a kiss, and we pull out. Dave is standing by his car looking at us.

I say, "Al. Stop the car."

He says, "What for?"

I say, "I'm going back with Dave. I don't want him to drive all that way alone."

He says, "Forget it. He needs time by himself. It'll clear his mind." And we keep going.

The whole way back Al and Kathy are cuddling up together. It makes me sick.

It shows you how desperate Dave was that at six o'clock the next day he came to the Green Leaf looking for Al Croppe. He's got nobody else to turn to.

Since my shift ends at six, I was also there. I sat at the bar and had a cup of coffee. No alcohol for me. I'm barely over my headache. I was so stuffed all that day that I didn't eat but by the time I got to the Green Leaf I was hungry, which is exactly what I knew would happen. I'm sitting at the bar in this grease joint remembering beef à la Roma, veal medallions, and the pastry which I never touched, which were all free and which I couldn't enjoy because I was so stuffed and which now, if I could have any one of them, would be a very nice meal. But if I'm going to eat now I've got to shell out my own money, which I don't want to do since I missed a day's work and things will be very tight this week. I'm not counting the thousand dollars in my pocket because I don't want to fritter it away. I didn't even give Brenda her five hundred yet. I'm still thinking about that because it's going to be something special. I'm not going to just plunk it down on the kitchen table. I want to do it in a way that she'll always remember. Believe me, I enjoyed thinking about it. As they say, anticipation is as good as the real thing. So I'm walking around with the thousand dollars rolled up in my pocket and every once in a while, when I'm in a bathroom or someplace where it's private, I take a look at it.

From where I'm sitting at the bar I can see Al and Dave at a table and they're talking. Al is talking. Dave is listening and shaking his head, no, no, no. This goes on for a long time. My coffee gets cold. Finally Al gets up and leaves. I wait a few minutes and then I go over and sit down with Dave. Al didn't finish his french fries so I eat them. I wouldn't normally do that but I didn't want to spend any money and I was hungry and he didn't put any ketchup on them or do anything to make them disgusting. Dave is watching but he doesn't say anything. He's in such bad shape that he doesn't realize what I'm doing. I say, "Did Al have any ideas for you?"

He says, "He wants me to declare bankruptcy."

I say, "What'll that do?"

He says, "That means they sell your assets and divide the money up to all the people you owe and they take whatever it comes to as full payment."

I say, "What assets do you have?"

He says, "I don't have any assets. If I declare bankruptcy,

that's it. The bank is stuck. They write it off as a bad debt."

I say, "Sounds like a good deal."

He says, "I think he's got that briefcase."

I say, "It wouldn't surprise me."

I didn't think of it before but now that he mentions it, it makes sense. Al must have spent five, six hundred dollars at that restaurant. Why would he do that? If he knew we'd all get so boozed up and sleepy and dazed that he could just lift the attaché case, it would make sense. It was probably in the trunk of the car the whole time we were riding back and forth. I said, "What are you going to do?"

He says, "What choice do I have?"

I say, "How do you declare bankruptcy? Maybe I'll do it myself."

He says, "Al is going to have his lawyer arrange it."

I said, "You mean Grenlily? The guy who's supposed to get you off in Atlantic City?"

He nods.

I say, "Doesn't it occur to you that you're getting in deeper and deeper?"

He says, "What do you think I'm so upset about?"

So I say, "Then why do you go on with it?"

He says, "What do you suggest?"

I'm stumped. I got no suggestions. The guy is trapped.

20

MEANWHILE, I HAD MY OWN PROBLEMS BECAUSE when I got back from Atlantic City it was around midnight, which is five hours later than I usually get home from work and I didn't have any money. I'm not counting that thousand dollars. It took a lot of will-power not to use that thousand, not even to mention it, because there was no money in the house until I earned some the next day. I told Brenda that I got so sick I had to go to the hospital. I told her they kept me for ob-servation in Elmhurst Hospital all day. I said I was so dizzy I couldn't even make a phone call. The way I looked you could believe it. I had a headache, a stomachache, and I'd been sleeping in the limousine for hours. I think she believed me when I told her the story but the next day I could see that she thought it over and didn't believe it any more. I wasn't worried. I figured when I pulled out those five hundred-dollar bills and gave them to her there'd be no more questions. Questions are not a problem from Brenda anyway. When I tell her something, she accepts it. I think she knows I lie to her sometimes, but she knows I never lie about anything important. I wouldn't do that. Brenda is a good person and I couldn't do that to her.

Maybe I should have just given her the five hundred right away. Maybe I shouldn't have made such a fuss over it. To some people a thousand dollars isn't much. Here's Dave with fifty thousand, Al Croppe fooling around with hundreds of thousands, and even people like the Blitnises must have a big bank account because they're retired and still living nicely. But I never had a thousand dollars in my pocket before and I don't think I ever will again so to me it's a lot of money and I wanted to get full satisfaction out of it. I didn't want to dribble it away. I wanted to do something so special that after it was done I could say, "If I had another thousand, I'd do the same thing over again." I never even thought of keeping it all to myself. Right from the start I wanted to give Brenda half. The only reason I didn't was because I couldn't think of the right way to do it. This was a once-in-a-lifetime thing.

All that week I had to hustle because I was trying to make five days' pay in four days. I'm driving fast and all the time I'm thinking about what to do with that thousand dollars. I was afraid I'd never think of anything good enough. It's like if you had just one wish. It was making me crazy. To show you how crazy I got, I started to wish I didn't have the money. But that was only a little part of the time. The rest of the time I was thinking just the opposite. I was wishing for more. Before this I was never a greedy person. I could have made more money in a different job but I liked being free, out in the open, on the streets, and that was important to me. But once I had that thousand, a thousand wasn't enough. I was afraid that as soon as I spent it I'd realize that I spent it on the wrong thing. What I needed was another thousand. If I could have another thousand then I'd feel easier about spending the original thousand. I wouldn't feel that it had to be perfect or that I couldn't make a mistake. So I'm debating with myself. Where can I get more money? Should I take, say, fifty dollars and buy lottery tickets? But the odds are so bad that fifty dollars doesn't mean anything in the lottery. Some people spend fifty dollars a week on lottery tickets and don't win. I'd have to risk five hundred or the whole thousand.

One day I'm walking home and my head is full of this kind of thing and who do I run into but Al Croppe. I don't keep the same hours as Al Croppe so I don't often run into him. When I see him now it strikes me as strange and I get suspicious. This is what happens when you've got money on your mind. You get suspicious and cagey. My first thought is, What's he doing here? But I gave him a nice hello, which is hypocritical, because I don't like him and I know he don't like me. And he gives me a nice hello back and walks along with me. I don't remember what we were talking about because the whole time I had on my mind that maybe this is an opportunity I should take advantage of and I'm afraid he'll leave me before I get a chance to. Finally I say, "By the way, Al, have you done the sheets lately?"

He says, "Where'd you hear about the sheets?"

I say, "You told me."

He says, "I don't do the sheets any more."

I say, "You told me you pick winners nine out of ten times."

He says, "That's absolutely true. But what's the payoff? My time is too valuable to spend on that kind of payoff. Russ, let me ask you something. I wouldn't ask this but, since you bring it up, do you ever think of that? What your time is worth?"

I say, "I work twelve hours a day, five days a week."

He says, "That's what I'm talking about. You put in sixty hours for less than most guys make in forty."

I'm insulted but I swallow it. You swallow things if you smell money. I say to him, "Well, the fact is I could use some extra money."

He says, "Sure. We all could. But the sheets are small time. It's no way to make money. Russ, let me tell you something. You impressed me down there in Atlantic City. I realized that maybe I been misunderestimating you. I found out what happened. I found out you took a day off and went down there out of loyalty to a friend. That's very impressive. There's not ten guys in a thousand that would do it."

I know Al Croppe is a liar, a con man, and everything else

but I appreciated him saying that. Dave Winger never showed any appreciation for what I did. In fact, Dave was suspicious. Even after his girlfriend dumped him he never dropped the suspicion she put in his head.

Al says, "I'll be honest with you, Russ. It made me sit up and take notice. I know what you think of me and I won't try to convince you different but I want you to know one thing. No matter what you think of me, I am an honest business-man. I am a businessman who operates on handshakes and word of honor, not written contracts. I don't trust written contracts. My word is my bond. When I see a man who is loyal, whose word is his bond, a man like me, I take an interest in him. That's what I liked about you. It was an act of honor. I'll tell you something—I don't knock what a man does for a living but I believe that you are not working up to your abilities. You could do a lot better than drive a cab. You got a little time?" he says. "I'd like to talk to you. Let's go in and have dinner."

We're in front of this nice restaurant and I know he's going to pick up the tab so how can I say no?

We go in and make ourselves comfortable and he says to me, "Russ, people have funny ideas about what is business. They don't realize that business is war. In war the idea is to win. If you're about to get killed you don't think about rules. You think about how to survive. The same in sports. Each team wants to win. On television it looks like they're fol-lowing the rules but down on the field they're doing every-thing they can get away with. They're doing it behind the ref's back or so the umpire won't see it but you and I know

they're doing it. And they got to because their livelihood's at
stake. It's the same in business. You understand me? Now
I'm an entrepen-ewer. My idea is to go out and make a buck.
There's no other reason to be in business. It's not a charity.
Now where do you make a buck? I'll tell you. The buck is
made in the marketplace. And the marketplace is open to
everybody. Everybody has an equal chance in the marketplace. It's free and democratic. The market don't look for
who's good or who's bad. It don't look for crooked or honest. All it looks for is the buck. That's a philosophy that goes
back to a man named Adam Smith. I don't know if you
know anything about philosophy or economics but this
Adam Smith invented the free market and he ran the first
free market in the world someplace in England. He set up
rules which haven't been changed to this day. It shows you
what kind of a genius the man was. Do you understand
what I'm telling you?"

I say, "Sure, Al, I understand." And I do. I understand a lot
of things. I see right through him. I know he's leading up to
something. He don't care about philosophy or marketplace
or anything else except making money. A few weeks ago I
would not have sat there. But things have changed because,
liar though he is, I know he don't lie about the amount of
money he deals with. I've seen proof of that. So I sit there
and listen to him. He says, "What is it you want, Russ? You
say you're looking for some extra money. What kind of
money do you have in mind?"

I'm too embarrassed to say a thousand dollars. I say, "I
could use about five hundred."

He says, "Do you know about the exchange Dave Winger worked with the hotel in Atlantic City?"

I say, "I have an idea."

He says, "It's a very simple system. I deposit money in a bank in your name. But everything, even your name, has my signature. You go to a casino. They fill out a card on your checking account to allow you to cash checks. They're not worried because they got you right there. You're a guest in the hotel. I write checks and I sign your name. You cash the checks I wrote as if you wrote them. Then I take the money out of the bank and the checks bounce. The casino has you arrested. You say nothing. You plead not guilty. You go to court. Donnie Grenlily is your lawyer. He asks you to show your driver's license, your ID. He even shows the hotel registration card. All these things have your signature and your signature is nothing like the one on the checks. So why are they blaming you? The cashier says you cashed them but it's his word against yours and one against one won't convict. That's in the United States Constitution. So the judge throws the case out of court. But we say we don't want it thrown out. We want an acquittal. We get an acquittal and then we sue the hotel for false arrest and deflamation of character. They don't want court cases like that so they settle out of court. We keep what we got for the checks plus maybe another hundred, two hundred thousand, maybe even a quarter of a million in damages.

"Now, with Dave, I never laid it all out for him because he couldn't handle it. I had to lead him step by step. With you, it's different. You're smart. You can handle it. I tell you the whole deal. I lay it out for you and let you decide from the beginning if you want to do it."

I say, "What's going to happen to Dave?"

He says, "As soon as he agrees to sue the hotel he's going to be okay. He's just got to sign some papers for Donnie Grenlily."

I say, "What about this guy Grenlily? I thought you said he messed you up."

"Russ," he says, "Donnie and me go back a long way. Sometimes I say things. It's all in the game. You understand me?"

I say, "Is Dave going to go bankrupt?"

He says, "Let me give you a piece of advice, Russ. I have a rule—if you don't know, don't ask. If you need to know something, somebody will tell you. Dave Winger will be taken care of. Dave Winger could have made himself a lot of money but he acts like a little boy. He talks like a little boy. Nobody hurts a little boy but nobody gives him money either. You understand me? That's all you need to know. Now let's talk about you. Are you ready for a trip to Atlantic City?"

I know that no matter how simple he makes it sound this is big trouble. I also know that it is illegal. It's not just illegal, it's crooked. And I know that if I touch it, I'm putting myself in Al Croppe's hands. I say to him, "That's not in my line of work."

He says, "Your share is twenty-five thousand in cash."

When I heard that my mouth must have fallen open.

He says to me, "This is not illegal. Nobody gets hurt. Nobody gets hit on the head. We do exactly the same thing the casinos do. People go down there to gamble but that's not really gambling. The casinos aren't gambling because the casinos set the odds. They make themselves automatic winners. All we do is reverse the procedure. We set the odds so we win. You follow what I'm saying?"

I don't follow what Al Croppe is saying. It doesn't matter what Al Croppe is saying. I know better than to listen to Al Croppe. But I'm being honest here so I'll tell you the truth. Al does not have to convince me. Once I heard twenty-five thousand dollars I can't turn it down.

21

IF YOU GO TO THE RACETRACK AND HIT THE DAILY
double, a really big daily double, for a couple of weeks you'll have money in your
pocket. You hit a football pool and you can
make a day's pay. But twenty-five thousand
dollars is different. That's like hitting the
lottery. The odds on the lottery are in the
millions but people play it because if you
hit the lottery it changes your life. That's
what twenty-five thousand dollars meant to
me. It was like offering me a college education. With that much cash I could do something. I could start my own business. I could
take the time to find a really good job. So

how could I turn it down? What would I turn it down for? So I could keep driving a cab?

Dave already told me the whole story of his time in Atlantic City. Every detail. That gave me a reference, something I could use to check what Al was telling me. I never trust Al but, in this case, because I knew Dave's story, I knew Al was telling the truth. I knew the whole deal ahead of time. So I'm not afraid of Al.

I knew it was not legal. I knew it was wrong. But I figured it was only a matter of four or five days, one very quick thing, in and out, and after that I'd have money. I'd be respectable. I could set myself up. I could breathe. So I told him I'd do it.

Just like Dave, we started by going to that basement in Astoria for clothes. We had a different guy, not Freddie, a thin guy named John. I could see right off that Al was not trying to pull things on me that he pulled on Dave. He didn't try to get me to pay. I got suits, jackets, pants, shirts, handkerchiefs, socks, everything. I filled up two very expensive suitcases and Al paid for the whole thing—a hundred dollars.

I didn't have to sign for a bank loan or put up any money. Al went to the bank, opened the account, put in his money in my name. He used his signature and naturally the account was in a different bank. And I was going to a different hotel in Atlantic City. We were also going for less money—twenty-five thousand, five thousand a day for five days. Sid General knew the printing company that printed the checks so we didn't have to wait for them. And they were the official checks. Everything went very smooth. I didn't hit a problem until I got home carrying those two suitcases.

This was the second time in a week that I came home after midnight and Brenda was up waiting for me both times. She didn't know what to think when she saw the suitcases. She didn't believe my hospital story and she knew that last time I came back late I had no money to give her. But that's all she knew. I never told her I went to Atlantic City. And I still hadn't mentioned that thousand dollars. Now I walk in with these two fancy suitcases. I put them down and the first thing I do is lay the money I earned driving that day on the kitchen table. When she sees that she knows I worked. Whatever she was thinking, that throws her off. She's looking at the money and she's looking at the suitcases. She says to me, "Russ, are you doing something you shouldn't?"

I laugh. I say, "What makes you think that?" and I'm acting as if those suitcases don't exist.

She says, "You don't have to do anything like that. We can get by on what you make driving. We done it so far."

I say, "Brenda, what are you talking about? I've been driving all day. There's the money."

She says, "Russ, don't do anything wrong. Don't get in trouble. I need you here, with me."

I give her a big hug. There are a lot of people in the world who make a lot more money than me who never heard that from their wife. Nobody tells Al Croppe they need him. He could drop dead tomorrow and nobody would miss him. I was tempted to pull out those five hundred-dollar bills and give them to her right then and there. But I didn't because it would be insulting. It would be like paying her for what she said.

So the suitcases sit there in the living room and nobody mentions them. This is a very small apartment so you can't miss them. The kids come in, look at them, I mean really look at them, then they look at Brenda but they don't look at me. And they don't say anything. Not to me anyway. Maybe they ask Brenda when I'm not there but I don't hear it. The more time that goes by with nobody saying anything, the more everybody's thinking about the suitcases. Like they're getting bigger and bigger. I feel like every time somebody moves they have to walk around them. It's getting me crazy. I feel like I should say something. But if I say one word it'll open the door and there'll be no place to stop. I'll have to tell the whole story. I don't want to do that. Maybe afterwards I'll tell them, but I can't now.

It's a funny thing about having money. All money is the same. A dollar is a dollar no matter how you got it. If you stole it off a dead body, if you won it on a horse, or if you earned it digging ditches it all buys the same things and it all gets you the same respect. When I walk in the door with twenty-five thousand dollars and tell my family we're moving to a better apartment, we're buying clothes, we're going out to dinner, and I'm going into business, I'll be a hero. But if I tell them now, before I go, when I don't have the money, I won't get the same respect. I won't be like a guy who could have twenty-five thousand dollars so they'll try to talk me out of it. I didn't want to listen to that. So all night long the suitcases sit there and nobody says a word about them.

The next morning I don't get up at five the way I usually do for my six o'clock shift. Al was coming later to take me to the airport. I was flying to Atlantic City instead of Sid driving me in the limo. At 6 A.M. I'm still home so Brenda knows that whatever I'm doing, I'm doing it that day. After the kids left for school I got up, opened one of the suitcases, took out a brand-new suit, a shirt, a tie, and shoes. Brenda is staring at me like I'm Cinderella. I think she would have asked me about it then but she was dumbstruck. I got all dressed up and I looked like a million dollars. And there she is in her old torn nightgown. I gave her a hug and I said, "Don't worry. This is a legitimate business deal. I'll be back in five days and I'm gonna bring you a brand-new nightgown. And we're gonna make money this time."

She says, "Russ, I don't care about money or the nightgown. I just don't want you to do anything wrong. Do you know what I mean? Don't do anything wrong."

I say to her, "Brenda, I don't have to worry about that because you're good enough for both of us."

She says, "No I'm not. That's just talk. Take off the suit. Please. You can still go in and drive half a shift."

I laugh. At least I try to laugh. I say, "Five days and we're gonna be a lot better off than ever before. Trust me just this once."

She says, "Five days? How will we eat? I don't have money for five days."

I hadn't thought of that. I'm leaving her with one day's pay. That won't get her through five days. I'm going to have to borrow something from Croppe. I figure he'll give me an advance on the twenty-five thousand. In fact, seeing how he is with money, I figure that if I ask him for a hundred for my wife he'll probably give it as a gift. So I say to her, "I'm going to leave you enough money to get through. Just think of this as a business trip. Imagine your husband is a businessman. I'd go away all the time."

She says, "You're not a businessman. You're a cabdriver. My husband don't run around on trips with fancy suitcases. He stays home with me. Don't go, Russ."

I can't listen to this any more. I pick up the suitcases and head downstairs. When I get to the street I see the limo with Sid in front and Al in the back. I go over to them and Al opens the door. He starts right in talking, the way he always does, so you don't get a chance to think. He tells me to get in and before I know it I'm inside and we're heading for the airport. When I finally get a chance to say something, I say to him, "Al, look, this is embarrassing but I forgot to leave my wife enough cash until I'm back. Could you do me a favor? Would you give her a hundred dollars and take it out of my twenty-five thousand? It'd be a big favor."

He says, "Would I mind? Russ, baby, how could I mind? You got kids. I love kids. Is a hundred enough? How about I leave her two hundred? And listen, this does not come out of your share. This is on me."

So I got on the plane feeling good. It was my first plane ride and I went first class. I did everything first class, the whole five days. First class was part of the operation because I was supposed to look like a big spender. I got to Atlantic City, got my hotel room, my credit check, and rented a safe deposit box. The next day I cashed the first check, put away forty-five hundred, and had five hundred to gamble with. I was also carrying my original thousand which I won in the slot machine. Nobody knew I had it but I had no place to hide it so I always kept it with me.

A few days went by and it turned out to be different for me down there than it was for Dave Winger. At first I thought it was great. I felt good rubbing elbows with all those rich people and big spenders. Everything I ate, every place I went, I went first class. I really enjoyed myself.

Then one night, I guess it was about the third night, I go out on the boardwalk and I decide to walk down to the beach. People don't do that much because you get sand in your shoes. I'm a little nervous because it's dark out there and I have my thousand rolled up in one pocket and five hundred for tonight's gambling in the other. But generally I was feeling very good. I just had a nice meal. I was sleeping late every day. I was relaxing. This was the first real vacation I ever had. I had vacations where you took a few days off but I never had one where you went away. So I'm really enjoying myself. I'm walking down on the beach and I can hear the waves breaking, louder and louder as I get near the water. Finally I'm standing right at the ocean. If I get any closer my shoes will get wet. I stand there and listen to the waves. It's an odd thing but it's almost like I have in mind that I'll just stand there and listen until the waves stop. Naturally I know they'll never stop. Any idiot knows that. But I never really thought about it before. The idea never hit me. It's very dark out there. There's nothing but a few little stars way overhead and the waves coming in and coming in, over and over and over again. I don't know why I got such a feeling about it. I feel like I'm standing at the edge of the world and these waves are going to keep coming in forever. They'll do it when I'm dead and gone. They'll do it a thousand years from now when the whole world will be so different you couldn't even imagine it, when nobody alive now will even be remembered. Somebody will stand here and these waves will keep coming in and coming in and coming in. I don't know why that got to me so much. I stood there thinking about it. Then finally I went back to the casino to gamble the way I was supposed to.

I don't know if it was because I was standing by the ocean for so long and breathing in the salt air or what, but as soon as I opened the door to the casino I got this smell up my nose which I can't exactly describe. Something like wet metal. But it was sickening to me. Maybe it was my imagination but I thought I was smelling the money. I went in to gamble and the whole time I was there I felt queasy, like this smell was making me nauseous. I figured it was something I ate. But the next day as soon as I went into the casino I smelled it again. I believe I really was smelling the money. I couldn't enjoy gambling any more because of it. It's like the money made me nauseous. That's a very bad condition to be in in Atlantic City. The whole place down there is nothing but money. Money is the whole purpose of everything down there. There is absolutely nothing to it except money. They don't produce anything, they don't do anything, they just move money back and forth, back and forth, and keep raking off the percent that the games are set to give them.

I'm watching this and I'm getting sick. I can't stand the smell. It's like I can feel that money going back and forth and it's making me nauseous all the time. A couple of days later, when the police finally came for me, I was actually relieved to get out of there. I don't say I'd have been relieved if I didn't know this was all a setup and I'd be free in a few hours. I'm not that stupid.

Right on schedule, according to plan, Grenlily sent somebody to bail me out. I got the cash from the safe deposit box, went back to New York, and gave it all to Al Croppe. He says to me, "This will cover our expenses and the law fees Donnie has to pay in New Jersey. After he gets you off and sues the hotel we get our share."

I'm patient. So far he's kept his word. He had Sid General deliver an envelope with a hundred dollars to Brenda right after they got back from the airport. He told her it was from a friend. She didn't want to take it but Sid forced her to. And naturally she used it. She had no choice. When I got back she asked me who was the fat guy in a white suit who gave her the money and what was it all about. I said, "Don't ask me yet. I'll tell you everything when it's settled."

She was glad to have me back. I put the clothes in the suitcases and put them both under the bed. I brought out the silk nightgown I got her in Atlantic City and gave it to her. But it turned into a letdown. She wasn't as happy as I thought she'd be. When I saw that I was glad I hadn't given her the five hundred yet because it proved I had to do it under the right circumstances or the whole thing would be spoiled. I'd feel very bad if I gave her five hundred dollars and she had the same look as when I gave her the silk night-gown. Of course, once I got the twenty-five thousand it would be different. That would throw everything into a different category.

I went back to driving a cab. A couple of times I ran into Dave Winger. He looked bad. I didn't ask him what was happening because I didn't want him to ask me any ques-tions. I was sure he didn't know that I went to Atlantic City but I didn't want to give him the opportunity to ask in case he did find out. Then one day he told me he was going back to Ohio. I wished him luck and I thought I'd never see him again. And I figured that was best for all concerned.

A couple of weeks went by. I had a little money that I kept for myself from all those five hundreds I was supposed to gamble away in Atlantic City. I used it to take Brenda to the movies and a nice dinner. But the main thing I did was I rented a safe deposit box and put my thousand dollars in it. I tied the keys on a string and from then on I kept those two keys around my neck like dog tags in the army.

Finally the court case came up and it goes just like Croppe said it would. We turn around and sue the hotel. It doesn't take long for them to offer a settlement. One day in May Al Croppe gets in touch with me and tells me it's time to go up to Donnie Grenlily's office, sign the papers, and collect our money.

22

~~~~~~

I MET AL ON ROOSEVELT, WE GET A CAB AND GO TO
Long Island City which is where Grenlily's
office is. He says to me, "You got something
to carry it in?"

I say, "I thought it'd be a check."

He says, "I don't take checks. This is a
strictly cash business. We'll have to find
you a bag to carry it in."

I'm not worried about that. I'm thinking
of my safe deposit box. That's where I'm
going to put this money. Right on top of the
original thousand. Croppe doesn't know I
have this box. Nobody knows. Not even
Brenda. I got the keys around my neck so

she knows I've got them but she doesn't know what they're for. I told her they're my lucky charm. I'm still deciding what to do with that original thousand but now, with twenty-six thousand, it's a whole different thing.

We get out at this fancy old building. Actually the building is not fancy, just the front of it is. What's going on in Long Island City is that they're taking these old factories and warehouses which used to be built with fancy stone fronts, they're steam cleaning them and converting them to offices. Like in Soho. The whole area was very run down but now all of a sudden it's "in."

We go though the glass doors into this little lobby and get the elevator to the second floor. We find a door which says "Donald H. Grenlily, Counselor-at-Law" and Croppe knocks. A buzzer unlocks the door and we go in. I'm a little surprised at the setup. It's a tiny room with no windows, silver wallpaper, and two metal doors, one opposite the other. It looks weird. Like a science fiction movie. There's nothing in there but a black table with a telephone on it. Al picks up the phone and says, "It's me. Me and Russ." A couple of seconds later the door opens. Originally I pictured Grenlily as a fat, bald guy with a big cigar. I don't know why but that was the picture I had of him. But when I saw that room with the silver wallpaper I didn't know what to expect. Somehow I didn't think a fat guy would have a little room like that. It turns out he's a tall, young guy who probably works out every day. Right there in the office he's got one of those exercise bikes and some weights. It's a very big office but there's hardly any furniture. Wall-to-wall carpet, but all he's got in there besides his bike and the weights at one end is a table with a chair for him, three chairs for visitors, and a filing cabinet. The whole middle of the floor is empty. The really impressive thing, the first thing you notice, besides how big and empty it is, is this huge semicircular window where you can see the Queensborough Bridge and the whole Manhattan skyline.

Al introduces me, we shake hands and sit down. Grenlily has his back to the window but we're facing it and I'm looking at the bridge, the ramps, the cars and trucks going up and down—you can see everything. I'm looking at them and I'm feeling like I've really come up in the world. This is the kind of view rich people get.

Grenlily says to me, "Russ, what's your average daily income?"

I thought he's going to tell me what this money will do for me, how it'll raise my income if I invest it right but I'm not so quick to answer questions. I say, "I don't know but I think today is going to be above average."

He gives me a smile like that's a funny remark and he says, "Do you have an approximate figure?"

I say, "No, I don't."

He says, "Think about it. What would you estimate?"

I estimate only one thing—this guy is a shark. When he asks me questions I get nervous. I came to collect twenty-five thousand dollars, according to an agreement, not to talk about average daily income. I want to sign, get the money, and get out of there. These guys pulled a scam on banks, hotels, and I don't know what else so there's no reason they wouldn't pull one on me. So I'm not going to answer questions. I say, "I can't say exactly how much. It varies from day to day."

He says, "About."

I say, "There's no 'about.' It depends on the season, the weather, the traffic, everything affects it."

He says, "The hotel asked me for a figure and what you just said is what I stated to them because I assumed that would be your answer. But in the absence of any figure from us they said they would use fifty dollars a day. How does that sound to you?"

I said, "What does my income have to do with this?"

He says, "I'll explain that in a minute. Are they wildly off with their fifty dollars a day?"

I don't know what's happening. Should I say it's low or it's high? I'm dealing with lawyers so I know there's an angle but I have no idea what it is. I say, "Sometimes yes and sometimes no."

He says, "Can you give me a better figure?"

I say, "I can't. Especially if I don't know what it's for."

He says, "All right. Let me ask you another question. Are you in any danger of losing your job?"

I say, "No. Why should I be in danger of losing my job?"

He says, "Are you having problems with any of your neighbors? Has anybody insulted you lately?"

I say, "Why are you asking me these questions? Al told me we were coming to sign papers and collect our money."

Grenlily says, "I called Al yesterday and told him the hotel is ready to settle. They made us an offer which they say is their final offer. If we don't take it they'll go to trial. They say they've been burned too often with this scam and they want to stop it. I'm just telling you their point of view, not mine, and I have to tell you honestly so you'll know what's happening and what you're up against. You may find some of this insulting so I remind you that this is the hotel's point of view, not mine. They feel that you are a weak opponent. They feel that if they get you into the witness box they can break you down. They'll keep you in that box for days, weeks, whatever it takes until you make a mistake and contradict yourself. Then they'll pin that check forgery on you and send you to jail. Even if they can't accomplish that, they will drive up the cost of this trial so far beyond any settlement they have to give you that you'll be financially ruined. You'll be in debt for the rest of your life. That will discourage other people from pulling this scam. You're the ideal person for them because your earnings are so low that you can't show much financial loss. Even if you should lose your job it's not a lot of money. So they can settle for very little. Do you follow what I'm saying? I want you to understand what you're up against."

I sat there looking at him. I knew this would happen. In the back of my mind I knew it all along. I came to collect the twenty-five thousand, but, all along, in the back of my mind, I knew that wasn't the kind of thing that happened to me. He's telling me I'm not worth that much money. Other people are but not me. And I knew that all along. If you say what people are worth in dollars, people like me don't count. People like me can't even make that kind of money as a crook.

He says, "Do you want to pursue the case or sign and settle now?"

I stare at him. I can't even talk.

He says, "It's up to you."

I'm choking. I'm afraid of how my voice will sound but I say, "I'll sign now."

Croppe says, "Oh, no. We're not signing. We're not signing anything. These guys don't scare me. I don't sign unless we get the settlement we want. I won't take less than a quarter of a million. And I'll tell you what else—if they try to pull a bluff on me I'll raise the ante. I'll ask for more money."

Grenlily says, "I'm afraid it's not your decision, Al. It's entirely up to Russ. Your signature isn't needed. Legally you aren't involved in this. The hotel, the police, the courts, nobody knows your name. Russ is the one they're after."

Croppe says, "Russ, don't listen to this. The man is trying to scare you. I've pulled this scam a dozen times and it's worked every time. There is nothing to worry about. Don't sign. They've got nothing on us."

Grenlily says, "All I'm doing is stating facts. You gentlemen have to draw your own conclusions. But, as I say, only Russ has to sign. He's the only one with authority in this case."

I say to Al, "You heard what the man said. You say you pulled this scam a dozen times. Now they're tired of it.

They're out to stop it and I'm the one they're going to get. I got to sign."

Al says to me, "You're chicken."

Grenlily says, "I don't know what arrangement you two gentlemen have but you must understand that by signing now you'll get much less than you expected. Their offer is not high. You won't have much money to cover your costs. My people in New Jersey have to be paid, my fee has to be paid, the expense account also has to be covered. Of course, if you reject the settlement and go to trial, the costs will be much higher. We're dealing with a major court case then. And, as in any trial, you risk losing. Since the money for all the fees and expenses was to come from the settlement and there would be no settlement, in fact there would be a risk of you getting no money at all, and since our bills are unpaid, we'd expect some payment immediately plus a guarantee, such as your house, if you own one, that you would be good for the further expenses."

I say, "I'm not going to trial. I'll sign."

Croppe says, "Listen, Russ, this lawyer is scaring you. There ain't gonna be a trial. Don, you go back to Atlantic City and tell them we're calling their bluff. We're not signing. We're fighting all the way."

I say, "I don't know who's bluffing who and I don't care. All I want is to sign and get out."

Croppe says, "Don't be chicken. I have pulled this deal ten, twelve times and nobody ever chickened out on me. Not even Dave Winger. We got a chance for some real money.

There's twenty-five thousand in it for you, Russ. Don't believe that crap about going to jail. Nobody I worked with ever went to jail. Even if you lost the case all you got to do is throw yourself on the mercy of the court and they'll never send you to jail. You're a family man. You're the breadwinner. You can't lose."

I say, "Al, you can't pull the same scam ten or twelve times. If I'd known you had I'd never have gone along with it. This man is your lawyer, you hired him, you work with him, and he's the one who's telling me to sign. I got to go by that. Just give me the papers and I'll sign."

Al says, "If you sign, you break our agreement. If you do that, by rights I don't owe you a cent."

I say, "You said you're a man of your word. If you're not, that's your problem. I can't help what you do."

He says, "But you put me in a bind, Russ. If you sign, we get no money. Where am I going to get twenty-five thousand dollars to give you? I'm in debt. I laid out a lot of money for you. I bought plane tickets, I paid for the clothes, I gave your wife two hundred, for God's sakes."

I start signing papers. At first I was so anxious to get it over with that I hardly looked at them but then I caught myself and stopped. I'm in the lion's den there. I started to read. I don't understand the legal language but I see that the settlement is for a hundred thousand dollars. I say, "Mr. Grenlily, this settlement is for a lot of money."

He says, "We had five negotiating sessions in Atlantic City that I personally attended. I had to stay overnight in order to prepare. You're paying me by the hour to represent you and those five days alone amount to thousands of dollars. I have travel expenses, research, New Jersey people who represent you to the New Jersey courts, and a lot more if you want an itemized list. I just hope the hundred thousand covers it all. I'd hate to have to send you a bill."

23

~~~~~~

FOR A WHILE I STAYED AWAY FROM THE GREEN LEAF
Tavern because I didn't want to run into Al
Croppe. I went to work, came home, and
stayed home. And I'll admit I was scared.
What scared me was that I'd get a bill from
Grenlily. He could have sent me a bill for
anything he wanted. He could have taken
my furniture, had my salary garnished—
anything—for the rest of my life. When a
guy like that gets you, you can't get away.
Sometimes, when I started my shift at six in
the morning I'd be filling the tank and
watching the sun come up and I'd feel like

taking off and never coming back. I was afraid to go home and see the mail.

When I went back to the Green Leaf I didn't see Al Croppe. It was a long time before I saw him anywhere. When I did he ignored me. That was fine with me. I didn't want to talk to him. But he let people know that he was mad at me for chickening out on him. He didn't say what it was all about but everybody knows what Al Croppe does. That doesn't matter. He makes a lot of money so people respect him. They respect his opinions. When he smears somebody it sticks. But I still go to the Green Leaf. It's on my way home. It's close to the OTB. So what else am I going to do?

I knew what happened in Grenlily's office. I knew what they were doing. It was all part of the scam. It was a performance. They did a con job on me right in front of my eyes and I was watching and knowing they were doing it but there was nothing I could do about it. They never intended to give me money. They must have been laughing at me the whole time. They probably split the hundred thousand, minus something for Sid General. I'm just glad Grenlily never sent me a bill.

After a while things went back to normal. I drive my cab up and down Queens Boulevard—the same business over and over. All I got going for me now is the keys to the safe deposit box with a thousand dollars. It's mine and nobody knows about it. People may look down on me but inside I know something about myself they don't know. I know I'm worth more than they think. I got my thousand dollars. The only thing that bothers me is that the longer I keep it the less valuable it is. I'm watching the news about inflation and there's nothing I can do about that either. I won't invest the money because when the market crashes or the banks go broke you get nothing.

So time goes by. I get older, Brenda gets older, the kids get older, and my money is worth a little less. My shifts are still twelve hours but they feel longer. Five, six, seven years go by. Once they start rolling away like that you can't remember which year it was when things happened.

One day I dropped a passenger in Manhattan and I'm heading back to Queens. I'm on Second Avenue in the Seventies and I stop for a light. All of a sudden I hear a loud bang and I see that a guy who was crossing the street has come over and banged on the hood of my car. He says, "Russ! Hey, Russ! I'd recognize you anywhere."

I'm wondering which of my fares this is because sometimes you make the same call two, three, four times a month and you get to know the customer and some of them like to pretend they think of you as a friend. This guy is very spiffy. He looks like he just came from the tailor or the barber. He says, "Don't tell me you don't remember me. It is Russ, isn't it?"

I almost drop dead. It's Dave Winger.

He opens the door and gets in. I'm not allowed to pick up people on the street but I'm not going to tell him that. I can't believe the way he looks. When I knew him he couldn't afford clothes. I say, "What are you doing here?"

He says, "I have an office on Madison Avenue. I came out

of law school, took the bar exam in New York, and here I am."

I say, "Madison Avenue. That's high rent."

He says, "You wouldn't believe how high." He says, "Russ, how come you're still driving a cab?"

I laugh. It's a fake laugh but it's the best I can do. I can't even think of an answer. We drive along for a few blocks and he's talking and telling me how great things are and I'm pretending that I feel good too.

Then he says, "I've got to get out here but, Russ, it's great seeing you. Let's get together one of these days and have lunch. How's the family?"

He gets out and I swing left and go over the bridge to Queens. I come down under the Els in Queensborough Plaza. That is such a sleazy place. I head down Queens Boulevard. I'm listening to calls coming over the radio.

"Car number one-ninety-two, Al. You get Fourteen-twenty Twenty-first Avenue for nine dollars."

"Car number one-fifty-five, John. Marine Air Terminal. Mr. Bumpers for fourteen dollars."

"Car number sixty-five, Bill, you get Ten-oh-five Ankena Avenue for eight dollars."

All I hear is dollars. I do three, four, maybe nine, ten dollars at a time, Al Croppe does thousands, maybe Dave is doing millions. But it's all dollars. Dollars. That's all anybody does. That's who you are, that's what you are, that's how smart you are. That's life. All of a sudden I realize the dispatcher is calling me on the radio. "Russ. Car number ninety-seven, Russ. Russ, where are you?" I don't know how long he's been calling me. I call back. He says, "Pay attention to the radio!" He gives me a customer in Sunnyside. I pick her up and she has one of those doggie baskets which she hands to me to put in for her. I can see the little dog in there all squinched up. He can hardly move. He's drooling and whining. It's pitiful. She tells me she's going to LaGuardia Airport. I pull out and she starts to talk. She tells me about the dog, how old it is, the pedigree, all the diseases, how much the vet charges. I'm trying to listen. I like to listen to my customers. You meet all kinds of people. But I can't concentrate. I keep remembering when Dave and I would sit and drink beer in the Green Leaf and talk. I remember what he said and what I said. And now I know where he is and where I am.

I get to LaGuardia. The lady pays for the ride with exact money and then starts looking for a tip. She's got a pocketbook as big as a suitcase. She can't find any money in it. All she's got is traveler's checks. She says, "I'm sorry I don't have any cash for you. Do you ever play the lottery?"

I say, "Occasionally."

She says, "Play these numbers—one, ten, eleven, twenty-one, thirty-one, and forty-one. Will you remember that?"

I say yes. On the way home I buy a lottery ticket. I play those numbers. I had a feeling it was just crazy enough that I might get something out of it.

Then I stopped off at the Green Leaf. Max is gone by now. He had a heart attack. The bartender is an ex-cop named Eddie. The place is as greasy as ever. Eddie is not my favorite guy and I don't talk to him much. I sit there with my beer. I finish it and order a second beer. Then I have a third. I didn't make much money that day so I shouldn't be drinking it up but I feel like I need it. And I don't feel like going home. I hang around until 10:30 when they do the lottery on television. Everybody in there plays so they always turn on the station that shows the drawing. They got little Ping-Pong balls with numbers on them blowing around in a glass case. The balls come up one at a time with the winning numbers. I don't have a single one of them.

I finish my beer and go. I decide to check out tomorrow's races at the OTB office. It's open late. Maybe they'll have something that sounds good. At that hour there's nobody in there but drunks and bums. Papers all over the floor. Guys sitting on the floor looking at racing sheets. They all have rotten teeth. They all know each other and they're laughing and coughing. If the office was closed they'd be under a bridge someplace. There's even some women in there.

I look at the charts but I can't concentrate on what I'm doing. Nothing looks good so I head home.

When I come in Brenda is watching television. The kids are out. They're always out now. I don't know where they are and neither does she.

I lay what's left of my money on the kitchen table. She'll take what she needs. If anything's left, that's mine. She knows I had a few beers on the way home but she doesn't complain. She trusts me and I trust her. You got to be able to trust somebody or you'll go out of your mind. She asks me if I ate. I have to stop and think about it. I'm so tired I can't tell if I'm hungry. She makes spaghetti and then sits down with me and we eat together. I'm looking at the apartment. The stuffing is coming out of the cushions. Paint is peeling off the walls.

I'm sitting there with Brenda and I'm so tired we're not even talking. It's almost midnight and I've been up since 5 A.M. I got to get up at 5 A.M. tomorrow. If I want any sleep I have to go to bed right now. But I can't do that. That's why I'm always so tired.

I take the string with the keys off my neck. It's been there I don't know how long—five, six, seven years. I plunk the keys down on the table in front of Brenda and I say, "Happy birthday."

She says, "It ain't my birthday."

I say, "Take 'em for God's sake before I change my mind."

24

A COUPLE OF DAYS GO BY, MAYBE A WEEK, AND where I used to have a pair of keys around my neck, instead I got nothing. And it's the usual thing—you don't know what something means until you don't have it any more. All the time I had that money I never made any plans. I never realized that thousand dollars was my chance in life. Now it's too late. It's gone because, as far as I'm concerned, I would never ask Brenda to give it back.

Meanwhile I'm waiting to see what Brenda does with the money. So far I see nothing. No clothes, no furniture, no steak dinners. Maybe she paid some bills. But she don't say and I don't ask because I don't want it to look like I'm sorry.

Then one night I come home from work and Brenda is sitting at the kitchen table. Just from looking at her I can tell she's waiting for me. She says to me, "Russ, sit down."

I say, "Brenda, when I want to sit down, I'll sit down. If you got something to tell me, I'm right here. I'm listening. What did you do with the money?"

That last part just slipped out because it was on my mind. I didn't mean to ask her that.

She says to me, "I didn't do anything with the money."

I say, "So what do you want to talk about?"

She says, "I want to buy a car."

Well I don't even know how to address that question. We can't afford a car and she should know that. And I'm feeling so low that I don't need to be put in a position where I have to explain it. I say to her, "Brenda, there's a thousand dollars in that box, not a million. You figure insurance and the rest of it and you don't have enough money for a car."

She says, "We could get a car for maybe five, six hundred dollars. Get it painted, put in nice seat covers, buy a CB radio. Then we put signs in the Green Leaf, the cleaner's, the grocer's, everyplace. 'Russ's Car Service.' We'll charge a dollar, maybe a dollar-fifty cheaper than the other car services. People will call me here and I'll give you the messages on the CB. We keep a hundred percent of the fares plus the tips and we'll be way ahead of where we are now."

Well if it was that simple everybody'd be rich. But things don't work that way. And I don't want to hear from Brenda how to operate a car service. I say to her, "You know who you sound like? You sound like Al Croppe. 'Invest a little money and you're a millionaire overnight.' Let me tell you something. The car service is a regulated industry. To operate a car service you need a permit from the city—which costs money. And you also need a special insurance policy which costs thousands of dollars. So you already don't have enough money." And as I'm saying this I'm getting very mad. I'm so mad that I have to go out and take a walk to calm down.

I go up Woodside Avenue to Northern Boulevard and out Northern past the Ronzoni plant. I'm walking and walking and as I'm walking I'm thinking to myself, Why am I so mad? It's not hard to figure out and I'm going to say it straight. I had that key around my neck a long time and in all those years that idea never occurred to me. So what am I supposed to think? That I'm stupid? That I got no ambition? I don't think that's true but what can I say? All I know is I feel like an idiot and that's why I'm mad. But I will say this about myself—I'm not afraid to give credit where credit is due. So I give Brenda full credit.

I go back home and I say to her, "Maybe you got a good idea after all," and I take the thousand dollars and invest in a car. I knew a guy in the used car business who gave me a very good deal. I put in seat covers, nice rugs, and a CB radio. Then I go around to some stores where they know me, put signs in the windows, and I'm in business.

As far as the law that I was telling Brenda about is concerned and the insurance policy and the rest of it, I take the attitude that until somebody bothers me I don't need it. So that means, without the permit and the insurance and the rest of it, and being only one car, I got no overhead. And that means I can be cheaper than anybody else. So pretty soon I'm doing a nice business.

The funny thing is that my clientele reminds me of Dave Winger. It's not just the same kind of people, it's the very same people themselves. For instance, I got the Blitnises as regular customers. The doctors are always giving Harry Blitnis tests. So between the round-trips to the gallbladder doctor and the cardiologist they're good for four to eight rides a month. On top of that, once a week, Wednesday morning, I got a standing order with them for a ride to the Georgia Diner where they get the bus to Atlantic City. They don't tip much but I keep the whole fare instead of just thirty-five percent, so it's still a big improvement.

I don't even have to advertise. Word of mouth does everything for me. These old people got nothing to do but talk and they got nothing to talk about. So whatever's new or a little bit different they talk about over and over until you could turn blue in the face. But for me it's good because they tell each other how nice I am or how nice Brenda is and from that alone I got more business than I can handle.

And Brenda is perfect in this line of work. The clientele love her. She gets on the phone and talks and she's so nice and friendly that she knows them all by name and she knows their whole business. Sometimes I'm tied up with rides for an hour and a half but they say they'll wait for me anyway. Not just because they want to save a dollar and a half on the ride but because they want to talk to Brenda.

So all of a sudden things are a little different in my house. I don't mean I'm rich. You don't get rich from driving one car for one shift. We got a little more money but we're in the same apartment and we got the same furniture. But, for me, it's a lot better than before because I feel different. I'm my own boss. There's no wise guy in the dispatch office who can insult me whenever he's in a bad mood.

From that time on I never heard of Dave Winger again and I'm not sorry because I already knew all about him from what I saw the last time he got in my car.

But I did hear from Al Croppe.

One day I get a call to pick up a customer on Twenty-first Avenue in Long Island City. This is unusual because it's way out of my area. I pull up there and who do I see? Not Al Croppe but his lawyer, Grenlily. He gets in the back seat, makes himself comfortable, and says hello like he expects I'm glad to see him.

I say, "Where do you want to go?"

He says, "Let's stay right here. I want to talk to you, Russ. How are you?"

I say, "I'm fine."

He says, "Russ, I'll come straight to the point. I'm here representing Al Croppe. Now before you say anything let me tell you that Al knows he did you dirty and he knows you've got a right to be angry. Okay? And, what's more, he apologizes. If you give him the chance he'll apologize to your face. Russ, things have happened to Al. He's a different man. If you see him you'll know what I'm talking about. Now I know you're impatient but, please, just give me a little time to explain why I called you."

What can I say? He's sitting in my car. I tell him, "Go ahead. Say what you want."

He says, "I don't have to tell you that Al Croppe was a con man. You also know that Al Croppe ran a lot of scams, not just the one in Atlantic City. And you probably know he made a lot of money. But, Russ, that's all beside the point now. Al can't do it anymore. He's very sick and he needs help. Believe it or not, the kind of help Al needs most is something only you can give him. I know how strange that must sound so let me explain. Russ, Al is hearing the voice of mortality and it makes him nervous. He's done a lot of bad things in his life and now he wants to do something good before it's too late. He hurt you, Russ, he knows that, and he wants to make it up to you. Listen to what he wants to do. Al would like to put his money in your business. Now I want to lay all the cards on the table right from the beginning so let me make this clear—there's something in it for him too. Here's what I mean. All of Al's money is cash. Cash is not legitimate money because it's not registered with the government. There are no taxes paid. So there are things you can't use this money for. He needs to invest his money to make it legitimate. He needs to have it on the books somewhere. Now, he could invest anyplace. He could invest in IBM. But he won't do that because he owes you. He wants to put at least fifty thousand dollars into your business. You remain the owner. You run the business. You become rich. But he gets a legitimate source of income. Al is in my office right now. You don't have to commit yourself to anything. Just come up and talk to him. Listen to what he has to say."

This is crazy. I've been through this with these guys already and I don't trust them. I'm not stupid. But he is talking about fifty thousand dollars so I don't like to just say no without hearing his story. I don't know what to say. I say, "I'm working, Mr. Grenlily. I came here because you called and said you wanted a car."

He says, "I'll pay your hourly rate. No problem. Just come up and talk to the man."

I don't want to do it. Only a sucker gets burned twice. But for fifty thousand dollars, which I know Al Croppe has, I can't just say, "No, forget it. I'm not interested." I have to go up and listen. Even if it's just out of curiosity.

I get out of the car and we go up to the office. First we come to that little silver room with the black telephone. Grenlily opens the inside door and there's the big room with the blue carpet, the view of Manhattan in the semicircular window, the bicycle, the weights, the desk, and the three chairs in front of it. Al is sitting in the middle chair.

I see right away that it's not the same Al. He looks like a very sick man. All dried up and shriveled. The jacket is two sizes too big on him. He gives me this weak smile and holds out his hand like it's hard for him to do that. I take his hand and I'm shocked. It's cold. And not just cold. It's shaking and weak so I feel like just by giving him a normal handshake I'll break his arm. Now, all of a sudden, I have to think that maybe this isn't a scam. And believe me, that doesn't make me happy. I still don't want to be mixed up with these guys.

But now I don't know what to think. I say, "How you doing, Al?"

His voice is low and he talks like he's got no strength. He says, "I'm okay, Russ. I'm grateful to you for coming. I've been wanting to apologize to you."

I say, "Ah, forget it."

He says, "Russ, you're a good man. I want you to do me a favor. Would you do me a favor?"

I say, "What is it?"

He says, "Russ, I don't know what's going to happen to me but I need help. Listen to me. I got cash. A lot of cash. But cash is not legitimate money. It's not listed with the government. I need legitimate money, Russ, so I can get top medical help. Russ, you're also off the books. I know that. Make me your partner. We'll both go legitimate. Fifty thousand dollars. More, if you want. New cars. An office. Air conditioned. Suits. Whatever you want." And as he's talking he gets weaker and weaker until he fades out and shuts his eyes.

What can I say? That I don't want fifty thousand dollars? Of course I want fifty thousand dollars. But I don't trust him. Maybe it's crazy. The man is sitting right in front of me and I can see how sick he is but I don't trust him. And to tell you the truth, I'm still thinking about how he humiliated me and I'd still like to get even with him for that. Not that I would actually do it now. The man is dying. He's apologizing. Offering me money. What else do I want? I should be grateful.

He's got his eyes shut and he says to me, "How 'bout it,

Russ? Fifty thousand. Donnie will draw up the papers."

I don't say anything.

His hand is shaking but he goes into his jacket pocket, pulls out a checkbook and a pen, writes a check, and hands it to me. I'm saying to myself, What is he pulling on me this time? And I'm worried he'll make a fool out of me again. I take the check and it's for fifty thousand dollars. I'm looking at it and as I'm looking at it I get so crazy that I tear it up and I say to him, "Al, how does this scam work? I don't understand it." And as I'm saying it, I'm thinking to myself, How can I talk to him like this? The man is dying.

Al is speechless. I never seen him speechless before. Grenlily doesn't believe it either but Grenlily is a different character. He looks at me like I'm slime. He opens his desk drawer, which I can see is full of money, and he tosses a hundred-dollar bill on the desk and says, "That's your hourly rate. Keep the change and get out of here."

But Al says to me, "Wait a minute. Why do you think this is a scam?" He sits up and, all of a sudden, right in front of me, he starts to turn into the old Al. It's fantastic. The man actually had made himself look smaller. And now, as I'm looking at him, it's like he's filling up with air. I can't believe it. He's not shriveled anymore. His voice is normal. Even the jacket fits him.

To this day I couldn't answer the question he asked me. In fact, I didn't know it was a scam. All I knew is that these guys were offering me fifty thousand dollars again and I knew I was never going to get that kind of money from them or anybody and so I went crazy. That's why I tore up the check. When he sat up and looked normal, that's when I knew it was a scam, not before. If they held out a little longer, maybe I would have gone along with them. I couldn't walk out on a sick man like that. But once I see him sitting there, the old Al, then I know what's happening.

And I've learned a few things myself. So I say to him, "Al, you better think this over. If a dumb guy like me sees it's a scam, everybody's gonna see it. You gotta figure out what you're doing wrong, otherwise you'll get caught."

I pick up the hundred from the desk, pull a ten from my pocket, slap it down, and say, "There's your change." I'm looking right at Grenlily. What I would like to do is say something to him that goes into his heart like a knife. But you know how that is. I can't think of anything. If I do, it'll be a week too late. So I turn around and walk out.

I go downstairs, get in the car, and call Brenda. I say, "That last customer was an hourly rate and he gave me a ninety-dollar tip."

This is like an extra day's pay so naturally she's excited. But I still got one more call to make before I'm finished. I drive over to Ketchem Street and pick up the Blitnises for Harry's doctor's appointment. The two of them get in the car and I say, "You know who I just saw? You remember Al Croppe?"

Mrs. Blitnis says, "Of course I remember Al Croppe. The gentleman from Philadelphia. How could I forget him?"

I say, "The guy is such a con artist you wouldn't believe it."

She says, "What do you mean 'con artist'?"

Harry says, "Never mind. Russ is right. I knew he was a con artist the first minute I saw him. Didn't I say it? Russ, sometimes a con artist can fool you because he's wearing sheep's clothing. But underneath, he's always a leopard. And you know the saying—The leopard does not change his seats."

I drop them off at the doctor's office and head home. On the way, I decide to do something special. I get Chinese take-out and a cold six-pack and bring it home. Me and Brenda sit down, go through the food and the six beers, and we're feeling pretty good.

She says to me, "How were you so sure he was faking?"

I say, "I wasn't sure."

She says, "Then how could you take such a chance to insult him?"

I say, "I had a feeling. It's like a horse race. Sometimes you go with your feeling. Not everything in this world is written on those philosophy cards they got in Paris."

She says, "What philosophy cards in Paris?"

I say, "They got philosophy cards in Paris with sayings on them."

She says, "How do you know about philosophy cards in Paris?"

I say, "I know about a lot of things."

She says, "That's true. In fact, I'm the one who always said that."

I say, "And you were right."

She laughs. So I start to laugh. I just hope we're both laughing for the same reason.